THE PROPERTY OF JOSEPH McBADEN

THE PROPERTY OF JOSEPH McBADEN

ATTORNEY AT LAW

A Novel

Peggy Reid Rhodes

Copyright © 2002 by Peggy Reid Rhodes.

Library of Congress Number: 2002093664
ISBN: Hardcover 1-4010-6881-2
Softcover 1-4010-6880-4

Also by Peggy Reid Rhodes
   Rosemary for Remembrance
      An Historical Novel
   Charlotte Greystone
      A Novel

All rights reserved. No part of this book may be reproduced or transmitted in any form or by any means, electronic or mechanical, including photocopying, recording, or by any information storage and retrieval system, without permission in writing from the copyright owner.

This is a work of fiction. Names, characters, places and incidents either are the product of the author's imagination or are used fictitiously, and any resemblance to any actual persons, living or dead, events, or locales is entirely coincidental.

This book was printed in the United States of America.

To order additional copies of this book, contact:
Xlibris Corporation
1-888-795-4274
www.Xlibris.com
Orders@Xlibris.com

Dedicated to Outstanding Attorneys

David B. Freedman

Carl F. Parrish

Wayne Shugart

William S. Taylor

... To give birth to an idea, to discover a great thought – an intellectual nugget, right under the dust of a field that many a brain plough had gone over before.
To find a new planet, to invent a new hinge,
To find a way to make the lightnings carry your messages.
To be the *first* – that is the idea.

...From Mark Twain *The Innocents Abroad* (1896)

CHAPTER 1

"One more action to justify," Joseph McBaden thought, repeating his motto slowly under his breath, for he never said it out loud. Not even now when no one was around to hear him. His next appointment was at 5:30. Checking his watch, he saw that was ten minutes away. What a day! Time to take a short respite in transferring files from cardboard boxes to steel filing cabinets along one wall. And that chore was being sandwiched between interviews.

He stretched back in his wooden swivel chair, extending his arms and reaching toward the ceiling. He brought his long, lean fingers into fists several times, then lowered his elbows, unfolded his shirt sleeve cuffs and buttoned them. Swiveling the chair, he took in the room, his private office in an upscale building in one of North Carolina's largest cities. No longer was he just another name in a firm in the uptown area he had just left. This was the new gateway to the upscale side of Windermere, a city widely admired for its beautiful trees and a variety of architecture in public and residential structures along curving streets and hills. It aptly represented the central section of the state – the Piedmont. Tomorrow his name would go on the door.

Estimating the time for dealing with a box and multiplying by a dozen, he knew he had several hours of work tonight. Or tomorrow.

Joseph decided to use the ten minutes to telephone a friend.

"Sam, I'm glad you're still in the office. Have a minute?"

"I do. What's up?" responded Sam as he closed a file folder on his cluttered desk. "Oh, can you hold a moment?"

"Yes."

Sam Littlegate rose from his leather chair, walked around his large mahogany desk and spoke to the woman who likewise had stood. "Could you wait a few minutes in here?" he asked, opening the door and indicating the receptionist room.

"Yes."

As she exited, Littlegate returned to the phone. "Hey, I'm here and listening."

"I'll make this brief. Someone will be here shortly and I assume you have someone leaving. Did you have a law clerk this summer, Watt Whitehurst?"

"I did."

"He graduates this spring. He was in for an interview today."

"He was?" In a noncommittal tone came the answer.

"What's your opinion of his work?"

"I heard you were looking for someone. Which do you want, a fellow with some family connections here in the Piedmont or a worker?"

McBaden considered the options, then replied. "Connections would be nice, but a worker is essential."

"My personal advice is to keep looking."

"Not putting words in your mouth, Sam, but I'm detecting he wouldn't put his feet to the pavement quickly, knock on those friendly doors without urging, or ring those phones as often as need be. Doesn't exert himself."

"Is that what you're hearing? I didn't say lazy, did I?" Littlegate chuckled.

"Just following up on this end," McBaden's voice bordered on disgust. He scratched through Whitehurst as he had all the other names.

"Are there any good candidates for another attorney yet?"

"Not a one."

"Would you consider taking on one of that sex you shy away from?" Littlegate grinned.

"Wipe that smirk off your face, friend. Why? Have you and Ruth found someone to set me up with as usual?" McBaden rested his head on the chair back.

"I don't know this one well enough yet. Doubt if Ruth does at all. She's just coming to town. Well, want to know more?" Littlegate teased.

"Listen, Sam, someone really is due in five minutes. So spill."

"Remember back a few months ago, I told you we were doing so well that we needed another attorney? I put the word out and received some possible replies and scheduled interviews. I overlooked getting back to one candidate and today she showed up." Littlegate paused.

"Go on."

"Her credentials read top notch. Her references are excellent. Her work experience, solid, and, I think, could fit in with what you are doing and planning to do."

"And you didn't hire her?"

"No. Couldn't. Two of our big clients were lost. One through a merger and the other in a change of management. The new man wants the firm he has always used. We had to cut, not enlarge, our staff."

"Well, it turns out a wise move for both of us that I didn't accept your offer. Okay, what else about that woman attorney of whom you were speaking?"

"So glad you asked. She's here now in the reception room. I expect she has had other interviews today. Do you have time to see her? She's staying overnight in The Patrick." He concluded with a vocal up-note.

McBaden, used to his friend's voice control, answered, "I'll make time. My five forty-five meeting should take no more than twenty minutes. That'll give her traveling time from your place to mine. Oh, what's her name?"

"Clarissa Bentley. Like that ritzy automobile. I'll give my best spiel about you. That way she can't say no to an immediate interview. Thanks, friend. So glad you can squeeze her in between your other applicants." Littlegate pressed the phone button quickly, knowing Joseph would catch the verb with its various definitions. Quickly, he scribbled a note, placed it and material from the folder he had closed minutes ago into a large envelope, sealed that, and walked into the outer room.

Clarissa Bentley folded a leather daybook and stood up.

"If you're up to one more interview, that was a good friend of mine who is searching for an attorney. He's a good man, excellent attorney. Opening his own office."

Littlegate told her that McBaden had been practicing general law with a large firm locally for several years. Now the time seemed right for making a change. He gave her the address, saying McBaden would be expecting her.

McBaden was replacing the phone receiver when he saw the door opening in the outer office. Purposefully, he had left the door from his office to the hall open. His secretary had already left. McBaden stood and walked to greet the man just entering.

The man was short, rather squat in frame and form, perhaps fifty years of age, bald on top with a frizzy fringe of coppery hair from one temple around the back of his head to the other temple. His cheeks were full and round, his neck short, as were his limbs. McBaden trusted he took primarily sign-painting jobs that required a minimum of reaching.

"Good evening, Mr. McBaden."

"Hello, Mr. Avery. You found the way all right?"

"I did. Even without a number or a name on the door. Pushed the elevator button with a 6 and wound to the left. All the offices appear let?"

"I believe I'm the last tenant for this floor."

"Mighty nice building. Those uptown will have to look to their maintenance and remodeling the way the construction is mushrooming in this area." Avery said as he looked around the room.

McBaden moved over to the entry door; Avery followed and they discussed exactly where to paint the sign. They decided on a script, size and a gold color. One inside door was designated as supply and another, restroom. McBaden decided not to place a name on his office, a second office to be used by one or two other attorneys or the conference room. Copiers, fax machines and such were to be placed tomorrow in a large niche in the hall immediately behind his secretary's desk.

"So, you'll be in tomorrow afternoon?"

"I plan to. If there's any delay with the machines getting placed, let me know. I wouldn't want to be in their way and it wouldn't help the paint either." Avery said agreeably.

McBaden acknowledged the logistics. Avery walked down the corridor in short, quick steps.

McBaden freshened his face with soap and water and combed his hair. He buttoned the collar and straightened his tie. He took the briefest glance at his reflection, reassuring that a shave wasn't necessary and that his hair hadn't grown to meet his shirt collar. He switched off the light. The image of his well-shaped head and his regular features, dark brown eyes always impressive with large black pupils and brown eyebrows, disappeared. His hair, light brown in winter, was almost blond in the last month of summer.

Picking his way around the boxes, he reached for his suit jacket and pulled it on. He could best be described as a regular guy — average in height, weight, proportions, complexion. His body structure came from the paternal side – his father differed in being taller and leaner, traits often associated with selfishness and injustice – but Joseph kept in shape by swimming at the YMCA pool, running primarily outside and eating a well-balanced diet. Although McBaden's eyes drew attention, it was his calmness, concentration and self-control, and winning his arguments with prepared presentations that his followers talked about. And those two features, eyes and comportment, elevated him above the rest of the crowd.

He headed down the hall, but stopped just short of the reception room as he watched a woman enter.

She was dressed in a becoming beige suit, light stockings and medium-heeled pumps, which, like her handbag, were a few shades darker. Her short hair was dark brown.

"Are you Joseph McBaden? I was told there may not be a sign on the door."

"I am. You are Clarissa Bentley?"

"Yes." At this point she turned, grasped the doorknob with her right hand and walked the door to a close. Turning again, she faced McBaden. "Thank you for seeing me on short notice."

"It is good of you to come so quickly." He took a step toward her. She immediately came forward. His eyes fully surveyed her: her walk, confident with good posture; her stride neither long nor minced; her size, neat; her facial expression, sincere and inquisitive. Overall, this first impression was positive. She held her hand out; he advanced a pace and shook it. She had smooth skin and a firm grasp.

"We're still in some disarray. There're boxes yet to be unpacked in my office, but I believe we can find a couple of chairs." McBaden said and returned to the end room. She followed.

He moved behind his desk and indicated a chair opposite. She sat down, maintaining erect posture. He noticed, then he eased into his chair.

"Mr. Littlegate regretted that his office forgot to get back with you. He spoke of your replying to an inquiry when he expected to expand his firm."

"He said the same to me. He appeared to be concerned, but it was really not an inconvenience."

While she spoke, McBaden continued to appraise her with his dark brown eyes intently focused on her face, especially her eyes. She focused on him also. She spoke evenly, giving him time to draw his conclusions. Never had she watched anyone with such penetrating eyes. It was as if he were filing every obvious feature and delving as deeply into another's core of being as the person was allowing him to approach. She remained still and let him make his evaluation. She knew when he was through. In an instant, he shuttered the wide-eyed stare, pulled his head slightly back, and replaced his expression with a "let's get down to business" aspect – albeit, in a general amicability.

"So you're thinking of coming south?"

Her countenance reflected a polite friendliness. "One state down, sir. Mr. Littlegate asked me to hand you this envelope." She leaned forward and passed it over.

He noticed her gestures were easy and controlled. "Thank you. Would you like coffee? The pot should still be on. Or water?"

"Water will be fine. I saw the bottled water stand in the hall. If I may, I'll get a cup."

"I'll get it for you," he offered. She had risen quicker. "Thank you, but I don't mind. Could I bring you one? Or some coffee?"

"Neither," he replied, standing. He watched her walk into the hall. She had a self-assuring manner that was acceptable, one without purposefully drawing attention or indicating aggressiveness. He quickly opened the large envelope and withdrew the papers. He recognized Littlegate's handwriting on the smaller envelope: Open later. He placed it on his desk and quickly scanned the resume, the references and her certificates.

She returned and they resumed their seats. He said, holding her résumé, and briefly referring to it, "Mr. Littlegate was correct in saying you have much experience. You have been connected with one firm since law school?"

"Correct."

"That has been quite a few years. I read that you have handled a number of different type cases."

"I have. The firm practices general law. The senior partners do have their specialties."

"Do you have a particular interest?" he inquired, again watching her carefully.

"General law. Not the most confrontational cases. There is one area that interests me."

"Which is . . ."

"Intellectual property."

His eyes narrowed slightly. He sat back in his chair. "Have you worked in this area?"

"Only a few times. It's a growing section, or it is in Virginia and D.C."

He thought a minute before speaking. "That's a specialty I intend to look into myself."

She smiled pleasantly. "The need must exist at times. Windermere has large companies. Some have merged or been bought out, or buying for themselves, so I have read. And there are universities and colleges here. Writings and scientific work that might need legal counsel."

"True. I have one case I'm wrapping up soon. One I started on with the previous firm. One they let come with me."

"And I trust, one they expect you to win," she said generously.

He smiled, while he thought that she was sharp, understanding and positive. He liked what he was seeing and hearing. He referred to her references again. First rate. He would ponder later why she was leaving. Surely, she couldn't be bored right outside D.C. The district was a great place for successful attorneys, or that was a general consensus.

He shifted to a more serious mode. "I am on my own here. I have some clients with rather standard situations that need attention. So I've been interviewing this week. Also I've been moving in."

"If this question is bold, forgive me, but are the intentions for the firm to remain small?"

"Yes. At least for several years. I have space here for one, perhaps two other attorneys."

"Would the others handle basically the bread-and-butter cases?"

"In the beginning, yes. There's always the possibility that whoever comes in could have a friend or be referred to by someone whose legal needs develop into a major case. May I ask if you have acquaintances in Windermere or this state?"

"No, not in either. No one who I know has need of counsel currently. Do you handle divorce cases?"

"No," he shot right back. More even tempered, he added, "I don't myself."

"Will you accept them? Or will you allow others in the firm to do so?"

"If an attorney wishes to take on a domestic case, it would be expected that the attorney plans to stay with the firm long enough to see it settled. If you have practiced in that area, you are aware matters can take years to resolve. I, personally, do not take them on."

She appeared faintly surprised at his decisiveness. "Yes, I realize that. However, with the high rate of divorce, there is a demand for representation." She too spoke with firmness. For a moment she thought she saw a flicker of a question on his face. Perhaps he wanted to know if she were divorced.

"There are few forms these days that ask for marital status. Except perhaps, income taxes and such. I do have a personal interest in those cases, for I have several friends who have needed attorneys. But I have no vendetta or soapbox stand on the issue. No more than fair representation of all parties. That's probably why I am interested in intellectual property, although the case there may more often be a little guy against a big business." She paused, looked at McBaden and asked, "Was that a short soapbox?"

He had been watching her and following her statements closely. "No." He stood up. "I appreciate your coming, Miss Bentley."

She also rose. "Again, thank you for seeing me. May I inquire if you would recommend the café in The Patrick for dinner?"

He said, "It is all right, but there are two or three excellent restaurants within two blocks. Are you staying over a day or two?"

"That depends, sir," she replied. "I do have a reservation tomorrow for an early afternoon flight into Dulles."

McBaden considered that a truth and a well-worded statement. One she knew that could be checked and one that gave the impression that she was open to a recall from him or one of the other firms she interviewed with today. The look they exchanged was an understanding between them: He would not appear to be too eager to hire, and she was not revealing any information about other possibilities. Both were capable of knowing when to cease an interview.

She said she had a rental car, and he phoned security downstairs to walk her to the parking lot. She thanked him.

He walked with her to the elevator, saying he hoped she would enjoy her dinner. On the way back to his office, he thought maybe he should have asked her to dinner. No, he decided this was the right way. He didn't need to see her on a social level to make his decision. He opened Littlegate's envelope and read the single-page enclosure: What do you think, pal? Looks like an attorney, speaks like an attorney, has all the credentials. I could wager she's the best prospect you've had all week without seeing the rest of the list. Grab her up quickly. Sam.

He laughed to himself. What a jokester, but Sam did keep life on the upbeat. And he was a pretty smart fellow when it came to sizing up people. McBaden almost e-mailed a reply: You're on, friend. But McBaden rarely bet; he didn't like to lose. Adding an attorney was a major decision; and it had to be his choice, not just a highly referred one such as Miss Bentley, the woman who looked upscale like the automobile.

CHAPTER 2

The following morning Joseph McBaden arrived early and cleared his desk. He unlocked his filing cabinet, opened a drawer and withdrew several expanded folders. He took off his suit jacket and hung it on the wooden tree in a corner. He carried the boxes he emptied last night to the hall, having arranged for them to be picked up today.

With the clutter removed, the office took on a ready-to-be-worked-in look. McBaden was pleased to have pressing work before him. His pleasure was increased when he saw Gretchen, his punctual secretary, come through the door.

"Hi, Mr. McBaden. You've really been busy, by the look of all those empty boxes."

"Well, Gretchen, you were thorough in labeling as you boxed the files. Transferring them to the cabinets was the easier task. Thank you for inserting the cards on the drawer fronts. I wrote in the name of the first client and the last. I stashed new hanging files and new folders in several drawers. The general information folders are filed temporarily according to box numbers, which you kept a record of?"

"I did. You could have left this for me, especially with the big case coming up tomorrow," she said with a mixture of gratitude and concern.

"It gave me time to think about the details. The business machine delivery and hook-up service is due soon. As much as possible, please, take care of them. The layouts we talked about are taped on the workroom wall."

"Yes, sir. Shall I open the mail when it comes; use our regular procedures?"

"Please, do. If you see some ways to improve things as we

adapt here, let me know. I have a few phone calls to make," he said, closing the door behind him. He checked the phone directory, punched in a number and asked for Clarissa Bentley.

"Hello," Clarissa spoke.

"Good morning. This is Joseph McBaden. I trust you had a pleasant dinner and evening."

"Thank you, I did. I found a nice restaurant with excellent food."

"I appreciated your coming by yesterday, and I would like to think you found Windermere a place you'd be comfortable working." He paused. There was no reply. "Miss Bentley, I would be pleased to have you come into the office as an attorney with me."

Quietly, in an even tenor, she said, "I would be pleased to accept your offer. Perhaps we could discuss more specifically the generalities we covered last evening."

"Are you still taking the flight this afternoon?"

"That can be cancelled. You spoke of a court case tomorrow. Would it be convenient anytime today for us to chat briefly?"

"That can be arranged. There will be service people in this morning, but they know what to do. We could talk awhile without too many interruptions."

"Will ten o'clock be suitable?"

"It will. I look forward to seeing you."

After he hung up, he thought, "may she live up to all the accolades in her folder and justify the hasty selection."

Then he swiveled his chair, fully facing the desk, and opened the top file. Once he entered a case mentally, he concentrated and absorbed facts with lightning speed. While this was a review of material he was familiar with, he let his eyes and mind as much as possible inspect it as if it were new, alert to some nugget or slant he could have missed.

He scrutinized copies of Bing Leroy's personal diary about his experiments at home. It had been handwritten, every entry dated; even margin notes were dated. Likewise, he opened and reread photocopies of the client's log from work. It had been meticulously kept. The time clock tickets had been also copied. Leroy had provided the first two records, while the employer had submitted, under subpoena, the latter. McBaden considered the time records to be the most convincing evidence of his client's declaration that he had not come to his research conclusions of a project on the employer's premises or the job. The records supported his statements that he never returned to the employer's premises in the evenings. Every half-hour of his work on the job was documented.

McBaden quickly thumbed through the file and brought up sworn statements of three of his co-workers that he was at all times fully engaged on projects assigned by the supervisor. He had the morning coffee break with the other technicians and they usually walked across the street to a café for lunch. There was no mention that any of the men ever met in the evenings. McBaden made a note on a blank legal pad: Ask the witnesses about this before they have to testify, if the case went that far. The client has no notation as such. But McBaden wanted no surprises.

His phone light blinked. He picked it up. Gretchen said, "Mr. McBaden, Clarissa Bentley is here to see you. Shall I send her in?"

"I'll be right out. Have the service people come?"

"Yes. They're bringing the equipment in."

McBaden placed the papers back into the folders. He put on his jacket and went into the hall where he stopped to speak to two men. He moved on to the reception room.

Clarissa was seated in a straight chair across from Gretchen's desk. As he walked through the hall, the workroom and across the reception area, she observed him. He had a confident, self-assured manner with enough ease not to be considered stuffy. His appearance was much more youthful than she had expected before seeing him yesterday. His friend, Sam Littlegate, would be about the same age, but Sam was older looking. From the years she knew McBaden had been practicing, she figured his age around forty-four if he began right out of law school. But he looked six years younger. He dresses well, but then most lawyers do.

"Hello. Did you have any difficulty changing your reservations?" he asked as she stood.

She smiled, "No."

"Or in keeping your room at The Patrick?"

"No problem."

"Shall we go back to the office?" He stopped. "Did you meet Gretchen Pearly?"

"We introduced ourselves."

When the two were seated, McBaden put his arms on the desk with his hands clasped together. "Just to review what we discussed last night: I see the office as a practice for two or three attorneys at least for the next few years. There are no ambitions here to build a large firm. I've been there. It was a profitable time in many ways. I made no attempt to locate anyone to go into a full partnership with me. A junior partnership may evolve later, if someone works out and likes what we do. Or, God willing, the clients and the workload merit such.

"Anyone who comes in has much at stake professionally and financially as I do. You may be interested, even if you refrain from asking directly, can a lone partner support an office? I've been at this for a number of years. I have no dependents. I have a comfortable lifestyle. I'm neither frugal nor a wastrel. I work long hours and I expect diligence from everyone in the office. But, I assure you, I will not keep a time clock or ask one of you. Other than the billing hours, we have to provide for clients."

He paused.

She asked, "Will Gretchen be secretary for both of us?"

He liked her use of the plural. "For the time being. If we get pressed, we can think about another person. Part time. Would you like to see your office?" He watched her response with wide-eyed intensity.

She looked directly into his eyes and, with the faintest of smiles, answered, "Yes, sir."

He led the way to the adjacent room on the right. Opening that door, he stood aside for her to enter first. He watched as she went in and looked at the walls and the furnishings.

"It's very nice. Quite roomy now and, I see, there would be space for another desk if needed."

"A computer will be installed this morning. It could be behind the desk. There's a small table that can be placed there. Or on the desktop. Is there a preference?"

She studied the arrangements then sat in the chair at the desk. She turned the chair around and contemplated the space between the wall and chair. She pretended to type on a small table then turned and repeated the motions at the desk. Looking up, she said, "On the desk. Left side. The phone on the right."

He nodded, thinking she was thorough. What a time saver it was not to have to be patient while she learned how to speak to the subject without being expansive or roundabout like many women.

Pulling up an armchair to the client's side, he sat opposite her. "The phone's connected. Gretchen will answer when she's here. You'll have voice mail and e-mail. The fax will be in the workroom. There are three in-trays: one for you, for me, for the office. You may either send your own faxes or leave them in the office tray. She will bring your mail to your desk as soon as she sorts it. Look around. Let her know if there's something you need."

"You both have anticipated quite nicely."

Gretchen came to the door. "The men are ready to install the computer equipment. Shall they start in here or your office?"

McBaden stood. "In here will be fine. We'll go to the conference room. I'll put away some files in my office." He walked out, then the women moved across the hall.

When Gretchen opened the door, Clarissa stared ahead. "How marvelous! Two large windows." She walked around the large table and gazed outward. "What a green view! And more buildings than I had noticed yesterday."

She scrutinized the room. The woodwork was dark, the walls a light tint of celery. The conference table centered the room. There were eight dark wood and deep green upholstered chairs. Very narrow tables were placed on two sides of the room.

Clarissa asked, "Are there plans for draperies or accessories?"

"Mr. McBaden hasn't said so." Gretchen walked to the window, placed a hand on the casing and looked out. A ring on her left hand reflected a light.

Clarissa noticed the sparkle. "What a lovely ring!"

Gretchen turned and eagerly extended her hand. "Thank you. It's an engagement ring. I got it in June. The wedding will be after Christmas." Effervescently, she added, "That month is almost as traditional as June."

Clarissa praised the ring, saying it had a clear sparkle like Gretchen's eyes. "I wish the most happiness to you and your fiancé. I look forward to meeting him."

"His name is Warren. He works a route across town, but he sometimes can run by in the morning. He's a UPS driver." Her voice held a note of pride.

"How important! We really need his company's service."

Gretchen suddenly asked, "The coffee's hot. Would you like a cup?"

"I would. Please, join me, unless the men need to connect something in here."

"No. They will be awhile in the offices." She scooted out and returned with two steaming mugs and packets of sugar, sweetener, dry creamer, and two plastic spoons. "I'll give you a hint about pleasing Mr. McBaden. He's – what's that long word, beginning with . . . a *c*?"

"Connoisseur?"

"That's the word. Thanks. I'll make regular coffee for the office, but it's top-quality, and it'll be full-bodied, as he prefers. That's so it'll suit clients or anybody else who comes in. We plan to offer coffee if they'll be here longer than twenty minutes." She began to drink her coffee.

Clarissa placed her mug on the table. "You can claim to be an excellent maker of coffee. Are there other traditions or procedures I need to know about?"

"No. Oh, he's a very good boss. His instructions are always clear. I like to get my work done so I never have to work overtime. I like to leave the to-do tray empty. And the best part is we get lots of holidays. All the federal ones. If court closes early on Friday, and I'm caught up, I leave early. That's one day, the boss does, too. Only, he does come back on weekends." She sighed.

"It has been kind of you to share all this with me. It certainly has begun as an agreeable environment." Clarissa rose. "I'll be on my way. If Mr. McBaden is busy, I won't interrupt him. I will be out hunting for a residence."

"Will you be returning?"

"I plan to."

CHAPTER 3

The trial procedures had started with jury selection at 9:30 A.M. The prospective jury had been assembled and queried. Surprisingly, not a person had begged off. Tom Kincaid, attorney for the plaintiff - officers of the Nu-Vue Techniques where Leroy Bing was formerly employed as a technician - had presented his arguments; and Joseph McBaden had answered for his client Leroy Bing, project designer.

The jurors had been told to consider what was presented here and whether the work in question was done in the scope of his employment. This work was by Leroy Bing, a technician employed for four years prior to being dismissed four months ago by the plaintiff Nu-Vue Techniques. The firm states Mr. Bing worked on his own projects during company time, using company equipment.

Further, the jurors were to consider the evidence presented. They should keep in mind three criteria that had to be met to substantiate Nu-Vue Techniques' claim that the experiments; the records of those experiments; and any designs, procedures and all products that are results from or are ready for production are the property of the Nu-Vue Techniques or Leroy Bing.

First criterion: Was the work the kind he was hired to do? Second criterion: Was or was not the work done in time or in place of employment? Third criterion: Did the work to some extent help his employer?

All three criteria have to be met for the plaintiff to be considered entitled to the work in question. If any one criterion is not met, the plaintiff has no claim on the work in question.

During the presentation by the defense, the defendant's detailed records of his work hours in his home workshop, his purchases of equipment and experiment materials, and his notations of results of experiments had been impressive. The records were a challenge. The opposing attorney had attempted to discredit them. He had not succeeded, nor did any of the three witnesses for the defense refute their statements. After McBaden's brief questioning of the three men who were co-workers of Bing's, the two attorneys approached the bench. Kincaid asked for time to talk with his clients. The judge granted him a half-hour. The jury was directed to wait in another room.

The judge read some papers, wrote on some others. McBaden explained what was happening to Bing.

"Our case looks airtight. Their attorney is pointing out the advantages of dropping the charges."

Bing relaxed visibly for a minute, but then tensed and placed his elbows on the table. Hoarsely, he said, "Is this unusual? It's been such a short time."

"It varies. We never know."

"If charges are dropped, do we ask them to cover my expenses? And back pay since my dismissal?"

McBaden replied. "We will."

Squirming again in his chair, Bing asked, "Why did they go through all this legal process?"

"Have they ever offered a reason to you?" Bing shook his head. McBaden added, "They are a small company, but one that is likely to grow. The technology field, as you know better than I, is expanding daily. Or merging, whichever is the most advantageous. They may consider your work to be highly profitable down the road. By bringing the experiments in question to the court for a decision, they know if they have any legal rights to use this particular work of yours. And if not, that is one issue that will not have to be dealt with if they are bought out. A clearing of the books."

Bing shook his head in disgust. "An expensive way to go about something. There have been a number of work days lost. For all of us." He looked around to McBaden. With a half-smile, he added, "Except for you, McBaden."

McBaden responded. "And now you can continue with your experiments. When did you say you could start your next position?"

"As soon as I am through with this trial. And, with a not-guilty verdict."

"Excuse me, Mr. Bing. Their attorney is signaling." McBaden rose and crossed the room. Even though he had spoken positively to Bing and felt they had enough data to support a not-guilty vote from the jury if the case went to them, he was experienced enough not to get elated. Ego could cloud the discussion, the negotiation that he probably was being called for. Kincaid nodded to him and opened the door to the hall. McBaden followed him out, and into a very small room.

"My clients are willing to drop the case and pay the legal fees and court costs."

"And what else?"

Kincaid blew out a deep breath. "Isn't that enough?"

"No. He wants back pay for the months since his discharge, expenses of job search covered. And, the amount we requested for defamation of character."

"Come on, Joseph. This is a struggling company."

"In a highly profitable industry. My client needs to recoup his living expenses for those months. Tom, face it; this is a small amount. He's no mercenary. Your clients should appreciate he's not greedy." McBaden spoke strongly and directly, focusing straight into Kincaid's eyes. He waited, his posture erect, tense.

Kincaid returned McBaden's stare trying to read his tenacity. He said, "Let me talk to them again." He returned to the room where his clients waited.

McBaden stopped at the water cooler to quench a drying throat. He withdrew a small notepad from his pocket and referred to some notations. Closing it, he saw Kincaid re-enter the hall, point to the small conference room and return there. Again McBaden followed.

Kincaid began speaking. "They've agreed to your client's conditions. We'll talk about when and where to direct the monies. As soon as all the figures are tallied, give me a call." Kincaid put his hand out. "Good to meet you in court on this case. I wish you the best in your new office."

McBaden shook his hand, thanked him for the comments, and returned to the courtroom. He told Bing of the company's agreement to all that had been requested. Relief was immediately visible on Bing's face. He extended both hands toward McBaden.

"How can I ever thank you enough? And you did this so quickly in here!"

"Your detailed, dated notes expedited the process. Those were hard to refute. Now, you can resume your work unencumbered with all this."

Bing looked around. "Do we sit here or what now?"

"Mr. Kincaid and people from Nu-Vue Techniques will be in shortly. He's letting them know we accept. And reviewing our requests. Giving us time to change our demands." McBaden looked intently at Bing.

"No changes. I'll be satisfied with what we asked for, as well as to end this wrangling."

Leaving the courthouse, McBaden felt a distinct sense of well-being. It wasn't the first case he had won in this building, but it was a milestone for him. The maiden trial in his independent practice ended with the settlement he and his client had sought. The old firm had been agreeable to his taking the case upon Bing's request. True, this was not a highly remunerative case; the plaintiff was a small industry. But McBaden liked cases that were decided in favor of his clients.

The news was out and other attorneys congratulated him in the hallways, on the elevator, and along the sidewalks. Many stopped and shook his hand.

Gretchen asked him the outcome when he walked into the office mid-afternoon.

He answered, "A win for us. Now our work is in the wrap-up. Mr. Bing is a much relaxed man."

"Good for you, Mr. McBaden. Your phone messages are on your desk."

"Thanks. Is Miss Bentley in?" He asked as he thumbed through the faxes.

"No, sir. But she said she'd be back."

He nodded to her and walked on to his office. He stopped, turned around and looked at the coffeepot. "Fresh?"

"Not really. I'll make a pot." She jumped up and started the process. "Drat! I should have ordered a cake."

"The thought is appreciated."

McBaden swung his briefcase on the desk then hung up his jacket. From the filing cabinet he withdrew four folders and sat in his swivel chair and fanned the folders on the desk. Quickly, he flipped through each one. Finished, he sat back a few minutes and thought about the clients. He leaned forward again, shuffled them, and wrote numerals 1, 2, 3, 4 on the tabs. After he restacked them to his left, he returned to the filing cabinet where he selected a few more folders.

He opened the top one and read with more concentration. He took a legal pad and pen from a drawer. He made several marginal notes. After he closed the folder, he picked up the phone messages. In the reply section, he made notes on four sheets and took those to Gretchen's desk.

"Coffee's ready, sir. Shall I get a cup for you?" She asked.

"Fine, if you're getting one for yourself." He walked behind her to the coffee area. "You can make these calls for me. If there's any problem, buzz me. Thanks. It smells great." Taking a couple of swallows, he pronounced, "It tastes perfect. And, Gretchen, anytime you're busy, I can pour my own. Don't worry about wasting coffee. A pot in the morning and one mid-afternoon are okay. Miss Bentley will get her own, too. No problem." Drinking several more swallows, he refilled his cup. "Is all the equipment working right?"

"So far, yes."

"Good news. I will depend on your letting me know when anything is not in working order, especially the electronic equipment, and everything else under warranty. We'll need to get the service people in here quickly. Later, routine services, you know, like lamps out, dripping faucets, clean-up – call building maintenance number; and when paper and other office supplies are low, call All Office Products. We'll open an account there tomorrow and let's try buying at one place. One bill. One deliverer."

McBaden drained his cup and placed it beside the pot. "When Miss Bentley comes in, please, tell her I'd like to see her."

When he was back in his office, Gretchen washed and dried his cup and spoon and stacked them with the other china and silverware. She didn't mind the small chore; she felt she was practicing for her housekeeping with Warren. She wanted to use china instead of paper or Styrofoam. Her mother had promised she could have her grandmother's everyday dishes when she married. Whenever there was a five-minute lull, she would daydream about setting a table with the lovely flowered pattern.

She wasn't prone to daydreaming in the office. She was a clock watcher who timed her tasks, for she wanted to leave at the end of her eight-hour day. Lifting the handset she began the telephone calls.

McBaden went to the work area, paused, held up some papers and said, "fax," as she held the receiver with one hand and scribbled notes with the other. She nodded her head. He gave a glance in Clarissa's office. It was empty.

Around four o'clock, Clarissa returned and stopped at Gretchen's desk. "Any messages?"

"A couple. I put them on your desk." Gretchen smiled.

"Thank you. Is Mr. McBaden back?" Gretchen nodded. "How did the case go?"

"We won. What could be better on our first court day? He's probably still on a high with all the strong coffee he drank."

"Well, that's good news. Oh, who handles the tax forms?"

"Mr. McBaden. He plans to do the billing, enter financial accounts in his computer. For now anyway. But I have some state and federal withholding forms. Here," she said as she pulled papers from her desk drawer and handed two over. "I knew we'd need a few so I picked 'em up when I was getting some other forms."

"Thanks. When I get a phone, I'll let you know. You can reach me now at The Patrick."

"I hear that's a swell place. As plush as you get in Windermere," she exuded.

"It's very nice." As she headed toward her office, Gretchen exclaimed that Mr. McBaden wanted to see her.

Clarissa put her handbag down. She pulled out a mirror and combed her hair and applied fresh lipstick. After a short debate whether or not to take a legal pad in, she decided no. Commit to memory what he has to say. Write pertinent data down afterwards.

His door was open a few inches; she knocked; he said come in.

"You wanted to see me?"

"Yes," he motioned to the chair opposite him

"Congratulations on the success of the trial. It was a short one according to Gretchen."

"It was and thank you, Miss Bentley." He said.

"Would you mind if we weren't so formal in the office? Could we talk on a first-name basis?"

"That's fine. Is it Clarissa? Or are you called Clare? Clara?"

She kept a composed countenance but he noticed it took a little effort. "Clarissa, please."

"All right, Clarissa. And I'm Joseph."

"Not Joe?" She took her turn to inquire.

"No. I've always been Joseph."

"Never had a nickname?"

He shook his head. "And you?"

"When we know each other better, maybe. Now, what do we need to confer about?"

He reached for a stack of folders and held them out to her. "There are four cases. Four possible clients. I had talked with all of them briefly, while I was still at Hadley Morgan. I have known them for some time. They had heard I would be setting up my own practice, and they asked me to consider these matters then. Each person is supposed to have written to the firm saying he was choosing our firm as his attorney. These should be rather direct, uncomplicated matters. Look them over. I'd like for you to handle them."

"You have numbered the tabs. This is in the order you would approach them?"

He nodded. "I'll be looking into contracts for a couple of clients. And I have a speech to prepare for a seminar next week. There's some research I plan to do while I'm away."

"I told Gretchen I could be reached at the hotel. When I decide on a residence, I'll give you the address and phone number."

"Did you apartment hunt today? Any luck?"

"Some maybes." She hugged the folders with one arm, rose and left his office.

CHAPTER 4

Gretchen knocked on McBaden's door. "Come in."
She walked in and partially closed the door. Standing near his desk, she said in a hushed manner. "There's a lady here who wants to speak with you."

"Did she say what it's about?" He asked with interest, closing a folder. Gretchen was not given to secretiveness; thus he looked at her intently.

"Well, she asked if you practiced general law. I said yes. Then she wanted to know if you handled divorce cases. I don't remember that you have. I thought I'd better ask."

"Your memory is perfect. I haven't. I appreciate your asking me. Wait a minute." He pressed a button on his phone base then lifted the receiver. "Clarissa, can you come to my office?" He hung up.

Clarissa opened the door, looked at McBaden and Gretchen. "There's a lady in the office who wants to know if we handle divorce," said McBaden. "Would you like to speak with her?"

"Yes, I would. Do you know anything about her?"

"I don't, but Gretchen has seen her. Any opinion, Gretchen?"

"She appears to be mid-twenties. Neat looking. Worried, I'd say. Maybe careful. Smart."

"Did she say how she found us?" McBaden inquired.

"No. What shall I tell her, sir?"

"Show her in. Clarissa, I'll introduce myself, make a few inquires and then tell her you will be handling the case. Unless, you signal me that you aren't interested."

Gretchen left the room and returned promptly, leading the neat young woman. "Mr. McBaden, Miss Bentley, this is Susan Phillips."

Gretchen had given a good description of Susan. The woman's carriage seemed weighted; her expression, worried; and her hands, tense on her purse.

McBaden scrutinized the woman while speaking calmly. "How did you select us, Mrs. Phillips?"

"From the directory board downstairs. I had come to the bank on the first floor. I read the listing with your name." She continued. "I need an attorney, and I don't want to go to a large firm."

"We are new to the building. The two of us are in practice together. What specifically are your needs?" He asked.

"I told the receptionist – a divorce." Her voice was terse and impatient.

"Mrs. Phillips, that's not an area of mine; however, Miss Bentley can talk with you."

Susan turned directly toward Clarissa and gave her a hard look, as if she were trying to make up her mind. Clarissa remained composed and watched as Susan sighed and lifted her shoulders. "Thank you, I'd like to talk with Miss Bentley," she told McBaden.

He stood up, and then Clarissa did likewise and said, "Let's go to my office."

As Susan stood, Clarissa walked to the door and into the hall and directed her to the office on the right. She pulled a chair up to the desk and Susan sat down, wearily.

"Would you like some coffee?" Clarissa asked.

Quickly, Susan was on the edge of the chair. "Heavens no. I'm too nervous now."

"How about some tea? Hot tea?"

Susan concentrated a few moments. Turning to Clarissa, she said, "Yes, thank you. Sugar, no lemon."

Clarissa said, "Excuse me," and left the room.

"Gretchen," she spoke quietly, approaching her desk. "Do we have tea bags?"

"No."

"Can you check with one of the other offices on the floor? Or with anyone you know here to scare up a couple? Then bring two cups to my office and whatever snack we have on hand. The bank should have a tea drinker if no one else does. Thanks. Leave your answering machine on."

Clarissa returned, closed the door and sat in her desk chair. "If it looks as if we've just moved in, we have. There's still unpacking to do."

"I'm usually not a nervous person. But this is something I need to do," Susan curled her fingers tightly around her purse and moved closer to the edge of the seat.

"Is this a sudden decision?" Clarissa spoke quietly and slowly.

"Not really. It's one I've put off much too long. Now, I need to take some action. I said a few minutes ago, I think I need a lawyer." She stopped. "I read an ad in the classifieds about quick divorces for fifty dollars. But those are for both parties being anxious to separate. That's something they agree on?"

"And that is not your situation?"

"No." She looked down, tucked her feet under the chair, and then lifted her gaze to Clarissa's face. "I haven't mentioned this to Garvey."

"He doesn't know you are thinking of a separation?"

"A separation with divorce is my intention. No, I think, he doesn't suspect that."

"What can you tell me about your relationship?" Clarissa asked calmly with an open, interested tone.

Clarissa watched Susan as she sighed deeply and collected her thoughts. Gretchen had sensed that Susan was smart and worried; Clarissa agreed from the short contact. She noticed a hardness of facial lines and expression that may have come with stress.

"It was good for the first couple of years. Gradually, the financial difficulties ate away the accord, the pleasantries, the togetherness." Having said that, she hunched her shoulders again. She stared at her hands.

"Do you think he's aware of how you feel?"

"I doubt if he cares anymore. We seldom see each other. We share the same apartment, the same name and honestly that's about all." Briefly, she looked Clarissa in the eyes, then lowered her focus to her lap and slid backward in the chair.

There was a knock on the door. Clarissa got up and opened it. Gretchen came in with a tray, two steaming mugs, and a plate of individually wrapped sweet shortbreads.

Clarissa thanked Gretchen, who closed the door, and handed a mug to Susan. "The shortbread makes a welcomed afternoon tea break." She opened a couple of sugar packets and stirred her tea.

Susan moved her purse beside her and leaned forward and fixed her tea and opened a shortbread. Holding the wrapper around it, she nibbled while the tea cooled. Clarissa prolonged stirring her tea, allowing Susan time to recoup her energy. The women sipped silently for several minutes. Susan's hand was smooth and strong, Clarissa knew from the handshake; now she saw dexterity.

"This is refreshing. I used to enjoy afternoon tea. Thank you. This is a ritual I would like to return to. Maybe after work."

"What kind of work are you in, Susan?"

"I'm a dental hygienist. I go to work early mornings and get off around three-thirty. But I'm so tired when I get home. Usually, I do errands after work. Maybe I'm too depressed to prepare tea. It's simple, isn't it? Boil water, drop in a tea bag, stir in some sugar. How can that be too much?" Susan lamented.

"Your work is probably a steady pressure. And if you don't look forward to going home, the pressure stays with you." Clarissa was attempting to be supportive and rephrasing what she was hearing, while at the same time not putting words in her mouth.

Susan drained the mug, dropped in the crumpled wrapper, and set it on the desk. She appeared more at ease.

"We are seldom at home the same time. I work long hours four days a week. I suspect he lost his job, because he stayed out of work those days. He tried to make up hours when I was off. Now he uses those days to do research at the library."

"What does he do?" Clarissa unobtrusively had begun making notes on a legal pad.

"He's a sociologist. Worked for the city part time in human resources. Led some seminars for the recreational department, too. But he's determined to . . ." she stopped short, sat upright. "I won't go into that now." She stood up. "I'm glad I read the directory and took a chance coming up. I haven't told anyone that I was going to do this. Will you represent me?"

Clarissa stood. "Yes."

"Thank you. There is something I want to do before we talk again. Could I see you the first of next week?"

Clarissa looked at her appointment book. "Tuesday afternoon? Will four o'clock be suitable?"

"It will. I'll come from work. I'll write my address. You can find the number in the phone book, but I prefer you don't call me at the apartment."

As Susan wrote, Clarissa said, "I understand."

Reaching the door, Susan turned back and said, trying to smile, "I feel comfortable with you." Then she walked out.

Clarissa resumed jotting notes on the legal pad. There was little information; however, she felt Susan would offer more considerable facts when she returned. The first step, the initial interview was the most difficult she had observed in her years of dealing with divorce cases. It was not unusual for an attorney to be the first person one confided in when wanting a separation.

Clarissa printed "Susan Phillips" on the tab of a new folder. She filed it at the front of a cabinet drawer, in front of the four folders McBaden had numbered for her. She had Gretchen make appointments for them Monday and Tuesday. Five cases. That was a comfortable number. And she would also have time to tend to some moving arrangements. She had an apartment guide and planned to continue surveying the areas that sounded appealing. There would be daylight until about seven. If she delayed dinner, she could have an hour or so to drive around. Saturday she would look most of the day.

CHAPTER 5

Saturday morning Clarissa arose early, showered and dressed comfortably in a skirt, blouse and low-heel shoes. She gathered yesterday's newspaper and her shoulder bag and headed toward the hotel coffee shop.

The shop was quiet; the few patrons appeared casual, unlike the weekday crowd that at the first meal had assumed their business-like mode. Clarissa had found the shop pleasant and comfortable. The hand-painted murals on the wall were eye-catching but not distracting. They depicted local scenes. This morning she chose a table that afforded a view of all of them.

She opened the menu that had been wedged between napkin and sugar containers. Thinking of a light and filling breakfast to fortify her for apartment searching, she scanned the menu.

A waitress walked up quietly in her soft-soled shoes. "May I bring you a cup of coffee while you decide?"

Clarissa looked up. "Yes, please."

When the waitress returned with a mug of coffee, Clarissa ordered a Belgian waffle, bacon strips, fresh fruit and a glass of milk. The waiting time, she used to review the apartment addresses and the city-county map then determined a route.

First would be complexes in the county. The newest buildings would be outlying. They would include fitness and activity rooms, a pool, perhaps security alarms. There were several gated communities advertised. She starred one. "I'll look at that for you, Dad."

Twenty- to thirty-year-old city buildings would be next. Unless these units had been refurbished, they would require heavy maintenance soon. These may be the best built, dating to a time brick exterior and plastered interiors were the rule of thumb. She penciled on the map: Stop only if recently remodeled. She had heard the horror of years of grease down the kitchen drains, wax layered on wood floors, lopsided windows and screens, and inadequate heat and air-conditioning.

Last would be any apartments in the center of Windermere.

She folded the map and papers and slid them into the outer pocket of her shoulder bag. Looking up, she viewed the first mural to the left. In its center was a town square with a bell on the upper left corner and a water pump on the diagonal corner. A walkway crossed from lower left to upper right. Around the square were a church, a school, various shops and residences. Second was a map centered with the Town Square. Spiked from it were meandering roads along elevated ridges that terminated in villages. No crossroads showed; however, Clarissa considered there must be a communality with footpaths between the villages.

The other murals were more typical of city development, but these either reproduced the appearance of the buildings' early history or would be easily recognized today. A tobacco factory was the third mural; a textile plant, fourth; a hospital and research center, fifth; an airport, sixth; and an auditorium, seventh.

Finished with mural gazing and breakfast, she gathered her things, left a tip and paid the bill. She sought her rental car in the parking deck.

The first two complexes she inspected had large living rooms and at least one large bedroom with private bath. "Do I need such a large bedroom? Now?" She queried. The answer saddened her so she gave it only momentary mental anguish. That door had been closed. She sat in her car and surveyed the sparkling clean exterior – bright, white paint, swept walkways, the short border of shrubbery, neatly clipped, resident doorways not visible or easily accessible from the parking lot or street. No tenants were outside. The sterility of it all caused her to shutter.

She stopped at the entry of one gated community and asked for the office. She was told to call for an appointment. She backed out and questioned if this were the type of place for her. Samuel Littlegate should be knowledgeable to the extent of how important security measures were to be weighed in Windermere.

Quickly, she realized that traveling was speedy and relatively easy along the interstate, but once she tried state and county roads, the results were speed, slow-and-stop cycles. She had not envisioned dwelling a stone's throw away from an interstate. Not again. Consideration of another's convenience was no longer a factor. Was her convenience of living quarters close to the office a prime requisite?

Consulting her notes, she headed the car well within the city limits and found an older apartment site. Slowly, she drove around the curving streets and scanned facades and along rear drives to look at parking spaces, back doors, waste bins, clotheslines and general upkeep. Finding the office, she parked and went in.

The leasing agent, occupied with a tenant, told Clarissa she would be with her shortly. Clarissa sat on a small, soft sofa and checked off the places she had been and reviewed those still to see. A female tenant was naming an assortment of problems that needed attention: Some were immediate; some could be delayed. She was speaking in a respectful tone with an effort to convince the agent to take care of the complaints. Clarissa surmised that the woman often would be placed on the delayed list, for she did not have a convincing aspect. Her appearance in general showed what the British writers so aptly described "one of genteel poverty." Her personality broadcast now one of not bothering others while it pled for needs to be met.

Two other apartment seekers opened the front door and strutted in. They were twenty-year-old guys, who barged right up beside the woman at the counter that separated the waiting room and the business office. The taller one asked for a layout of the floor plans; the other piped over his shoulder, "and a price list."

The tenant moved over. The leasing agent spoke directly and levelly. "I'll help you after I have finished with this lady and the one seated."

The guys turned around, gave sweeping glances at Clarissa and leaned backward with elbows upon the counter. They were similarly dressed, not only like each other but also like many teens, in baggy cargo pants and long white tee shirts. Their hair was shaggy and their facial expressions were sour. After the brief look at Clarissa they kept their eyes down.

The woman kept her distance from the guys as she passed and turned a weak smile toward Clarissa. As the woman exited, Clarissa stood up. The guys did not move.

"I also would like to see your floor plans." The agent handed her a paper. "Thank you. I'll look them over." She walked back to the sofa.

It was easy for Clarissa to hear the agent explain as she gave one of the guys a paper and then said, "If there's one you're interested in, I will look up the rental fee."

He shoved it over. His friend said, "They look kinda small." "Yeah, but bigger than what we got now." "What about this one bedroom? We could get bunks." "If you want a top one." "Not me!" "Let's ask the price. Ma'm, what's the rent?"

The agent flipped through some charts and wrote the amount on the paper.

"A month!" said the tall one in disbelief.

"Yes."

The shorter one whispered, "No way, buddy." They left the paper on the counter and walked out dejectedly.

Clarissa approached the agent. "Do you have a vacancy for a two-room, one-and-a half bath?"

"I do. Do you prefer a first- or second-floor unit?"

"First. Is there one I could inspect this morning?"

"There is. The monthly rental and the deposit I'll jot beside the model," she said as she wrote. "And if you'll give me your name and current local address, I'll get the key." When Clarissa took the key, the agent commented, "We really have some very nice people here. I wouldn't want you to get the wrong impression from the young men."

"I'm sure you do. Thank you. What time do you close today?"

"One o'clock. Just drop the key through the door slot if you are later than that."

Clarissa parked in front of the apartment building. She noticed each had mini-blinds and some also had draperies. The brick exterior lent a somewhat stately appearance, but the window frames needed painting. There was a mellowness about the buildings provided by tall, old trees ranging from narrow-leafed native pines to broad-leafed white oaks.

Cars parked along the streets and in the rear lots were low and mid-budget models, economy vans and pickup trucks. They were a contrast to the expensive vehicles that people on the fast track drove and which dominated the newer developments that she had seen earlier.

Still, she toured the vacant apartment and considered it an excellent unit for the money. In D.C., it would be a real find and probably be grabbed immediately by the new guys in town. The updates had been carefully designed and executed to keep as close as possible to what she expected had been originally planned. She knew her budget allowed for a steeper monthly rent and decided to keep on looking. She just had not found the place to suit her yet.

A glance at the dashboard clock showed it was lunchtime. However, as she was driving toward the center of town, she slowed down for a better view of the houses and yards along the older streets. There were grassy strips and cement sidewalks, and small lawns. Large shrubbery ran across the front of the houses; many had some type of porch. Set along the curving streets, they were quite charming.

At the first signs of businesses, she spotted a small restaurant and parked at the curb. Lettering on the door read Six-day Café. It appeared a popular lunch place, for all the booths were filled. One stool was empty at the counter and she opted for it. She read the chalkboard menu above the pass-through between the kitchen and eating area. The selection was varied. She felt conservative today with more looking around ahead.

A young man in white – shirt, trousers, apron and a hat of sorts – walked down the counter and asked what she'd have.

"Number 5 if the chicken salad was made today."

"It was. I made it myself."

"I'll take it and a glass of iced tea."

"Coming right up."

When he walked away, Clarissa once again pulled out her notes and map. She ran a finger along the downtown streets until she came to Six-day's location, a convenient restaurant to downtown and to the older residential area. Turning to look out the front and side windows, she noticed a fine old two-story brick home directly across the street. There was a simple, tasteful sign over the door; thus, she thought it could be a business. Further to the left was an expanse of lawn with a fountain and a gazebo, which probably served as a community park. The open space was pleasing to the eye and it appeared accessible also from another street just to its rear.

The waiter returned and she pivoted toward the counter. "It looks delicious," she said as she folded her papers into her bag.

She ate slowly, realizing it was a treat not to hurry. The entire afternoon could be devoted to the hunt. The waiter asked her if she were through. She answered yes, but she would like a refill of tea. "Do you have any lemon desserts?"

"Lemon meringue pie. Also fresh baked today," he smiled.

"I'll take a slice." When he placed the dessert in front of her, she exclaimed, "Fresh strawberries on the side."

"They're from California. I noticed your map and newspaper. Are you new to Windermere?"

"Yes. Oh, the pie is so tart and tasty. And the crust crispy." She ate a couple of bites, and as he was standing nearby filling sugar containers, she asked, "Are there any apartments tucked away in this area?"

"One strip of maybe a dozen down about four blocks." He had noticed her nice clothes and her refined way of speaking. "They are small and not updated. There is one section of townhouses that folks say are very nice. A lot of couples who work downtown like them. They're two blocks over. Can't miss 'em. Right on the street. No yards. Three stories high, I think."

"Thank you for the descriptions. Probably not what I'm looking for. This is a charming area. It's nice to see people strolling around and coming in for lunch."

"We think it's a nice section of town. High Street is a Historic

District now. So there will only be remodeling and changes that will preserve its character."

"That's nice."

He asked, "What are you looking for? You asked about apartments?"

"I haven't seen what I want yet. The newest complexes are without personality, and the exclusive communities weren't very appealing and the older ones seem to be for transients before they find a small house or some other place."

"You must have seen a lot of 'em." He began filling the napkins holders. "Would you be interested in a duplex? Rooms on first and second floors?"

"I might. Do you know of a place?"

"My landlady recently remodeled one side of her house and she's hoping to rent to some single person or a couple."

"What else can you tell me? It sounds like a possibility." Clarissa spoke enthusiastically.

"It hasn't been rented before. Her daughter had lived there for years. She married a few months ago and moved out west. It's only a few blocks away."

"You said she was your landlady?"

"Yes, I have what used to be the garage, which always had living quarters overhead. Intended for helpers, I suspect. That was their first remodeling. I've been the only tenant. Very convenient for me."

"Do you think she'd let me look at it today?"

"I'll give her a call," he said. He refilled her tea glass before going to the kitchen to use a wall phone.

Clarissa thought what a stroke of good fortune it would be to locate a place so easily. It could have the advantages of a condo without the commitment of ownership. And the sidewalks would offer ample walking routes.

The waiter returned. "Mrs. Hughes was at home. She said to tell you come on. Hand me your map and I'll mark the house. I'm sorry I didn't ask your name to tell her, but I'll call her back and let her know you're coming and your name. Okay?"

"I'm Clarissa Bentley from Northern Virginia. I'm an attorney and will be in practice with Joseph McBaden. You are most kind to do this for me, a stranger."

"No problem. The house has gray-green siding with dark green shutters. A porch runs across the front. Good luck. Oh, yes, I'm Phil." Someone called him from the kitchen, and he nodded to Clarissa while walking away.

The blocks were short with side streets crossing every fourth or fifth house. Phil had marked an X on the third block down, and she pulled over to the right hand side when she located 306. It was an attractive place nestled between two very different-styled houses. One was half brick with a second story of clapboard painted a soft ivory, while the other house was a story and a half of gray-painted shingles and white trim.

What a picturesque grouping, Clarissa mused. She walked upon the wide-planked porch flooring and caught the echoing wooden notes. She lifted the brass knocker and liked the solid sound. In a few seconds, a tall, thin woman about fifty years old opened the door. She was dressed neatly in straight gray skirt and a long-sleeved, white oxford shirt.

"Good afternoon. I'm Clarissa Bentley. Phil at Six-day Café gave me this address. Am I speaking with Mrs. Hughes?"

"Please come in," the woman said as she opened the screened door. "Yes, I'm Mrs. Hughes. Welcome to Windermere. I hope you will like it here."

"Thank you. I am appreciating kindly, friendly people such as Phil and you. He said that you had an apartment, or a duplex, you may wish to rent?"

"We've just finished the remodeling. Would you like to see it?"

"I would."

"Well, let us go back out on the porch. There are separate entrances for the two living quarters." Mrs. Hughes led the way. They walked left, turned, and continued on a narrower porch to a door at the end. Clarissa recalled doors like this in her hometown that usually led into the family dining room or a small anteroom.

"This is the duplex entry. The mailing address is 306 B. My daughter started that. Here is the living room, and just beyond is a dining room. To its left is a kitchen, and to its right is a bathroom with a shower, and a study or it could be used for a guestroom."

"The colors are nice and the rooms are quite large. I like the high ceilings."

"Shall we go upstairs?" The steps were just beyond the bathroom. The upstairs bathroom was above the first-floor one. It had an old clawfoot tub with a shower overhead. "We had quite a debate about the tub. My daughter and I think this tub is lovely; but Daddy Burl, my husband, was all for a modern tub and shower." She looked apprehensively at Clarissa.

Clarissa smiled. "I would have sided with the women. It is a lovely fixture. So deep. What a way to relax after a long day. And the small octagonal window above to let the bather see the blue sky or the stars at night. The basin in the oak dresser adds a distinctive touch."

"There are two bedrooms on this level. One at the back is larger and offers a grand view of the back garden. And the room at the front is smaller, allowing space for two large storage closets as well as a regular one for clothes. All of this may appear too much for a single tenant; however, after having my daughter here for many years, I know there are some women who like to spread out. Who enjoy their space. Of course, it would also be adequate for a young couple."

Clarissa felt a question in the last statement. "I am not engaged or planning to be married anytime . . . soon. And I plan to live by myself. I assume you prefer no subletting."

"That would be our preference. This is a quiet neighborhood. People will be friendly and speak to other residents. They are generally not nosy. Somehow it manages to come out a comfortable place to reside." Mrs. Hughes said evenly, not boasting or apologizing.

Clarissa quickly retraced each room, looked out the windows, opened a door off the kitchen, and stood on a deck that ran the width of her side of the duplex. She found Mrs. Hughes waiting for her in the living room.

"I would love to stay here." Clarissa spoke earnestly.

"Would you like to know the monthly rental?"

Clarissa laughed. "Yes, thank you. I would not want you to think an attorney is careless in money matters. But I just have a feeling it's right for me."

The fee was well within her budget and the women agreed upon terms with a shake of hands until a contract could be written.

CHAPTER 6

Saturday found McBaden enjoying a new experience, even though the routine was quite familiar. He spent the day at the office. His own office. From the first sighting of his name on the outside door, he felt he had moved up in the world. He affirmed that this was what he wanted; his own practice with all its responsibilities and possibilities: He was equally aware that many tongues uttered that he had walked away from a prestigious firm where one was automatically granted respect just from being associated with its name. Now McBaden closed the door tightly, just as he had the door of his mind when friends asked him to consider all he was leaving.

After weeks of handling details for moving in, he glanced around the reception room and smiled with approval. Gretchen was not sitting there this morning, but he knew she could be counted on to greet his clients with a friendly, welcoming face. He briefly envisioned her today darting about the city, fulfilling some needs for her wedding. "Good luck to you!" he muttered and moved down the hall.

He stopped by the fax machine, saw there were several messages and carried them down to his office. He plopped the briefcase and faxes on his desk, then walked back into the hall.

Opening the conference room door, he saw it was empty. Turning, he knocked on Clarissa's door. There was no answer. He opened it and it too was empty. He hadn't been sure what to expect. Would she be there studying the notes he had handed to her or was she still out apartment hunting? Why not a condo? His read of her indicated enough funds. Surely, she planned to stay? No time for such questioning, he reassured himself she'd stay: He would be justified in his attorney selection. Still, taking a few moments to look around, he wondered what Clarissa would put up on the walls or around the windows, or what her mother would suggest putting up. He shuddered slightly, closed the door then returned to his own space.

Decorating was low on his list of priorities. He was not attempting to wow his clients with office décor. He was counting on his years of experience and his creditable record of favorable handling of client's needs to keep them coming through his door. And he trusted some of them would refer friends and other contacts to him.

He picked up the faxes and started reading them as he sat in his chair. He scribbled notes in the margins. Several he headed, "Gretchen, reply as noted." Those remaining he took with him to his current filing cabinet, thumbed the tabs, found the names he was hunting and dropped the relevant fax in the front.

On the desk calendar, he jotted his arrival time and names of clients he had just handled papers for. He pulled his briefcase forward, opened it, withdrew folders and legal pads, then shoved the case aside. Reviewing the notes he had made late last evening, he was pleased they were still intelligible this morning. He would be ready for his first appointment Monday morning. Quickly, he opened another folder and scanned the few pages. On a legal pad he penciled a statement that needed to be checked with the register of deeds office.

He leaned back in his chair; his eyebrows pulled center. I need to be in the courthouse, he cogitated. Don't let many days go by without being seen among the active attorneys. Always show purpose. Never appear to be pursuing clients. He mulled over a dictate of Hadley, Morgan & Jamison – always have a client represented by the firm when a court appearance is scheduled. On that score, he could be backed up with an attorney from his own office. And down the road he would have a paralegal to research records and do some of the nitty-gritty work. A waste of time, he scowled, you've already considered all of that. Don't steal today's minutes replotting the future.

With that admonition he opened the next folder and gave it his full attention.

Mid-morning Saturday, Gretchen Pearly and her mother began the search for the perfect wedding invitation. They had circled with a red pen four businesses that advertised invitations, stationery, photograph albums and bridal books.

Being efficient and knowing all the locations, Gretchen had planned the route with the first stop at a shopping center near their home. A clerk at the front register of the bookstore pointed them to the rear of the shop and told them the stationery manager could help them.

The manager kindly greeted them and, learning their interest, showed them a shelf stacked with albums. She drew one down, placed it on a small table below, and pulled out two chairs. After opening the album, she pointed to the order numbers and where to look up the cost of invitations.

When she walked away to help another customer, Gretchen and Mrs. Pearly sat down and immediately began to pore over the sample invitations. "This is beautiful, Mom!" "But so large, dear." "Look at this on the next page. A blue border." "Too stiff." "They are all so formal." "How many have we decided we need?" "Two hundred." "Mercy, Gretchen. The prices." "Let's check another album."

By the time they had scanned several albums, they agreed to look elsewhere. The second place on the list was also in a shopping center. The results were similar: Invitations were costly and very formal.

Driving downtown to the third location of a small independent shop, Gretchen said as they entered. "Mom, my wedding dress didn't cost as much as the invitations, thank-you notes, and the price of stamps. What will Warren say?"

"He's not buying them!"

"No, but he'll fuss."

"Maybe he was right to say you should have stayed with Hadley Morgan. There would be a lot more chances of advancement. Regular salary increases, weren't there?"

Gretchen sighed. "I like working for Mr. McB. You all know, I told you how harried the day's work is in a big firm."

"What was it Warren said? Yes, I remember. 'It's hard to make it by yourself in business.' I know you like your boss, but don't forget you two are counting on your paycheck!"

While they opened the albums, which had been spread out over books on a counter, a young male clerk stood nearby. He wasn't busy, appeared bored and not happy to be working on a Saturday morning. Gretchen wished he'd go find something to do since he told them he didn't know about the invitations.

Mrs. Pearly exclaimed. "Look, here're some of the types we're looking for."

Gretchen looked. "Closer, but not right. Let's try the next place."

As they drove on, Gretchen said, "Some place has to carry other styles. We've had enough from friends to know that."

"We should have asked somebody."

"We may be in luck," she said. "This is a Christian bookstore."

Inside, a smiling middle-aged woman immediately greeted them. "Yes, we have a lovely line of invitations. Please, sit right here at this table and I'll bring some over." She asked what month would the wedding be.

"December."

"Oh, a lovely time. Let's skip over the first half of the album. That's for spring and summer. Ah, here we are."

Mother and daughter became excited as they turned several pages. "The bells along the top and ribbons down the sides . . ." "Look at this one, dear. A bride and groom and a candle being lit." "And here, Mom, this one in color and the design raised. And the printing is slanted. I like the script. It reads more personal." "Oh, that's lovely."

Gretchen pulled out a notepad and copied the prices as her mother read them. The clerk complimented the designs. "Did you see the notes that can be enclosed for guests to check how many will be attending? And you can pre-address the envelopes to be returned to you."

Mrs. Pearly exclaimed. "But that will be so much extra cost."

"In the mailing, yes. Mothers of the bride often tell me that it was worth the cost because they could give a more accurate count to the caterer." She gave the information time to register, then added. "We have a full selection of bridal books, photo albums, registers for gifts and for guests at the wedding and reception. White Bibles. Let me show you where they are." As she led them to a display stand, she offered to help them any way she could and handed them her business card.

Gretchen wrote in her notepad the price of each item that she considered essential and some others she would like to buy. Mrs. Pearly borrowed a page and did likewise with bridal napkins, a figurine for the caketop, and other decorations.

Back in the car, they decided to have lunch at McDonald's nearby. While munching hamburgers and French fries, they went over the figures. Gretchen moaned. "My budget is so tight. The invitations are a lot more expensive than I ever allowed for. Warren will just throw up his hands."

"Will he help?"

"No. He's got his things to pay for, too. And he's paying for the ring."

"Can you pay monthly for the invitations?"

"No. I have all the payments scheduled . . . the dress, veil, shoes and the bridesmaids' gifts. And we agreed not to go in the marriage with any debts."

"Can't you get overtime work?"

Dejected, Gretchen answered. "Mr. McB has just started his own firm. He probably has everything itemized. I really don't want to start overtime."

"He can put it under miscellaneous expenses. Remember, overtime pays time and a half. That would be better than some low-paying part-time elsewhere. That is if you're not on the lookout for one better-paying job." Mrs. Pearly stared smugly.

"Yeah." Gretchen sighed then brightened. "I'll ask him Monday. Those invitations are perfect. And the return cards will help you."

"If you get those, I'll fork over the cost of the stamps."

"Mom, you're the greatest." She drained her soft drink. "Let's go. We can talk about the cake in the car."

Samuel Littlegate was experiencing some proud moments on Saturday morning. First were during his younger son's two saves that gave his team a victory in the soccer match. Jerome, an eighth grader in his last year of middle school, weighed more and was taller than most of his teammates. He easily was selected as goalie. Samuel predicted to his wife Ruth that if Jerome kept maturing this year that he might have a chance for the high school team next fall. She had squeezed his arm, smiled at him, and said cheerfully, "Let's enjoy his successes this year." Samuel pressed her hand, all the while thinking, "She's a love. But in this, she just doesn't have a clue to how important each year is toward landing that position next year."

Meanwhile, Ruth was remembering all the games she had sat through with their older son, Sam, and his moving from team to team whenever he aged out of community leagues or changed schools. This year he was a starter for his high school, which was considered an honor for a sophomore where competition was keen.

During Sam Junior's game, the second one they attended this glorious fall day where the grass on the field was still green, the surrounding poplar trees were turning golden amid interspersed native pines, and the sky domed over in a heavenly Carolina Blue, Samuel checked his shirt several times. He yelled so loudly, breathed so expansively, jumped up from the bleacher so often, he knew the buttons had to be coming out of the buttonholes. Never again would he wear a sport shirt. No sir! He was going to be a pullover man. Yes sir! His son was making him proud as a peacock with his interceptions and his two scores and he certainly did not want to look like a slob.

Littlegate was feeling conflicting emotions, wanting Sam to repeat all the great moves and wishing the referee's whistle would blow "the end of the game" while their team was ahead. Jerome, along with one of his soccer buddies, was sitting a row below and cheering for Sam's team as vocally as his dad. The brothers jousted and picked on each other at home, but in sports there was total support.

When the final whistle blew, Jerome eyed his dad and gave a big grin. Ruth leaned forward and said, "Two good wins today." Jerome nodded to her, appreciating her comments, but reluctant to say so with his friend beside him.

They scrambled down the few rows of bleachers and made their way through the spectators to find Sam. There were several groups of students congratulating the players, and parents had to squeeze in between the teenagers.

"Great game!" Littlegate shouted as he put his arm around his son who stood several inches shorter than Littlegate. The teen was slighter in build and darker in coloring than his dad was and showing skills in a different sport. Ruth, Jerome and the friend praised Sam, also. Then they yielded ground to others wanting to congratulate him.

Parents had learned not to mention they would be waiting at the car for their teenager. Travel plans would have been decided before anyone left home. As usual, both boys knew to look for the car in whatever parking lot was near the field. After all, they had been accustomed to this for years.

Jerome knew he had time to be with his buddies while Sam showered and changed. That was a switch from walking straight off the playing field in community leagues.

Sam and Ruth stood around and chatted with other parents. He replayed the game; she discussed car pools, school activities and dinner plans. Camaraderie was one of the rewards for being involved with children's sports.

On the way home, still in high spirits Samuel asked, "Honey, how about stopping at McDonald's?"

Ready to accept a meal she didn't have to prepare, she replied, "Sounds fine to me. How about you guys?" When no answer was immediate, she added, "The drive-through." Hearing "yeas" she said, "Be ready with your order when we get to the call box."

CHAPTER 7

"Susan, you have been busy and thorough since you were here last week." Clarissa exclaimed as she stacked three stationery boxes on her desk. "I'll take good care of these."

"The floppy disk copies I sent registered mail are going to my mother's house. And she knows not to open them. Is there anything else I need to do?" Susan asked.

"Just notifying the credit card companies the same way. You'll want the receipt signed and returned to you. And the apartment leasing agent should be notified with a written confirmation."

Susan hastily wrote her mother's address and phone number, as well as her work schedule and phone number, and handed the index card to Clarissa.

"You will contact me when you leave your apartment?"

"I will. Thank you for the time today. Mother will transfer the funds and will write you a check in a few days. Miss Bentley, I may not have made some right choices the past few years, but I think giving my mother money every month to put away was one of the best things I ever did. Otherwise, I wouldn't have you representing me." Susan managed a weak smile, picked up her purse, and moved toward the door.

Clarissa walked to the outer door with her. She stopped and spoke to Gretchen. "Does Mr. McBaden have a client with him?"

"Yes. Do you have any mail? I can drop it in the box for the last pick up when I leave."

"No, thank you. But I will pour some coffee before the pot is washed." Clarissa was adding creamer to the cup when McBaden's door opened and he and a client emerged.

After seeing the client leave, McBaden joined her at the coffee area.

"If you're free, may I talk with you?" she asked.

"Sure, come in," he said and went to his office.

She followed and started talking. "Remember Susan Phillips, the young woman who came in about a divorce. She was back today. She's quite serious about leaving her husband whom she has basically been supporting the four and a half years of the marriage."

He paused and waved his free hand outward. "No. I don't need to hear. If you take the case, it's yours."

"But she has . . ."

"Do you understand *no!*" His eyes darkened and his tone was hostile.

She thought it a miracle he had held his cup in the other hand without its contents splashing across the room. Physically, she did not flinch, but her eyes showed an attitude of tenaciously digging into and holding her own position. She placed her cup on his desk and walked out. Within ten seconds she returned with Susan's three boxes and her notes.

She closed his office door and walked back and faced him, serious and determined. "Will you give me the professional courtesy to point out something unusual in this case? You made your point clear at the interview and again before Mrs. Phillips talked with us. You handed the matter over to me. However, when I am presented with some material that I think might be of interest to you, I would like to know that I can consult you." She finished in a strong, direct voice.

He put his cup down, placed both palms on the desk and spoke grimly. "Consultation granted."

She squared herself opposite him. "These boxes represent creative work her husband has produced during their marriage. Three novel-length manuscripts and fifteen short stories. They have not been published. In the event any of them are later, she wants to know, can she ask for half their value?"

He glared at her, then at the boxes. "How did she get them?"

"She had typed two of his novels and the short stories which are part of a collection of twenty. She printed copies this weekend from the home computer."

"Wouldn't it have been easier to copy the material to disks?" He continued in a terse manner.

"Those she has sent registered mail to her mother's house. She has her own ideas of insurance." Clarissa stood her ground, spoke for her client.

McBaden's eyes widened into his engrossing assessment of a person. The moment he found what he wanted, his eyes changed. "All right. Have a seat. How do you see this creative work?" He waved his hand toward the boxes and sank into his chair.

She considered his yielding to be tentative and marginal. With the poise of a seasoned competitor, she lowered herself onto the upright chair with her head and upper body erect, her hands in her lap. She returned his direct stare.

"I have not had time to open the boxes. She said they were fiction. How do I see the work in the scope of her divorce? The work is creative; it's joint property; the property is an intellectual production." She paused to assess his response. His eyes showed interest. She continued, "And money earned from any and all media with this work may be the only remuneration she will receive."

"He's broke?"

"Has no money except what he earns from pick-up work."

"Their occupations?"

"He is a graduate in sociology and has a year of post-grad courses in writing. He worked with the city human resources for about a year. His job was eliminated and he wasn't offered another. She's a dental hygienist, drawing a good salary, but not enough for their needs."

"So his time is spent writing and to date no sales?"

She nodded affirmative.

"Dividing the money from future sales could be written into the settlement."

"Yes, only there's one aspect that bothers me."

"That would be?" He asked, settling back in his chair.

Clarissa detected a note of impatience in his voice. "She didn't make it sound like a major issue and I didn't point out that it might be. I wanted to consult you first." She referred to notes on her legal pad, then looked at him. "He's mentioned two or three times lately that they should declare bankruptcy."

"Are they deeply in debt?"

"From what she said, without reading any financial statements, I would say no. There are outstanding bills. He has run up a balance on her credit card. Their cars are not paid for. If she leaves and he files for bankruptcy, what about the manuscripts?" she asked and nodded toward the boxes.

"Um," he pondered. "They are property and the creditors could claim them."

"What if he doesn't list them?"

"What if they are sold down the road?"

"She could list them if he doesn't."

"If the debts are joint, the manuscripts could be seized."

"Lot of *ifs* here."

"But my role is to do the best for my client."

"Are the works any good? Will he find a publisher?" McBaden asked.

"Judging the quality of the work, or its market value, is not a question I can answer. Susan says they are very good. Not many writers succeed at making a living with writing. They usually have a full-time job. The few who do turn out best sellers are rewarded handsomely. And it's that slight chance that Garvey Phillips' work could be in the elite category that concerns me."

"Well, think about it. I will, too. We may locate a precedent. It is an interesting section of law. This is a different approach to intellectual property, and the bankruptcy filing is a complication. She may want to talk him out of that, even if she has to pay off his debts."

"She's smart enough to know when to leave a losing situation," Clarissa retorted as she picked up the boxes.

"Ah! A judgment?" He rejoined.

In the hall she bumped into Gretchen and the boxes shifted in her arms. Quickly, Gretchen reached out and restacked them. "I'm so sorry. I'm ready to leave and wanted to let you know. In case, you're expecting a phone call or anything."

"No, I'm not expecting a call. Do whatever you usually do

about the phone," she spoke shortly. Stopping at her doorway, Clarissa turned her head and added, "Have a nice weekend. See you Monday."

After topping her file cabinet with the manuscript boxes, Clarissa sank into her desk chair. She stared at the boxes, bewildered and disappointed. "What's Joseph's problem with this case? Why doesn't he handle any divorces? Is he divorced?"

As she reviewed the scene in his office, she shook her shoulders to loosen the chastisement of his intense reprimand. "Do you understand no!" She hadn't heard that phrase since first grade. He was one teed-off fellow. In an instant, he had strayed from his reputed trait of composure.

She declared that if Vernon Taylor weren't such a good friend and an excellent attorney, she would doubt Taylor's recommendation of Samuel Littlegate and Littlegate's of Joseph. Even though Samuel was a personal friend of Joseph's, she had to rely on her instincts that he would not have praised Joseph and set up the interview purely out of loyalty. "What have I gotten myself into?" she mouthed. "Discord I don't want in the workplace." Again she shook her head, this time to straighten her thinking. "It's too early to get upset. What happened could be his personal problem." As long as she was in practice with him, she would keep the relationship as even-keeled as possible. But by Jove, if she had to stand up to him, she would. So much in law is adversarial that the attitude overflowing in the office shouldn't be a surprise.

She swung her chair around and surveyed the room. Bleak and sterile, she tagged it. No personality. Where can I start? Artwork? Draperies? Colorful magazines? She spun the chair, facing each wall. No windows! Number one omission! Her environment had always been a priority. Her bedroom at home, her college dorm room, her apartment, her office – each had been personalized. Each had been a pleasant, welcoming retreat and work space and always with windows. She laughed at herself, thinking anyone would call her spoiled. Really, she didn't believe she deserved a window; the fact is she liked windows. Being somewhat relieved by her turn of outlook, she noted mentally that Joseph had not had time to decorate. There was a lot involved in setting up an office. And furthermore, maybe he intended to let the person who would occupy the room choose the accessories.

As she turned again to face the doorway, Samuel Littlegate approached. "Hi," he called. "Busy?"

"No, come in." She stood up.

"Just dropped by to see the new office. Are you settling in?" He asked as he looked around.

"Beginning to."

"Nice layout. This is becoming a very desirable business location."

She replied, "It does have an appeal. The section and the building. And the office will, too, later." She glanced around. "A few touches here and there."

He grinned. "Planning some decorating, eh?"

"When it's through, you're invited back for an open house, or should I say an open office?" She smiled.

"Glory be! Joseph is going to have a reception?"

A quizzical expression crossed her face. "Would that be unusual?"

"Well, when I spread his highest qualities before you, a social one wasn't tucked in there, was there? Oh, he's not a pure recluse. He attends functions he has to. But host a party? Well, that will be a new day or evening," he said, without malice or degradation.

"I trust it will not be out of line for a fellow attorney to host her own reception. It seems very appropriate to have friends in to see where you work. And in our profession, a friendly gathering is as welcomed as a session with opponents."

"No wonder so many of our cohorts set their sights on D.C. or northern Virginia. Clarissa, bring all that social culture you want to, here to Windermere. I accept your invitation right now."

"And your lovely wife, too. Vernon speaks well of her. His words were 'a sweetheart of a wife and a charming hostess.'"

"I thank him for that. You'll have to come to dinner some evening. Well, it'll be a suspense, waiting to see how you decorate this room."

The word, *decorate*, echoed from the doorway. Joseph stood there.

For a moment neither Samuel nor Clarissa spoke. Then she said, "I was saying I would add a few things if there is no objection."

Lacking enthusiasm, he replied, "None."

She said, looking first at Joseph, next to Samuel, "My mother will be down soon. She enjoys decorating. I may ask her for a few suggestions for draperies and pictures in the office."

Joseph looked at Clarissa without commenting. He turned to Samuel. "It's good to see you."

"When I came in, you weren't in any office, so I stopped to chat with Clarissa. You must be treating her in your usual gentlemanly manner. She was smiling when I stopped at the door," Samuel said to Joseph and turned to Clarissa and grinned.

"Well, come along. My office is next door, end of the hall." There was a note of brittleness that Samuel picked up on. He maintained his smile while he tried to read Joseph's expression. He nodded to Clarissa and followed Joseph into the next office.

Clarissa also had caught the change of tone. The word gentlemanly was not the most appropriate choice. The day had been long and she was ready for an early dinner, a hot bath, calls to her mother and sisters and a good night's sleep.

CHAPTER 8

Mid-morning on Monday, McBaden had already conferred with Clarissa on some points in the cases she was handling for him and checked with Gretchen that the machines were functioning properly then dictated a few letters. He decided to take a break and drive down to the courthouse to look up a record.

If there were any inconveniences about his new office location, heading the list would be driving to do something he could have walked a block to accomplish from Hadley, Morgan & Jamison. The schedule he was tentatively following began with a stop by his office, downtown to court as needed, lunch either downtown or in West Points Center, afternoons for case work, gathering data for the legal forms that Gretchen would type, appointments, and returning phone calls.

Entering a gravel lot behind a brick office building, he stopped close to the landscape timber marked reserved #8. He considered himself fortunate to be leased this parking place. Soon after the word was out that he was setting up an office at Price Tower, his friend and accountant, Charles Fortescue, approached him. Fortescue, a partner in the firm that owned the building and property, asked if he would be interested in the space, which would be available September 1. The location was great, a block from the county courthouse. Not a step further than Hadley Morgan. From there he had walked north; from here, he walked east. The sun would warm him and the rain would pelt him just the same.

He entered the county courthouse at the lowest street level, passed through security, and entered the clerk's office. He scanned the dockets of the courts, mentally noting some of the cases. His search for some dates in the records took about twenty minutes. Glancing at the wall clock and seeing it was a few minutes before twelve, he decided to take an early lunch downtown and walked to the elevators.

The traffic flow was its typical pace for a Monday morning, he observed. A few bewildered women wandered about as if they were in a foreign country. To them it was, he thought. Perhaps their first encounter with the Halls of Justice. Some soul more kindly than he stopped to ask what they were looking for then gave directions. McBaden recognized two attorneys; each seated alone at a booth in the small snack area. In front of each were paper cups of coffee and a file folder, unopened. He debated whether they were dragging out a late break or eluding someone. McBaden considered nodding recognition to them, but they didn't look toward him. Yet he knew those seats could be a spot to see who was coming and going on this floor. People headed to criminal court would take a left, to the clerk of court office a right, or to domestic court straight across from the elevators.

"Good to see you're not deserting us now that you've moved out to Five Points West," friendly tones resounded.

McBaden turned, recognizing the voice. "Can't do that, Mike. The elevators are slow this morning."

Mike Monahan had a genial face to match his voice. Both were disarming in a man built solid as some rocky cliffs of Ireland. He stood several inches taller than most men of Irish descent; however, he had inherited their typical somewhat short neck. McBaden had known him since law school days, respected his views, and honored him as a judge. He also counted Mike a friend.

"I hear the buildings are first class in that area," Mike commented. "I haven't been inside Price Tower yet."

McBaden said, "When you're out that way, stop in. I'm on the sixth floor."

"I plan to take you up on that. Soon as the moving dust settles. But before that appointment book is heavily inked. You'll jot 'The Party' in a few slots, right?" Monahan looked McBaden directly in the eyes.

"Is it an election year?"

"There's always something to talk over. Next year starts today."

One set of elevator doors opened and the packed-in crowd began to emerge. McBaden stepped back a few paces.

A tall man walked toward him, "Joseph, do you have a minute? I thought I'd run into you upstairs."

"Sure, Grant."

"The Jordan contract case was handed to me last week. Do you have a copy of the paperwork?" The man's face was tense, but the question was quietly asked.

"All the transactions are there." When McBaden saw him cast his eyes down and slightly shake his head, McBaden continued. "The data will be in the computer. Nothing was deleted. Not by Gretchen or me. Ask the girl who took Gretchen's place to search by dates after the entry name. Probably three weeks ago was our last work on that case."

"Thanks," came the response, but the voice sounded unconvinced.

The attorney moved toward the outside exit. McBaden watched him a few moments and remembered long hours that he had dug for documents the year he had started with Hadley Morgan. Grant Addison, who was a new face fresh out of law school, would have to scramble to stand out among the half-dozen recruited this year. You have a few pluses – height, you won't be unnoticed . . . and a distinguished-sounding name – McBaden thought. Learn to keep your head up, show confidence when you talk, he wanted to tell Grant. Turning around he saw the doors close to two sets of elevators.

He walked briskly over and pushed the up arrow button. Stepping back again he caught peripherally a figure hastening up the hallway. It was a young woman glancing toward the walls, briefly disappearing down another hallway and reappearing, still hurrying. As she looked toward the elevators, she exchanged a quick look with McBaden. She passed behind him.

Suddenly, the click of her heels ceased. A quick drawing of breath was audible. She retraced her steps and stopped beside McBaden.

"Hello!" she spoke, excited and expectantly.

He turned and looked into the prettiest face he had seen in Lord knows how long.

Again she said hello in anticipation of a response.

McBaden echoed, "Hello."

"Aren't you?" she spoke. She moved back and looked at him intently. "I'm sorry. I thought you were someone I know."

"Is there someone you were looking for?" He scrutinized her. Gorgeous blonde hair around a sun-tanned face with lively blue eyes, very shapely legs and in between a nicely fitted lightweight linen suit and a white knit blouse.

"I was to meet someone at the snack machines."

"They are around the corner from the booths over there," he said and pointed.

"Thank you." She repositioned the very large shoulder bag, handsome, brown leather and obviously expensive with brass initials *BC*. She withdrew from a narrow front slot a brown leather notebook. Opening the cover, she asked as she read, "Do you know where courtroom 4A is located?"

"The fourth floor and to the left as you exit the elevator."

Thus informed, her perplexed expression switched into one of gratitude followed by a dazzling smile. "So sorry about mistaking you for someone else. Thank you again. And your name?"

"Joseph McBaden."

She jotted something in her notebook as she pivoted easily. Joseph admired her energetic gait and formed his own questions in the seconds it took her to gain the corner and move out of sight. He heard the elevator doors opening again. A crowd was converging to board. This time he kept his position up front and his focus on having lunch as scheduled.

During lunch at a restaurant in Five Points West Plaza, Clarissa looked over the city map. Beside it was a bank's listing of its branches. One was a couple of blocks from her house and another was very near the office. She decided to walk to the Plaza branch after lunch. The sun was bright, the sky cloudless, and she wanted to stretch her legs.

She ambled along the brick walkways, paused at display windows, entered a few shops, and gathered in general the atmosphere of the businesses. She liked it. There was an interesting mix of restaurants, women's clothing boutiques, linens and bath items, jewelry and gift shops, and art galleries. All upscale. Unless one was familiar with the business names, a passerby might not drive in for shopping, for there was an absence of oversized signs that chain stores displayed, gaudy colors or other attention-getting devices. She walked to the far edge of the Plaza where she spotted the bank. The freestanding building was attractive and well placed, she decided. People with only banking business could easily drive in, park or drive through and avoid the more congested egresses.

She admired the Plaza's brick selection of a warm clay color with enough yellow tones to mimic aging; she surmised that the buildings were recently erected.

The doors were not electronic; she had to pull to open and she liked that. There were three other customers inside, two tellers at the drive-in windows and two tellers at a high counter facing the lobby. A lone woman was seated at one of the two desks opposite the counter. While Clarissa waited, she reviewed in her head the costs of moving, anticipated expenses for the current and next month, and determined the amount she needed to transfer from her bank in Virginia, which had merged with this bank two years ago.

When the woman hung up the phone, she stood and asked Clarissa how she could help her.

"May I speak with the manager, please."

"Just a moment. May I tell her your name?"

"Clarissa Bentley."

The woman returned quickly. "Celia Trawick will see you now." She said and showed Clarissa to the first of three small offices at the side of the lobby.

Celia walked forward and greeted Clarissa then indicated a

seat and returned to the chair behind the desk.

"I'm moving to Windermere and will be in Price Tower in practice with attorney Joseph McBaden. I have accounts with your bank in Northern Virginia and would like to open a checking account here."

"Welcome to our city and to our branch." She withdrew forms from a desk drawer and checked several lines to be filled out.

Clarissa extended her banking card and took the papers to read while the account was being brought up on the computer.

"Yes. Here we are. How do you want to handle this? A transfer or a check?"

"A transfer from the money market please."

Clarissa stated the amount and asked when the transaction would occur.

"By Thursday. This is your account number, and here are some temporary checks to use. Your Virginia checks on our bank should be acceptable here. Have you located a place to stay?"

"I have. A charming half of a house in High Street District on Hillside Street. I'll be 306-B. The Hughes, Lydia and Burl, the owners are listed as 306 Hillside."

"I know the area. It's friendly and quiet. Do you have a phone number?"

"No. I just talked with the owners on Saturday. Could you delay the check printing until I have a number? The phone may be the first item I'll have there."

"Certainly. I hope everything goes smoothly with the moving in." And Celia looked at Clarissa and spoke with warmth. "Let me know how it goes. I look forward to seeing you around the Plaza."

"Thank you. My first stroll today was a delight. Such lovely shops and landscaping. I'll be at The Patrick until my furniture is moved."

Clarissa walked back to the office, musing perhaps Celia could become a friend. She was wearing a wedding ring; still, perhaps they could have lunch together. The thought brought a smile to her face and lightness to her walk.

When Gretchen was free, Clarissa asked for a standard form

for real estate or apartment rental. She read it and made notations. With her door open, she spotted McBaden as he left his office. Suspecting it was coffee time, she followed him.

"Would you have time to look something over for me? Personally?"

He poured coffee, asked whether she wanted one. With her reply he filled a second cup.

She accepted it saying, "Our hymnal has a selection that is a thanksgiving for coffee to start each morning."

"Amen. Come into my office," he said as he headed back down the hall.

She picked up the contract from her desk and took it and the coffee across the hall. He was seated and leaning back in his chair with his cup in hand. Again, she was aware of his penetrating gaze. Wondering what personal issue I'll bring up, she thought. How often will he be scrutinizing me? Remember to comb your hair and generally tidy up before leaving your own space, she instructed herself. She sat opposite him.

"This is a standard form. A leasing agreement."

"You found an apartment?" he said and drank his coffee.

"A half of a house. I stopped in Six-day Café Saturday and the waiter told me about a place, not advertised, but available."

"Sounds interesting. Top floor?"

"Top and first. It's not a duplex. It's an older house that the family's son lived in, then their daughter. She married recently and moved out of state. So half of the house has been remodeled. I told Mrs. Hughes I would take it. The verbal agreement is probably fine, but this is her first rental. I told her I would check on leasing forms for this state and so forth. Any suggestions?" She drank her coffee and watched him review the contract.

"You chose an old house? Well, it's a convenient, short drive from here. This appears okay," he said as he handed her the papers.

She thanked him but kept its other conveniences to herself.

CHAPTER 9

For the first time in several weeks Joseph McBaden took time to dine in his favorite restaurant. He had ordered a steak, enjoyed it thoroughly, and, at the moment, wished he smoked to give him a reason to sit and relax a few minutes longer. Well, he concluded, the third cup of coffee had been drunk, it must be time to get back to work.

He scanned the ticket, pulled out his wallet and left a generous tip along with payment on the tray. As soon as he pocketed his wallet, the waitress scooted over. He told her to keep the tray.

There was a crowd around the reception stand, so he waited for the people to move. Coming at a right angle from another area of the dining room, he saw Breear Callum. She caught his glance, recognized him and smiled.

"Hello, there. Joseph McBaden, isn't it?"

"A good memory, Miss Callum."

She laughed in a sparkling manner, and the heads around them turned. "Well, it's only been a couple of days, and you were one of my first interviews. And you know my name."

"From Channel 6 News."

The waiting people were asked to follow the hostess. She led them around Breear, who stepped closer to McBaden. He in turn caught her elbow. The way clear, the two walked toward the door. In the lobby, she opened her purse and reached inside.

"Oh, no!" She fumbled through the contents briefly. "I forgot, I don't have the vehicle."

"The vehicle?"

"The station's sports vehicle. I often drive it to and from assignments. I told Kirk, the cameraman – he was at the courthouse with me – to drop me here and drive on back to the station. Drat!"

"Do you need a ride?"

"No. I'll go back and call a cab." She turned around.

He reached out and gently placed a hand on her arm. "I'll be glad to take you wherever you need to go."

She looked hesitant a moment then lowered her shoulders in surrender. "Thank you. I appreciate the offer."

As they walked to his car, he asked if she often took cabs. "A few times. I don't have a car. My mother is quite frantic about my safety. She calls often to be sure I'm still alive in the new city."

"Do you want a car?"

"There's not a dire need yet. There's always someone going on assignment with me. He can easily pick me up or bring me home."

"What about errands?" McBaden asked and stopped beside his car, unlocking it with a remote. He opened the door and she slid in.

Buckling his seat belt, he turned. "Where to?"

"Oh, my apartment. The Cloisters. Do you know where they are?"

"I do."

"I partly chose it for its name. It was sure to impress Mother with respectability. It's small, but a step above an efficiency. And after a dorm for years, it's quite luxurious."

"So you're settled in?"

"I am." She looked out the window. "This is a nice route. I shall have to drive Mother this way when she comes up. Have you lived here long?"

"Many years. How did you select Windermere?"

"The media conglomerate I interviewed with owns the station here. I had interned for them last summer. Channel 6 had an opening."

McBaden glanced at her. "We are very fortunate you came to fill the vacancy."

She seemed pleased. "Mr. McBaden, I accept the compliment, even though it does sound very formal. Here we are. My unit is the last one on the front. There's a parking space with my number, 108, just right of the front walk."

He pulled in slowly and stopped, leaving the engine running. "May I walk you to the door?"

"Concerned for my safety like my mother?" she teased, looking at him.

"Perhaps more like a friend?" He waited.

"That's very considerate. Yes."

He switched off the engine and walked around to open her door. Because she sat until he came around, he knew she was accustomed to being treated in this manner.

They walked up the steps and walkway and stopped at the entry. There were no numbers outside.

"If your apartment opens from a common hallway, would you like for me to see you that far?"

She handed him the keys. "Yes."

He unlocked the front door. Her apartment was fourth on the right side. He handed her the keys. She selected one, fitted it into the keyhole, and turned her head. "Would you like to come in? Since we've just had dinner, I won't ask if you'd like anything to eat or drink."

He appeared surprised. She quickly added, "Today, the maids came so the place will be tidy. Just thought you could view one of the newest living complexes."

She pushed the door open and he followed her. It was small as she had said, and very neat. The few furnishings were modern, linear, with striped fabric in orange, tan and gold. There was a desk with brass bookends holding an assortment of books, black binders, a lamp, and a portable phone and answering machine on top; and below, were two deep drawers on the right side. A straight, slatted chair was pushed up under it. An area rug with big cats: lions, cheetahs, leopards, panthers parading in the border, centered the living room floor. A similar, smaller one was beneath a glass-topped modern dining table and four seats.

While he continued his tour to the kitchen, she walked into the bedroom, put her purse down and took off her jacket. She changed to lower-heeled shoes and paused to run a comb through her hair.

"Well, how does it look?" She placed some loose notepad sheets into a black binder and wedged it between the bookends. He didn't answer. Puzzled, she asked, "Are you certain we have never met? You seem so familiar." She stared at him intently.

"We haven't. Where do you think it was?"

He took a step closer to her and she to him. She tried to recall, as her eyes moved from his head to his shoes and back to his face. She went right up to him and kissed him.

"You don't remember this?" She asked, watching his expression.

This time her action caught him off guard. He drew in his breath and leaned back. "No. We've not met." He leaned forward, put his arms around her, and drew her close. He kissed her vigorously on the lips long enough for her to respond. "Do you remember that?"

Breathless, she mumbled, "No. But I'll never forget it." She didn't move away.

He kissed her again. "I like being kissed by a, ah, mature man." She spoke with a lively energy, as if she surprised herself. Her smile widened, parting her lips. She tilted her head backward. He didn't feel mature at all; for him, primal passion mingled with a youthful lust.

"Um . . . whoa. This is time for us to part." She backed away, stood behind a chair. "Let's say goodnight. And thank you . . ."

"Joseph. Joseph to you."

"Except on official encounters," she said.

"Right. I'll see you again?"

"Yes." As he took a step forward, she held up a hand and pointed toward the front door. He nodded and left.

He hardly remembered moving down the hall or along the walkway to the parking space. Inside his car, he pulled the visor down and viewed his face. Same guy. Even in the unearthly glow of the security lights overhead, he noticed blotches on his face. A wipe of his handkerchief showed smudges of lipstick. My God, the color was so natural, but it's makeup. Careful, there, my man. It's best not to saunter into the office and have the night crew snickering. When did I last use that word? When was the last time I had lipstick on a handkerchief? So long, I don't remember.

Some things were evident tonight to him; he could still feel, still desire and get a response. It had been short, but he knew he didn't dream it. He had the handkerchief by Jove. Mature? Well, what's to worry, if a beautiful young girl says *yes* to seeing you again?

The Littlegates were both long-time, generous hosts.

Traditionally, Ruth considered Sunday dinner the most important of the week. She could time a beef roast, baked chicken, turkey or ham meal to be ready forty-five minutes after the close of church worship. Albeit, she planned and prepared some dishes the day before. There was always enough to feed more than her family of four. This Sunday, Sam and Jerome were both to be away.

Samuel invited Joseph to dinner and the church service. As expected, Joseph accepted the first invitation while declining the second.

Ruth, his like-minded wife, in not wanting someone who lived alone to have to eat Sunday dinner by herself, asked Clarissa to come. Earlier, Samuel had spoken of her as someone he thought Ruth would enjoy knowing, and he had emphasized that Joseph and Clarissa were just co-workers. She had nodded that she understood. After all, she was not matchmaking without knowing one of the people involved. She'd have to wait and see about that. Thus, she didn't alert her husband of Clarissa's joining them until they drove home after the service.

At first, Samuel whistled. "Wow! Stand by for our composed friend's shock and disdain."

Ruth gleamed. "Oh, you can handle him."

Joseph arrived shortly after the Littlegates and parked in front of their house. He rang the bell and was soon greeted by Samuel.

"Hi, there. Come on in. The boys said to tell you hello. They miss you at the games."

"Tell them that I'll surprise them soon. They are both starters this year?"

"They are." Making his way back to the kitchen with Joseph following, he called out enthusiastically. "Ruth, anything two starving men can do to help?"

Ruth replied, "Not at the moment. Here," she handed over a small basket of assorted crackers and nuts. "Munch on these until everything is ready."

Samuel and Joseph stayed in the kitchen rehashing yesterday's sports events while Ruth finished the lunch preparations. Their idling there appeared not to bother her; on the contrary she smiled at their analysis of the games. Her bustling about didn't seem to bother them either; they were so accustomed to it. However, when she needed them to shift their positions or perform some duty, they felt comfortable that she would give them a sign. The doorbell rang and she did just that.

"Samuel, will you answer the door? Joseph, could you get the vegetable bowl from the cabinet? The pattern is on the table. Look on the middle shelf. Thanks."

Ruth turned to stir a couple of simmering pots on the range and Joseph walked into the dining room to look at the china. Ruth used three different serving sets. Today it was the ivory with a turquoise band around the edges. He paused to look over the familiar dining room. Everything was in harmony. The colors, the furnishings, the table setting, the flowers. Just like his favorite people. Samuel and Ruth.

McBaden heard Littlegate's booming voice, louder than usual, greeting someone at the door. "Hello, Clarissa. Welcome to the house. Have any trouble with directions?"

"Hello. No trouble."

McBaden froze like one of the figurines on the buffet. The name registered. The voice was softer than Littlegate's and he couldn't be sure it was his Clarissa's. But she was the only woman he knew with that name. *His Clarissa.* His mind began to thaw. He corrected himself. His co-attorney. His breathing resumed. His eyes focused on the china with the turquoise edge. What have they done? Set me up again? No, not without some warning. God, if it weren't Sunday, I'd say damn my friends. He grabbed the closest chair back, letting his anger seep into something inanimate. The movement helped. He squeezed the wooden frame several times, adjusted the chair a fraction of an inch so that it was more in line with the one beside it. He glanced forward knowing a mirror hung above the buffet. His reflection bore a hard, fierce expression. Deeply, he exhaled, took a few controlled breaths. Okay, my expression is passable. He returned to the kitchen.

He walked directly to the cabinet, reached up and pulled out a bowl. As he pivoted, he asked, "Is this the one, Ruth?"

"It is. Thank you." She placed it on the counter top beside the range.

Standing immediately behind her was Clarissa. Samuel lagged a few steps and watched Joseph's face. Yep, he caught the name, Samuel realized.

"Hello," Clarissa said. "I thought that might be your car outside." She moved a bit forward, but more to the left. McBaden sensed she was clearing the front of the oven and allowing room for Samuel to enter the kitchen easily. Damn, what grace, and damn again, she had brought a gift. As always he had crossed the threshold empty-handed.

Ruth checked the oven. She donned a pair of terry mitts and took out a steaming casserole. She put a pan of rolls inside and closed the door. She turned to the others. "The rolls will take about twelve minutes."

Clarissa asked, "What may I do to help you? Oh, I heard you were tea drinkers. This is a blend my family likes."

Ruth accepted the package, admiring the unusual print of the wrapping paper secured with sisal twine. "It smells heavenly. It'll be a treat for the chilly evenings we'll have soon. Thank you so much."

Samuel said, "Joseph, there's something I want you to see outside. Ruth, call if you need us."

She nodded to Samuel then said to Clarissa, "I'm so glad you could come."

"Thank you for the call."

That was all of their conversation Joseph heard before he and

Samuel walked out the door from the dining room to a sun porch and through another door to a patio. Several steps away from the house, Joseph stopped. Aware he was walking by himself, Samuel slowed and turned around.

"The boys are building a cart for us to use in the garden."

"I'll see it later. What did I tell you about these set-ups?"

"Oh, come on friend!" Samuel exclaimed. "Would I do that?"

"Didn't you? Tell me that you didn't know she was coming?"

Samuel walked toward the seating surround of the patio and poked at the potted plants on the top. Joseph approached.

Samuel said, "I did. Ruth called her. But I didn't think it would make a difference."

"After I said, forget it? I'm not interested. Listen, Samuel. I like visiting you and Ruth and the boys. I don't need a girl. You are wise enough to know this is different. We, Clarissa and I, are in the same office. And I'm the boss."

"Lord have mercy! That gold lettering on the front door got to your head in a hurry."

"Cut the nonsense, Littlegate!" Joseph said defiantly and crossed his arms.

"You don't know enough about her," retorted Samuel.

"Resumes are sterile. What can you tell me that will make a difference?"

"You're safe."

"Eh?"

"You don't have to worry about her as if she's seeking a man down here. Or being instantly drawn to one she's working for."

Joseph gave him a puzzled stare.

"Not that you're over the hill, yet," Sam laughed. In a straightforward voice he added, "It'll be a long time before she's looking around."

"Did your Virginia buddy tell you that?" Samuel didn't reply. Joseph continued. "I did you two a favor, didn't I? Hired her on your recommendations."

"You did. This I can pass along. She's just out of a long-term relationship."

"Oh. I'm surprised she's keen on divorce cases."

"She's not divorced."

"Separated with intentions of filing?"

"Nope. Not married."

"Samuel, cut to the chase."

"That's all that needs to be said now. But you understand, don't you? She's left a great firm, the area she grew up in, she's moving beyond her past. It'll be a long time before she's ready to commit to anyone." Samuel waved toward the sunroom where Ruth beckoned them.

He started toward the house. "You know Ruth. She'll do more than her share of introducing Clarissa in the area and to people. Now, relax. Enjoy your undeserved good fortunes. An excellent attorney on your staff. And if she never adds a painting or a drape to your office walls, she's a lovely addition herself. And, God knows, if she can put up with your scrutiny of all that passes above or around you, there'll be stars in her crown. Now, let's go taste the best meal in town today."

CHAPTER 10

It was shut down time. The evening news was winding up. He aimed the remote at the set, but halted his action. Breear appeared. He turned up the volume.

"A human interest incident was caught in action uptown about nine o'clock. It happened right in this block behind me. Two cars collided. Both drivers got out of their cars and decided to call the police. While the men talked with the policeman, a male passenger in each car got out to inspect damages. These two men looked at each other and recognized a friend from high school days. They were delighted with the chance encounter. Damages to cars were minor and both passengers asked their drivers, who are their sons, not to prefer charges. They will attend to repairs. Sometimes accidents bring about unexpected happy reunions."

Breear had a terrific television presence, McBaden noted. Her blonde hair blew in the slight breeze, her unbuttoned linen jacket did likewise and her knee-length skirt fit snuggly. Her voice was clear, her pronunciation almost general American with enough mellow southern accents retained to make her as easy to listen to as to look at.

He wished her schedule were not so unpredictable. Usually, she learned of an assignment at the station in the morning. With her ambition she kept herself sleep fulfilled, careful of her calorie intake, and clear of stressful involvement. McBaden had a growing awareness that she was beginning to be a stress element in his own life. He waited until her segment ended to power off the remote.

He stood there staring at the black screen, wanting her so much. Wanting to be in her apartment. Holding her tight. How long had it been since he had been so aroused by a woman?

Walking around his house, switching off lights, checking doors, his thoughts clung to the night he had taken her to her apartment. When he went to bed and stretched out, other memories crept forward – hazy faces and half-formed places – overlayering the golden-haired girl and dimming her voice. Another face, laughing, curly hair falling over her school sweater. Then the image swirled. Another followed. Although the face was out of focus he could see her shoulders were bare. Her hair fell back, her eyes closed. As that image was floating away, he could hear the sound of water turning on and off. Loud then fainter and fainter.

McBaden kicked off the sheet and bounded out of bed. He shook his head as he walked to the bathroom and sought the aspirin bottle in the medicine cabinet. He filled a glass with water and took two tablets. Staring at himself in the mirror, he tried to guess how old Breear thought he was. Did it matter? Yes, he barked at the reflection. Well, tossing about in the bed and dragging up the past is not going to improve the present.

So he did what he typically resorted to on nights when he and sleep were not immediate partners. He pulled file folders from his briefcase and opened the one that most demanded concentration and pen and paper.

An hour later, only one plan outside of legal matters was formed. He would telephone Breear tomorrow before she left her apartment and invite her to dinner. At a plush restaurant. He didn't want a refusal.

He did just that and hung up the phone with a pleased countenance. He couldn't resist looking in the mirror as he put his jacket on. That's much better. Sleep and resolution tightened those muscles. And anticipation is a sign of youth, eh?

When Samuel Littlegate's secretary buzzed him that she had Joseph McBaden on the line, he lifted the handset. "Joseph, are you free for lunch today?"

Peering at his calendar, McBaden asked, "What did you have in mind? Any surprises?" It wasn't unusual for them to lunch together, but it was more typical if they were at the courthouse and finishing up at the same time.

"How about say we'll grab a table for two?"
"Where?"
"Shipley? I hear they have fried oysters now."
"Sounds fine. What time?"
"Twelve forty-five okay?"
"It is. See you there."

McBaden worked steadily till mid-morning then stood up, stretched and walked down the hall to collect the contents of his in-tray and to fill his coffee mug. Returning, he knocked on Clarissa's door.

"Come in." She looked up from papers she was reading.

"I'm going out of town Friday to do the research I didn't get to do last week. My parking space will be free if you'd like to use it."

"Thank you. I appreciate it."

"It's two blocks south of the courthouse on the same side of the street. Behind the Carolinas Accounting Firm office building. Charles Fortescue is my accountant and a friend. I expect to have some records for you to look up for me."

"I'll be pleased to do that for you."

The tone was even but the slight emphasis on *you* caused McBaden to stare at her seeking some meaning. What? I'm returning a favor? Am I your paralegal? It certainly wasn't sexy. Her facial expression offered no answer.

He said, "I'll be out of the office for lunch today. Then I'm going to the university law library."

"I hear that it has a very good library. I'll go out some time soon."

He turned to leave. After two steps he half-turned backward. "Would you like to go this afternoon? I could stop back here."

"Yes, thank you."

"I'll call from the car phone when I head this way."

"I'll wait outside the front door."

Clarissa took an early lunch hour and enjoyed a salad at the plaza. McBaden was leaving as she returned. He gave her a nod as if to say I'm glad you're back so we're covered here. She smiled as if to reply I planned it that way.

As soon as Clarissa was settled, Gretchen poked her head in the doorway. "Have you got a minute?" Her voice sounded worried.

"Yes. Come in. Isn't this your lunch hour?"

"I'll run down to the snack machines. I'll grab a fruit drink and eat down there." Gretchen twitched in her chair a few minutes.

Clarissa waited for her to speak.

"Is Mr. McB in a good mood today?"

"Yes, he appears to be."

She breathed a sigh of relief. Nevertheless, her voice sounded unsteady. "I need to ask him for overtime work. I've never done this, but I want to order some invitations for the wedding, and the ones I like cost more than what I expected."

"You're very efficient with your work. And I remember your saying you liked to leave on time."

"I do. I only need a half hour more each day."

"And you can't pay by the month or . . ."

"No way. And Warren says we won't go into debt to pay for a wedding."

"Can he help with the invitations?"

"He won't. He says they are too expensive. And I agree that the invitations, the return cards, thank-you notes and all that kind of stuff is way overpriced. But Miss Bentley, it's custom here. In my church. With my friends. Do you know what Warren told me to do?"

Clarissa answered no.

Exasperated, Gretchen spoke. "He said well type up one and copy it at the office. And put some clip art on it if I wanted some decorations."

Gretchen was almost in tears. Clarissa said sympathetically, "Men don't always understand. And there are so many things to consider and to purchase for a wedding. I know when my sister was married a few months ago, she had all these decisions. Sometimes it comes down to give up one item to buy something else."

"I know. I hope it's not selfish of me to ask for more time here. Mr. McB has a lot on him setting up this office. He pays me well. I won't ask for a raise. I only want enough to cover all the stationary items. And taking on a second job would mean learning new skills, making adjustments. Warren really wanted me to stay at Hadley Morgan. He warned . . ." She paused and looked as if she had said too much. She had a frantic expression as she rushed on. "Do you think Mr. McB would mind my asking?"

"You appear to have thought this through. Asking him seems the first solution to try."

"I appreciate your understanding. I really do. I love Warren to death, but I wish he could understand what this means to me. I'll dash out to lunch. Thank you so much."

"Gretchen, I'll be leaving as soon as Mr. McBaden finishes a lunch appointment uptown. I'm going out to the university law library with him. He's to call before he gets here and I'll meet him downstairs. You'll be back to cover the phones?"

"Oh, yes." She scooted out. In a minute, Clarissa heard the outer door close.

She glanced down at her desk and pulled Susan Phillips's file folder toward her. "Susan, what you could tell Gretchen about men you thought you could love forever. You are fortunate to have been a co-worker. He may have called you a convenient, free typist, but he didn't know what a smart one you were. While typing his works, you learned some valuable lessons."

Clarissa proofed the papers she had ready for Susan to sign tomorrow. She hoped Susan had made the best choice to present the papers to Garvey in person. Some men did not take kindly to receiving them. So far she had planned well. If she has cleared her personal items from the apartment and makes a quick exit, she might leave without abuse.

A blinking light on the phone caught her eye. She pulled over a notepad with one hand and picked up the phone with the other. "Good afternoon. McBaden attorney office."

"Yes. A friend gave me Mr. McBaden's name. He had a will

drawn up by Mr. McBaden when he was with Hadley, Morgan and Jamison. I want to have a will made, too. Is he taking clients now?"

"Yes, he is. Would you like to make an appointment to see him?"

"Yes. Could he see me this week?"

"His appointment secretary is out of the office now. If you will leave me your name and phone number, she can call you probably in the next hour?"

"I'm Lane Hoots."

Clarissa wrote the name and number. Hanging up, she pushed the chair back. The phone rang again.

"Good afternoon. Joseph McBaden attorney office."

"Hello. Is Mr. McBaden in?" asked a young female voice.

"He's out of the office. May I take a message?"

"Maybe you could answer a question for me. I know him slightly. We live in the same neighborhood, but he may not remember me by name. He's said to be a very good attorney. What I want to know, does he take divorce cases?"

"The firm does."

"Oh," she hesitated. "Which attorney handles them?"

"I do. I'm Clarissa Bentley. Would you like to come by the office for a talk?" When the caller didn't respond immediately, Clarissa added, "You will not be committing for us to handle the matter. There will be no charge for a brief conference."

"Thank you. That is most kind. I called information for the phone number. Will you give me directions to your office? And can you see me tomorrow afternoon around one o'clock?"

Clarissa said that time would be fine then gave the office location and floor with room number. Gratefully, the caller knew the building and Clarissa did not have the task of plotting a route on her local map.

Well, this is a productive lunch hour. Thanks be, I ate early. This is a claustrophobic room. She pushed her chair back once more and looked around for some relief for her eyes. The four wainscoted walls squeezed in on her and she walked out and down the hall to Gretchen's desk. In the center of it, she placed the number to call as soon as possible and weighted it with a stapler. Gretchen's words about Warren's wanting her to stay with the big firm had been disturbing not only to Gretchen but also to Clarissa. A good, efficient secretary who suited her boss would be a major loss.

Back in her room, she dialed a familiar phone number. She waited for the answering machine to pick up. "Mom, this is Clarissa. Can you come next weekend to help with the office décor? First on the list is a large picture of an outdoor scene. Maybe an English landscape. And half-house needs all your expertise. I want some new accessories and window treatments. Have a good week. Love to Dad and all."

Littlegate was already seated when McBaden arrived at Shipley, a popular café at noon. It catered to the business crowd in the restaurant and with take-out meals. Littlegate spotted McBaden and signaled him.

"I knew you'd be on time, so I took the first table open. See, two chairs."

"Thanks. I think I smell the oysters. Do you have a menu?"

Littlegate handed it over. McBaden read it with his typical amazing speed.

"What I'd give to have that reading rate. And that accuracy. Cut my work hours in half," he said jovially. He caught a waiter's eye and beckoned him over.

Both men ordered oysters and house salad, coffee and lemon pie.

McBaden unfolded his napkin and placed the silverware beside where the plate would be set. "How were the Saturday games? I've missed not being there."

"Great. Both boys. Jerome made some spectacular saves. He's growing so fast. He's going to be larger than Sam is. Sam scored two goals for the high school. They seem adjusted to their classes. Looks like it'll be a good year."

"Tell 'em I'll be out to see them as soon as things are a little more organized in the office. How's Ruth?"

"Busy and beautiful as ever. She said to tell you hello." He saw McBaden's quick narrowing of eyes. Everything about his friend was quick. Most everything. "I told her I would probably call you."

The waiter came and carefully set down the hot platters, then the salads. He returned with a basket of cornbread squares and an assortment of dressings. He made a third trip with coffee and cream.

"Enjoy your oysters," he said.

They were silent as they relished the piping hot oysters and cornbread. With satisfied expressions, the men tackled the salads more slowly, talking almost in turns about their work and sports.

After the waiter refilled their coffee cups and removed the plates, Littlegate put his elbows on the table. "I told you we had a new minister, didn't I?"

"I recall your mentioning the conference was assigning you a new man. When was that change? Last of June?"

"Right. You've been so tied up with the move I hadn't thought to tell you about him. But I'm glad the news was delayed."

"Why?"

"Yesterday, I learned he knows you. Was a former pastor of yours."

McBaden showed his surprise. "In this conference?" He knew Littlegate was well aware that he hadn't been to church in years. God knows his friend had hounded him often enough to go with him to First Methodist, now First United Methodist.

The waiter appeared with the pies and the bills.

Left alone, Littlegate resumed the conversation. "That's what he said. I told him I'd give you his regards. Mitchell Rockland. Do you remember him?"

He took a bite of pie and watched McBaden. He recognized an immediate withdrawal in his friend, who also took a bit of pie on his fork, savored it, and next a sip of coffee. McBaden looked him squarely in the face.

"A long time ago. But that was back east. It wasn't this conference, or has there been a joining of conferences as well as denominations?"

"No to the latter. Maybe he switched conferences."

"Tell me about him. What he said."

"Well, he's a big fellow, probably was an athlete at one time. Basketball I think. Great personality. The congregation likes him. He has an attractive wife, Ginny. She's not as active yet in the church as the past ministers' wives were. But we heard that before she came here. But she's friendly. From the short time here, I would say she's more the pastor's wife than the church's. They have three mighty fine boys. Very normal guys. Sure they try their parents, but Ginny keeps them in line when Mitchell is busy. The boys are all M's: Mason, Morris and Manly."

"What are their ages, the boys?"

Wiping his mouth after the last forkful of pie, Littlegate sat back in his chair. "Oh, twenty, eighteen and sixteen. The youngest has a good shot at making the basketball team. Course they haven't begun practice, but several of the guys have seen him shooting baskets at the parsonage and in the gym."

"It sounds like Mitch, the youth pastor when I was a teen. So he told you he remembered me." McBaden swallowed the last of his coffee and eyed Littlegate.

"He knows I'm an attorney. He said he read in the newspaper that a Joseph McBaden had opened a law practice in Price Tower. He asked if I knew you, and I said yes. That's how it all came about. I told him I'd tell you, he is now in Windermere."

"You should have yourself a good fellow. Strange how when you're young and you don't see anyone for a long time, you continue to picture him the same age, in the same role. Tell him hello for me."

"I will." Littlegate picked up his bill and McBaden did his. As they waited in a short line at the cashier counter, Littlegate said, "Why not come to a service soon? He gives a good sermon."

"Thanks. When all the dust settles in the tower."

They paid their bills and walked back in the direction of the courthouse. Littlegate's office was on High Street and McBaden left him and turned a corner toward the courthouse.

He walked briskly with his thoughts in time, short and choppy.

Mitch here. Three months now. Twenty years – clipped away – in a few steps. Mitch his hero for four years. A shaper of his moral life. Do good, set worthy goals. His model in academics. Study hard, grades will follow. An athletic example. Play to build your body, to have fun, to release tension. McBaden walked by a building with a revolving front door. He kept his eyes focused on it until it disappeared from his peripheral vision. He increased his pace to resist the urge to push it in and watch the sections swing round again and imagined himself entering an opening, then being flung back on the sidewalk. That was the feeling in the pit of his stomach about Mitch. There was a time he had needed Mitch, and had walked through his door, but Mitch hadn't come through for him. Having been rejected, McBaden had exited the door. He had not seen Mitch since.

By this time McBaden had crossed the street and walked around the side of the accounting building to the parking lot. He heard his shoes crunching the gravel and realized for the first time the unevenness of the surface. The bits of gray granite were tangibles underfoot, comparable to the figurative annoyance in his mind of Mitch's presence in Windermere.

CHAPTER 11

Joseph McBaden found it difficult to understand how he could have been unaware of Mitchell Rockland's being assigned to First United Methodist Church in Windermere. He prided himself on staying current with local news. First Methodist was the largest of its denomination; its membership numbered more than its share of top business and professional men and women, as well as politicians. The church was frequently in the news with its social outreach programs.

Surely, one of the Littlegates had mentioned his name. Or had closing out the work with Hadley Morgan and opening the practice in Price Tower made me oblivious to news in print and conversations? Well, today he had heard the name and now considered that might explain Samuel's lunch invitation. Why would he want me to know this? What might Mitch have said to him? About me? Well, for sure he wasn't going to prod Samuel.

If Mitch was the man and minister that he remembered, then McBaden knew much of the past wasn't discussed. However, only one course was obvious – McBaden had to go to church and he should go soon. This coming Sunday. Somehow he would bring a conversation around to the subject of church and accept Littlegate's predictable encouragement to come to the service. He certainly didn't want to run into Mitch on the street or at some public occasion. His connection had been in the church so there would be the logical place to meet again.

Thus, a decision reached, he turned his attention to the telephone calls. First, he had Gretchen call to make appointments for Lane Hoots and two other clients. Then he organized his notes for a late-afternoon conference.

He had asked Breear to call if her schedule was changed. When a light on the phone base glowed red at five, he wondered if she were calling. Gretchen would be staying thirty minutes later so he wouldn't have to listen for the phone or to monitor the messages for a while. The light ceased to blink.

Clarissa had picked up the phone. "Hello. Are you just getting in from school? Oh, a teacher's meeting. You can come this weekend. Great. Yes, I can meet the plane. Friday noon. Joseph will be out of town so I won't get off early. But you can keep the car, and I'll get some addresses of decorators and furniture stores. And do go by half-house and look around. You'll like it, Mom. I know you will. Give Dad a kiss for doing without you this weekend."

Knowing her mother was coming to perk up the office and give her advice about the house, Clarissa smiled and began humming to herself. She walked over to the conference room and stared out the windows. What a lovely glow the late afternoon sun cast over the buildings across the street and it deepened the autumn tints of the trees that hid the residences nearby. She drew her shoulders up, breathed deeply and felt a loosening of her spirit and body.

Gretchen met her in the hall. With bright eyes, Gretchen said, "I'm going in a few minutes. Anything you need? Any mail to drop off?" Then she whispered, "I'm so relieved he said yes to overtime. Thanks for letting me talk."

"No. There's nothing I need. I'm pleased it worked out for you."

Clarissa telephoned Ruth and asked for recommendations of a decorator and shops for various home furnishings. Ruth suggested Clarissa open the phone directory to the Yellow Pages and furniture shops. While Ruth said the names of the shops, Clarissa placed a checkmark beside them and those of two interior decorators under that section.

"So you're getting ready for your move?"

"I am. Mom is coming Friday. She loves decorating projects."

"That's super. If you all have time, there are some fantastic places in Eastford. Prices are more reasonable on a wide range of furnishings, especially the high-end items. Eastford is one of the largest furniture-manufacturing cities in the country. And we often look there when we're shopping for furniture, fabrics or accessories."

"I've heard of the city. It's not far, is it?"

"No. Only thirty minutes. I don't want to impose on your shopping, but I'd be happy to go over with you Saturday morning."

"Ruth, that's very kind of you. And it wouldn't be an imposition at all."

"Samuel is going on the school bus with Jerome's soccer team to an out-of-town game. And Sam has an evening game and plans to work on a paper and read a novel for his English class. Both reports are due Monday so I know he'll be buried in the work. It will be something to look forward to – a day off with female companionship."

Another blessing, Clarissa hummed cheerfully as she gathered her things for leaving.

McBaden came to her door. "Just checking if a radio was on somewhere."

"No," she smiled.

He cast an inquiring look, but otherwise bore a pleased countenance. She opted not to displace that with decorating plans. She bid him good evening and left. Tonight she would redo her makeup at The Patrick then stroll down to one of the nearby restaurants for a seafood dinner.

At the Cloisters, Breear dashed into her apartment pulling off her jacket as she made for the bedroom. Stripping off her clothes, she turned on the shower and tied her hair back. She washed away the stress of the day with a citrus-scent gel that foamed as she scrubbed from neck to toe. After she toweled herself dry, she noticed in the large mirror that her summer tan was rapidly fading. A few trips to the tanning salon would change that. The mirror reflection and the scales showed a two-pound gain. As she dressed, she decided first to cut out breads for a few days and weigh again, same time and before dinner.

She was putting on earrings when the doorbell sounded. She

switched off the bedroom light, grabbed her shoulder bag, and turned the living room three-way lamp low.

"Hello," said McBaden with a broad smile.

"Hi. I'm starving," she said, closing the door quickly behind her.

"Good. So am I."

As he drove toward Five Points Plaza, they chatted about their day. He commented about having oysters for lunch at Shipley with Littlegate. She asked who Littlegate was. She told him about riding out to a suburb to do a piece about remodeling of a school building that had not been completed when school reopened.

After the hostess showed them to a table, Breear scanned the room, pausing at tables, which were occupied by men who either looked important or well-to-do. She looked pleased.

"Joseph, I like this place. It has a nice feel to it." She opened her menu and read the listings on the two pages, then flipped to the back. "What a varied selection! Have you tried the pork chops?"

"Yes. They are thick and very good. Would you like an appetizer, a salad?"

"A salad, yes. Let's see. The apple-nut salad with honey dressing on the side. And unsweetened tea."

McBaden ordered a rib-eye steak, medium, baked potato and house salad with ranch dressing, and coffee.

Breear once again looked around. "Joseph, who are the men seated three tables over on the right? My right."

After the waiter placed the beverages on the table and walked away, McBaden added a packet of sugar and poured cream into his cup, turned his head slightly, then back again and tasted the coffee.

"The one in the blue shirt is a judge, the one in the middle is a university professor, and on the end in the tan sweater is a doctor."

"Do you know them?"

"You could say I'm acquainted with them."

"What do you think they are talking about?"

He was a bit impatient with this inquiry. He hadn't asked her to dinner to talk about other men. He said as evenly as he could, "Is it important? They all have connections with the university."

"Maybe something important is being planned."

"Or they could be replaying Saturday's football game."

The waiter brought their salads. She finished hers first and unobtrusively withdrew her notebook and pen from her shoulder bag.

"Could you tell me their names?" She was writing in the book. She looked up.

"Are you being a reporter?"

She laughed and kept her voice low. "Joseph, knowing people or at least recognizing a face and having a name to go with it, it could be helpful someday." In a feminine, pleading manner, she added, "I don't know anybody in Windermere. There are so many people to learn. Some of these assignments may have me interviewing these men. I will appreciate your help." Her eyes softened and focused on his.

He laughed, choosing to convey the feeling of a congenial twosome rather than a discordant couple. He told her the names and she penciled them in the book. She seemed so delighted that he asked if there were others in the room she wanted him to identify.

Continuing an appreciative note, she responded. "I'll take a look around and I promise not to point. You know what would be better? You look over the diners and tell me who should be in my little book."

So as if it were a conspiracy, he said a name and an occupation for a dozen other people. Twice he nodded at diners. She glanced over and smiled their way.

McBaden was relieved when she closed the book and replaced the pen in her bag. "All through?"

"Yes. The meal was delicious. Thank you."

"I was thinking of your recording. Would you like a dessert?"

"No." She patted her waist. "TV has a wicked way of adding pounds to you."

"Well, it doesn't show."

"Not in person, but it does on air."

McBaden signed the credit card slip, and they made their way among the tables. He stopped briefly to speak with people at two tables. He introduced Breear to them. At each table, someone spoke up and said he had seen her on television. To all the people at the tables, she vivaciously said that she was so pleased to have met them.

Walking to the car, she locked her arm around McBaden's nearer her. "That was so thoughtful of you. The marvelous dinner at the beginning of the week and introducing me to your friends. Someday, maybe I can return the favors."

To McBaden, the drive back to the Cloisters was long. She was so tantalizing he wanted only to be there and back in her apartment.

As soon as he parked and switched off the engine, Breear put a hand on his arm. "Joseph, I know you want to walk me to the door, but tonight how about just waiting to leave after I'm inside?"

"You don't want me to walk with you?"

"It's not that I don't want you to." She saw his expression mixed with disappointment and bewilderment. "I need an early night in. There was talk as I left the station that tomorrow would be full of assignments. And if you came in . . . well, I remember the night you did . . ."

McBaden turned toward her as he slid his free arm around her shoulder with his hand on the back of her neck and pulled her toward him. "I recall that night. This time I'll be the first to ask 'do you remember this?'" And he embraced her with firmness and kissed her with passion.

At first she quietly accepted his kiss, then responded with warmth. She pulled away to shift more directly toward him. "Joseph, we've known each other a short time."

He was listening to her body, not her words. He didn't want to argue. He gazed at her parted lips and once again drew her toward him and kissed her. She did not struggle. He felt her arms slide around his back and she moved against him. He felt hot and yearned to press her tighter, but feared crushing her. He was the aggressor and he was the captive. He moved his face and begged in her ear, "Breear, Breear."

She slowly stilled her body and kissed his ear. "I'll stop. Joseph, I'm sorry. Forgive me."

He placed his hands on the sides of her face. "Dear, dear, Breear. Don't be sorry." He kissed her again. Her hands squeezed his waist. His ardor returned, but as she released her grasp, he drew back. He turned to open the car door, took a look at the fogged windshield, and pointed to the condensation.

"I should have considered your reputation. We're directly under the security light, but perhaps any passers-by will not know who was in the car. I'm going to open my door, then walk around and open yours. But I'll watch you walk up."

"Okay. Thanks."

After she emerged from her side, McBaden closed the car door. "I was right. You shouldn't come in tonight."

"Next time." He said and watched her intently and listened for nuances.

"There's never been anyone like you." She went up the walkway without looking back.

He drove home a changed man. There was more to life than law and clients. There had been a reawakening of sensations that had long been dead. The feelings tonight were a cross between the devil and pure pleasure.

CHAPTER 12

Friday mid-morning Clarissa drove into McBaden's uptown parking space. Exiting her car, she saw a well-dressed man approaching. He was tall, with dark hair and she guessed he would be in his mid-thirties. He glanced at her car then at her. As he was walking directly toward her, she paused.

"Hello," he said.

"Hello. Are you with the accounting firm?"

"I am."

"Mr. McBaden offered me the use of his space today."

In a friendly voice he said, "I'd like to think that workaholic friend of mine is taking a vacation." He extended his hand. "I'm Charles Fortescue."

She shook his hand and noticed how clean it was. No trace of ink or carbons. And the skin was tight and smooth. "I'm glad to meet you. Joseph has spoken of you."

"And you are?"

"Clarissa Bentley. An attorney in his firm."

His expression was a mixture of smile and question. "I am trying to remember where I've seen you."

"I've been here a few weeks. I'm from northern Virginia. Thank you for introducing yourself, Mr. Fortescue." She took a step forward then stopped as he spoke.

"Please, call me Charlie."

"Charlie. I was about to think the Windermere men used full Christian names. Joseph, Samuel. Have a good day."

"You, too." He walked around the car parked beside hers and stared at her crunching across the lot. What an attractive creature. A lot of class. And no wedding ring. Fortescue suddenly felt the day was brighter, and he hastily unlocked his car door and drove away quickly with the intention of completing his errand swiftly.

An hour-and-a-half later, Clarissa reentered the parking lot behind the accounting office. Fortescue had been watching for her from his office window. He intended to do something impulsive. If she worked with Joseph and knew Samuel on a first-name basis, his move had pre-approved stamped on it. And Joseph had already mentioned his name. This was not a pickup per se. Why wait for gossip to discover if she were dating his friend? He considered that unlikely for Joseph had never been linked seriously with any girl.

As soon as he spotted her coming, he rushed to the back door. However, he sauntered onto the lot while she was unlocking the trunk of her car. She heard him call her name as she was tossing in her briefcase.

Closing the lid, she turned around.

"Do you have a minute?" He walked over.

She looked at her watch. "A minute, yes."

"Are you looking for a parking place near the courthouse?"

"I'm not sure how often I will be down here. I've been parking at Price Tower. I appreciate your asking." She walked around and unlocked her car door.

"If you're free tonight, would you like to have dinner?"

She was surprised and pleased. "Why that's a nice invitation. But I'm on the way to the airport to pick up my mother. She'll be here for the weekend." She opened the door and with an afterthought said, "Some other time."

Instantly, he shot back. "What about Sunday evening?"

"Her flight out is early Sunday afternoon. Would around seven suit?"

"It would. Where shall I call for you?"

"The Patrick. I'll meet you in the lobby."

Not wanting to appear overly pleased, he turned and walked back into his office. Scoring on the first try, man it was his day. He spent a few minutes recalling her attractive face, especially the hazel eyes surrounded by shining brown hair, and her overall physical appearance that indicated good health and femininity.

Fortescue had a purpose for staying on task with the work in front of him–freeing up Sunday evening.

At the airport Clarissa parked in a short-term metered space, inserted two quarters and checked the arrival information data in the terminal lobby. The flight from Dulles Airport was on time. She walked through security check and down to the gate where passengers departed or arrived. She went to the window and saw little activity on the paved area, but knew as soon as the plane taxied in, it would be abuzz with vehicles and trolleys, some bearing luggage and boxes, food services, clean-up crews, as well as attendants directing the plane to the gate.

Clarissa liked the convenience of the Piedmont Airport. It had easy parking, inside layout with direct-traffic pattern in a basic H, only a few shops and those on the lower floor grouped together. The waiting area was beginning to fill up. A queue of businessmen formed at the counter to show their boarding passes or electronic tickets. Two college-age students dropped large duffel bags on the floor and stepped over them to sit down. The other people seated opposite the windows, Clarissa considered, were likely meeting the plane.

When it landed, Clarissa moved near where the passengers would disembark. She saw an attendant open the door and secure it with a floor latch then back up against it as the passengers entered the terminal. She looked forward to seeing her mom, always a pleasant person, even when she had to make comments that opposed some position or choice of Clarissa's. She had tact in asking a question instead of giving an order. Clarissa had watched her in discussion with the younger girls and learned to appreciate the technique and adopted it with some of her clients. The middle daughter, Opal, now thirty-two and married with two children, a boy seven and a girl five, was the most like their mother. She was a real homemaker who had married a couple of years after her college graduation. Visiting Opal's home, which was about a two-hour drive from her parents' house, was always a treat, chaotic at times, especially so at Christmas. The past few years, the family had alternated Christmas at Mom and Dad's with Opal's. Packing up the children's Santa gifts was the main argument used to get the family to travel. However, the wise mother had spoken.

"Wouldn't Opal want the family to see all the decorations she had made for the house?" Her brother Ralph, the oldest sibling and still a bachelor, was always agreeable with wherever the family chose to gather. Holidays were often his busiest seasons at the large department store where he was manager. He routinely told them "you plan where and I'll show up, exhausted surely, but your bright spirits will revive me in a couple of days."

Clarissa saw her mother through the gateway door and waved. Her mother, luggage in both hands, nodded and smiled. Her hair was neatly cut, her makeup understated, her clothing conservative and appropriate for most any occasion – all hallmarks of the fifty-plus-year-old teacher. As educators had labeled them, the backbone of public school education, many upheld the title while bearing the burden of passing on knowledge under increasing difficulties in the classroom.

Clarissa and Louise Bentley exchanged close hugs and warm words. Clarissa took one of Louise's carry-on bags and they chatted as they walked to the car.

"So tell me everything! How's the job? The half-house? And is there another name we can refer to it? Someone could misunderstand and think it's a half-way house." Louise kept up a steady stream of questions that Clarissa answered readily.

As she drove off one of the exits to Windermere, Clarissa shifted the conversation. "Here's what I thought about for the afternoon. I'll drive to the office, then drive to my half-house," she turned and smiled at her mom, "then I'll go back to the office so you'll have a better feel of how to get there. It's a fairly short route. Then we'll go by the shops you see listed on the pad on the seat beside you. The addresses are written down, too. If there's any particular salesperson to ask for, the name will be under the shop."

"Organized and thoughtful as always."

"Ruth Littlegate gave me these names. I told you about her. Samuel's wife. He's Vernon's friend. The Littlegates are delightful people. Ruth offered to go with us to Eastford, one of the area's foremost furniture cities. It will save us precious time."

"How generous of her. So you're meeting people quickly?"

"Yes and in the strangest places. Mom, can you believe I accepted an invitation to dinner for Sunday night while talking with a stranger in a parking lot this morning?"

"No!" Louise peered at Clarissa. "Truth?"

Clarissa laughed. "True. Joseph offered his uptown parking place while I checked records for him at the courthouse. His friend Charlie was leaving as I arrived, and, as I returned, he came out of the office building and asked me out."

"He certainly has good taste," she said. Louise looked out the side window with a pleased expression and released a deep breath.

Completing the drive to the shop sites, Clarissa drove again to the office and stopped the car in front of Price Tower. "Mom, when you're all done with the shops, take time to swing by the house. Or drive to The Patrick and take a nap, whatever you want to do. I'll be through by five o'clock."

"Will I get to meet Joseph when I come back?"

"He said he wouldn't be in the office today." Clarissa opened the door and got out. Louise slid over to the driver's side.

"Um. A new office and not dropping by later. I'm excited about seeing the office. I think you had a good idea just to survey what's available here today before I see what we're to decorate. This way I won't get bogged down with swatches, prices and so forth."

"And we'll be back before closing time tomorrow if we don't decide on items in Eastford. Do stop for a snack or a beverage." Clarissa said as she closed the door.

Louise checked to be sure there was no car approaching or coming up from the rear, then she smoothly drove away.

Joseph McBaden knew there was no escaping an encounter with Mitchell Rockland once Samuel Littlegate got hold of the information that the two had a prior connection. Therefore, McBaden decided to go to church Sunday, eliminating a surprise meeting on the street or a planned one at the Littlegates' house. He left a message on their answering machine saying he would see them at the eleven o'clock service and added he might be a little late so don't wait for him. The family was out of town.

It was after eleven o'clock when McBaden walked into the narthex of the large church building. The congregation was praying the Lord's Prayer: After finishing they stood to affirm the Apostles' Creed. When the prayer ended, McBaden moved forward and accepted a bulletin from an usher. As the congregation resettled on the pews, the usher led McBaden through the open double doors.

The sanctuary was filled except for the back two pews on the right-hand side. McBaden indicated with a nod that he would sit there. He moved down the vacant pew until there was a space between two people on the row immediately in front of him. It was as important to McBaden to see Rockland as to hear him.

With the ministers seated and only a single one visible from Joseph's vantage point, he was in suspense during the offering collection and the choir's anthem. The music was more modern in lyrics and melody and the voices more powerful than any he had heard before. Every aspect of this church was grander than any Methodist church he recalled in the eastern part of the state, beginning with the exterior of this impressive, mellow limestone structure without a steeple. The sanctuary ceilings were roofline high. Along side walls, tall, brilliant-colored quartets of stained-glass windows depicted scenes of Christ's earthly life and ascension. Eight massive columns that required two grown, long-armed men to reach around them stood in solid support of the wooden-beamed ceiling and marked the outer aisles. Wooden flooring beneath wooden pews echoed different sounds than those from the outer stone corridors and central aisle. Straight down the center from the front door across the narthex and through the length of the sanctuary, the path for eyes and feet went to the altar where gleamed a simple brass cross. That was the focus of all the churches of this denomination. There were few symbols in evidence. There were always an altar and a pulpit

The final hymn "Take My Life and Let It Be" was familiar to Joseph; he had sung it many times as a teenager. However, the last line of the second verse caught his attention anew this morning: *Take my intellect, and use every power as thou shalt choose.*

After the benediction, music from the organ swelled as befitting the spacious granite-wall sanctuary and multi-pillar-shaped columns; the wooden flooring and pews absorbing but little of the sound.

Rockland stood down front to shake hands with the congregation.

McBaden folded the bulletin and waited for the crowd to thin before making his way down the long aisle. Several men spoke to him, some shook hands. Two couples stopped and chatted. Both bespoke genuine pleasure at his coming to their church and said they looked forward to seeing him again.

The line had dwindled to a lone handshaker with a funny story to share with his minister. Rockland gave the man full attention. McBaden slowed his last steps at the front pew. Finally, the storyteller laughed heartily at his own story and the minister did likewise. Then catching sight of another person to greet, Rockland clapped the man on the shoulder and said, "I'll remember that one." The man walked down the center aisle still chuckling.

Typically, ministers expected to see church members who thanked them for the good sermon, said a friendly "hello," conversed briefly about a minor church matter, or shared a bit of good news about themselves or another member of First Methodist. Now, Rockland faced with a welcoming grin the final person in line. Although a puzzled expression crept into his eyes, his face was still uplifted in a smile.

McBaden stared straight at Rockland's eyes, extended his hand.

"I know you?" Rockland said.

"From many years ago. In the eastern conference."

Rockland pumped McBaden's hand. "Joseph. Joseph McBaden. You look the same. I know people say that, but in your case, it's true. And you're an attorney in Windermere now."

"Yes. And you're senior minister in this imposing church."

"Imposing?"

"Well, we never did say our grand edifices, did we?"

Rockland laughed. "No, t'wouldn't be humble." He quickly glanced around and up. "But it is a fine piece of architecture, well constructed, well maintained. Inspiring, like the message it calls to tell." He turned again to McBaden. "It's so good to see you again."

"I've been tied up with opening the office and missed your being appointed here. Samuel told me you read the newspaper article."

"Yes, I thought it might be you. I had lost track since we both left the east."

"How did you switch conferences?"

"Ginny wanted to be nearer her family. And it has had its blessings. Especially with the children. We're both from this part of the state. I liked the east and just slid into the youth pastor position after serving as a summer intern during divinity school."

"Well, I'm glad it worked out for you two." McBaden smiled then shifted his weight backwards preparing to say goodbye.

Quickly, Rockland's face reflected serious thought. "Joseph, this is late, but I am sorry that things didn't work out well for you."

McBaden took a step backward. He didn't answer; this was the dreaded moment.

"You know she called me about South Carolina, didn't you?"

"No," he answered with surprise.

"Not immediately. Maybe a year later."

"She never told me. Any particular reason?"

"That she didn't say. Her mother told her the conference was moving me."

"We never told anybody."

"And I've honored that. Still do."

"Thanks."

"Is the situation generally known?"

"No!"

"No?"

Joseph peered at Rockland. "Never has been necessary to talk about it."

"Personal questions a taboo nowadays."

"No one ever asks about your religious preferences either?"

McBaden asked, diverting the focus of the talk.

The minister said lightheartedly, "True. Divinity schools have students who intend serving churches different from the college's denomination." Reverting to a serious tone, he said, "I was really sad to hear of the accident."

"Thank you. It was a low, rough time for all of us."

"Did her parents ever know?"

"Not until after . . . the accident."

"How did they find out?"

McBaden shook his head side to side briefly, took a deep breath and frowned slightly. "Look, Mitch, I haven't thought about this in years. Can we talk about it later?"

Two teenage boys, laughing in good fellowship, swung open the doors from the transept to the right. They were half-dozen paces forward before one of them slowed down and became quiet. He nudged his friend. Rockland waved to them, but turned back to McBaden. McBaden was facing the boys. He watched as the two agreed without speaking to retreat. He admired their tact.

"Sure. No problem." On second thought, Rockland added, "How about lunch someday or breakfast?"

"Breakfast sounds fine."

Rockland thought a minute. "How about Tuesday? There's a small café on Maple Street. It's not crowded around seven. Maple Kitchen."

"I know where it is. See you then." McBaden briskly turned avoiding another handshake. Every step down the center aisle toward the exit trod upon the memory of his last interview with Rockland. And McBaden kept that encounter in check now as he had done for twenty years. How much longer would his will be conqueror of his past was a question he now asked himself.

CHAPTER 13

Clarissa Bentley was proofing a contract that she had drawn up for Mr. and Mrs. Russell, neighbors in High District and friends of the Hughes. They were adding on to their house. Mrs. Hughes had told them that her contractor delayed work on their addition numerous times, and she wished she had some agreement about completion date on paper. Then, she related to her neighbors how pleased she and Burl were with the rental agreement Clarissa had drawn for them.

Thus, Clarissa was settling into the firm and her expectations were lifting. As she finished proofing and attached a note for Gretchen to make three copies, she heard her name spoken and looked up.

Samuel Littlegate walked into her office.

"Hello, Samuel. What brings you out this way?" she said and stood.

"Lunch with Joseph in the Plaza. Are your decorating plans on schedule?"

"They are. My mother's almost finished with the draperies. She'll be here soon with those and whatever else she has unearthed in her favorite haunts."

"Ruth said she volunteered the boys to help put up rods and hang pictures."

"She did. I'll check with maintenance here whether there's a stepladder available. Is next Saturday afternoon still open for them?"

"Whatever she said. She keeps up with their schedules. That's their fall break, I presume, and they won't have games. So, when's the open house?"

Clarissa laughed. "That decision's not made."

"That's the important one, lady!" he joked.

"Why not, the next day? Sunday late afternoon? I'd like Mom to be here and meet the few people we'll invite. Check with Ruth. And I'll ask Mom to take the evening flight back."

"Sounds good." He withdrew his cell phone and punched in a few numbers.

While waiting for a pickup, he said, lowering the mouthpiece, "She should be home now. Her day for inside chores." He nodded to Clarissa and then spoke into the phone. "Ruth, I'm in Price Tower talking with Clarissa. Do we have anything scheduled for Sunday afternoon around five o'clock the day following the decorating of her office? Clarissa asks if that's a good time for her open house up here. Well, pencil us in. The boys, too, she's saying to me. Don't work too hard, sweetheart." Pocketing his phone, he said, "We're setting the date aside. Let us know how we can help."

"I will. And thank you for sharing your family."

"Joseph says you're bringing in clients on your own. Congratulations."

From the doorway McBaden said, "Congratulations?" And he walked into Clarissa's office.

"Hi, there. Lots of news around here," Littlegate said to McBaden then turned and smiled knowingly at Clarissa.

She returned his smile before she spoke to McBaden. "Jerome and Sam are pledged to help with hanging draperies and pictures during their fall break. And Samuel and I have just planned to have an open house here the next day. Five o'clock Sunday afternoon."

Joseph eyed them both. "That is news."

"Just the few people I've met to date. And anyone you suggest that should be invited," she said.

Still absorbing the news, he said, "No names at the moment, but I'll give it some thought."

Littlegate said, "I'll wash my hands before we walk over to the Plaza." He walked around McBaden and down the hall.

As McBaden turned, Clarissa quickly stopped him. "Joseph! This will be a small gathering. There's no intention to have it mushroomed into something you would feel, in any way, forced to do beyond what you'd normally do. But I would like very much for you to come."

He gazed hard at her then nodded.

Littlegate stood outside her door. He stepped aside for McBaden to walk into his office, then came just inside her office. With a thumbs-up sign, he spoke softly. "Be sure to ask our friend, the accountant."

Seeing McBaden reenter the hall, she merely reflected an understanding look. After hearing the outer office door close, Clarissa took the documents to be copied and placed them in Gretchen's tray. Gretchen was typing at her desk and Clarissa walked over.

"I have a contract that I would appreciate your making some copies of for mailing tomorrow morning. Mr. McBaden will be out for lunch, but I will be here until one if you want to go now."

"Gee, thanks. I do have a couple of errands to run." Gretchen finished the letter, ran an envelope, then switched off the machine. She withdrew her purse from a drawer, took out a lipstick, applied a fresh coat of color, then dropped the tube in her purse. "Bye, now."

Clarissa filled a cup with water from the bottle and returned to her office. From her shoulder bag, she extracted a granola bar. She took the water and bar to the conference room and stood in front of the large windows. She enjoyed this view and wished this were her office. On the shopping trip to Eastford, she found a glorious colored fabric of gold, russet and magnolia-leaf green that was perfect for this room. And a world globe on a magnolia wood stand, two scenic prints of the Blue Ridge Mountains – one springtime, one a winter snow. How lovely it will be to have conferences in here. Or to enjoy her coffee breaks. She really wished for a tea set to have an alternative to offer her clients. Tea is such an inexpensive beverage, which relaxes the body and refreshes the spirit.

She stood beside a window, eating the granola bar, and noticed that the dogwoods were turning red and the maples showed a progression of yellows and flame red while still retaining stripes of deep green. Across the intersection on the upper right corner, tall pines stood like a deep green hedge between the deciduous trees and the bright blue sky. She sighed, not from sorrow or loneliness. The sigh was symbolic of a deep breath of clean air on a clear, sun-filled day.

Back in her office, she scooped the folders from her desk to put in the filing cabinet. She counted the cases she was working on. There were enough to keep her busy, including a number of clients she had seen first, giving her comfort that she was adding to the practice. True, they were not highly remunerative cases, but she believed they were clients who would pay their statements within a reasonable time. She would welcome a steady practice of bread-and-butter-type cases for some time yet and anticipated, down the road, a few clients with legal needs that would involve a large financial settlement. She accepted that you paid your dues in one firm; and, if you pulled up stakes, you had to start over. She prayed that this start would be of short duration and bring good fortune more ways than in the practice of law.

She withdrew Susan Phillips's folder for she needed to talk with her husband's attorney about the assets listings. Fortunately, Susan had been foresighted enough to make copies of the literary work of her husband, move her clothing and a few personal possessions before she left their apartment. She was living with her mother and pleased to have the emotional and physical support offered, but she wanted her own apartment. She did not dare commit to any monthly payments until she knew whether Garvey was going to declare bankruptcy. His attorney was not advising that action; he was encouraging Garvey to settle with Susan even if she may someday share any monies resulting from his creative work during the time of the marriage. If he went the bankruptcy route, then creditors could claim the manuscripts.

Clarissa learned during the telephone conversation with the attorney that Garvey was leaning toward signing the papers since he wasn't being asked for alimony. He had come around to realizing he should be responsible for his own debts and payments on the car he drove. His debts were more than Susan's but the attorneys showed figures that Susan's car payments were more, and that she had paid the majority of the bills since their marriage.

Garvey's attorney had strongly advised him to talk with the Consumer Credit counselors to set up a schedule for debt payments. He had done that and was more actively seeking a part-time job or full-time position.

All this news was favorable and Clarissa looked forward to phoning Susan with an update around five o'clock when she would be at her mother's.

She spent the next hour telephoning on behalf of clients. Afterwards, as she organized her notes, she recognized some headway was being made for most of them. This afternoon she planned to file some documents at the courthouse. Mentally, she made a note to ask Joseph if he would need his parking space.

Gretchen rushed in and appeared at Clarissa's door saying she was back and would be in the restroom a few minutes. The telephone rang and Clarissa answered.

"Hi. It is Clarissa, right?" asked Charles Fortescue.

"It is. How are you?"

"I'm okay, but by dinner time I shall be very hungry. And the twilight view from the Schaffer Club should be awesome." He paused. "It is a sight to share. I'd like you to join me."

"I've just been admiring the noon beauty from Price Tower. And I'd be twice blessed to see the setting sun."

"I'll look forward to it. Shall I pick you up at The Patrick at six fifteen? That should give us a half-hour of view before dusk and street lights."

"I'll be in the lobby. And thank you for thinking about me."

"It's a pleasure." He hung up with a happy smile and resurgence of energy to tackle his adding machine and computer.

Likewise, Clarissa felt brighter in spite of her dark office. Gretchen returned to her typing and copying duties. McBaden entered with a lighter pitch of voice and seemed in a good mood. Clarissa got up and followed him into his office.

"I have to go to the courthouse to file some papers. Will you be uptown in the next hour or so?" She asked.

"No. I'll be here at the desk most of the afternoon. I have several appointments."

"If you're not using your parking space, may I park there?"

"Yes." He directed a curious look at her. "I've heard from several sources that Charlie and you are dinner partners."

"We have been out. And he's taking me early this evening to see the city from the Schaffer Club."

"That should be quite a view. I hope you enjoy the evening. And Charlie is a super-nice fellow." He felt he owed her an assurance that his friend was a suitable companion.

"Thank you for saying that. He is a good conversationalist with a happy temperament. Is there any errand you'd like me to do while I'm uptown?"

"No. Have you moved into your place yet?" he asked.

"Next weekend, I'm delighted to say. The movers will be here on Thursday so I'll be out of the office for several hours. Some pieces from local dealers have arrived, but not enough for me to set up housekeeping."

"Well, you will keep your mother very busy next weekend."

"She's very well organized and gets an adrenaline boost from this avocation. I know what I like around me and she knows, too. She's so much better at shopping and sewing that I've just put learning those skills aside. My sister married a few months ago, and Mom helped her decorate an apartment. I'm catching her between that and her own preparations for Christmas."

"For Christmas?" he asked, curious.

"That's a big holiday for us. It's worth a trip just to see her newest creations. But we really go to enjoy the whole family being together." She had a sparkle in her eyes and joy in her voice. A personae of anticipation. Suddenly, he wondered if that would linger until her dinner date or was that a contributing factor. He shook his head, dislodged the matter with an air of "it's no concern of mine."

He rejoined indifferently in a manner that equaled Scrooge's *Bah! Humbug!* for an attitude toward the season. "Well, let Gretchen know when there's an address change and a phone number." He pulled out his chair and sat down.

Clarissa shivered and left. Is he really cold of heart? Does he ever warm up to any occasion? Again, she glanced around her dark, impersonal office. I'll be glad to see some cheerful objects in here. They'll be welcomed after chilly encounters.

The following week Joseph picked up Breear from work. As they looked over the menu in a popular restaurant located between the station and the Cloisters, he asked how her day had been. "Long and interesting. I made pages of notes."

"Well, let's get you something to eat." He signaled the waiter. He nodded to Breear, who told him she wanted a nice, juicy, rib-eye steak, medium, and a house salad with no dressing, no potatoes, and a basket of hot, soft rolls and butter."

Joseph joked. "No potatoes but bread and butter!"

"Yes. Trading off like diets allow."

The waiter asked what she'd like to drink. "Coffee, now, please." She spoke in a pleading voice that had the magic to spur him to the coffee carafes and scoot back. He fetched a basket of rolls in double time. Looking at her as if he were a knight granting her every wish, he promised to bring more rolls later. He didn't say on a silver platter riding a white charger, but his attitude projected a desire to serve in whatever way to please her.

Breear dug into the basket and placed a large roll on the small bread and butter plate and began to coat it thinly and evenly. "See," she held it a few inches above the plate and made a show of the action. "I am being conservative with the butter."

She took a bite and savored the fragrant yeasty bread. Joseph enjoyed watching her. "Mind if I have one?" He asked as he reached in the basket.

"No, please do. We can get more." She tantalized by stretching out the word "more."

"The lady has worked up an appetite."

"She has and who knows what the evening will bring. Isn't it a good practice to refuel against any eventualities?" She watched him across the table while she spooned a little sugar and poured half-and-half into her coffee.

Joseph looked over his coffee cup before drinking. He tried to interpret her meaning. Her manner offered no clue. However, Joseph was beginning to program a read on her sentence structure and voice quality. He noticed that she hadn't quite learned the skill of asking a question with the dropped pitch that clearly bespoke: "It is a statement we know the answer to." Her phraseology and delivery were getting there but hadn't quite arrived at the traditional rhetoric stage.

While she was eating her salad, she asked Joseph to tell her about his practice of intellectual property.

"You probably heard about it in one of your journalism classes. Property being the work of writers. It applies to unique ideas of people in the arts, as well as those of inventors. Companies like to register their name and or identifying marks."

"Do you register the work for them?"

"Anyone can apply for a copyright to his creative work. There are books with sample forms you can look at." He added with emphasis, "Copyright protects the expression of an idea, not the idea itself."

Breear asked with interest. "What's the advantage in having a copyright other than no one can reproduce the work without written permission of the author or publisher as I see in novels?"

"It establishes a public record of who owns the property and who has the say of how it can be used." Joseph looked at her and her show of interest prompted him to continue. "The copyright, be it the word or the symbol you see – a *c* in a circle followed by a date – is next to the owner."

"When did copyrights begin?" She paused after chewing a piece of steak. "If you see our waiter, I'd like some more coffee."

Joseph signaled to the young man who was refilling coffee cups at a nearby table. "The current statute was passed in 1976 . . ."

Breear grinned. "That's the year I was born."

Joseph's expression was a mixture of chagrin and amusement. "And it was enacted in 1978. However, for a brief history of intellectual property dates, the first one in America was in 1790. Great Britain first adopted one in 1710. But it was a statute passed in France in 1793 that most European countries used as a model."

He concluded in an attempt at glee. "And those latter dates were all before I was born."

The waiter appeared with a full pot of coffee. He held it toward her and she said, "Yes."

She laughed, looking back to Joseph. "Where do you as an attorney come in?"

"Well, a copyright is necessary prior to filing a suit in court for any infringement of your work. That's when an attorney can be consulted. And when timing is important if the work has been copied or used without permission."

Breear smiled broadly at the waiter and thanked him. He hardly took his eyes off her as he asked Joseph if he wanted a refill. Joseph nodded and watched the young server giving partial attention to the hot coffee being poured.

"That's enough," he said, and quickly the waiter tipped the carafe up. He smiled sheepishly at Breear and walked to the next table. "You have an admirer."

She laughed smoothly. "Timing is important?" Her remark could have referred to the young man as a waiter or an admirer, or to the copyright information. Joseph chose to address the latter.

"Yes. It determines what kind of settlement you can ask for."

"And anybody can copyright his work?" Her eyes showed a thoughtful inquisitiveness.

"The copyright is to protect published and unpublished work. Works in progress are protected."

She glanced at her shoulder bag. "You mean my notes are protected?"

"Yes. If you ever decide to put them into an article or use them in some other form of literary work, you are protected."

"Why should I, say for example, copyright these pages," she pointed at her bag even though he couldn't see it on the seat, "if they are already protected?"

"If you register the work within or before five years of publication, there will be prima facie evidence in court of its validity."

"Ah, ha! I'll make a note of that bit of information." She wiped the corners of her mouth, reached in the bag and pulled out her notebook. Scanning the room while flipping to a blank page, she noticed a woman seated alone at a table across the room. The woman turned her head, and they exchanged a brief glance.

"Joseph, do you know the woman dining by herself to your left a few tables over? She has short brown hair, a beautiful tobacco-colored suit, probably cashmere, and a cream-colored blouse, probably silk."

Joseph scrunched up his face. "From here I couldn't say what the fabrics are." He casually turned in the direction she had indicated. Immediately, he knew which woman she was referring to. He averted his eyes until he focused again on Breear.

She was writing in her notebook, which was beside her plate on the table. When he didn't speak, she asked without looking up. "Do you know her?"

"I do. She's an attorney in practice with me."

Still with her attention on the notebook, she asked, "What's her name and where's she from?"

"Clarissa Bentley. Two *s*'s in the first name and the last name spelled like the car." His tone was terse. "She's from Virginia and the District of Columbia."

After she scribbled another line or two, she laid the pen down and peered at him. "I thought she was not from here. Her clothes are very classy."

"You amaze me."

She crinkled her nose as she leaned forward. "She's a lovely woman."

"So are you."

"Will I get to meet her?"

"Tonight?"

She shrugged her shoulders. "Sometime."

"Sometime. Any particular reason?"

"I need to know people in Windermere." She reached over and touched his fingertips. "I know so few people. And I'd like to know those who work with you." She stroked his fingers slightly before removing her hand. "This was a delicious meal. Thank you."

As they stood to leave, Breear directed her eyes intently toward Clarissa who returned the contact for a second time. Breear's countenance was one of satisfaction as she smiled at Clarissa.

Joseph had been occupied with taking the ticket from the table and leaving a tip and had not witnessed the exchange between them. He put his hand forward and guided Breear around an adjacent table, giving her arm a gentle squeeze.

CHAPTER 14

Monday started off with a quick pelting rain just before rush-hour traffic. School bus pickups were off schedule as children waited under trees or in their own doorways till their ride was in view. Some commuters insisted on being dropped at their work sites instead of sloshing through streams of runoff water along the sidewalks and curbs. City buses and early delivery trucks emitted heavy exhaust to an already dense atmosphere.

Vehicle delays caused tardiness community-wide. However, after a few minutes of shaking soaked raincoats and umbrellas, throughout the city the general tone was one of thankfulness for the rain which would clear pollens from the air, eliminate the need to water lawns after work, loosen soil for setting fall plants in flower beds or gardens, and raise the water table after a dry summer.

On the sixth floor of Price Tower, Gretchen Pearly scurried from the elevator to the office. When she saw the lights were on, she said under her breath. "Drat! My only day late and someone's already here. Well, I'll stay thirty-five minutes later."

Joseph McBaden, standing at the fax machine, peered toward the doorway when he heard the door open and close. "Hello. Still raining hard I see."

"It is. Sorry to be late. I'll make it up," she called out as she hung her wet coat on the bentwood tree and dropped her umbrella in the umbrella stand. "I'll go dry my shoes with some paper towels." She scooted by McBaden and into the rest room.

Clarissa Bentley came into the hall. "Is Gretchen here?"

"She is. Thank you for the research on Friday. Any problems?"

"No. Was your trip profitable?"

"It was. Any developments I need to know about?"

"There were two phone inquiries Friday afternoon. Both men made appointments. One for eleven this morning. He needs a contract drawn up. The other wants to come in with a man he's going into partnership with. They want to be sure they're covering everything that should be addressed in an agreement."

"Gretchen left memos about several calls. Bring your notes from Friday," he said as he walked toward his office.

Clarissa picked up a legal pad from her office and joined him at his desk. She turned the pad toward him. "First page is regarding the contract and the second, the partnership. The information is sketchy, but the callers' names and phone numbers are there. I checked the phone directory and added the addresses. Both are likely residential."

Reading the notes, he said, "I'm not familiar with the names, but I agree about the addresses. You're learning Windermere quickly."

"Via the city map. The man coming today said he had heard you spoken of highly. And tomorrow's appointment had read the newspaper article. He took a chance with the recent opening that you could see him quickly. Is there any problem with my making the appointments for you? I couldn't reach him until after Gretchen left."

"No. I didn't see any notations on my desk calendar about them." He looked at her across the desk.

"I didn't take that liberty. Wasn't there a white card, four-by-six index, inserted over today's page?" She asked with a frown.

"No." As he searched his desktop, she came closer and looked, too. She walked around to the right side and quickly spotted a white card on the carpet. She held it up.

"Here it is." She made no excuses, offered no guesses how it ended there. "I'll use Post-it notes next time."

"How are the cases I handed you shaping up?" He inquired as he sorted faxes.

"Fine. I will have them ready for your review tomorrow morning. One very possible client stopped me in the courthouse. She wants a pre-nuptial agreement. That being akin to divorce – either a wand to ward it off or a lever if it comes – I agreed to see her tomorrow." She waited for his yea or nay.

He nodded his head slightly then glanced intently at her, though his tone was level. "She just approached you out of the blue?"

"She had been talking to Ruth Littlegate, who said I handled those cases. And she saw Samuel at the elevator, and he told her I was in the records room."

"A generous gesture."

"Yes, from both of them."

"A newspaper ad about your joining the firm may be another way to announce you. Hand me any suggestions you have for copy. We'll go over your experience. If we run it in the business section of the local paper, the area's business news weekly may pick it up. It would be expedient to have a few more facts ready to hand 'em or fax, if they inquire." He watched her for an agreement or suggestion.

"I'll work on it. And I appreciate your proposing the announcement."

He caught a lilt in her voice and watched her walk out of the room with a jaunty gait for a soggy Monday morning.

Soon afterwards, he donned his trench coat, slipped two file folders and his collapsible umbrella into his briefcase. He stopped by Gretchen's desk to say he was going to his accountant's and would be back in time for his eleven o'clock appointment.

Being near the end of the quarter, he wanted to check some figures with Fortescue. Rain still beating steadily, McBaden chose to drive the expressway, the quickest route uptown. After parking in Fortescue's gravel lot, he dashed around a number of puddles and entered through the back door.

He held the door open to release his umbrella and give it a quick shake.

"Well, come in and dry off, Joseph!" Charles Fortescue urged pleasantly.

"A good morning to you, too. I'll leave these here on your

pegs," McBaden said, placing his coat on the top row on the wall and his umbrella on the lower.

"Fine. Come in. Do you want some coffee to warm you on such a good soaker of a day?"

"I just had some. But no, thanks."

The two friends worked over the account for forty-five minutes then McBaden shoved the originals back in his folders and Fortescue the copies into a folder on his desk.

Fortescue leaned back in his chair, locked his hands at his waist, and smiled. "Thanks for allowing Clarissa to use your parking space."

McBaden eyed him with surprise. "Oh, you saw her, did you?"

"I did. A couple of weeks ago, I was leaving as she arrived."

"Oh. Chance meeting?" He knew that was possible, remembering his running into Breear.

Fortescue chose his next words carefully. "Yeah. We had dinner on Sunday. And again last night."

"Thank you for taking care of my attorney." McBaden was a stranger to this kind of small talk. He trusted his friend did not think that remark had been a possessive one.

"It was my pleasure. She's really a nice person, Joseph." The words were sincere, but implied a bit more than a generality.

Finding the conversation awkward, he replied, "She comes highly recommended. She and Samuel have a mutual attorney friend. And she's already drawing in clients of her own."

"That's good news for the firm, speaking as your accountant. And for myself, I'm hearing you have only a business arrangement." Fortescue's eyes glinted.

"Right, you are," stated McBaden, snapping his briefcase firmly.

Fortescue rose from his chair. "In all the years I've known you man, don't you ever get excited about a girl?"

McBaden squared himself in front of Fortescue and attempted to sound nonchalant, but the manner bore his typical seriousness. "You may be in for a surprise one day."

"Good. I look forward to that. And soon." Fortescue clapped McBaden on the back as they returned to the hall. McBaden put on his coat and grabbed his umbrella while Fortescue opened the rear door.

"It's slacked a bit now. I'll see you soon."

"Yeah," McBaden uttered, opened the umbrella and left. As he walked across the parking lot, Harry Wooten, an attorney who also parked in the lot, hailed him.

"Hi. Think Charlie will pave this lot someday? I hear he's squiring your lady around."

"My lady? Oh, Clarissa. They've been out to dinner. Watch the puddles there!" McBaden warned too late. Wooten, not looking where he stepped, splashed water over his shoes and onto his trouser cuffs. Good naturedly, he waved a thank you and hurried on choosing his way more circumspectly.

The rain continued on Tuesday in a steady drizzle that Joseph McBaden predicted could turn into a heavy downpour anytime. He dashed to his car with his raincoat on but his umbrella still furled in his briefcase. He started the engine, turned on the windshield wipers and headlights, and backed around in his driveway.

Traffic was moderate at six forty-five in the morning as he drove to Maple Kitchen on Maple Street. He arrived before Mitch and chose a booth at the rear of the small room. After hanging his coat on the hook beside the booth, he sat facing the door.

The café had a comfortable atmosphere with simple furnishings, sturdy and worn, but not shabby. It held nothing pretentious; it was simply a neighborhood, medium-priced café serving three basic meals. The single waitress approached his booth.

"Good morning. Can I bring you some coffee?"

"Thank you, yes."

He scanned the menu and decided on the scrambled eggs, bacon and whole-wheat toast and orange juice. The eggs and bacon could be eaten quickly and the bread and juice consumed according to the pace of the conversation.

The front door opened and Mitch appeared, large and imposing in his unbuttoned all-weather coat. Joseph signaled and Mitch strode down the aisle. Hanging up his coat, he greeted Joseph with a hearty hello.

The waitress returned with the cup of coffee. "Hi, Reverend Rockland. Still raining, is it?"

"Coming right down, Judy. I'll take coffee, too. Have you ordered, Joseph?"

"No." He looked to Judy, who was pulling her order pad from her apron waistband and pencil from her pocket. "I'm ready." She nodded and wrote down his order. She looked over to Mitch.

"I'll have the sausage, two once-over lightly eggs, grits and a cinnamon roll."

They placed the menus at the end of the table.

Joseph commented. "You still eat a big breakfast."

"You remember those before-Sunday school breakfasts we cooked for a fund raiser for our youth trips; and those we had on our trips?"

"It comes back. And how we all marveled that you consumed everything left over."

"I had some help from you teens who were always hungry."

Joseph drank his coffee, put the cup in the saucer and said, "This place gives good service at reasonable prices, but it could use a good coffee maker."

"Be it person or equipment, eh?"

"So how are you finding your Windermere assignment?"

Mitch replied easily. "The city is beautiful. Rolling terrain, lots of tall trees, many elegant homes and wide lawns, and attractive, more modest real estate, too. The culture menu is varied and has something for every taste. It's a modern city which keeps us reminded of its historic past, one that was primarily church-oriented, I'm pleased to say.

"The church is the biggest I've been assigned to. It's a challenge, but I have a large and capable staff. In this first stage, I'd say the family and I like the assignment. And few serious complaints about my handling matters or my preaching have reached my ears."

"That sounds as if you and the church are off to a good start,"

Joseph said. He waited, sipping his coffee, for Mitch to ask him how he was, to which he would answer doing fine. Then Joseph would wait for what was on Mitch's mind.

Mitch thanked Judy for the coffee refill. Joseph refused the offer.

"Joseph, I didn't ask you here to pry about the past. In spite of what was said the last time we met in the east, I considered you as close a friend as I had in that church. There was some reserve due to my position and your age. Back then, seven years difference seemed vastly more widespread than it does today. I was charged with advising youth when I was just beginning my ministry."

"You were our mentor. We followed you right down the line." Joseph reflected before continuing. "You were right when you told us where some actions, some crossing of the line, would lead us." Again, he paused and thought. "Times have changed, haven't they? We would be babies beside the youth today."

"I would find that job tough if I were just starting out now." Finishing his coffee, he moved the cup and saucer aside. "I'm glad life has turned out well for you. Samuel tells me your practice is off to a good start and you have an experienced woman attorney in the office. I hear she's also a Methodist. Samuel or Ruth has most likely extended her an invitation to go with them to First Methodist. Samuel says you are not married and as far as he knows that you've never been."

"He's my closest friend. He and his wife are good, good people. If they have a fault, it's trying to find me a wife. Ginny and Ruth are very similar, and I haven't seen anyone even close to them."

"Frances was an outstanding girl, Joseph. You chose well. Both of you had a tremendous capacity for love. The ability for love is innate; it's still with you. The years with Frances were important; they helped shape you. Although that chapter in your life is over and cannot be changed, you can open it at times, remember the best, learn from it, close it back up. You are still a young man. You look healthy, you're in good shape, and you're successful in a meaningful career. When you're ready for a partner, socially or in your home, she'll show up. I have faith in you, and faith you'll know her."

Joseph concentrated on his former minister while he spoke. And the years melted and he could see Mitch and hear him as he talked to the youth long ago, with conviction and sincerity and believability. When Mitch stopped, Joseph sensed his own throat was filled. He bent his head and swallowed hard. After a deep breath, he said, "Samuel says you have three boys; he speaks well of them. You were just expecting your first when I left for college?"

"Right. Mason. You'll have to come to the house and meet the three M's. When there were two, you can imagine all the M&M jokes. Mason is a junior in college and Morris is a freshman. The one at home is Manley."

"He's the high school's most promising basketball prospect."

"Well, he's practicing every spare minute to get and keep a spot on the team."

"I know that has to make you proud."

"He's a good kid. You know the downside. He doesn't want to stop to study. I have to hand any achievement he has in the classroom, and that includes handing in daily homework, writing reports and studying for tests, to Ginny. Those boys have been a full-time job for her."

Judy approached with the coffee carafe. Both said no and she laid the tickets on the table.

Joseph dropped a tip and picked up his ticket. "Well, it's work time, Mitch. It was good to see you. Tell Ginny hello."

"I will. And thanks for coming today and last Sunday. Do come back. Think about bringing Clarissa."

"We have a business relationship."

"I've noticed here that relationships – doesn't that word have vast modern implications? – are more niched than they are in some towns. We didn't feel so much that way in the east, did we?" Mitch stood up and put on his coat.

"I hadn't compared them. Perhaps I was too young to assess that part of the community."

They dealt with the cashier and dashed for their cars as the rain fell heavily.

CHAPTER 15

Friday morning Ruth Littlegate phoned Clarissa at the office. Gretchen put her through and Ruth apologized for calling there.

"I am in a small quandary of my own making and I know this is last minute, but could you join us for dinner tonight?" Ruth asked as she stood at her kitchen counter unloading groceries from the day's marketing.

"Is there something special happening?" Clarissa asked, signing some forms on her desk.

"A new guy moved in last week a few doors from us. I started to take some cake or something to him. But I saw the realtor leaving his house yesterday and she stopped for a chat. She told me he was new in town, well, comparatively new, recently joining a local firm. She hoped Samuel and I could drop by to see him. I decided a single fellow didn't need a whole cake, so why not have him over for dinner. Well, tonight he's free. And the boys are going to be off with friends. So will you please come and help us greet him. A table setting is so much more congenial with four."

When Ruth paused, Clarissa said, "The conversation is easier. I'd love to help you out, Ruth. Can you tell me a little more about the guy?" She stacked the forms and attached a note to Gretchen to mail them today.

"Blessings on you. His name is Rush Newton. He's single, never married, nice chap, and mid-thirties. He seems temperate, I mean, not boisterous, but not withdrawn either. Well, he's really cheerful and chubby. Joseph always accuses Samuel and me of trying to set single folks up. Let's say that tonight I'm trying to be a good neighbor to one, and saying to a friend that I appreciated the trip to Eastford. It was a marvelous day for me, escaping the regular Saturday routine."

"Mother and I enjoyed it, too. What may I bring tonight?"

"Only yourself. See you about six thirty?" Ruth opened the refrigerator and shelved the meat and vegetables.

"I look forward to it."

After Clarissa hung up the phone, she took the forms to the reception room. "Gretchen, these need to be mailed today. The addresses should be on your Rolodex."

Gretchen pushed her swivel chair to the side and asked, "Do you have a minute? There're some dresses I'd like to show you in a bridal magazine I bought today."

"Is there one like you selected?" Clarissa asked and stood beside the desk.

Gretchen pulled open her lower desk drawer and withdrew a thick, slick magazine. *Brides of the Mid-Atlantic States and the District of Columbia.* She placed the magazine on the desktop and caressed the cover.

"Isn't she gorgeous!"

"She is lovely. This is the most recent issue," she commented, noting the date.

Gretchen turned a few pages and pointed to an elegant gown of very simple lines, which Clarissa knew required exceptional skill to create. Gretchen flipped through a few pages searching for a particular dress. Quickly, she stopped. "This one. Isn't it heavenly! The satin bodice with pearls sewn around the neck and to a point at the waist and the full skirt with its chapel-length train. I just love it."

"Is that similar to yours?"

"Well, kind of. But this one has a better beading pattern and a longer train. And look at the price. Mine is no way near that amount." The phone rang and Gretchen said to Clarissa, "Take a look through."

While Gretchen talked with the caller and took notes, Clarissa thumbed over several pages. She passed one, then turned back. The two-page spread was headlined *Washingtonian Summer Wed-*

dings. Clarissa scanned the layouts and read the captions. Suddenly, she swallowed hard. Her finger stiffened beneath one caption; her eyes froze on one photograph. Her complexion drained of all color.

Joseph had come quietly down the hall for his morning coffee. Something about Clarissa's ridged stance caught his attention. He stood still beside the coffee area. She leaned her weight against the desk. As Gretchen hung up the phone and finished making notes, Clarissa pushed with her hands and slowly shifted her weight from the desk. Deftly, she turned several pages over.

In a strained voice, she managed to say, "Thanks Gretchen, for showing me your magazine." Without waiting for Gretchen to show her more photographs, Clarissa turned.

Joseph caught a quick look at her face; it was pale and drawn; eyes downcast, so as not to have to see another's eyes, hiding all thoughts. He swung toward the coffee cups, lifted the pot and filled one. She skirted past, went into her office and closed the door.

Very curious, he considered, remembering her lively expressions all week. Approaching Gretchen's desk, he looked for the magazine, but it was not there. Probably tucked in her desk somewhere, he deduced. Well, it was Friday and there were still papers on his desk to attend to. He had dinner plans with Breear and no thoughts of staying late himself, so he dropped his cup on the tray for wash up. Back in his office, he, too, closed his door; thus, he forgot Clarissa and her trauma.

Mid-afternoon Clarissa had a headache and was the first to leave the office.

Before the five-o'clock mail pickup in the outside box, Gretchen walked down with the letters that needed sending. Joseph came out to get some paper clips from the storage shelf and noticed the office was empty. Contrary to his nature of not meddling in staff matters, he quickly crossed to Gretchen's desk and opened the bottom drawer. There was a bridal magazine. He pulled it out, propped a hand on the spine and let the pages fall free from front to back without creasing them. All brides. What could bring such a shock to Clarissa? Scanning the front cover the only content information that read of a specific topic was about Washington weddings. He replaced the magazine and closed the drawer a minute before Gretchen returned.

"It's going to be a lovely evening. Did you need anything Mr. McBaden?" she asked, seeing him near the desk.

"No. Do you and Warren have big plans for the weekend?" he inquired and looked at her as if he were interested.

She found that strange for he seldom asked personal questions. "We're going to shop for the apartment. Maybe register some of our selections for a couple of the showers some friends are planning."

"Well good luck." He walked back down the hall.

The light was blinking on the phone in her room in The Patrick when Clarissa walked in. After dropping her briefcase and stepping out of her pumps, she called the desk. There was a message from Mrs. Bentley. Clarissa thanked the operator, pressed the off button then punched in her mother's number.

Waiting for a pickup, she pulled the bedspread down and propped the pillows against the headboard.

"Hello." Her mother answered.

"Hi, Mom. Did your Friday end peacefully with all those students kept in line?"

"Dream on, dear. If you're back in your room, you must have had a shorter day."

"I did."

"Is there anything wrong? I know it's a strain to be cheerful at this time, but you sound a bit low."

There was a silence. Mrs. Bentley waited patiently.

"Gretchen brought a brides' magazine in and wanted me to look at it with her. You can guess whose wedding was pictured in the Washington section."

"But that was only a few months ago. Doesn't it usually take six months or more to get a writeup?"

Rather wearily, Clarissa responded. "Not if you pose in a studio earlier. And know the wedding is a done deal beforehand. No possibility either party will back out."

"Dear, I'm so sorry. You seem to be handling everything so well. And saying everything was over."

"It is. I came to terms with it. I knew even before. There were signs. Thanks for letting me talk to you about it."

Relieved, she said with compassion, "Anytime. Have you some fun plans for the weekend?"

"Ruth Littlegate called today. She talked about the fun trip to Eastford. And she asked me to dinner tonight. I think mainly to have me meet a new neighbor, eligible bachelor. She describes him as someone a girl might want to know."

"Are you going?"

"I am. First, I'm going to soak in a bubble bath, then put on something bright and stylish and plan to enjoy myself. Did I tell you I had dinner with Charlie again? And he's asked me out for tomorrow, too."

"Windermere sounds like a very sociable city. I look forward to seeing both, it and you, again next weekend. And I did get the evening flight out on Sunday. I hope you won't do too much for the open house."

"I won't. I found a caterer, which surprised me for Sunday afternoon. It'll be simple, but filling enough to hold folks till dinner. We have the Littlegate boys to help with the office Saturday. And Phil and some of his friends are coming over Sunday morning to move anything that needs rearranging in the house."

"I know you'll be glad to move in."

"Yes, except it'll be back to some cleaning and meal preparation."

"Well, my dear, you always managed that with the least effort I ever saw!" Instantly, Mrs. Bentley regretted the statement.

"I'm not as accomplished in the kitchen as you and Opal. As you say, I keep the restaurants open. The half-house kitchen is charming and larger than city apartment ones. Maybe I'll get inspired. But don't expect home cooking next weekend; our energies will be consumed with decorating. I look forward to seeing you."

"Me, too, dear. Take care of yourself. I love you."

"And I love you, Mom."

On a Saturday afternoon Joseph drove Breear around to several automobile dealerships, where they strolled through the blacktop lots and inspected the latest models offered. The salesmen continually pointed at the hottest new cars. Joseph murmured to Breear that the hottest item was the paving they were walking on.

Both of them acted like people who enjoyed the shopping around as an adventure. They did appear to be basking from some source, perhaps the heated lots and the autumn sunshine. They even doffed their lightweight sweaters.

As the sun turned more bronze in color and dipped westward, the salesman, showing them the last of his offerings, began to pull up his shirtsleeve and read his watch closely. Joseph asked Breear if she wanted to look again at any cars on this lot.

"No. I'll have to think about all of the ones we've seen today." She turned and thanked the salesman for his time and said she would get back with him when she made a decision. He in turn thanked her for coming then hastened to the office to hang up the keys.

During the afternoon, as Breear had test-driven a few cars, Joseph had sat in the back seat allowing the salesman to sit up front and prolong his spiel about the advantages of the particular model. Meanwhile, Joseph thought about how he used to spend Saturdays watching Littlegates' boys play ball or a college game in the area. Today there was a big game in the city stadium. He had asked Breear to go. She had said no that she needed to check out cars. Her mother was pushing her to get one and her dad had offered to make the down payment, as well as monthly payments until she had worked several more months. Young people who weren't burdened with paying for cars, rent and meals were lucky folks.

When Breear had declared – according to her girlfriends – car salesmen were difficult for women to deal with, Joseph had offered to go with her. She accepted his offer quickly then hugged him when he suggested they could grab a bite later.

Leaving the dealership, Breear remarked, "I feel so hot and sticky after tramping about all afternoon. Can you drop me by the Cloisters? I want a shower and a change of clothes before dinner."

"Certainly. I could stand to do the same. How about my picking you up at six forty-five? We can eat at seven and catch a movie at nine."

She reached over and kissed him on the cheek. "That's for being so sweet about the cars." Then she nuzzled his neck. "That's for the rest of the day and evening."

"That's not fair! I'm driving!"

The crowds were larger at the Plaza than Joseph had expected. He hadn't factored in the football spectators swelling the usual weekend restaurants.

"Let's grab a pizza and a salad and we'll still have time for a movie," Joseph said.

"Okay."

Breear had changed into a pair of casual jeans and a pullover sweater in varying shades of orange, gold and rusty brown that were quite flattering to her hair and skin. He, too, was neat in tan twill slacks and a blue and green small checked, long-sleeved shirt. Both had brought along cardigan sweaters. His was on the back seat, and when he parked the car, she tossed her sweater beside his. "Looks as if they're reserving our places."

He grinned at her then went around to open her door.

There were a number of people standing around the entry. Joseph threaded his way to the receptionist and asked how long for a table for two. She scanned the list and said about ten minutes. He returned to Breear and reported it would be a short wait.

Several people were exiting the dining area and Joseph and Breear were pushed against each other. "Sorry about this," he spoke quietly to her.

She flashed a smile of understanding.

"Are you excited about getting a car?"

Before she could answer, the press of people was over and the receptionist called his name.

"That was quick," she said to the hostess who led them to a table.

She replied over her shoulder. "There was one vacancy for a couple." She stopped at a booth and placed two menus on the table and announced their waitress would be Jeannie.

The local Italian restaurant was well known for its pizza, but its regular customers also knew it prepared other Italian dishes and many traditional chicken and beef offerings, each served with a choice of salad or fresh vegetables. The atmosphere was comfortable; the receptionist spoke to customers as they entered; people chatted quietly at the tables and low-backed booths; a pungent aroma of tomato, spices and yeast breads permeated the air. The room was longer than wide, and one could easily see all the dining area.

The traffic being heavy, Jeannie was quick to take her customers' orders. The more turnover, the better her tips.

Although Joseph planned to get pizza, he highly recommended the chicken cooked on a rotisserie, and Breear agreed to try it. When the orders arrived, Breear took a deep sniff of the chicken.

Looking up, she pronounced the smell was heavenly. "Jeannie, is this a secret recipe?"

Jeannie smiled. "It is. The owners won't even tell us everything in it nor will they let us watch them make it. Enjoy your dinner. More tea?" She noticed their glasses were half filled.

Both said yes and she left the table.

Breear cut into the white meat, lifted a forkful and again took a deep breath. "This is divine. Thank you for recommending it. Do you think the owners have copyrighted the recipe?"

"I have no idea. I'm glad you like it," Joseph answered. "The pizza is very good, too."

"Wouldn't it be their intellectual property if they wrote it down and printed it?"

"Depends on the circumstances. There are so many recipes available. A lot of them are very similar. People pass them around, and grandmother's old cookbook is handed down."

Pausing after emptying her tea glass as Jeannie approached the table with the pitcher, Breear commented that many stories were alike. She thought while the glasses were refilled then resumed. "How about my notebook? Would that be something to copyright?"

"Your notebook?" Joseph frowned.

"Yes. It is a record of my observations on situations I see."

"If you make the notes while you're on assignment for the station, then they may be considered property of the station. The story you turn in would be their property unless you have some other arrangement." While he ate another slice of pizza, he stared at her and waited for her to continue for she had an expression indicating she was mulling over something.

"Okay. I understand that. What if I had boiled the facts down to what was pertinent for the news slant for that broadcast, and I hadn't used all the information? There may not have been time to include everything or it wasn't wanted." She stopped and appeared to be thinking again. "Say I made some observations that I knew were irrelevant to a news assignment, but I recorded them for my own . . . well, reflection?"

She studied his face. He waited for her to continue. She didn't. She just showed anxiousness.

"Those notes are most likely your property. Do you keep them separate from the facts you know you'll need?"

"Not necessarily. That is a procedure I can start. I can rip out the station notes and keep my own on the pad until I finish, then file them. I've been keeping them all together. You know the facts I hand in are not returned. It is not as if I have a newspaper sheet I can save for a scrapbook. The copy is kept at the station. When assignments are simple and we're back at the station early enough, I'll write up the material. I never save a copy."

"Do you have any plans for those personal observations? For further writing?"

She hunched her shoulders. "No, but there are possibilities." She relaxed and leaned back.

"Such as?" He showed curiosity.

"As my sources often say to me, 'let me get back to you.'"

He laughed. "Well, when you're ready to go public or publish, let me know."

"Oh, I will. You can help me with all the copyright procedures." She leaned across the table and stroked his hand then caressed his chin with the back of her hand. As she pulled her hand away, he took and squeezed it.

"Thank you for the confidence and gesture." He looked at her. "Do you want anything else?"

"No. The dinner was filling." Her eyes teased him. Over his shoulder, she saw someone she thought she recognized. "There's a woman sitting at a table at the rear of the room. She looks familiar. I know! She resembles your attorney. When we get up, take a look. There's a man seated with her."

Joseph lifted the ticket from the table, knowing it was to be handled by the cashier. He turned and glanced toward the back before walking up front.

As they waited for the receptionist to appear at the register, Breear asked who the woman was. He said it was Clarissa. Next, she inquired who the man was.

"My accountant. And a friend of hers, too."

"Um," she hummed.

The cashier finished boxing an order to go, placed it on the counter, then rang up Joseph's ticket and handed him the change. She inquired, "Was everything all right?"

Joseph said, "As always."

Breear beamed. "What a marvelous basting sauce on the chicken! Do you share the recipe?"

"Thank you. No. It's one that's been in my husband's family for years."

"Do you make it here?"

"Yes, we do."

"If you ever decide to bottle it for the customers, I want to be the first in line." She smiled again and received a pleased look in return.

As they were walking to his car, Joseph looped his arm around her waist, guiding her through the parking lot traffic. "You're something else, Breear. Next thing, you'll be her agent."

"Well, once a cheerleader, always a cheerleader. If you don't play sports and can't cook, you support those who do. Right?"

He didn't answer but he gave her a wink.

CHAPTER 16

In the middle of the week Jarvis Randolph telephoned Clarissa at the office. "Hello, Clarissa. We haven't met, but our dads are old friends. They were in medical school together. I'm a junior to his senior."

"I've heard Dad speak of your father. He's in Richmond?"

"Yes. He and Mother have been there a long time. He saw your dad at a convention in Richmond recently and each realized they have an offspring in Windermere. And that explains how I have your phone number. So, you're still in a hotel."

Clarissa liked his voice quality, carrying but not loud; he sounded pleasant and phrased his words conversationally, yet informing. "Thank you for calling, Jarvis. You are living here now?" He sounded much like the kind of guys she had grown up with.

"I am. Have been in the city since mid-August. I'm on the staff at the medical school."

"Teaching or clinical? Here, I'm assuming you are a doctor also."

He sounded as if he was amused. "Yes. I can say yes to all those named. Dad said you were an attorney and joined a newly opened firm."

"True. The attorney, Joseph McBaden had been with Hadley, Morgan and Jamison for years. Now he's by himself in Price Tower."

"Not by himself. He has you, and, from what I hear, you had a successful stint with one of the nation's best legal firms. Are you liking Windermere?"

"Very much. I hope you are?"

"Yes. Are you free tomorrow for dinner? We could get together and compare newcomer impressions of Windermere?"

"Let me look at the calendar." She scanned the one on the desk then her personal daybook. "Yes, if seven-thirty is all right. I have an appointment at six-thirty."

Jarvis sounded pleased. "Good. I'll pick you up at the hotel. The lobby or . . ."

"The lobby will be fine. Oh, could I have your number just in case there is any delay?" She poised her pen over her daybook and wrote it down. "Is this your office?"

"My home, which is an apartment. Bring your calendar and we'll see if you have an opening to go house-hunting with me soon. Our dads really traded news. You have a half-house. That sounds interesting. And Dad says the picture he saw of you, but I'll tell you that at dinner."

She hung up feeling she'd been handed a bouquet. Now why didn't Mom tell me Jarvis would be calling? Or did Dad even tell Mom? What photograph did he have of me? Not the bridesmaid shot!

From habit she recorded the dinner appointment on the desk calendar, a sure reminder to make no plans for working late. Also, his phone number. A caterer, whom Ruth had recommended for the office open house, was located in a shopping center two blocks away, and she wanted to pop by to meet her and finalize the order. They had discussed on the phone an assortment of cheeses and crackers, fresh vegetables and a dip, ham sandwiches, hot apple cider, and gingerbread squares. The caterer would be responsible for napkins, plates, cups, and serving utensils. Clarissa would bring the wine. Because the affair was informal, Clarissa chose the option of disposable plastic ware that she would bag and take to the Dumpster behind the tower. This was cost effective, too.

At noon Clarissa told Gretchen she would be out longer at lunchtime. The telephones were to be connected and some furniture and other items were to be delivered.

"Oh, Miss Bentley, I'm excited for you. Warren and I are thrilled with everything we have bought. The big pieces like the bedroom suite and mattresses are on layaway. We didn't want to pay rent before we had to. Our apartment will be vacant and cleaned for us two weeks before the wedding." Gretchen was so enthusiastic that she scurried around her desk and gave Clarissa an affectionate squeeze on an arm.

Clarissa parked one house below the Hughes' leaving room for the delivery van. She knocked on the Hughes' glass-paned front door. When Mrs. Hughes opened the door, Clarissa reminded her the phone company and the furniture delivery van were due anytime.

"It will be so nice to have you settled in," Mrs. Hughes spoke brightly. "Your mailbox is so attractive and what a clever idea to place your address numbers on the front of it."

"That was my younger sister's doing. It is a house-warming gift."

Clarissa walked around to her entrance and lifted the front of the mailbox and was surprised to see several pieces of mail. After opening her storm door and the front door, she left the inner one open. She noted the return address on the letters; one was from her mother and father, one from her brother, one from her former law firm and one forwarded from her college.

She walked to the dining room and stood beside the large window with a view of the deck and glimpses of lawn, shrubbery and blue sky at the rear of the main house and her half-house. She ripped the envelope flaps with her house key. Her parents had selected an attractive welcome-to-your-new-house card, which showed a picturesque cottage with lots of flowers and enclosed a check for a special dinner out. Her brother's was more humorous, showing a frantic woman standing in the middle of a roomful of furniture with large question marks around the words "where would it look best?" As she guessed before opening, the alumni were asking for money. The law firm was pleased to have her address and wished her success with the firm of Joseph McBaden. Her friend and lead attorney had signed the letter, a gesture she very much appreciated.

From her shoulder bag she took a package of trail mix and headed for the kitchen to put the kettle on. She had purchased some staples and placed them in an overhead cabinet during the weekend. She located the box of tea bags, took one, and dropped it in a teacup. The refrigerator had been turned on last week when she had the power hooked up. The soft hum was reassuring that all was working well. She reached in for a lemon to slice for the tea. She liked the feeling of preparing something this simple in her own quarters. Really the first residence that was truly hers.

She had lived with her parents after law school until she had saved enough to sign her name to a condo. But that wasn't the only reason she moved. And the ultra-modern condo wasn't her choice. She had lived there without complaint.

The kettle whistled. She placed a metal spoon in the cup to absorb some of the heat then poured in boiling water.

The doorbell rang. The telephone installer was right on time. She thanked him for his promptness and showed him where she wanted the phones. One in the living room, one in the study, a wall phone in the kitchen, and one in the large bedroom upstairs. And she wanted a separate incoming line in the study for the computer and fax. She emphasized that the line that served rooms other than the study was also to have a jack in the study. She wanted to have the convenience of using the computer on-line and answering the regular phone at the same time.

The installer had to run a second line. She had floor plans for each room and could show him where she needed outlets added. Having subscribed to the telephone company's inside-wiring plan, she wanted to be sure all outlets and whatever was needed be done correctly. She had purchased the phones and placed them on the floor where they were to be used. The answering machine would be in the bedroom. Might as well test them today, she decided.

The cable company was scheduled tomorrow noon. The week couldn't be any more crowded. She amazed herself that she was moving into the house, decorating the office and hosting an open house all in one week. Plus, having accepted a dinner invitation for tomorrow with a stranger. She would have preferred a time she would be less harried. Jarvis sounded too suave to meet at less than her best. She had seen a hair salon just up the street from Six-day. As soon as she left here, she would detour there and ask for a cut and style, maybe even a manicure, tomorrow at one o'clock. She could change at noon. Surely, among the clothes already moved here, there would be an outfit for dinner.

The furniture delivery van arrived as the telephone installer finished the downstairs wiring and outlets. He worked upstairs while the men brought in the furniture.

Clarissa pulled her floor plans for furnishings from her handbag and directed the men where to place the pieces. The walnut drop-leaf dining table was set in the middle of the dining room floor. While they went back for the six chairs, Clarissa raised the end leaves and pulled the supporting leg forward to a right angle. Four chairs were arranged at the ends and sides. The extra two were placed on the outside wall. A waist-high cabinet of walnut with some curly maple inlay on the two doors was set between the chairs. Next, a corner cupboard of walnut, which had an antique finish, was placed against the walls that backed up to the hall and living room.

She stepped to all sides of the room and admired the effect. Very pleasing. It was not a large dining room, but accommodated the pieces easily with enough room to add two more chairs if she wanted to seat eight.

The telephone installer stopped at the door and said the furniture looked handsome. He was going outside and would be calling to check the phones. He didn't want her to answer on the first testing. He would come back in to let her know when he was ready for her to pick up.

The deliverymen came in with pieces of a four-poster cherry bed and carried them upstairs. "Show us exactly where you want these," one of them said as they brought in the box-spring mattress. She hurried upstairs ahead of them and stood where it should go. They brought in the top mattress and began to assemble it all.

The phones rang. She ignored them. In a few minutes the installer came in and told her to answer the next time. He would call enough times for her to check that each phone was operating. While she was answering the phones, the movers brought in a box of window shades and some small pieces. She pointed to each item and signaled its location on the paper she was holding. Finally, the phones were all approved and the deliverymen had brought in the last piece.

As the driver handed her an invoice to sign, he said he had called the decorator twenty minutes ago that they were finishing. "She said to tell you she would be here probably about this time."

Seeing them out, Clarissa returned to the kitchen, reheated the water, and made a fresh cup of tea. She ate the trail mix and hunted some cheese and crackers. The doorbell rang just as she finished the food. She took the teacup with her.

"Well, the men finished. How does everything look?" the decorator asked. She had an enthusiastic manner that encouraged the customer to say positive things.

"They were right on time and worked steadily. I like everything we picked out. I haven't had time to check the small items. I was tied up with the phones."

"We can do that. Did they leave a ladder for putting up the shades?"

"Not that I can see."

"No matter, I carry a two-step one. I'll get it from the car." Clarissa admired her well-fitting, tiny-checkered suit of dark colors, softened with a jewel-neckline beige blouse. Her dark pumps were a sensible heel height.

Surprisingly, all the windows in the house where shades were to be hung were the same size, so hanging the linen, old-fashion, pull-down shades was quickly accomplished. The kitchen and bathroom windows had narrow wooden shutters. Other windows had cornices and new, double draw rods that the Hughes had put in. Clarissa and her mother were overjoyed with that bit of luck. Mrs. Bentley was only making, or having made draperies, and Clarissa could later add sheers to the other rods if she wanted them.

"Is your mother still coming this weekend?" the decorator asked, folding her ladder and picking it up along with her handbag.

"She is. Driving down in my car with the draperies. She will probably be here about the time the moving van arrives, give or take an hour or two."

"Give her my regards. She is a lovely person. Call us if there are any problems, and if there's any way we can help you further." Clarissa walked to the door with her, then closed both doors and walked through her rooms. Everything was taking shape. She went upstairs and stood at the bedroom door. The bed stood square in the middle of the outside wall between two tall windows. She had a bedside table coming for one side and a lovely old cherry chest that had been her grandmother's on the other. To top them were lovely crystal lamps with cut-through designs on the shades. Every covering of the bed was new: mattress, sheets, blankets, spread. At first her family didn't understand why she wasn't taking the bedroom furniture that had been so in style when she bought it and still much admired now – it was also very expensive. Finally, they stopped questioning her. Clarissa thought her mom must have given them a clue to the importance of a woman's bed in her life. Clarissa did not give it to a family member, although Liza recently married could have used it and wanted it, and she didn't want to deal with selling it herself and have people come in and gawk at it. She offered it for a charity auction to the medical guild through her mother. The guild was delighted and it was bought last month for a high sum. Now it was only a tax deduction to her.

She lifted the phone from the floor beside the bed and dialed her parents' number. The answering machine picked up. She spoke: Mom and Dad, I'm halfway home in my half-house. It's looking great. See you Thursday afternoon, Mom. Oh, Dad. Thanks for giving Dr. Randolph Sr. my phone number. He gave it to Jarvis Jr. We're having dinner tomorrow. I'll use your generous check later. Clarissa.

The next evening Clarissa was pleased with her decision to have her hair and nails done. She had splurged with a makeover in a new cosmetic line at the salon. The specialist had selected eye shadows, cheek and lip colors and powder that complimented the lapis blue wool dress and matching short jacket she was wearing.

When Jarvis met her in The Patrick lobby, she could see he approved her appearance. He walked directly toward her.

"You have to be Clarissa Bentley. The lovely daughter of Dad's friend of many years."

"I am Clarissa. And you are the face of the thoughtful voice that announced himself as Jarvis Randolph Jr., MD."

He smiled, amused. "I am. We must dine somewhere quite elegant tonight. You look ravishing."

She had to look up to him. He was tall, above six feet, and slender and handsome as well as mannerly. His light hazel eyes were lively and intelligent looking; his blond hair was smooth along his forehead and was naturally waved over the rest of his head and neatly trimmed above his collar at the neck. He wore a sport coat woven of subtle shades of beige, tan, gold and pink over a maize-colored shirt. His beige wool gabardine trousers were perfectly pressed.

During dinner he entertained her with stories of his family. His two older brothers had rebelled against becoming doctors. After college both had refused to go to med school. "Dad asked, 'What can you boys do?' Well, the first thing both did was to marry their college sweethearts. Next he asked, 'How will you make a living?' Thus my brothers cast their lot with firms that made money. The oldest one with a bank. The middle son in a brokerage. And Dad has finally stopped hassling them. They are both doing well. Now he can brag, that he has one to advise him how to make more of what he's got by investing and the other to stash it away until monthly bills jam the mailbox. And he gives my mother a hard look, which we know is not serious."

Clarissa said, "And he has one son that he can say followed in his footsteps and is helping mankind. And like his brothers making money, I trust."

"Not quite. Helping womankind, but roundabout, that helps mankind." He watched her. Seeing her not quite following him, he added, "I'm a gynecologist."

"Oh, I see. You deliver babies."

"Not if I don't have to. I don't mention the OB initials. That practice interrupts the rest of life." The waiter approached the table with the coffee carafe. Jarvis said, "Yes, please." Clarissa indicated yes with a nod. After the waiter left, Jarvis asked about her family.

"I have two sisters, both younger. The middle one, Opal, married right out of college a fine young man who has been successful in business, and Opal has been busy with two children now ages seven and five. She's most like our mother in disposition and homemaking interests. Maternal, kind, confident, multi-talented. Liza, the younger, is an elementary teacher and in that way is following my mother's profession. She married this past summer a high school teacher. They don't expect to be well-to-do financially, but they are both dedicated teachers with masters degrees. They are good money managers and have the advantage of living near colleges where they can attend concerts and lectures, which they enjoy. And sports events. They have many friends in academics so all the family thinks it's a good match. My brother Ralph had an interest in business even as a young person. He loved making sales. Boy Scouts, class money-raising projects, selling everything from doughnuts to wrapping paper. He worked two or three retail jobs on weekends while in school. Now he's the manager of a large department store in Washington. Single. He says he's too busy for a home life. We have difficulty convincing him to leave early for Thanksgiving and Christmas with the family. And the day after those holidays are two of the busiest in the year for retailers."

"And you?" He leaned on his elbows and looked straight at her.

"I didn't want to follow Dad or Mom although I admire both of them immensely. They gave my brother and sisters and me a warm, stable family life, and, I believe, a sound set of values to test whatever the world has to offer."

"Or throws at us."

"Or throws at us. Law. Why law? It requires thinking. It involves rules to go by to tell people who want to know what can be done when they have a problem they can't see their way through. A legal problem. And often times, they are forced to reconsider their moral stand."

"What type of law do you practice? Or what interests you most?" He focused on her, genuinely interested in her answer.

"Intellectual property. What man's mind produces. Of course, it includes what the public considers to be simple, direct matters such as contracts, copyrights, bankruptcy–though that's not simple, is it, for a man to declare he can't pay what he owes. Nor can he see any way for doing so."

"Intellectual property is a growing category, I hear. We had a talk a few weeks ago at the hospital about not sharing clinical data in research outside of the designated channels and contacts. Taking records is forbidden, you know, or certain printed materials outside the facility. Work of the mind done in medical school or hospital belongs there. Unless there is some prior written agreement otherwise."

"And involvement is growing constantly. Think about the technical research being done in this area. Joseph had an interesting case the first week I was in his office. Defending a technician who had developed some new ways to do something. The company accused him of developing the ideas during his working hours. He was such a good record keeper at work and in his home workshop that he could document how he spent his time and on which experiments."

"That was smart. Foresighted. How did it end?"

"Joseph's client was found not guilty. It was a good way to start off his own office opening. We're getting new clients each week." Her enthusiasm was evident in her cheerful voice and sparkling eyes.

"Is Joseph a good attorney?"

"He is. And I've been with the best."

"You have."

"In this profession one doesn't change to someone less accomplished."

Jarvis lifted his arm with his hand above his head. "You place him way up there."

"Jarvis, there're medical personnel who are saying the same about you."

"Do you think so?"

"I do!" Clarissa made no other response. Her eyes looked puzzled as if she didn't know what to add. His voice had a ring of soberness, somewhat akin to portentousness. A pricking on the edge of consciousness momentarily annoyed her, but the cause eluded her mental grasp and the sensations disappeared. His face relaxed and his smile returned. Other diners had noticed the attractive man and woman who were very attentive to each other as they conversed. They seemed not only at ease but also quietly excited in their exchanges. Good manners, as well as being comfortable socially, were obvious. It appeared that they knew what to expect and what was expected of them and they played by the rules.

"Well, I shall know where to go if I get intellectual." He leaned back in his chair. "If I write an article, or even a book, I may need some procedural assistance with copyright laws. Oh, I asked you about house hunting with me. I'm serious. I've been in apartments too long. And my brothers are concerned about my tossing money at landlords and tell me the interest rates are low and it's a good time to buy. They said it doesn't matter whether I stay here or move on, a house is a good investment."

"I didn't look at houses. I'm not quite there, but I do prefer houses. Right now I have what suits me. More a home than an apartment or a condo, but not the responsibilities of a house, yard, repairs, taxes. I'd best hush the negatives." Now, she sat back and looked at him. Seriously, with a question, she had puzzled without solution. "There are many men around your age here in Windermere, doing well in business and professions who are not married yet buying houses."

"The question?"

"I'm curious. Why? Is it really just an investment?"

"That's a major reason. Maybe, you're really seeking 'why aren't they marrying younger, like our parents?'"

"Perhaps. This appears from all the places one goes, to be a town full of men."

"A paradise for the women seeking a partner," he said lightly, somewhat amused. "That may be. I really haven't noticed. I see women all day. I'm not trying to turn this into a personal probing, and I didn't think you were, and I can hope you won't consider it to be, but I'd like to ask about you. You're not married. I doubt you would have come to dinner even with the family connection had you been engaged. And your dad never mentioned your being divorced."

"Neither engaged nor divorced. I haven't met the right man to marry. I do like my work. I find it exciting to tackle problems new to me. And the feeling of helping someone sort out his legal problems is rewarding. It gives you a lift as if you've done something good for mankind."

He reached over the table and pressed his hand over hers. "I like your attitude toward your work. My diagnosis is you have good values, kept what your parents instilled, and added your own measure in the field of your choice, and I like your humor and your trust of people. This has been a tremendous pleasure. I'll thank Dad for your number."

She smiled. "And I'll tell my Dad, I'll return the favor and invite you for dinner one evening. He sent me a check today to enjoy a dinner out tonight. Together we'll toast our Dads soon."

"You have my number," he grinned and pressed her hand again then withdrew it, stood up, and walked around to pull her chair back from the table.

During the drive to the hotel, Clarissa thought how comfortable the evening had been. They shared similar backgrounds that immediately put them in sync with what the other was saying, catching the nuances of the conversation, being familiar with the vocabulary, exchanging and responding to facts in a lightness of manner, all pleasant.

Inside The Patrick he walked her to the elevator, punched the up arrow, and waited for the door to open. No one exited and no one else waited to enter. Jarvis stepped inside after her and pressed the hold door button; keeping his hand there he leaned toward her. He focused on her lips.

"Did I tell you I am a lipstick inspector?" And he bent and kissed her lightly. He stepped back. "Thank you for the dessert. Delicious!" He winked, released the hold button and stood smiling at her until the doors closed.

He didn't hear her words as the elevator began its ascent. "Ditto delicious."

CHAPTER 17

While Clarissa Bentley waited for Joseph McBaden to return from court before she left for the day, she checked her calendar ascertaining all was in readiness for Monday. Three appointments were scheduled for that afternoon and she had promised to be at Civil Court for the calendar call at 9:00 A.M. for Joseph who had a schedule conflict. Afterwards, she planned to talk with an attorney representing the husband of one of her clients.

The letters for Gretchen to type when she came back from lunch were stacked on the desk. On an index card Clarissa wrote the names of the people invited and expected for the Sunday afternoon open house. On another card she wrote Joseph at the top; below the caterer, address and phone number and a few lines about her own responsibility for cleanup afterwards. She reminded him she would be in court Monday morning.

Gretchen came in making an unusually loud commotion. Banging her desk drawers, slamming a door, running the water rapidly. Clarissa pushed her chair back and stepped to the doorway. The restroom door was jerked open, and Gretchen, with a wretched expression, snapped the light switch.

"Gretchen," Clarissa spoke in a note of concern. "Are you all right?"

"No, I'm not!" She yanked a tissue from her skirt pocket and wiped her eyes.

"Come in here, please," Clarissa said kindly.

Gretchen stumbled in and Clarissa closed the door quietly. She pointed to the two chairs in front of the desk. When Gretchen dropped onto one, Clarissa took the other. "Is it something you can talk about?"

"Towels! Towels for the apartment!"

"Towels?"

"Yes." She was red in the face. "I met Warren for lunch. He called that he had several deliveries over here and had a surprise. He pulled a hand towel from a bag. It is awful looking. Bright green! He read about a sale and went and bought two of every size!"

"The color wasn't what you wanted?" Clarissa asked.

"No. He knew I was planning on light blue. I have registered my selection at a department store in West Mall. He shouldn't have done that. Don't you think it's the wife's, the fiancée's decision about colors?"

"Usually women are more interested in colors around the house. Had you two talked about what kind of linens you wanted to use?"

"Linens? Oh, yes, they are in that department. We had. I told him that I wanted light blue and the brand. The ones that are so soft and thick. We wouldn't buy those ourselves, but some relatives would give them to us for a wedding present. Those towels would last for years. My mom even said they would. The tacky ones Warren got, well, I won't use them!"

Gretchen was so mad she burst into tears. Clarissa pulled a tissue packet from her pock, withdrew one, and handed it to Gretchen. She had forgotten the small issues that younger people fought over.

When Gretchen ceased crying and dried her eyes, Clarissa asked as a matter-of-fact. "If Warren purchased them today, then he would still have the receipt, wouldn't he?"

"He's very good about keeping those."

"He should be allowed to return them for a refund." Clarissa sounded cheerfully, "After all, he hasn't had time to use them, has he?"

Gretchen brightened. "That's right. He could after he finishes the deliveries. I'll call him at work and leave a message for him to call me. Oh, thanks, you're such a help." She stood up. "I did sound silly, I know. But when I thought I'd have to see those awful towels everyday, I wouldn't even want to dry my hands and face."

"It's an emotional time for you both."

"You wouldn't believe how mad he got when I blew up at him!" She hastened to the door then turned back. "Miss Bentley, we'll work it out, and, I promise, I won't let this slow me down today. I wish Warren could understand it's much calmer working here."

"Good. Oh, here's a stack of letters. I'll run back in tomorrow before the last mail pickup to sign them. If you need me, call the house. Oh, wait a minute. My mom is driving my car down. I'll jot the license number, in case security asks about it or whatever. I need to check about getting a North Carolina car tag and a driver's license."

Taking the letters and cards, Gretchen eagerly offered to call for the information and leave it on Clarissa's desk. Clarissa thanked her and said that would be a big help. Clarissa wished all problems were that easy to approach, and so immediately, as well as to witness a person so quickly see a way to repay a kindness. Thus, there was no carrying even a slight burden of repayment.

Clarissa chose to place the index card about Saturday's plans in Joseph's tray. As she was getting mail from her tray, he walked in, said hello to Gretchen and her. She asked how the hearing went.

"It was resolved in our favor. You're leaving early and won't be in tomorrow?" He paused at his doorway and looked at her.

"Right. But I'll be at the house if you need me. The numbers and address are on your Rolodex, and on Gretchen's."

"Numbers?"

"Telephone, fax, e-mail." She smiled. "The changes from The Patrick switchboard to half-house communication center."

Joseph gave a knowing look. "No cell phone number?"

"Soon. Hallelujah! I'll have my car back today."

"Best wishes to you and your mother in the settling in."

"Thanks."

Joseph walked into his office and tossed his briefcase onto the desk. Shedding his coat and loosening his tie and collar button, he opened the briefcase and pulled out the folders and legal pad.

While the hearing was fresh in his mind, he filled in gaps in his notes and wrote a couple of follow-up letters. The time spent during the morning and at his desk was recorded on his desk calendar. Later, he'd enter it in the computer.

Gretchen buzzed him that a client was on the line.

Again, Clarissa parked below her house, leaving space for a moving van and a car. She bounded up the sidewalk, the front steps and to her entrance. She stopped suddenly. There sat a large floral arrangement under her mailbox.

Before checking for mail, she reached down and lifted a card from the arrangement. "Clarissa, Welcome Home. I look forward to seeing you – often. Your neighbor, Charlie Fortescue." She slipped the card in her pocket and the mail into her handbag and carried the flowers into the house.

After setting the arrangement on the living room mantel and tucking the card under the vase, she went upstairs and changed into slacks and a turtleneck sweater. She was tying her sneakers when she heard a car horn outside. Quickly, she finished and darted down the steps and out on the porch. She had to go on the sidewalk to locate where her car was: She had surely recognized the sound of the horn and the toot-toot-toot pattern of Louise Bentley's signal.

"Hello. Am I too far up?" Yes. She had been right. Louise stood in the street with the car door open.

"Back down. We can unload here."

Clarissa waited while the car rolled back with Louise looking out the rear window. Clarissa held her hand up and signaled stop. She walked onto the street to the front of the car, gave it a welcoming pat.

As her mother got out and closed the door, she said, "I'm just thanking my car for getting you here safely. Now a hug to thank you for coming."

Mother and daughter embraced fondly, then began talking rapidly, overlapping each other's final words. It was a harmonious pattern for two women who understood and appreciated each other and were delighted to be together.

"It was an easy trip. Only two stops. No, three. I filled the tank when I left the expressway."

"Oh, you shouldn't."

"We'll need it. Oh, it's so good to see you. The neighborhood is charming. Now show me the house."

"Mom, let me take in an armload."

Louise pressed the remote to unlock the car doors and trunk. "The draperies are on the back seat. Let's do those last."

Clarissa walked to the rear of her two-door sedan. Admiring its excellent design, its dark blue body and white top with a sunroof, white-walled tires and sporty, spoked wheel caps. It was a recent purchase, a consolation gift to herself.

After each trip to and from the car, Louise found something inside the house to praise: the new furniture and its placement, the linen shades and the freshness and cleanliness of the rooms. "The bed looks perfect in here. What an excellent choice! And mother's table and your cabinet will complete this setting. One can stand here at the door and just feel comfort waiting."

Clarissa laughed at the bed comment. "Mom, only you could see all that with nothing but a bed here."

"A beautifully made-up bed. The spread, the soft pink throw, the array of pillows are so attractive. Dear, you had the vision when you saw the bed. Now, I can see it, too." She touched her temple. "Clarissa, this already feels like a happy place." She hugged her daughter tightly. "Come on, let's bring the rest of the things in. Then I'll move the car. The van should be here soon."

"Yes, let's do. But I'll move the car. I want to drive it."

Mrs. Hughes was taking mail from her box when they walked out onto the porch. "Well, hello. It's so nice to see you again. Clarissa has been looking forward to your trip down. And what a sporty car. It'll give a youthful character to our old neighborhood."

"Mrs. Hughes, it's good to see you. I'm so glad to help her move in." She turned to Clarissa. "What time does the rental car have to be turned in?"

"Before five."

Mrs. Hughes spoke. "Would you like to return it when you're

unloaded? I will be here. If the movers come, I'll let them know you'll be right back."

"Clarissa, that sounds like a super offer." Louise exclaimed. Clarissa agreed. They thanked Mrs. Hughes then finished the unloading, carrying the draperies and decorative pillows last and putting them on her bed, out of the way of movers.

At six o'clock Clarissa and Louise collapsed onto the two deep-seated chairs on either side of the fireplace and shared the ottoman between them.

"Wouldn't a fire put the finishing touches on charm right now?" Louise exclaimed.

"I'm so thankful the Hughes put in the gas logs. Why not try them out now?" She jumped up and moved the fire screen aside and flipped the lever. After the blaze was adjusted, she sat back down. "Lovely, isn't it?"

They relaxed quietly and gazed at the flames. After some minutes of silence, both looked around the room. Clarissa asked, "What would you like for dinner? There's a booklet of order-in or take-out that was in the mailbox today. Or we can go out?"

"Order-in sounds good to me."

Clarissa stretched her arms over her head, brought them down and pulled herself to the edge of the chair then swung her feet to the floor. "Mom, the chairs were a great find. A bit deep for me but all right when I lean back."

"That's why I made the extra pillows. They are still up on your bed."

Clarissa walked over to the couch and sat on it, ran her hand over the fabric. "It really does not look or feel like the old sofa. The fabric is lovely. I would never have found any couch to suit me better. Thank you for talking me into keeping this one."

"The upholsterer did a magnificent remaking. He lowered the arms, made them rounder, curved the sides of the top a little and added plumper seat cushions. It's not too informal for your living room, is it?" Louise glanced up at Clarissa.

"Not a bit. I think it has a casual elegance. It suits the room, the house."

"I can see you entertaining in here." Louise tried to say casually, but embedded a trace of hopefulness.

Clarissa stated, "The fabric has a nice hand. It'll be cheerful to have flowers all year long. Big pink—and rose-colored roses. The pink throw or the bed comforter would be pretty down here."

"I'm pleased you like it. Did I hear a bell? The phone or the door?" Louise asked listening.

"The door. I'll get it."

Louise could hear her talking to someone and thought she heard a thank you. The door closed and Clarissa returned with a large basket.

"Phil, the fellow who lives in the house behind us here sent this. I told you about his café, didn't I? Come in the kitchen and let's inspect the contents."

Underneath a blue-and-white checkered napkin were two large sectioned plastic plates with clear plastic tops, two smaller containers with salad, dressing in paper cups, and rolls and cornbread wrapped in paper napkins. Clarissa uncovered the plates and salads.

"A whole meal. What a neighborly gesture! I'm very impressed with these welcome gifts! Thin-sliced beef, rice with beans, and stewed apples. Well-chosen fare for two hungry working girls."

"That was very nice of Phil. Shall we eat while it's hot? At the kitchen table?"

"I like both suggestions. Oh, you put the dishes out." Louise left the room and came back with the floral arrangement, which she placed on the table.

As they were eating, Louise asked, "Tell me about Jarvis. Dad thinks highly of his father."

"He's very nice." Clarissa bit into a roll and chewed slowly.

"Is that all? Nice?"

"He's smooth. Knows how to talk. Excellent manners. An interesting conversationalist. Very tall, handsome, has a good tailor and wears the expensive clothing well. What else? Oh, and he appreciated my lapis blue dress and all the handiwork of the stylist and cosmetologist from an hour-and-a-half salon visit and chose an elegant restaurant for dinner."

"Well," Louise let out a long-held breath and leaned against the chair back. "That is a flattering description. I like your haircut and the new make-up shades. Is he someone you'd like to see again?"

"I invited him to the open house Sunday. I hope you find him trustworthy." Clarissa waited a few moments as if to tease her mother a bit. Louise was familiar with the speech pattern and continued eating her salad. "Because he has offered to drive you to the airport."

"If your dad didn't have a long-time friendship with Jarvis Senior, I don't know what I'd say. Smooth? Um, that's an adjective that I'll have to think upon."

"Not oily or deceitful, Mom. He comes across as one who was well schooled from youth on conversing with adults in social situations. He gets information and gives some in a pleasant exchange."

"Thank you for explaining. Seriously, you know I'm happy for you to have found some men to take you out. Rather I think I'm hearing they found you. Even better."

The doorbell rang again. Clarissa wiped her mouth and hands on a napkin then went to answer. Louise tossed the plastic ware into the garbage bag. Clarissa returned.

"It was Mrs. Hughes, but she wouldn't come in. She and Burl are just before having dinner themselves. She made this cake for us." She set the cake plate on the cleared table and removed the cover.

"A pound cake. How grand-looking."

"She said it was still warm but could be cut if we wanted a piece with supper. I had told her about the open house and she thought I might like to take some slices."

"This hospitality is amazing even for the south. Shall we cut it?"

Clarissa responded. "Indeed. You do the honors, while I put the kettle on. Let's take the tea and cake in by the fire."

"After this refueling meal, we will be recharged to tackle the draperies," Louise proposed.

"Not till tomorrow, please. I want a long, soaking bubble bath. We can test the efficiency of the hot water heater. You go first. I can wait."

"A quick shower is all I need. Would you rather unpack one or two of your boxes and leave the rest until tomorrow? We don't have to do the office and conference room before Saturday, do we?"

"Right."

It was a small open house by standards the Bentleys were accustomed to attending or hosting, but the gathering turned out to be appropriate for the suite of rooms in Price Tower; traffic flowed easily and the mix of business acquaintances, neighbors and social friends was congenial. The sunny day lingered for the guests' arrival; and, to outdo itself, the sun painted the sky brilliantly and treated them to a breathtakingly colorful view from the double windows in the conference room.

Joseph mingled like a proper host, welcoming everyone and introducing himself to those who were strangers to him. No one would have thought he had no interest in the planning and had offered no help. He had come in Friday night when the clean-up crew was scheduled and insisted they do the whole spectrum of cleaning, which they sometimes slighted the end of the week. He had personally arranged his desk, tops of filing cabinets and bookcases so that all were straight and neat. He hung a framed print that some clients had presented him of a city park surrounded with tall green trees. A track was in the center of the park and one man was spotted running. Trailing some distance behind the runner was a second runner, who appeared to be a female.

Joseph had thanked them. The clients, two women, admitted to him that they thought the man running was like Joseph. The girl they had reasoned was no one they knew. Joseph gallantly replied, "Then I will look at the painting and think of both of you."

Ruth admired how the conference room took on a more formal and business appearance with the draperies and paintings. "The updated globe is a nice touch," added Samuel. "With the way the world boundaries are changing, it'll be handy to have a reference right out in the open."

The Hughes and their neighbors the Russells, who were clients of Clarissa, complimented her office and her swift handling of their contract. Mr. Russell claimed, "It has saved us a lot of money by having that contract. The contractor only tried once to substitute a fixture we had chosen, which was not as good as what we specified. And he's running on schedule, I'm happy to say."

Gretchen ran in for about fifteen minutes. Warren wouldn't come in and waited in the car for her. Gretchen whispered to Clarissa that she was very put out with Warren for his bad manners. He said it was her work place and everybody would be a lot older than he was.

Charlie Fortescue was pleased to see Clarissa had placed the floral arrangement in her office. She thanked him and hoped to see him sometime when she was out walking. He promised to call her next week; he'd give her time to settle in.

Jarvis Randolph walked up as they were talking. He introduced himself. "Did I hear you say you live in the Historic District?"

"Yes, two blocks down from Clarissa. In a townhouse."

"A very attractive area of the city. Clarissa, we'll have to drive around your neighborhood when we're out looking at real estate. Is your mother around? I need to introduce myself."

"She's checking the food table in the conference room."

Jarvis excused himself and left. A couple of Joseph's attorney friends joined her in the office. She had seen them around the courthouse. Joseph introduced her to Judge Mike Monahan. The judge clasped one of her hands with both of his large, strong hands. "It's such a pleasure to meet the attorney whose reputation preceded her. You were associated with some mighty fine legal minds up there in the District. Some of them I know to be strong for the party. I hope you will be active down here."

"Which party, Judge Monahan?" She asked directly, but without hostility.

"The Democrats, my dear lady. Your colleague here," he released Clarissa's hand and clapped one arm around Joseph's shoulders. "He is registered with us, but he stays so busy winning cases for his clients that he gives the party short shift. Maybe the two of us can move him to political action."

Clarissa smiled without commitment. Joseph said, "You have to watch out for this big Irish politician. I've known him a long time and can report that in the long run he regales workers and voters."

"While you two are settling party issues, I'll greet a friend who's just arrived." She walked over to Celia Trawick. "How good of you to come."

"I've been looking forward to it. The offices are lovely. You must have had an excellent decorator."

"I did. My mother and Ruth Littlegate."

"I can't do much with my office. The bank has a staff for the interiors, but my living room and study need updating, something fresh."

"Well, you can ask them, but I'll warn you, neither are in the field professionally. It is just an interest for them."

Celia walked over to talk with Ruth, while Clarissa went in search of her mother.

Meanwhile, Joseph had been standing in the conference room watching Louise Bentley greet guests. When they were alone and she was checking the refreshment table, she looked up at him.

"Well, do I pass muster?" His face tensed in a baffled expression. "Muster, yes. Doug and I paid our dues to Uncle Sam. After medical school, and a year of interning and residency, he served his two years as a doctor in the Army."

Joseph recovered an amicable expression. "I'm glad to meet you. Clarissa speaks often of you and praises your skills. All this," he looked around the room, "both rooms justify her comments. Thank you."

"My pleasure. One spends so much time on the job that a setting should be comfortable and attractive as well as functional."

"Your students should look forward to going to school."

She answered merrily. "Most days. But the environment occasionally loses its charm. Your conference room is handsome, especially the tables and chairs. Clarissa said you selected them."

"Thank you again. The conference table isn't too long?"

"It's perfect."

Joseph smiled, deciding she's a likeable person. It may be flattery, but she comes across as sincere. He glanced at the wall clock. "How are you getting to the airport?"

Louise replied. "Jarvis has offered to take me."

"Jarvis?"

"Jarvis Randolph. The tall fellow, slender, blond. Clarissa is most likely giving him a tour. His father and Doug were in medical school together. I think Clarissa and Jarvis had dinner together this week. Excuse me, there is an empty tray that needs replenishing." She picked up the tray and walked out.

Joseph counted Clarissa's dinner companions: Charlie, Jarvis, the Littlegates' neighbor, those were the ones he knew of. And she'd only been in town a few weeks. Well! He breathed a sigh of relief. He could stop worrying that his buddies would attempt pairing the two of them together. Furthermore, enough people had seen Breear and him out to bug him about snatching the gorgeous television reporter. "We're all watching the news and keeping the remote away from our wives."

As the last guests left, Clarissa encouraged Jarvis and her mother to start for the airport. She walked with them to the elevator. Louise was opening her purse to check that she had her ticket when the doors opened, and she stepped inside and continued to concentrate on locating the ticket. The doors closed.

Jarvis turned his back to the doors and leaned toward Clarissa. "Lipstick inspection."

She smiled and he kissed her upper lip, then the lower. "Um. Twice delicious."

The doors reopened. He said goodnight, walked into the elevator and stood beside Louise. Reaching over he pressed #1. All three said goodbye in unison. Each grinned as the doors were closing.

Joseph stayed and helped Clarissa put the office back in order for Monday. They rode the elevator down, he with two large plastic trash bags and she with a hamper of leftover edibles. He watched her safely to her car then dumped the trash in the bin and drove himself home.

CHAPTER 18

The days shortened in late fall and the office calendars filled with clients at Joseph McBaden Law Firm. Joseph McBaden and Clarissa Bentley were inwardly pleased but so occupied dealing with new surroundings and people that neither showed the trait to its fullest measure.

McBaden spent considerable time researching cases similar to intellectual property matters his clients brought to him. Many questions asked of him pertained to ways to protect their data from being stolen, copied or pirated. McBaden scanned daily newspapers, weekly business and newsmagazines, and legal and engineering journals. He began to listen to news programs that included clips of medical, scientific, and electronic experiments or new products.

Although Clarissa kept eyes and ears open for any references to intellectual property, she earnestly reviewed North Carolina laws of divorce, child custody, and related issues that deviated from those in Virginia or the District of Columbia. She didn't ask Joseph about divorce but consulted books or Littlegate. She learned about local judges by listening when people who were familiar with them talked. Gretchen explained the rotation of judges for divorce cases and the court scheduling. When she had time to spare while in the courthouse, she sat in the courtrooms during hearings and trials where she could expect to be some time.

She wrote brief notes on index cards, which she filed in her office.

Her knowledge of the Windermere real estate scene increased as she rode around with Jarvis Randolph checking neighborhoods that he considered possibilities for buying a house. She accompanied him when realtors showed him properties. He introduced her as his attorney and friend.

Thanksgiving, they flew to spend the long weekend holiday with their families, each sending greetings to the other's parents. A week after returning, the whirl of holiday parties was initiated with a dinner at a private club for doctors in Jarvis's department at the hospital. Clarissa was "the guest" on his invitation. She observed that the men appeared sincerely friendly and conversed easily with Jarvis: The older wives gave approving glances back toward their husbands when introduced to the new man on the team; the younger women, be they wives or "a guest" like herself, stared intently with brightened expressions at him.

Likewise, Jarvis was checking the attention both sexes gave Clarissa. She accepted the female compliments upon her dress, an appropriate choice of style with jewel neckline, long sleeves, bodice and skirt close enough in fit to show her healthy, feminine contours but still modest with a bit of flare at the hem, making a gentle sway as she moved. And Christmas red brought a lovely flush to her skin. He had taken her a pair of pearl earrings and kissed each ear before she put them on, saying, "I choose not to smear that daring red lipstick before this big to-do."

The admiration that was obvious on the faces of the men she returned only with a polite friendliness. Her customary poise and grace consistent throughout the evening were comments Jarvis heard often at the hospital the following few days. And during the holiday season, wherever she accompanied him.

Jarvis drew excited comments from female guests at a party Celia hosted and invited Clarissa and guest. Afterwards, they stopped at a club that had a live band and a dance floor.

While they were dancing to a slow number, Jarvis asked, "Is this pace too slow for you? Not the music."

"No. Puzzling perhaps."

"It's not for lack of your attractiveness. You're always a temptation and have been since you stepped out of The Patrick elevator."

She waited. After an uncomfortable pause for her, she spoke.

"Any questions, I pushed away. It was your lead." She couldn't tell him that if a fault were mine, chastisement I didn't need. If this was his typical date style, I accept it. If it's respect for me, that's a compliment. Instead she said, "Your company is enjoyable and you never pressure me. We part always with laughter and good cheer."

"We do. You are excellent company. There are many functions remaining on the calendar. I'll be proud and personally pleased to have you with me."

Being paid a compliment and offered an invitation to a full social schedule, she returned a pleasurable expression; however, underneath images stirred in her memory, triggered sensations that tightened her heart muscles and compressed her lungs. Speaking would be an effort. Veiling her inner visions was paramount. After a deep breath, she managed, "Thank you," then forced herself to say his name, "Jarvis." He wasn't responsible for her pain. She added, "It's an honor."

He replied, "It would be callous of me to monopolize your social calendar. Attorneys have their quasi-social functions with their firms and legal organizations. Joseph may want you with him."

"Ours is a business relationship. But you are thoughtful."

Jarvis continued. "And there are other men you know."

"It seems someone has been filling your ears."

He laughed with his unique amusement. "Newcomers do receive a lion's share of attention. By next year this time, we shall be scarcely noticed."

Clarissa rejoined, "That may be. But if we expect to be successful in our fields, there will be patients and clients, as well as colleagues and talk."

"Getting back to the pace, I don't want to jeopardize our relationship by pushing one aspect too quickly. Shall we opt to enjoy the festivities as we have been doing?" He gazed directly at her.

"That is an agreeable course," she answered.

Clarissa had shopped in a boutique near her mother's house

during Thanksgiving and had selected two dresses. This year she knew her clothes would be new to Windermere and were still stylish; thus, she limited her purchases. She wore an emerald green dress of cashmere to an open house with Joseph where he anticipated the guests would be mostly attorneys and their wives or husbands. After Joseph introduced her to several people, he more or less conversed with people by himself. He did keep a watchful eye in her direction; ready to rescue her if she got stuck with a bore. He never had to. She was an asset in social situations; he was pleased to note. She filled the "bring a guest" invitation yet did not require his constant presence.

Before he received a written invitation to the Littlegates' more informal holiday open house, Samuel urged him to bring Clarissa. "Joseph, be kind to her. She might have a problem deciding which of the current squires to escort her. I'll do you both a favor. There'll be no mention of bringing a guest. Okay?"

"Samuel, this is another favor to you. Hear? If I bring Clarissa, at least I can be assured you won't spring some other female on me."

"When was the last time, man? Must have been six months or a year. Pickings are getting slim, Joseph."

"Why is it all you married guys want us to be like you? Can't you see I'm doing great by myself?"

Samuel laughed heartily. "Yeah. Well, as the old saw goes, if you haven't tried it, don't knock it."

Suddenly, Joseph's face contoured into a deep frown. Someone called to Samuel; he turned and didn't notice the change of expression. He waved then excused himself to Joseph and walked away.

At the Littlegates' open house, after seeing that Clarissa knew several people to chat with, Joseph made his way to the dining table and picked up a plate, which he filled with ham biscuits, cheese wedges, crackers and coconut cake. Foods that would require chewing and time eating. He had to guard against talking off the cuff.

Clarissa strolled over. "Ruth has a decorator's touch. What an unusual centerpiece." She reached for some butter mints. "Will you be going home for Christmas?"

Joseph prolonged his chewing of a bite of ham biscuit. He shook his head.

"Will they be coming up here?"

"No. We don't visit often." He spoke without emotion and turned his head as if searching for someone.

"I hope you have someone to share the holiday with," she said with a compassion that caused him to look intently at her.

"Give my best wishes to your mother."

"I shall. She will appreciate being remembered. They, Mom and Dad will be down for New Years. We're thinking of having a small open house. Perhaps you can join us?"

"Thank you. We'll see how the calendar shapes up."

Littlegates' neighbor Rush Newton approached them. "Hi. Looks like a great party."

Clarissa greeted him. "I'm glad you could make it." She introduced the two men, then said to Newton, "Ruth said you had an earlier dinner scheduled."

"I did." He leaned over to the table, paused while lifting a piece of fruitcake, and said low and soft, "And I'm glad it was over in time to make this party. Have you been enjoying the season?"

"Indeed. Windermere has an abundance of sparkle. The street decorations. And so many bare trees wrapped in strands of tiny clear lights outside offices and stores. Downtown is enchanting." Clarissa spoke enthusiastically.

"Hey, we may solicit you to write ad copy for the Chamber of Commerce," Rush retorted. "That is if Counselor McBaden can spare you."

Joseph laughed. "She might be costly."

"Have you seen ad agency costs lately? Well, excuse me to go say hello to the hosts. Those biscuits are delicious," he said, took another and moved on down the table surveying the offerings.

Sam wove his way among the guests, pausing to exchange greetings with those he knew, and stopped beside Joseph to ask if he could come into the study. "You, too, if you'd like to, that is," he said to Clarissa.

The three cut through groups of guests who were merrily chatting and munching desserts in the dining room and hall.

"Thank y'all. Joseph, Jerome wanted to talk with you." Sam turned toward Jerome, who was seated on the sofa, but jumped up when they entered the room. Joseph walked over to Jerome and they sat on the sofa. Slightly embarrassed, Sam said to Clarissa, "I'm sorry about interrupting you," he lifted his shoulders, "but I thought maybe it would look more casual if the two of you came along." Here the usually articulate Sam didn't know what else to say.

Clarissa spoke. "No problem. It will give me a minute to sit down. Isn't it surprising that in a lovely home with lots of comfortable chairs, guests like to stand?"

Sam grinned and stuffed his hands in his pockets. Clarissa, glancing around, noted a basket of Christmas magazines on a table. She selected one then sat in a straight chair at a small desk.

"I'll be okay," she said to Sam.

He nodded and strode to the music center. He removed the CDs, replaced them in cases, and chose different music, but still seasonal holiday pieces. Meanwhile, Clarissa turned pages in the magazine, quietly, lifting her head occasionally, nonchalantly to glance at Joseph and Jerome. The teen was tense, his expression serious, even when not speaking, merely listening, his hands were clutched together.

"You're sure Dad won't mind? He won't think I'm a quitter? He's been so solid behind my soccer."

"Not at all. You'll be changing schools. It's a logical time to try different sports." Joseph pronounced.

"He won't have as many games to come to. You know how he's always ready to spend his Saturdays watching any sport Sam and I play."

Joseph said in good spirits. "I think he can handle that. If you were to continue soccer next year, he'd just have one sport to watch in the fall. If you choose football, he'll have two anyway."

Still unsure, Jerome continued, "But soccer can be played all year in a league somewhere! Football is one season! And I've never been on a Little League team."

"There are a number of months before sport season is on us again. After you talk with your Dad, you two could check with the high school coach. He'll give some advice about physical conditioning. He'll most likely let you work out in the summer before school starts with the team."

Jerome straightened his shoulders. "Really?"

"You bet. After he checks out your abilities with the soccer coaches, he'll know you're a reliable player. Strong. And if you grow as much this coming summer as you did last summer, he'll watch you seriously. I'll bet you'll get to play in a few games."

"Gee, thanks. You've heard that Dad was one of the best in high school and college?" Joseph nodded. "I wouldn't want to be just a bench warmer. He'd be..."

Joseph reached over and put his arm around Jerome's shoulder. "Your Dad will always be proud of you. You're a sportsman. He'll want you to make your choice and he'll support you. And, remember, he knows the game and can give you tried-and-proven pointers. It may not be easy to listen to a father all the time, but you two can work things out."

"Yeah. Would you be with me when I tell him?" Jerome asked.

Joseph was silent as he assessed Jerome, his face and his question. "Think about it a few days. If you decide you can't approach him by yourself, let me know. I believe you can do it alone." He clapped Jerome on the shoulder and stood up. Sam walked over with relief on his face. "And you have Sam here to stand in the wings."

Sam concurred. "He really wants to give football a try." Sam shook Joseph's hand and gave him a grateful look.

Clarissa folded her magazine, rose, and replaced it in the basket. The two boys left the room. Joseph stood with a far-away expression. Slowly, she walked near him.

"Counselor, you did that well. With a touch of fatherliness." She saw him swallow hard.

"There're good boys. Samuel has a right to be proud of them." He turned, stared at her briefly before speaking. "Shall we call it the end of the evening?"

"That's fine with me. I'll tell our hosts goodnight and get my coat. It's a warm, comfortable home. The fire is cheerful." She left the room.

Joseph stepped to the hearth and wondered why no one was poking the logs. Fixing his sight on the logs and flames, he realized they were gas logs. Surveying the room, he considered how his own study lacked the homey touch; and hearing the merry laughter, he recalled how quiet his house was. He shook his head to disperse comparisons.

He joined Clarissa in thanking Samuel and Ruth and taking their leave. After dropping her off at her front door, he drove himself to his quiet house.

On Christmas Day, he had dinner with the Littlegates. He listened with surprise as Samuel told him that Jerome was switching to football next year. Samuel grinned, Joseph gave a thumbs up to Jerome, and Sam said, "Great choice, little brother."

Immediately, Jerome sidled up to his brother. The younger one was over an inch taller and pounds heavier. "Watch your adjectives!" The two teens stood with arms around each other's shoulders.

Samuel started toward them. Together they backed away. Jerome joked, "Wait till next year to measure." Sam challenged, "Give us another year to catch up to you."

Such merriment continued that day.

Breear, overjoyed with a couple of extra days off, had caught a flight to Georgia to spend Christmas with her family.

Clarissa, in order to spend as much time with her family as possible, also flew instead of driving. The family had Christmas Eve and early Christmas morning together at Louise and Doug's home, then everyone drove to Opal's to view the decorations in her home. Liza declared that next year they must squeeze in a jaunt to her place. And everyone told Clarissa when she left that they would be down to Windermere for New Year's Eve.

Though reluctant to leave her family, Clarissa had promised Gretchen that she would return in time for her wedding two days after Christmas.

The weather was biting cold that afternoon. Clarissa rechecked the directions to the church and arrived a quarter-hour early to hear the music that Gretchen had chosen. The music was unfamiliar and sounded quite modern to Clarissa. The church was filled with people bundled in topcoats. Everyone eagerly took in the numerous stands of lighted candles, baskets of poinsettias, red and green ribbons tied in bows on the railings, and a single candle on a tall stand in the area where the ministers typically sit.

After the bridesmaids and ushers entered and took their place down front and faced the guests, the bride, unsmiling, walked down the aisle with her father. Her dress, chosen with such care, was lovely. The service was the longest one Clarissa had ever attended. Many songs were sung. Clarissa felt sorry that the couple had to stand there with nothing to say or do while everyone stared at them during two very long solos. She glanced, side to side at other people, and realized they expected this type of ceremony. Clarissa emptied her memory and mind of all other weddings. She slightly shook her head and forced herself to concentrate on what was happening here. She wanted to be able to converse later with Gretchen upon her return from the honeymoon. After the wedding party and family were out of the auditorium, Clarissa stood.

She heard a voice speak low and softly near her right ear. The breath was warm. Turning, she met Joseph's dark brown eyes.

"Gretchen will be pleased you returned for her big day. How was your Christmas?"

"I promised Gretchen. Christmas was splendid as ever. And yours?"

They were walking up the aisle. He replied, "Friendly, as for years. The Littlegates send their holidays greetings. You'll be pleased to hear Jerome's news was well received by Samuel."

"How good to hear. And Jerome appreciates your gift of listening and advising. Oh, the receiving line is forming in the foyer. How thoughtful."

Joseph peered at her.

She said, "We can shake hands here. The reception will be speedy."

"We won't have to go, will we?"

"Just for a few minutes. See the decorations, taste the refreshments, and sign the guest book."

"Oh," Joseph muttered under his breath.

"I haven't met Warren. Have you?" He shook his head. She said quietly, "This is a good time."

Clarissa looked at the groom. He stood erect and appeared comfortable wearing the tuxedo, perhaps the stance and uniform transposed from his UPS delivery position. His expression was so serious as he exchanged vows at the altar; now, he was greeting people with an open countenance. He was a nice-looking young man. And Gretchen was smiling.

They were the next to greet the couple. She warmly introduced Clarissa and Joseph to him. "I'm so happy you both came. I've told Warren so much about you. And how great you are to work for." Clarissa said, "And we are pleased to meet you, Warren. Gretchen is a lovely young woman." She congratulated them both, hugged Gretchen gently and complimented the church decorations, the music and the wedding gown and veil. Joseph shortened his greetings with "best wishes."

Joseph followed Clarissa down the steps to the fellowship hall and listened to her comments about the punch, cake and assorted sandwiches, mints and nuts, and then the side tables topped with numerous pictures of the couple recording their lives from babyhood until their engagement. Later, he was glad he had listened for he had no visual recall of anything. It was too much for him.

CHAPTER 19

Joseph McBaden thought about the conversation with Clarissa during which she asked if he were going to see his family at Christmas. It had been a long time since anyone mentioned his family; perhaps his friends in Windermere sensed his discomfort when family was first mentioned. And Joseph steered clear of the topic.

But it was about this time of year when he had a major break with his dad. After the first semester of his senior year, report cards had been received and college applications needed to be mailed. He broached the subject of college and financing one Sunday after dinner. His mother was in the kitchen washing up. Joseph knew she would be on his side; likewise, he conceded that it was always difficult for her whenever his dad took a negative position. He had a premonition that his college tuition would not be easily attained.

"Dad," the seventeen-year-old senior began, "my grades are good for the semester and I need to send off the application for next year."

"Application? Do you need me for filling it out?" His dad lowered the city section of the Sunday paper and peered over the tiny saw-tooth edges.

"I can fill out most of it. What about the registration fee?"

"Are you asking me if I'm going to pay it?" Jonathan McBaden asked and shook the side edges of the papers with his long fingers.

"Yes, sir. And how much I can count on for tuition, room and board and books?"

Jonathan cleared his throat. "Won't those scholarships you spent so much time last fall writing for and sending back take care of all your expenses?"

Joseph moved nearer the edge of his chair, cater-cornered from his dad. "No, Sir. Even if I get the best one I am eligible for, it will only cover a third of the expenses."

"You couldn't make the top scholarships? Too much ball playing and socializing." He grunted.

"I'm not big enough for a sports scholarship. Colleges want tall guys for basketball."

"So why waste time on the teams? If you'd buckled down to the books the past four years, you'd have stood a better chance. But you didn't. Now you want me to fork over what you didn't study for." Jonathan held the paper firmly still in front of him.

Joseph leaned his shoulders forward and clasped his hands at his waist. "Dad, all the guys I know get help from parents. Many of them have everything paid for. Even allowances, spending money."

"Ho, ho. So now you're asking for money to go to movies, money to take Frances out. You two at the same university," Jonathan shook his head and tightened his lips. With grimness he continued. "You won't be studying; you'll be seeing her."

"Oh, Dad, I'll study. I've done that the last two years. My work has always been in on time. My grades are good enough that the school counselor is almost certain I'll be awarded at least one scholarship at university. Frances will have her classes to study for and I'll have mine." Joseph made a valiant effort to keep his voice from registering an argumentative pitch.

"Son, I've done my thinking about this 'cause I'm the one who's going to have to pay out. After the scholarship kicks in, I'll put in the bank the remainder of tuition cost, half of the book fees, and basic room and meal card. Any other expenses, be they health, student activities, transportation, clothing, will be your responsibility."

"Dad! I've worked for the past two years and three summers all through high school, and it took all I made to have any extras all this time." He looked and spoke exasperated. With his eyes closed and head down, he let out a few heavy breaths. "Can't you spare a little extra? Even for clothes? Getting back and forth for the holidays?"

"I made my offer. One more thing."

Joseph raised his head.

"You are not to ask your mother for one cent. I'll know if you do. I keep the books. Her allowance will not be increased." There was a hardness to his eyes and mouth. "Don't put her in a position to jeopardize what she receives."

Clinching his teeth, Joseph nodded, pushed himself out of his chair and tramped toward his bedroom. In the hallway, his sister, Margaret, fifteen, stood at the door of her room. She put out her hand as Joseph came close.

"Oh, dear Joseph. I am so sorry. Why does he have to be so stingy?" She put her arms around his neck and he hugged her. "You've worked so hard. You don't complain."

"It's good to have you care. I used to complain, but it never changed his dictates. He's a dictator, Sis. Everything is his way in his house."

"I know."

"I'm concerned about you when I leave. You have two more years here. Next year you'll be old enough to work, and he'll make you find a job."

"It's all right. Lots of my friends will go to work. They'll use the money for gas and the latest style clothes and make up. I won't take work as seriously as you have. I'll spend the least of my take-home pay possible. Part with enough so as not to be left out of the social scene. And I won't have to spend for dates." She weakly attempted humor.

"God, I hate to think of you stinting; these will be your best high school years!"

"That's okay. I'll save every penny I can, go to a state school like you, and get out as soon as I can. Then I'll move so far away . . ." She dropped her head on his chest and began to cry.

Fearing his father, or worse his mother, might hear her, Joseph backed her into her bedroom and reached behind and closed the door. "Go ahead. Cry. God knows I want to do that often myself." He held her close and stroked her hair. His shirt was wet with her tears. As she ceased crying, he kissed the top of her head – the first time he had done that since she fell and skinned her knee when she was four years old.

"Joseph, we don't have any rights."

"Not here, Sis. But we do have them. We'll get them later. Hang in there. You're a good kid."

The day Joseph was notified that he won a scholarship, he read the amount and shouted "All right!" He reviewed the conditions of continuance for four years: Attend two semesters per academic year, carry a full course load, maintain a B average. "I can do that," he said aloud.

Happily, he consulted his dad after supper with the scholarship news.

"That's a relief for both of us. Knowing the conditions at the outset, I can plan my deposits to your account. Let me know two weeks ahead of the payment-due date."

"A deposit for a room has to go in this week. Here's the notice; it states the amount."

"I may as well start the dole now." He hoisted his tall, sparse frame from his leather armchair and strode across the room to his desk. He pulled a ring of keys from his pocket. After unlocking the top drawer and taking out a black ledger and a blue book of checks, he closed the drawer and pulled down a writing panel. He took a black pen from a pigeonhole, flipped the ledger open, and entered some figures. Next, he wrote a check and slowly creased the perforated edges until it came free of the book.

Jonathan took his time putting everything back in order then crossed the room again. Joseph stood up somewhat anxious to get the check. He was biting the inner edges of his lips; his brow was moist. He waited for a signal from his father to extend his hand.

The older man, being several inches taller, stood over his son. Barely, he lifted his hand from his side. A gesture so slight that Joseph knew it was not the moment to reach. Jonathan honed on Joseph's eyes.

"Son, the checks will be put in your account the next four years while you're in the university. If you lose your scholarship, there will be no increase in money from me. If you leave the university, the deposits will stop and not be resumed later. And if you marry while you're still in school, all financial assistance ends." He waited, watching for a change in expression or listening for an argument. All he saw were eyes that shifted from attentive assessment to a cold, hard stare. "Do you understand the rules? I will hand you a written copy the day we open your account."

"I understand," Joseph delayed his required salutation, but it had the cold tone of the first two words, "Sir."

Maggie McBaden entered the room and saw the check change hands. She looked pleased. "Well, Joseph, I see your father is being generous."

Joseph, holding eye contact with his dad, replied, "In his typical manner." He turned and faced her. "I want to put this check for a room next fall in the mail."

She searched the faces of father and son. There was hardness in each. It was familiar in Jonathan, but newly obvious in her son's. No matter what conflict he had had with his father, Joseph's face was always softer to her. Instinctively, she drew a fist and clutched it close to her breastbone.

Later, Joseph recalled very little about the remainder of that day except that he walked to Frances's house after posting the letters. Standing on her front porch, he told her the mandates concerning the money.

"I'm strapped. Tied down. By the scholarship. By Dad."

"I'm so sorry, sorry," Frances said. She stepped back and leaned against the clapboards between the front door and windows of the living room. Her mom was inside. She pulled him against her and held him tight. He felt her swell against him, her jacket open, and he pressed against her briefly, before she pushed him away, leaving space between them. "It's going to be a long wait. We'll make it. We will."

"We'll try to. Four years. It looms now as the horizon, no matter how close it appears, it's never within reach." He uttered then leaned over and quickly kissed her lips. "You're the only soft, sweet part of my life."

"You go run around the block. I'll go push the vacuum in my room."

Running hard an uncounted number of blocks, he questioned how he could love Frances as deeply as he did. He'd had no role model to map the game of love. He heard no words, saw no transferring of affections, to imitate. Where did his passion for Frances come from? He felt it acutely, no not acutely, chronically. He burned inside during their encounters. Often they single-dated because they needed some unobserved minutes of close contact. She told him recently that many nights she hungered for him after he had left her. He knew the feeling.

As he ran, he visualized her strong arms pushing the upright vacuum with her body moving in ultimate synchronization, all her motions were well developed by years of cheerleading. Her spirit, as her body, had been disciplined. And, thanks be to God, his had, too.

Shortly before end of school, senior cheerleaders spent a weekend on the Outer Banks. One of the girl's parents had a house; the girls stayed on the second floor, and their boyfriends on the first. The parents, known for their strictness with their daughter, occupied a room at the foot of the stairs and assured the other parents they would see that everybody followed the rule: No visiting bedrooms on a level they weren't assigned to.

Frances's parents selected a car for a graduation gift and gave it to her the first of May. They knew she'd enjoy driving her friends about town. When she begged to take it to the beach, the Smiths consented as long as she drove in a caravan with the other boys and girls.

Returning home Sunday, Joseph and Frances went to their houses and dropped their weekend luggage. They told their respective parents that they had promised to meet the youth pastor at church to talk about a project as soon as the MYF was over. This statement was so typical of them that no objections were raised.

By the time Joseph rang the doorbell at the Smiths' house, Frances had showered and put on a flowered jumper and short-sleeve knit blouse. Joseph wore neatly pressed khakis and a narrow-striped cotton sport shirt.

Joseph and Frances walked slowly to the church recreation hall entrance, timing their appearance with the closing song of the program. They could hear the shuffling of chairs, then feet on the tile floor. Soon they saw the heavy oak doors swing open.

Squeezing Frances's hand, Joseph moved forward. She followed. As their friends surged out the door, there was a wave of greetings.

"Hi, you beach bums!" "Are you sunburned?" "Did you just get back?"

"Yeah, we got back too late to catch the group," answered Joseph.

"Well, we won't have many more of these fellowships. Come June, the juniors will be taking over," said one of Joseph's basketball buddies.

A girl faked a sob. "Frances, won't you be in despair when you don't have to go to cheerleading camp or practice during the summer heat in the gym without any AC?"

"You want to drive by some night and wish them good luck with the pyramids and the coaches shouting, smile even when it hurts," Frances answered without much enthusiasm. She darted glances toward the door. When no more people came out, she tugged Joseph's arm. "Mitch may be free now."

"Okay," Joseph said to her, then to the group, "sorry gang we can't go for pizza with you or wherever it is tonight. We need to discuss a project with Mitch."

A boy groaned, "Plan something special for our last night before graduation, 'cause we'll be headed for the beach early Saturday morning."

"You bet!" "Yeah!" "Right about that. Ocean, here we come!" Their friends shouted as they walked lively to cars in the parking lot.

One of the girls said to another, "Do you think Frances looked different? Sort of hanging back. Golly, she's usually so exuberant?" "Yeah. Kind of like she was dreading something."

And a boy said not quite so quietly. "Say what was with Joseph? He held her hand as if she might run away." "Frances? No way. Those two are thick as fleas." "They never miss MYF. Too good a time at the beach." "It'll be the same with us in two weeks. Yahoo!"

Frances and Joseph walked into the fellowship hall and saw Mitch at the other end stacking songbooks on top of the piano.

Frances whispered. "Joseph, it doesn't feel the same, not like a usual Sunday night."

He looked at her. "I know. We're not the same, honey." His lips offered a mock kiss. She blushed.

"Come on over," called Mitch. "How was the beach? Did you save some sun and sand for us?"

"A lot of both," rejoined Joseph. "All finished here?"

"Yes. Don't spot anything I've missed, do you?"

Each of the three scanned the large room; one side was filled with long tables and steel folding-style chairs neatly pushed under and against the tables. On the opposite wall, cabinets were built in to store games, equipment, and general supplies. No items were lying about.

"Looks like you took care of everything." Frances stated, still holding Joseph's hand, which she squeezed tightly.

"We need to talk with you." Joseph said, dropping his voice as deeply as he could get it.

Mitch immediately sensed something was on their minds. "You want to sit down at a table or just stand here?"

"May we go to your office?" Joseph asked.

"Sure. I'll walk ahead and switch the lights on."

Frances reached over and touched Joseph on his upper arm. "I'm nervous. But I'm excited, too."

"Same here."

Inside the study, Mitch pointed them to the sofa and he sat in an armchair facing them. "What's on your minds?"

Without preliminary, Joseph put forth his request. "We want you to marry us. Tomorrow."

Joseph and Frances focused on Mitch. Mitch jerked upright, his shoulders high and his back against the chair. He stared first at one and then the other. Neither changed their intense countenances.

"Marry you?" He waited a moment. "Isn't this an impulse? A sudden thought?"

"Frances and I have talked about marriage for a year. We know that is what we want to do."

"But you two are about to graduate in two weeks. And you're headed toward college in a few months."

"We know that. None of that has to change." Joseph sat stiffly, leaning forward.

Frances spoke in wavering tones. "We love each other, Mitch."

"I think you two do love one another. You're kind and thoughtful in the way you speak to and treat each other. You're good kids."

"Please, Mitch, don't call us kids. We've followed your examples, been glad to have a leader like you, but we've thought of you as a friend."

"Well, you should. I respect you as friends. Kids was not disrespectful. 'You're good youths' didn't sound right to run off my tongue."

Unexpectedly, Frances said, "We were good people until this weekend." She turned and looked at Joseph. She smiled and her mouth curved upward. "And we're still people intending to be good." She turned again to Mitch. "It's because of so many things you have said to us, that we want to get married."

Joseph added, "We may need to, Mitch. We won't feel right or honest about ourselves if we take a risk and live in suspense for the next few weeks."

"Don't you want to graduate with your class?"

"We could," Joseph said.

"You'd have to drop out of school. Maybe not take exams. That could mess up your college plans," Mitch eyed them both, then only Joseph, "cut you out of the scholarship."

Frances broke in. "We'll wait until after graduation to announce our marriage."

"What do your parents say about this?"

Joseph glanced at Frances, who nodded her head. "We haven't told them."

"You're planning to go through with a ceremony without their knowledge?"

"Yes," they spoke in unison.

"Why? Frances, you know your parents will want to see you when you wed."

She didn't respond.

Curious, Mitch questioned Joseph. "And yours, Joseph?"

"It won't matter to them." Joseph jumped up and walked halfway down the room. He stopped and clinched his fists before spinning about and stalking back to face Mitch. "I don't matter to my dad."

"Hold on, Joseph. You know you do. Why?"

"Why are you telling me 'you know'? You don't know my parents at all. They don't come here to church. You're a newcomer. You haven't been here long enough to see inside all these houses. I'll let you in on a truth – you like to point them out to us a lot; now here is one – and if you respect me as you confess you do – listen. Dad doesn't give a damn about me. He's hard and cold and loveless. He hands out commandments that chisel what he will do and will not do, and in so doing he chisels the heart from his family."

With tears spilling onto her face, Frances stood up and put her arms around him. "It's okay." She looked at Mitch. "Will you marry us?"

Mitch stood but stayed where he was. "I can't. Not without your parents' permission."

"Is that final?" Joseph asked him face to face.

"Yes. But if you wait a few days and think it over, you might change your minds. Wait until after graduation. Talk with your families."

"Come on, Frances. We'll get no help from the church." Again, he sought her hand, clasped it tightly, and led her through the room and out the door.

This was the last time he exchanged words with Mitch. Although he saw him at baccalaureate and graduation, he avoided speaking with him.

He and Frances did get married the following day. They spent an hour Sunday night after leaving the church planning how to bring it off. Monday was a teacher workday so there was no school. Students had a reading day preparing for exams or finishing senior projects. Frances and Joseph had completed their projects early.

She would tell her parents she was going to pick up Joseph for breakfast at the doughnut shop, drop him off to check about a summer job, then head for the public library where she would meet Julie, a classmate and fellow cheerleader. They would first study in the library, then write their routines for cheering to hand over to the coach, who would go over the list with them before handing out copies to next year's squad.

Joseph checked the map to the closest South Carolina town where they could get married. The laws there did not require a three-day wait. They could find a justice of the peace and be married in a few hours and get back to town by suppertime. He declared, "It'll be close, but it's possible. It would be suspicious if we started before seven thirty."

"I have a credit card so I'll put in gas and pick up breakfast at a drive-through before I meet you. No, scratch all that. I'll pick you up first on a cross street four blocks from your house. Wear your running clothes and bring a change in your duffel. Your mom will know you wouldn't be out about a job in running shorts. Someone could see us getting gas or breakfast. We'll buy both down the road."

Joseph said, "God, I love you, Frances."

"Me, too. You don't want to change your mind?"

"No. And when we see each other after that we'll be married and can behave like man and wife."

"Joseph, you'll use protection, won't you?"

"The first item I'll buy." He kissed her passionately.

"And when we go to the university health center, I'll ask for birth control pills. Students don't need parents' permission. We'll be living two lives. I'll pray, you do, too, that we don't give ourselves away to anybody."

"Right. You don't mind taking the pills?"

"It will be better not to think of the consequences. It may be four years."

"It may be. Do you believe you can still pray after a minister wouldn't marry us?"

"Yes. He's a good friend and a good pastor. We have to decide in the end for ourselves. And we're doing this because we hold it to be right. The secret may be hard to carry, but as long as we know we are acting right and can pray, Joseph, I feel it is right."

"Frances, Frances. Sleep well. I'll see you early tomorrow."

During the past twenty years Joseph had attempted a few times to recall, almost to relive, the final breaking scene with his father, but he could never completely go through the trauma for anguish ballooned in his heart and his mind with each effort. Now he considered telling the scene to someone else, to Mitch. He was a compassionate person by nature and, Joseph believed, more experienced in dealing with other people's tragedies.

So with his agitation and his desire for relief, he visited Mitch again in his study. This room was not unlike the one in which he and Frances had talked with him that May evening. Prominent in Joseph's mind was that both were in a church, a site where ideas and emotions could be presented, discussed, and even argued, with hope of resolution. Consequently, such talks took on an official nature.

"Mitch, a few weeks before the beach weekend, Dad had spelled out to the last detail the conditions under which he would give partial financial support in college. Four consecutive years of attendance, keeping the scholarship, my working for half the book fee, all student activities and health services, transportation and spending money. And the absolute dictum was there would be no support of any kind if I married before graduation.

"That left me in the tightest bind. Frances and I were very emotionally involved. We listened to you, acknowledged our parents' and their generation's codes: abstinence until marriage. And succeeded until the beach weekend. I swear we never drank before then, but the last night someone brought beer and we just were caught up in the party mood. We consumed too much for beginners. And wrapped up in a beach blanket, the fire burning, the ocean lulling its magic over and over. Our bathing suits on. Well, you know the rest.

"Frances hadn't checked her cycle, there never had been a need for her to, for we'd never transgressed. After that closeness neither of us wanted to wait it out: A had-to-get-married situation was abhorrent to us. We'd talked about getting married after college, so we just moved up the date. No, we were not going to announce we were married. We were going on to college just as planned. If she were pregnant, then we'd reassess the secret marriage. As it turned out, she wasn't, and we continued to be merely sweethearts for the public. For four very long years."

Mitch had listened without interrupting. Now Joseph was quiet. Mitch said, "Thank you for sharing all this with me. You had as much as told me about consummating your love, and I, personally, was proud of the two of you for taking responsibility seriously. As your pastor, I felt I couldn't marry you without your parents knowing I was doing so. Frances was under age, only seventeen; you were barely eighteen. An early marriage can have far-reaching consequences for college life. Setting up housekeeping, forgoing insurance under parents' plans – there are hundreds of expenses unknown before you get into the situation. There had been no pre-marital counseling. I was young myself. I had to consider where I had been remiss in my leadership."

"No way! I regret being so hard on you that night. After we started at the university, I dug my heels into studying and being with Frances every hour possible. My grades had to be maintained to keep the scholarship. The freshman year that B average was a strain academically. And satisfying our physical and emotional needs, was paradoxically a pressure and a release."

"I appreciate your telling me this, but you don't have to go on."

Joseph, still in a talkative mode, said, "There are a few more disclosures that may help me to shake the ghosts and guilt if I can verbalize them. Later, you can forget anything I say that isn't relevant to the picture for you. At night I sometimes wake up either sweaty or disturbed by images darting forth, then receding, one following another. I never see clearly the woman's face that comes in the dream, but I feel it's Frances's."

Mitch asked, "And there's no peace in the dream? You said it was disturbing? Do you wake up? What do you do?"

"Yes, I wake up. I get out of bed and go to my study and work on whatever files I've brought home."

"Like hitting the homework as you did in college. Now solving problems that were, are, basically someone else's problems."

Joseph looked surprised. "Yes. You think there's a parallel?"

Mitch shrugged his shoulders. "Maybe. Was there an unresolved situation with Frances?"

"I asked myself that. Let me go back to the college years. I found a small two—bedroom apartment in town and rented it with another student, male. I told Dad it would be the same price of the dorm so he didn't balk. The guy also had a steady girl and we had an understanding that the girls, his girl and Frances, could come and go as each pleased. Frances came frequently. We felt more married as if we were keeping house but without the myriad of chores. However, after the first year, the intense passions subsided gradually.

"She decided at the end of the sophomore year to transfer to another school that offered a better teacher-training course in elementary education, her declared major. She went home for the summer, but I stayed at university and worked with one of my professors who was writing a book. I did errands, proofed copy, and researched materials in the library.

"The junior year classes are tougher with concentration in your major field. I was recognized as pre-law but pursued history and economics for the BA. There was so much reading, then numerous papers to write. Frances found the same demands, in addition to starting a lot of psychology courses. She rarely came over weeknights but managed many weekends. We had to give so much time to studying. We were determined to finish in four years. So many of our classmates were taking five years. That was not an option for me.

"The senior year, well, we just didn't see each other regularly after Thanksgiving. Tests, papers, projects, senior meetings. Already graduation-oriented decisions were being made. I was checking out law schools, getting references and all that entails. Frances was scheduled to student-teach during the last semester in an elementary school near her college."

"Both of you graduated on schedule?"

"We did. I know this is taking a long time. Do you have to be somewhere now?"

"No. Let me get us some coffee. I'll be right back," Mitch said and walked downstairs to the kitchen and returned with two steaming mugs.

Joseph took his and walked around the room stretching his legs as the coffee cooled a bit. Taking a long swallow, he pronounced the coffee very good and thanked Mitch for it.

"I'll speed this up." He sat down on the sofa, took a big swallow and set the mug on the table in front of him. "Frances really threw a shocker at me when she said in March that she was going out west for the summer to work in a program for young children. She had applied to the college's graduate school to enter the Masters in Education program and had been accepted. She wanted a close, firsthand experience with children and planned to use her notes about the program and the students for an independent study. It would merit six hours. With scheduling of finals and graduation, we saw each other twice after late April. She went west and I took my first summer off since after my freshman year in high school. I went bicycling from the mountains to the coast. Along the way, I had pre-arranged invitations from several guys I knew in college. Those were great stops with showers, washing clothes and eating home-cooked meals.

"I had been accepted to law school, and that trip, devoted to replenishing my physical reserves and freeing my mind from academic worries, probably saved my life. I stopped in my hometown and stayed a few days with my parents. My sister was there with her boyfriend, Austin Trulove. She had started college two years after me and planned to finish the next year; taking courses each summer, she could do this in only three years. She told me privately that she was going to marry her guy the day after graduation and they were going to move to California and she intended never coming back. I hugged her and wished her well. She said she would welcome a visit from me anytime I could get out. We promised to stay in touch."

"I'm glad you did and hope you still see her family." Mitch smiled and asked if Joseph would like more coffee.

"No, but I'd like some water. All this talking has me thirsty. I know why you preachers have glasses on the pulpit." Mitch got up and poured water from a pitcher on a side table and brought a glass to Joseph.

Sipping the water, then placing the glass on the table beside the mug, Joseph resumed. "I stayed at the house so that I could visit with Mom. She was okay, but didn't appear very happy, except in talking with Margaret and me. And I needed to talk with Dad about funding for law school. His rules for undergraduate days were fulfilled and any chance of support for three more years was slim. This time I brought up the subject after dinner my second night there while mother was in the room. She was rocking and resting after a full day of activity in the hottest part of the summer.

"'Dad, I wrote you that I was accepted in law school and it starts in about three weeks. Can you help me with finances?'

"Dad shifted his position in his chair and stared in surprise at me. 'Help? My arrangement with you is completed.'

"'For college, yes. Can you help with law school?' I repeated. This was important to me.

"'You want too much from me. Not a word of thanks all these four years. Not a letter.'

"There was no answer I could give him. We had seldom spoken the summer before I left home.

"'And from me there'll not be a cent. Go do something else now that you're a college graduate. Save your money. Put yourself through this time.' He closed his mouth and glared.

"Mom spoke up. 'Jonathan, don't be so hard. Give Joseph the money. He's had to work since he was fifteen. Don't make him work years to get his law degree.'

"'Stay out of this, Maggie. It's between us.' He pointed a finger at her.

"She stilled the rocker. 'Jonathan, this is a family matter. I am part of this family. I've never asked you for much. I've let you have your way when it came to setting limits on the children and on our money.'

"'Our money? It's my money. Do you hear that? I decide what to do with it.' He was showing a rare minute of heated chastising. 'Don't interfere,' he warned her.

"'A marriage is about sharing, Jonathan. What's yours is mine.' She, too, spoke sternly.

"'Since when? It won't start now. You're not to give him a cent of our money!'

"She stood up and walked directly toward him, stopping a couple of feet in front of his chair. 'I will give him my money. Not your money. My money!'

"He gasped. 'You won't do that.' He looked crossly at her. She didn't flinch. 'You can't give him your inheritance.'

"Mom turned to me and came over and took my hand as I stood up. 'I have money my mother left me, Joseph. It is yours. All yours. Go on to law school. You won't have to work. There's enough for school and for everything else you need.'

"In awe, I stammered. 'Mom, law school is very expensive.'

"'I know. I checked out the costs. I talked with my broker. He said there's enough in the account for the three years. A lot more. I congratulated him on investing it wisely. I know you and Frances want to marry and nothing could make me happier than to see the two of you not have to struggle for those years.'

"I hugged her and I swear we both cried in joy as I had never done and have not since."

"God bless your mom," Mitch said.

"Mitch, this is the hard part to tell to anyone. But you may still not understand the final break of relationships and penalty it has cost. Dad was so furious he stalked over to us and jerked her away from me. He was red-faced and seething. He didn't shout, but the deep, grating noise he made sounded like some animal warning you of a dangerous attack to follow if you didn't cower and retreat. I stood there poised for whatever he thrust at me."

"'You conniving, thieving blackguard! Take from me all your life. Robbing your mother of every cent that belongs to her. It's all she's got.'

"Mom started to protest, and he wrenched her arm and she cried out. I reached toward his free arm and he swung mightily at me, but I leaned back and he couldn't land a blow. Mom screamed for him to stop. He brought his hand around and slapped her hard on the face. Her eyes showed terror, and she could only manage a whimper. She dipped the shoulder of the upper arm my father was still grasping. I could feel her pain. I stepped up and grabbed his wrist so tightly and I must have hit a nerve, for he let her go and I moved between them. I could feel her back inches away yet stand behind me. At that moment, I was her shield.

"I became the commanding one, telling my father if he ever touched her in anger again I would see that she left his house. 'You do not have the right to abuse anyone physically. And God gives us the right to refuse anyone who abuses us mentally and emotionally. I'm not going to ask you if you understand. Whether you understand or not, those are truths: You don't abuse her in any manner. I'll come for her straightaway if I ever hear that you do.'

"Then I took her out on the porch. When we were calm, I thanked her for the gift. Afterward she told me I was the only beneficiary of her inheritance and that Sis would get whatever Dad had at his death. I said I would accept. I asked her to write me monthly, even a mere two lines, to say she was all right. And she has. Mom and I went to Margaret's and Austin's graduation, and immediately afterwards in the campus chapel, to their marriage. We went to California when their children were baptized. Annie is now sixteen and Tommy is fourteen.

"That's about all, Mitch, except for a guilt that lives with me. Mom is trapped in that house, trapped with an unloving man as stingy as ever walked. And it is because she gave her inheritance that could buy her freedom to me. To me! There are times when I doubt I've been worth the trade."

"It was her decision. Don't flog yourself, Joseph."

"How many times I've said those words to myself. But the guilt abates only to haunt me when I least expect it."

Mitch asked if he could repay it now.

"I've tried. She says his bitterness couldn't be dissolved. She asked me not to put the sum with her old broker because Dad might find out. There are few secrets in that town. I have replaced the amount that her broker transferred to my account the day after that terrible scene, with a local broker into a fund with a good return in our names jointly so that Dad could not raid it. Mitch, I'm exhausted. Thanks for hearing all this. I don't wish to transfer any burdens, but I do feel some relief."

"Thank you for the honor of trust as your minister and your friend. Your mother would be proud of her investment in her son who spends his days helping people in his own way."

Joseph stood up then had a sudden thought. "You asked me if anyone knew about the marriage. The wreck happened a few weeks after that encounter with Dad. Mom called to tell me and I went right home. I stayed at a friend's house. Mom went with me to the funeral home. She gave me some private time at the open casket.

"Before I went back to school, Mom and I went over to see Frances's parents. When I walked in, I knew something wasn't right. The Smiths asked us to sit down. They sat opposite me. She held out a fist, fingers curled topmost, and opened it. Lying on her palm was a wedding band. She gave me the most longing, sorrowful look. 'It was in Frances's luggage, hidden in one of the side pouches. It's hers, isn't it?'

"I answered truthfully. She asked why hadn't we told her? All

I could do was tell her how much we loved each other and the restrictions Dad laid down. I said that we planned to tell everyone as soon as we were in our graduate programs and that we were going to rent an apartment convenient to both our campuses.

"Mitch, the Smiths and I and Mom had grieving and rejoicing there that night. They didn't scold or blame, saying nothing could be changed. They agreed, feeling some relief knowing she had had someone to love her those four years. The four of us talked about the pros and cons of making a statement about the marriage or putting it on the headstone. Finally, we concurred that she had only been known as Frances Smith and had been buried with that name, so we'd leave it at that. There were no joint possessions to consider or names to change on college records. It was what we concluded was best for everyone, but that isn't to say it was easy for us.

"I suppose you heard that Mrs. Smith died several years ago. Mom says he has remarried a younger woman. Half the town says that is a compliment to Mrs. Smith, a showing that he had a good first marriage. The other half of the population says Mr. Smith wants someone to look after him in his old age."

Mitch laughed. "That sounds about the right percentage. I'm glad you keep up with some of the goings-on back east."

"And now, I really am weary. Surprising how until we unload the excess baggage, we don't realize how heavy it was. It'll take a few days to stand up straight again, to adjust to what we don't have to carry." Joseph shook Mitch's hand and they walked to the church entrance together.

CHAPTER 20

Joseph McBaden opened the door to a cold and dark office. Momentarily, he was disconcerted. There were no sounds, no people. He closed the door then flipped the wall switch and the overhead lights came on. Going into the hall, he pushed the thermostat lever up. He glanced at the empty fax trays and Gretchen's vacant chair. When she returned next week, she would have a different last name on her paychecks.

He gave a somber look at her chair and desk. He tipped his head and brought his hand up. "Gretchen, I salute you. May your new life be as you wish it."

He moved down the hall and paused briefly at Clarissa's closed door.

Going through the morning routine, he reviewed mentally the days since he had opened his office. He made short notations on a legal pad and must have been at it some time, for when he heard a knock on his open door, his first visual awareness was a numeral 4 at the top of the page facing him. Startled, he lifted his head. Clarissa was standing in the doorway.

"Am I disturbing you?" She remained there poised, yet calm, considerate of his privacy, her brown hair framing her fair skin, stylishly dressed in suit and sweater. He recalled Samuel's comment that "if you never hang a painting, Clarissa is decoration enough," and Joseph compared the scene before him now to a long, narrow John Singer Sargent portrait.

"No. I thought you'd be home getting ready for your guests and the New Year's Eve celebration." He flipped the legal pad to a blank page and sat erect.

"I had a maid service in before I left and everything is still tidy." She walked to his desk. "I thought you might take a few days off. Give yourself a vacation."

"Your invitations are all out?"

"They are only verbal. Yes, to answer more directly. I came in to double check I had all the billing in for the year. If I work on any case this week, I'll add those figures later. And I wanted to check if there are any fax or phone messages."

Joseph stood. "The fax trays were empty. Shall we see what the machine ejected? And make a pot of coffee?"

The next two mornings both of them worked consistently in their respective offices. Once he stopped at her doorway to ask a question. He noticed a china tea set on a lacquered tray atop a table against the wall.

"A Christmas gift?" He pointed. She nodded.

"How many of your family are coming tomorrow?"

"Everybody except Ralph. There will be eight beside myself."

With a quizzical expression, he asked, "Do you have room for that many in your half-house?"

She laughed. "Not quite. Opal's family will stay in Phil's cottage. He goes to visit his mother a week every Christmas and will return January second. He's a swell guy."

"Single, I recall. Did you have to get maid service for his place?"

"No. He's actually very neat. His cottage like Six-day Cafe could hang up an A-rating award. Opal and I will tidy up before they leave."

Joseph and Clarissa shared phone-answering duty for two days.

Clarissa had three phone calls from women who made appointments to discuss separation procedures. Experience had taught her that many women are ready to leave a marital situation after an unhappy Christmas.

Joseph had, among his calls, a few of his new clients requesting advice about taxes. He opened the office mail so that he could deposit any checks received before the end of the year. He had not given Clarissa the customary Christmas bonus, having decided to wait until he reviewed the practice's financial situation at year's end. The two days he was in the office by himself, he dug into the account ledgers.

Clarissa spent a day shopping for an artificial tree, small New Year's favors, and thematic paper supplies for serving. She selected a wreath of dried vines with a decorative horn and bright multi-colored ribbon to tie on her front door. Last, she purchased a variety of snack foods, then confirmed that her New Year's Day dinner would be ready to pick up the day before: The meal was reheatable.

Unpacking at half-house, she wished she had proper china and everything else to set a fine table like her mother and Opal. Liza, too, had more service ware with all the wedding gifts. "Cheer up!" she instructed herself. "With a few years here and more clients, I will get those things. No negatives. The family is not traveling down here to witness a long-faced, apologetic woman. Smile! Remember that – smile. Let them believe everything is A-okay."

And the family did find her half-house inviting with Opal and Doug's seven-year-old son Ben standing on tiptoe to blow the horn on the front door upon arrival. His sister, five-year-old Ellie, immediately was enchanted with the tree and the variety of small favors tied to the branches. Louise became an assistant house guide, telling tales of their shopping in Eastford and hanging draperies and repeating how the grandmothers had used the tables and chests that had been brought down from Virginia.

Doug and his sons-in-law, Glen and Bert, not only inspected the interior of the house, but after unloading the van, left the women to unpack while they surveyed the front and backyards of the Hughes property and on around the block. The back gardens, though not at their peak, Doug found well planned for the sloping hillside. Large evergreens gave a full and lively appearance now and would offer a pleasing background for perennials and annuals in other seasons.

Nearby houses seen from the front and rear of the Hughes' drew favorable comments from Glen, an architect. "Quite a variety of designs and building material. The colors are unusual. The soft yellows and medium grays on the wooden houses and the blue green trim on the brick one-and-a-half-story house, together give a quaint appearance without an artificial, tourist-type tableau," he commented.

Being a history teacher, Bert added, "The community likely started with families of varying economic levels; the brick homes of the more well-to-do and the clapboard for those of medium financial circumstances. Either the builders or the owners show their individuality in the trim, banister and railing designs, porch locations."

Each expressed an interest in walking around the Historic District the following day before the first football game on television.

Ellie bounced around the cottage inspecting every nook and cranny of the all-purpose, largest room of the three. It had a couch, one club and one desk chair, one daybed, tables for propping feet up between couch and club chair, one for a telephone, computer, television and other electronic devices, and a narrow one for dining with a bench slid underneath. Ellie peeked around a folding screen and shouted back to Opal, "Come see this little bitsy kitchen. It's like for the seven dwarfs." Opal peered over Ellie. "Ah, you can be Snow White come to visit!"

Opal assigned Ben the very small bedroom, Ellie the daybed, while she and Bert would take the other bedroom.

Throughout the holiday, Ellie called herself Snow White, but when she asked Ben to be Prince Charming, he backed away, insisting he didn't play make-believe with kindergartners. She kept trying to entice him until he shucked off the seven-year-oldie's why-pick-on-me attitude, lifted his arms, and with a menacing face claimed that he was the woodsman sent by the wicked witch to kill Snow White. Ellie went screaming to Opal, who settled the dispute by saying, "the next outburst like that Ben, and Ellie will have the little room and you will sleep on the daybed." Thus the sibling undercurrent conflict was kept from erupting again.

New Year's Eve was cold, clear and sunny. Everybody bundled

up for a walk downhill to the park. The children ran off some of their pent-up energy; the men briskly paced the cinder track; and the ladies strolled along a walking path around a playground and up and onto a bridge that spanned a narrow creek and its adjacent low banks. Always, someone was keeping the children in view.

Liza and Clarissa walked side by side. "You look happy," Clarissa commented. "Married life has brought a new glow to your lovely face."

"I am happy. Bert was always such a nice person, now he's even better, a nice, considerate husband."

"You made a good choice."

"Sis, I won't ever mention this again, but I'm so sorry things ended as they did for you. I knew things were cooling for you and Lester, but I was shocked when we returned from the Falls and found out he had left while you were home helping me with the wedding. What is it we learned in English? An irony. That's it." Liza, an inch taller than Clarissa, leaned sideways and put her head against her sister's.

"I know you care. It was a surprise to all of us. But it's okay. At best it was a clean break. There's no agony wondering about getting back together."

Liza squeezed Clarissa's arm. "You're more than generous to that despicable man." Liza threw her hands up. "All right! That man who disappointed our whole family. Better?"

"Yes. Thanks for caring. It gets easier every week. I've made good friends here."

"Mom says you have some beaux."

"You know Mom. I have had dinner with an accountant several times. He lives in those condos perched on the side of the hill at the end of the second block from me. He's very nice and polite."

"Doesn't sound like much of a prospect for a future."

Clarissa replied, "He is for someone, but it is nice to share dinner with a good conversationalist."

Opal crossed the bridge and stopped beside her sisters. "What are you two so serious about?"

Liza answered. "What else but men?"

"Yours or Clarissa's?" asked Opal.

"Both."

"Oh, what have I missed big sister?"

"Nothing really. I've just told Opal I have had dinner several times with an accountant who is nice and talks about a variety of topics. He appreciates my many interests." Clarissa looked from one to the other. "Don't be shy, I know Mom or Dad told you about Jarvis Randolph, the son of one of Dad's friends. He's a doctor in Windermere."

Opal smiled. "Yes, we did hear their version of his calling up and you two went somewhere elegant to dine, and, furthermore, that you bought a new outfit and got all dolled up. Do you see him much?"

Clarissa suggested they walk back toward half-house, and she would entertain them with her social adventures with Jarvis. She signaled with her hand to the others that they were going back uphill. Opal watched till Bert called Ellie and Ben and had them at his side for the return trek.

"Yes, I've seen him several times. Always for dinner until the holiday parties began. He asked me if I would be his guest whenever he received an invitation to a function. We have been to some uptown-style parties and medical school department celebrations."

"Any parties on your own?" asked Liza.

"Yes. Who did I take? Jarvis to Celia's party; she's my banker. I went with Joseph to the Littlegates' reception."

Liza prodded. "Was that any fun? From what Mom said he's been rather a cold dish to you."

Clarissa searched Liza's face for hidden implications. Not seeing any, she admitted, "He had an opportunity to give advice to one of Samuel's sons. The boy had something he wanted to ask his father and laid the matter before Joseph, who handled it very wisely. Or so I thought. Like I know what young fellows want to hear. Anyway, Jerome was very happy after he talked with his dad, so something helped."

"Will we get to meet all these guys tonight?" Opal asked.

"They all plan to come. We'll see."

Louise joined her daughters and piped up. "Clarissa, run the guest list by us once more."

"Mr. and Mrs. Hughes, Mr. and Mrs. Russell, who are neighbors and clients; Charles Fortescue, the accountant; Jarvis; Joseph; all the four Littlegates; and five Rockfords. Mitchell Rockford is our minister at First Methodist. That's twenty-four people. That's all I felt I could manage this year. I do miss Ralph for the party."

Liza spoke as if in a whisper, but loud enough for the other women walking alongside to hear. "Am I the only one who sees a pattern of just single men in our big sister's guest list?"

"Shush, that libelous talk, young lady," Louise chided, but not too harshly, her youngest daughter. "Clarissa says they are all just friends, except Joseph, who is her boss."

Opal posed a question. "Doesn't Joseph have a date he could bring?"

Clarissa avoided Opal's question and looked askance. Opal's eyes squinted, her head tilted, as she attempted to read Clarissa's face. She couldn't for Clarissa dropped back and continued the walk home beside her father.

Ellie and Ben raced the last block to the Hughes' house and clattered across the front porch with Ben a dozen steps ahead.

"Hi!" He shouted, scooting back toward the banister. Ellie changed direction and ran beside him. He held up a package. "Look, Aunt Sassa! We've got a present!"

"Let me see!" begged Ellie, jumping to grab it. Teasing her, Ben held it out over the banister until Opal reached the porch and rescued the package.

As Clarissa mounted the steps, the children clamored toward her. "Mom's got it! What is it?"

Clarissa gave the house key to Louise, who opened the door and waited until Clarissa was abreast of her then Louise turned over to Doug the door duty. Inside, Clarissa stopped at the entry closet and hung up her outdoor wear. The family staying in halfhouse did likewise; others looped theirs on the hall pegs.

"Is there a card?" Liza quizzed.

"Yes," Clarissa answered, taking the gift to the coffee table in the living room. Sitting on the sofa, she pulled the card from its envelope and read it silently then announced, "It's from Jarvis."

"What does it say?" "Open the package." "Girls, it's a bag. You don't need to guess?" "Clarissa, come on."

"Unfortunately, he will miss our party," she said. "He has unexpectedly drawn hospital duty tonight and tomorrow."

Louise with sympathy said, "Well, that's to be expected some time." She glanced over at Doug and he nodded in agreement.

"I'm so disappointed I won't meet him," Liza sighed. Then huffy, she added, "And to think I came down here just to see...." Clarissa reached over, hugged her shoulders and finished the sentence, "to see me and all my new friends bring in the New Year."

Ellie leaned over the back of the sofa intent on the card. "Those are a lot of words. I can read some of them."

Clarissa lifted a hand and stroked Ellie's head. "Good for you, young lady." Casually, Clarissa tucked the note into the envelope and began to ease the bag down.

Opal chided. "And young ladies don't read other people's cards or mail without permission."

"She was holding it out."

Clarissa held the bottle of champagne forward for everyone to see. "Okay, who has the lunch detail? The kitchen is yours. Everybody else do what you please until then."

Bert and Glen went to the kitchen. Doug ambled over to the gas logs and set them aglow. The children sat on the floor with one of their Christmas games. Seeing them settled and her dad agreeing to oversee the pair, Opal went upstairs after her mother and sister to talk about what each was wearing tonight and deciding if any clothes needed pressing.

Clarissa followed the men in case they needed to locate anything. She placed the champagne on an open shelf. She took the ribbon from the packaging, threaded it through the envelope and retied it around the neck of the bottle.

"Jarvis selects the finest," Bert commented. "Dad thinks highly of his family."

Glen opened the refrigerator and took out lettuce, cheese, cold cuts and a bowl of cut-up fruit. "Any particular dressing for the fruit?"

"There's a container of sour cream dressing I made up in the glass bowl with plastic wrap. Mayonnaise on the door."

"Are you sure there's enough room for the turkey dinner in the fridge?" Glen asked.

"Oh, don't let me forget to pick it up by three o'clock. If we're short of space, Mrs. Hughes has offered to refrigerate some dishes. I wish Ralph were here. He loves turkey dinners."

"True. He could zap a frozen one," Glen said and winked at Bert.

The remainder of the day was filled with putting the house in order for the night, clearing the table before the caterers arrived, freshening the downstairs guest bathroom, and running last-minute errands. Ben and Ellie protested afternoon naps but yielded when given a choice of no nap and early to bed, or nap and staying up later that night.

The men kept their pledge of canvassing the neighborhood. At four thirty, Glen and Bert drove off for cigarettes.

At five o'clock Clarissa put a big pot of New England clam chowder on the range to warm. Louise placed Styrofoam cups and plastic spoons on a tray and a basket of crackers to the side.

Around five-thirty everyone stood around the kitchen consuming the chowder. Louise queried Opal. "Where did those men go to shop?"

As if on cue, Glen and Bert opened the front door and called out. "Is anyone at home?"

Liza intoned mischievously, "Where have you two been?"

Bert entered and hugged Liza. "Wouldn't you like to know?"

Glen appeared with a serious face. "One could get lost on this strange layout of streets! Did you know, Clarissa, that First Street crosses Fourth?"

The phone rang. Everyone started talking in twosomes, thus Clarissa answered. "Hello. Ralph, how good to hear you. The only thing better would be to see you. Happy New Year's Eve." She stirred the soup on the range.

"Well, Sassa, Happy New Year's Eve to you!" He stood in the kitchen doorway. "Turn around and tell me in person."

She dropped the ladle against the edge of the pot and spun toward the door. She gasped and moved quickly to him.

Ralph, the tallest and overall largest of the family, pressed disconnect and pocketed his cell phone in his all-weather coat pocket. After a fond hug, Clarissa smiled broadly at everyone and with tears said, "You knew! How could you keep a secret so well? You are all so dear to come for the holiday."

"The Bentley clan is all assembled. We're ready to roll out the old and ring in the New Year. Right?" Ralph challenged with good-natured gusto.

Again everyone chattered happily and merrily–one person topping another so a question was asked and answered several times over.

By nine o'clock the guests were knocking on the door. The night was very cold and they welcomed the instant heat from the gas logs, taking turns huddling around the hearth. The atmosphere of friendliness and the excitement that comes when everyone is conversant with a show of interest in what others are saying has the effect of renewing warmth.

From the obvious relish everyone had for the food and beverages, Clarissa felt good about the menu she and the caterer had selected. The interaction of her family and friends pleased her even more so. She was especially happy that Ralph was enjoying himself and talking with the Littlegates about some mutual Washington interests and friends, which included Vernon Taylor.

One person was missing. Clarissa checked the time; it was 9:45 P.M. She was wondering if something had happened to Joseph when the doorbell rang. Her dad answered before she could get there. From the other side of the living room, she glimpsed Doug introducing himself and shaking Joseph's hand then showing him where to hang his topcoat. After a few minutes' chat, Doug led Joseph into the room and introduced him to Liza and Opal, who were standing nearby.

Shortly, Bert appeared, joined in the chat. Opal excused herself to check on the refreshment table. Bert asked Joseph if he were a native of Windermere.

"No, I'm from Eastern Carolina. The northeastern part."

"The Bentleys go to the Outer Banks every summer in August. Last summer was my first time with them. They love it."

"Do they have a place there?"

"They rent a big – I mean big – house. There's enough room so no one stumbles over anyone else. The beach is nice in spite of the hurricanes the past few years. I expect you're familiar with the beaches, though?"

Joseph answered. "I used to be, but haven't been back for many years."

Louise brought Glen over and introduced him.

Bert quickly interjected. "Joseph is from Eastern Carolina. You were wondering about some of those houses on the beach last summer. He may be able to tell you about them."

"There were several that interested me. I have some photographs at home. I'll hunt them and mail them to Clarissa. What I'd like to know is who built a couple of them and where they obtained the shakes or shingles. They are different from the majority on the old houses. The finishes are more mellow than grayed."

"I'll do what I can. To me, most of those summer places look the same. Right offhand, I can't remember who owned the places we went to, but I can contact mother. She may know or have some references." Joseph offered.

Louise suddenly spoke. "Joseph, I don't know where my manners are. Please, get some thing to eat or drink." She began leading the way to the dining room. Just as she approached, Ben came up and whispered to her. She said, "Joseph, please help yourself." She turned and walked away with Ben.

Joseph took a plate and filled it with sandwiches, raw vegetables, and hot sausages rolls. He by-passed the buffet with an assortment of wines and hot cider, moseyed to the end of the room, and peered through the partially opened doorway. Ellie was seated at the kitchen table munching butter mints.

"Hello. Mind if I come in?"

"No. Not *no* don't come. *No*, I don't mind. Have a mint?" She offered as he placed his plate on the table.

"Thank you. Not *thank you* I'll have a mint. Thank you for asking. I'm going to get something to drink."

Ellie watched him find a glass on a shelf where Clarissa had placed the champagne. He picked it up.

"I know who you are! You left *that* for Aunt Sassa." She hopped up in a jiffy and ran over to him. "I can read some words on the card. Let me show you." She reached up and slipped the ribbon over the top.

"Wait a minute. That's not from . . ."

"It's okay. I read some over Aunt Sassa's shoulder." Ellie pulled the card from the envelope and began sounding the letters. "R-e-g-r-e-t-s. Regrets. I'm not sure what that means."

"It means 'you're sorry.'" He put the glass on the counter.

"OB. D-u-t-y. Dutty?" She spelled, sounded, made a puzzled face.

Joseph pronounced it correctly.

"Oh, like my duty at home is to set the table?"

"Right. Maybe you would like to put the card away now. I know you can spell and read."

"Wait! NY E-v-e. We had Christmas Eve and tonight is New Year's Eve." She grinned as if proud of her knowledge. S-a-v-e." She eyed Joseph for help.

"It tells someone to *save*, that is put away. That's what we should do," he politely retrieved the card. Turning toward the shelf and trying to tuck the now-bent card into the envelope, his attention was caught with the words *till the 2nd to toast and taste – Your lipstick inspector.*

He replaced the bottle, picked up the glass and was filling it from the faucet when Clarissa appeared.

Ellie ran to her. "Aunt Sassa, aren't you glad your boyfriend came? Now Aunt Liza won't have to be sorry. She'll get to see Jarvis." She beamed at Joseph. "He helped me read . . ."

Clarissa held Ellie's shoulders and quickly stopped her flow of words. "Ellie, dear, this is Joseph. He's the attorney I work with. Ellie meet Joseph McBaden. Joseph this is my niece Ellie Smith. Opal's daughter. Ellie, go find your mother. She was looking for you."

"Okay."

"What do you say to Mr. McBaden?" Clarissa asked her.

"I'm glad to meet you. You can be Aunt Sassa's boyfriend tonight."

Clarissa gently guided Ellie through the doorway. Joseph drank from the glass.

"She's really a sociable child," Clarissa said, somewhat embarrassed.

"Sassa. So that's your nickname. Quite unusual." He bit his sausage roll, chewed slowly and assessed her in this state of embarrassment. He wondered whether it was because of the revelation of her family name, or because Ellie spilled the news about her relationship with Jarvis.

She did not watch him staring at her. She pushed the champagne bottle to the back of the shelf, then walked over to the table and took up a box. "Have you tried the brownies? They are very . . ." She couldn't get out "delicious." Instead she finished, "They are double chocolate." Even those words echoed Jarvis's comment and she blushed.

He didn't answer immediately. She lifted another box. "Or some mints? Ellie must have been digging in." She held out both boxes.

Slyly, he smiled. "No sweets, thank you." He held her gaze a few seconds, gloating that he had broken her composure. He knew moments later that he should feel guilty for she was trying to be nice. He ate the sandwich. "It's very tasty."

She darted a glance at the bottle and remembered the feel of the rumpled card. Her pleasantness dissolved and her shield returned. She replaced the boxes on the table. After checking the contents of a few others, she faced him.

"Is there anything I can get you? Ice in your water?" She shot at him.

"I think it's cold enough. But thank you." He drained the glass and placed it and his plate, half full, on the counter. "I shall bid your kind family goodnight. Sassa. It fits." And he walked past her.

Joseph turned the car key and the digital clock blinked ten thirty-five. Breear wouldn't be finished with the news until 11:30 P.M. He had almost an hour to drive around. Hungry and chilly, he cursed himself for acting like a jackass. The challenge to her was socially unforgivable, but his pleasure in cracking her armor that should have warmed him, didn't. Why not? This was the second time he had hurt her with words. The first she had been angry and confronted him with the manuscripts Susan had copied. Not tonight. She had turned as chilly as the night's below freezing temperature.

He thought of stopping for something hot to eat; only he knew that would spoil his appetite for a late bite with Breear. He rode around awhile until he chose to drive through a fastfood place for a cup of coffee. The attendant said, "Happy New Year," handed him the coffee and shut the glass window. He pulled to a side parking space to drink the coffee. Damn, it was cold. After a few swallows he got out of the car and dumped the cup, coffee and all into a trash container and cast a disgusted frown toward the drive-through window. There was nobody there to take note.

Getting back into the car, he restarted it, flipped the heat switch on high and tuned in the radio station that was affiliated with Breear's television station. A sentimental song was playing. Joseph listened to a few more before he pulled out of the parking lot, figuring if he lingered longer, the night shift might grow suspicious and call the police. Police cars would be patrolling the city all night and, who could tell, one might be nearby.

As he drove around, he thought about other New Year's Eves in Windermere. Usually he was with the Littlegates or some other friends. During the years that most of them had young kids, they often begged out of parties. Joseph realized the social groups had always been changing. The few constant people on the scene were single men. Tonight had been quite different. There was a family, a group by itself, many of whom he had never been with or even met before, as well as other strangers.

Without planning, he had circled back to Clarissa's half-house. He stopped when he saw a familiar car pull up just below the house. The car lights went off, the driver's door was opened and Mitch got out. Both back doors opened and the boys emerged. Mitch walked around and pulled the passenger front door outward and Ginny stepped onto the sidewalk.

Joseph assumed they had been somewhere else first for it was very late. He scolded himself. "Stupid! It's New Year's Eve. A lot of people will be circulating for several more hours. Think of your own plans. Breear, a quick dinner, and then I don't know," he admitted with disgust. As soon as the foursome entered half-house, Joseph turned a corner to avoid passing by it.

At the television station, he waited in his car, until he saw Breear come to the door, before getting out and walking to the entry. He knew it would be locked and waited a few feet back. Soon she returned and pushed the door.

"Hi. You didn't get cold waiting, did you? Brrr, what freezing weather!" She shivered and walked very close to him.

"No," he lied. After they were in his car, he asked, "How about a bite to eat?"

"Fine. Nowhere posh. It's been a long day. Something quick and somewhere warm."

"We don't have reservations so what are you hungry for?"

"Pizza. We haven't done that recently. It'll feel like college days."

He remembered. "It will."

After they chose their toppings from the menu, Joseph asked the waiter to bring his coffee. "Breear, you want coffee?"

"Just hot water, thank you."

Joseph asked with surprise. "Hot water?"

"Yes." She poked around in her bag and withdrew a small

white packet. "I've learned to carry tea bags. Often I find places that don't keep tea. God, I'm tense."

"The night shift getting too much?" He looked at her intently.

"No. I think it's a good exposure for me. I'm on air longer. It's still covering the trite stuff for the morning or noon news that is tiring." She leaned back against the booth.

"You did say there'll be a new reporter starting next week? That should give you some relief."

"I have to decide if I want to keep this special holiday and weekend news slot if it's offered to me on a regular basis. Or back to only daytime assignments."

Joseph attempted to put a positive slant on the job. "This year ends well. You have your degree and a job you prepared for and like. We should make a toast?"

"With coffee and tea? How very chic on this night!" She was almost sarcastic. "Sorry. I'm not knocking us or the pizza parlor. You are sweet to have waited for me. Was the party fun?"

"I wasn't there very long. Just made a quick stop."

"You know what we need Joseph? A bottle of champagne. Here're our hot drinks. Thank you," she said to the waiter. He watched her drop the bag into the water then walked away shaking his head.

After the pizza was devoured, they chatted during a second cup of coffee and tea. Breear yawned. "Excuse me."

"It's bedtime, I see." He helped her with her coat, which she buttoned while he put on his. On the way to her apartment, he asked, "Were you serious about the champagne? I can stop somewhere."

"I'd love it. But, no, it was a longing. But no."

Joseph dropped the subject although his memory was jogged. Clarissa had asked if there was anyone he wanted to bring to the open house. He had hesitated a bit while he debated whether or not to let her invite Breear. When he replied no, he could swear relief crossed her face momentarily. And there was plenty of champagne at half-house. A touch of jealousy crept into his thoughts. Would Breear be more her energetic, bouncy self if they were going to a party?

He drove the car to a spot where the security lights did not shine directly on the vehicles. After parking, he turned toward her, leaned over, and kissed her cheek.

She smiled weakly. "This isn't a joyful celebration for you. Sorry, you're a good guy." She took his hand and brought it to her cheek, then to her lips.

He pulled her close and kissed her. She put her arm around his neck, held him tightly.

"Too many layers," he muttered and unbuttoned her coat. She wore a heavy sweater over a turtleneck shirt. He kissed her again. She relaxed. His hand searched for the end of the sweater and shirt and found its way upward. She brought her hands to the back of his neck and held his face against hers. The car began to feel warm. She drew her head back before placing the side of her face against his and whispered in his ear, "Joseph, Joseph."

His coat was open and a hand dropped to his waist and pulled his shirt until she touched his skin. "God, you're so warm." Her breath in his ear was hot and moist.

His hand crept lower. "You're hot and . . ."

She drew her breath in. "No. No!" And she jerked her hand away from him and grasped his hand that was exploring. She pulled it away and sat up and back. "We can't."

"Why? Why not?"

"I just can't." She closed her eyes.

"Are you afraid of getting pregnant?" he asked.

"Pregnancy is not in my plans anytime soon."

"What about the pill?"

"What about it?" she snapped.

"Can't you take that?"

"Why should I?" She flung the words vehemently.

"To let you follow through on what you start or what you want." He countered.

"I won't take it. Why should I assume the responsibility? What if one day I forgot? Would there be sympathy for me if I got pregnant? I doubt it. The gossip would be 'careless girl.' And if I took it, the word would be out. Attacks happen everyday."

That was the strongest speech he had ever heard her utter.

"You've thought about it, haven't you?"

"Yes." Through tight lips, she said so deeply that her abdominal muscles contracted and the word hissed.

"Does it have to do with the champagne night and your not remembering?"

She faced the side window and did not answer.

"Did you get pregnant that night?" He asked with concern.

With a touch of contempt she said, "No."

He pushed, knowing it was too personal. "Did you wish you had?"

She stared at him with amazement. "Joseph, have you taken leave of your sense? Do I look like someone who wants a baby, a child now?"

"I apologize. Forgive me. This loving and stopping, without some satisfaction, is agony for both of us. Right?"

She shook her head. "But it's this or nothing. I've liked our kissing and closeness, but this is one of those nights I'm vulnerable. Please understand."

"What other choice do you give me?" he lamented. Then fiercely he added, "If tonight's lack of celebration is because of the New Year's Eve you can't remember, think about this: What will you have to remember tomorrow – not much!"

She jerked the door open, stepped out and told him, "I'll go up by myself. Think about your own problem and choice. I'm not asking why or throwing that in your face!" She slammed the door and ran up the walk and into the apartments' corridor.

He watched her disappear.

"Well, I loused up this evening. First being rude to Clarissa and leaving the party abruptly. Now pressing Breear too hard." He never noticed when the New Year rang in. Were there bells or horns? He did not remember any ringing. "Man, I've missed the whole party. I'll have to start this year mending the fences or finding new orchards. Thank God, these weren't public actions. It'd be harder to justify my behavior. It'll have to be done soon with one woman who works with me daily and one with the power of the media behind her. I was counting my successes too soon. What a great year I've had – did I say that this afternoon? You tallied your gains too soon, old man."

CHAPTER 21

The second evening of February, Clarissa was humming "Let it rain, let it rain, let it rain" in time with the raindrops pinging on her kitchen window. She was stirring chocolate chip cookie dough and enjoying the circular rhythm. Every element in life seemed to be harmonizing at this moment. She felt contentment with her own place, snug, the doors closed against the showers and suddenly dropping temperature. The room smelled of vanilla and brown sugar, and she already anticipated the added aroma of the baking chocolate chips.

Classical music, hot chocolate, freshly baked cookies – what a treat with a new novel to read. If it's cold enough, a fire would be perfect. Then the telephone rang. She put the bowl down and reached for the wall phone handset.

"Hello."

"Clarissa. Joseph. Sorry to bother you at home."

"That's all right."

"I need some translation on your shorthand notes. And Gretchen was upset about some papers she had forgotten to put in your tray and was literally wringing her hands. She was babbling about your planning to work on them tonight."

"Those notes will be difficult to interpret over the phone since I don't have a copy of them."

"I can bring the notes and papers by your place. I'm leaving in a few minutes."

"It's really raining, Joseph. I wouldn't want you to go out of the way. I can deal with my papers tomorrow. Go in earlier." She returned to the mixing bowl and stirred in the chocolate chips. Trying to clamp the cordless handset between her ear and shoulder, it shifted and fell, but she caught it before it landed on the table. "Sorry, I dropped the phone. I'm mixing some batter."

"Keep on with whatever it is you're doing. I'll be there shortly."

She replaced the handset to keep the work surface clear and to locate it if there was another call. With a wrapper from a stick of margarine, she greased two large cookie sheets and set one aside. She dropped tablespoons of dough in rows down the pan, then evenly spaced rows crosswise. The oven pre-heated, she opened the door and slid the pan in and set a timer for ten minutes.

She placed the second pan on the counter. Before greasing the surface, she wiped her sticky hands, deciding to unlock the front door and leave it open. The rain was still falling. She unlatched the storm door where condensation was quickly covering the glass. She scooted back to the kitchen and resumed spooning dough. The timer rang. She opened the oven door and pulled the middle rack forward a few inches.

Another minute, she decided, as she shoved the rack forward and closed the door. She counted to sixty as she located a wire rack to set the hot sheet on. As she pulled the hot cookies out, the doorbell rang. She turned her head and called out, "Come in."

The second cookie sheet went into the hot oven. She was searching for a long-handle spatula when she heard Joseph calling to her. "Back here. Close the front door, please."

Finding a spatula, she grabbed an edge of the pan with a heavy terry mitten and transferred the cookies to the cooling rack.

"Have I wandered into a piece of paradise? That must be chocolate chip cookies. Nothing else smells like this. Nothing so delicious and tempting!" Joseph smiled and his naturally tight face showed signs of relaxing: corners of the mouth up, nose lifted, sniffing, and the corners of eyes merrily crinkled.

"Hang your coat in the front hall on the rack. There's an umbrella stand if you need one." As he turned to retrace his way, she called out, "Then come back and yield to temptation."

Just as she finished removing the cookies, she gasped, "Whoops. I forgot to set the timer." She estimated the time at four minutes.

She located a cookie tin in her narrow pantry and set it on the table.

Joseph reentered the room.

"There's a plate in the cabinet just overhead here." She motioned to the left of where she was standing. First, he reached over, took a cookie, smelled then bit it. "This is the way to eat 'em. Hot, standing in the kitchen, while the chocolate is still melting."

"I agree. But it's hard for the cook."

He took up another one. "Open," he said, holding it in front of her mouth. She leaned over and he inserted it part way. She bit and nodded a thank you.

Joseph took down a saucer then placed two cookies on it. "This way I won't drop crumbs on your floor."

The timer rang again. She put the empty pan in the sink, then seeing the cookies were evenly browned, she began the cooling and removing process again.

To Joseph she said, "Would you put the cooling rack on the table near the tin?" He did and she said, "Thanks."

"Do you want some wax paper inside?"

"Yes. The roll is on top of the fridge. I'm impressed you know your way around the kitchen."

"Barely. It's a transfer process. I see the bags from the bakery and the boxes from the grocer have paper around the goodies." He ripped off a large square and pressed it around the sides of the tin. He took another cookie from the plate and stretched his hand again for her to eat. She did, savoring the crispy chocolate-studded cookie.

After she swallowed, she said, "There's milk in the saucepan for hot chocolate. Is that tempting, too?"

"Yes, ma'am."

She turned the knob to medium setting. "Please, watch it and when bubbles rise to the surface, stir and let me know. I'll wash the baking sheets."

He pulled a stool near the range and sat and enjoyed the moments of rest and warmth of the kitchen. He couldn't remember when he had been a part of a baking scene. Childhood memories of his home life were kept behind mental doors. But this fragrance was once associated with his mother's kitchen. That was far away, out of reach. This feeling of euphoria was in the present and he let associations recede.

"It's boiling."

"Thanks. Stir it a little." She dried the pans, then her hands. She took a cup from the countertop and moved to the range. "Spoon a little hot milk into the cup. I'll make a paste." The process was repeated three times. "Now carefully pour till the cup is two-thirds full. Fine." She stirred the dark chocolate, sugar mixture into the saucepan and in one minute turned off the unit and moved the pan. She poured the contents into two tall ceramic mugs. From the refrigerator she took a bowl of heavy whipped cream and spooned a large dollop into the mugs and placed them on a tray.

"Fill up the cookie plate and there are napkins in the right hand drawer of the counter. Shall we go into the living room?" She led the way and he came behind her.

She set the tray on the ottoman between the two deep chairs. "Brrr. It's chilly."

She turned the gas logs on. For the time being, the cookies had banished the rudeness he showed the last time he was here. She hoped the warmth of the fire would assuage her feeling that he was imposing on her time tonight, as well as spoiling the solitude needed for reading.

He commented, "Half-house has charms. It could be a retreat from the world and its demands."

She faced him, showing gratitude for his remark, ironic though it was.

"Hey, the gas logs are neat." Joseph put the plate down and walked closer to the fireplace. "A fire is nice. Even more so when there are no logs to bring in. Or ashes to shovel."

"True. But I still enjoy the smell of wood burning." She sat and leaned back in a chair and siphoned at the whipped cream. "And the texture of whipped cream."

Joseph sat on the edge of the opposite chair, reached over for a cookie. "And the anticipation of still-warm chocolate." The cookie disappeared in two bites. "You have a talent in the kitchen." He drank deeply from the mug. "Correction. Talents."

"You've partaken of them all. Thank you. Now that the decorating is almost complete and the grasp of the North Carolina legal variations is a bit firmer, I may tackle cookbooks. Eating out for so many years has spoiled me." She drank from the mug, ate another cookie and gazed at the bright flames. "I wouldn't have made a good mistress in the plantation days." She had a faraway look.

Joseph settled against the back of his chair. He wondered why she had chosen that phrase for herself. "If you had been in that position, I expect you would have learned whatever you were in charge of. And done well." She made no reply.

He continued. "This is certainly a comfortable chair. Deep, roomy and perfect for a headrest." He put his head back, breathed deeply and relaxed a bit more. "A great napping chair."

Clarissa leaned forward and scooted the tray aside. "Put your feet up."

"Ho! Do that, and I'll be dozing in a minute."

"It's allowable. Your schedule has been hectic this week. Here, let me take your mug," she said and reached over.

"It's still warm. I'll hold on. But if I do close my eyes . . ."

"I'll rescue the mug." She placed her own empty mug on the tray, then lifted her feet, crossed her ankles on the ottoman.

He followed her example. He stared at the gas logs, felt warmed by them and the chocolate and recognized the knots in his stomach loosening. When he stirred, the cushions adjusted to his body. There was comfort in the furniture, the burning flames, the foods. He let his mind wander. This she planned for herself. Just herself? Or is she expecting someone else to share this evening? She has steadily maintained that she's no cook. Could she have baked for Charlie, or the businessman or the doctor or someone he didn't know about? Why had he come? The papers, rather the notes he couldn't decipher. Some papers Gretchen sent. Rouse yourself, be a good fellow, get to the business that brought you here.

He brought his head around to look at Clarissa. She, too, had been flame gazing. She is a lovely woman, he said to himself. People had told him this, and he had known since she first entered his office back in September that she made a good impression. Calm, confident, poised, well groomed, with a healthy feminine shape and a walk that was pleasing to watch. Clear complexion, intelligent eyes. Since she had let her hair grow a little longer, there were deep waves that compelled the eye to travel the curves, to linger upon the dark brown tresses. But now he was seeing a lovely face with its unique charm. Mistress of a plantation? What had Littlegate said that first week she was in the office: If you never add a drape or a picture, she's attraction enough. That was before his intimacy with Breear who reawakened his desire for a woman. Breear who had burned him like the flames in the fire logs. How long could they continue as they were? The switch-on lever was not moved often nor kept in position very long.

Shaking his head and bringing his mind back to business, he sat up and leaned forward to place his mug on the tray. "This is very pleasant, but I was forgetting why I came."

He retrieved his briefcase from the hall. Clarissa took the tray back to the kitchen and rinsed the mugs and plate before stashing them in the dishwasher. In the bathroom she combed her hair and applied lipstick.

Back in the living room, she said, "Now let me see if I can read my own handwriting. It really is getting cooler in here," she shivered, then continued. "And the sound against the windows is more that of sleet than rain."

Joseph had stacked the papers on the ottoman. He pointed to a circled section, she studied it, then stated what she meant. When all the circled material was clarified, he put the papers back into his case. Saying thank you, he pulled out the envelope Gretchen had sent. "I will leave these with you."

"Yes. I'll get to them tomorrow."

"Clarissa, I apologize if I've held you up by coming and by staying so long. You may have company on the way expecting tollhouse cookies."

"Not tonight. This was 'treat myself' evening. Hot bubble bath, baking, fire and a new novel. Thank you for sharing it with me." Immediately, she blushed.

He smiled and turned toward the door, and she walked behind him and waited while he put on his coat and took his umbrella in hand. He unlocked the doors, went out and she stepped onto the porch.

"Well, it is sleeting!" Clarissa went over and touched the banister. "This is coated. Be careful. This wooden floor can be very slick," she cautioned Joseph.

The front edge of the porch was iced. He stepped carefully down and turned his head back toward Clarissa. "It's cold. You should get back in." He was reaching for the handrail on the steps when his foot slipped and his forehead struck the porch column. He fell against the rail and banged his knee, which in turn kept him from falling farther down the steps.

Clarissa called, "Are you all right?" and started toward him.

"Don't come any closer. The porch is solid ice." He tried to right his body by pulling on the narrow, iron railing but his hand slid down. He reached up again and grabbed the top rail and wrapped his hand around it where it joined the vertical-supporting rail. "God, it's too cold to hold."

He steadied himself and withdrew his hand and blew on it. Clarissa urged him to stay were he was. She stepped carefully, slowly to the Hughes entrance, took up their bristled mat and placed it near the porch edge.

"Don't move yet." She got her own astroturf doormat and returned to the front porch. She placed her feet on the bristled mat, then stooped and laid hers from there to the edge. "Now, I'm going to sit on these mats. I'm going to reach over and grab your coat. Can you pivot a little from the waist and sit down on the mat? Try."

She pulled her sweater sleeve over her hand, and clamped it around the porch upright rail that had not frozen all around. Then she caught his coat and held tightly.

"Okay. Ease down. You're right on target. Now walk it back

on the count of three. I'll do the same. One, two, three."

Together they moved the mats back twice. Slowly, she stood. He pulled his knees up, lifted his feet and swung to the left. She reached over and helped him up.

"I'm okay," he mumbled, but as he took a step his knee buckled. She caught his arm. "Put your arm around my shoulder."

He did and they walked and hobbled to her door and inside the hall.

The storm door came shut by itself, but she halted to close the inside door and lock it. Joseph put a hand out and supported himself on a table.

"Thanks. God, it hurts," he moaned and looked down.

She watched him as he tested the injured knee. She spotted a lump rising on his forehead. "Which? Your head or your knee?"

"My head?" He raised a hand and felt his face. He looked in the mirror over the table. She switched on an overhead light. "Oh. The leg was all I felt hurting. The bump is tender to touch."

Switching off the light, she came over and helped him remove his coat. She laughed as she saw he still clutched the briefcase. "Good job, counselor. Holding on to what's important."

He made a weak attempt to laugh and released the case. She placed it on the table. "We'll look for the umbrella tomorrow. Come, use my shoulder as a crutch." She steered him back to the same chair.

After he settled himself and lifted his injured knee and leg upon the ottoman, Clarissa went to the kitchen and opened the freezer compartment of the refrigerator. She found the sport gel pack and slipped it into its cloth cover.

"Here. Put this around your knee. It will be more effective if you place it next to your skin." She handed it to him and went back to the kitchen, where she crushed several ice cubes, placed the fragments inside a plastic bag and wrapped a tea towel around it.

She lifted the phone handset and went back into the living room.

"Hold the ice pack against your forehead. I'm going upstairs for a safety pin. Are you okay?" She bent and gazed into his eyes. "Can you see me?" He nodded. "How many fingers am I holding up?" She raised two fingers

"Two."

"Right answer."

She rushed up the stairs. She took her telephone directory from her handbag and a safety pin from a small sewing kit. She shivered and realized her clothes were wet and that she needed to turn the central heat up. She changed into a fuchsia, knit lounge, two-piece outfit and slipped her feet into soft-suede, cream-colored inside boots. She briefly toweled her hair, shaking it loose. It framed her face attractively, but she wasn't aware of that.

"Here, sit forward." She pinned the towel. "We need to watch the clock. Only twenty minutes for the cold packs. How's the knee? Was the skin broken? I saw you could bend so it must not be dislocated or broken."

"It looked okay. No blood." He leaned his head back. He had pushed his trouser leg above the knee. Without staring she noticed he had fair skin, golden haired, and firm calves. He works out somewhere, somehow.

She turned up the gas logs, then the central unit.

"Tell me if you get chilly or too hot. My knowledge of first aid is skimpy. Look for signs of blurred vision, unconsciousness, slurred talk, vomiting. Do you know anything else?"

"You are more knowledgeable than I. Medical acquaintances?"

"Well, you can speak. Clearly. Remember that my dad's a doctor. I could call him to ask what to do."

"I'll leave soon. Nothing is broken."

"How? The streets are slick. We're on a hillside. It's thrill hill for snow sleds, but you don't see them out on ice."

"Well, I can't stay here!"

"Well, I'm not offering to drive anywhere tonight!"

She walked over to the television and picked up the remote. "Push the weather station. Tell me what it says." She handed it to him. "I'm going to call Jarvis Randolph. Ask if he has any advice." She punched in a number.

"What if he's entertaining, too? Or away from home?"

"I have his numbers," she replied. "Hi, Jarvis. This is Clarissa. I have a little emergency. Could you give me a call." She said her number clearly.

"He might tell you to throw me out."

"What? And lose my employer? And perhaps be disbarred for inappropriate behavior?"

"Having me overnight doesn't fall into the latter category, does it?" He said that in a manner Clarissa couldn't interpret.

She waited a few moments to answer. "The accident has to be of primary consideration."

Joseph watched the television. When the phone rang, he pressed mute.

"Thanks so much for calling so quickly. No, I'm fine. Joseph McBaden came by to bring some papers that needed reviewing. The rain changed to sleet while he was here. The porch and steps are icy. When he was leaving, he slipped and his forehead hit the banister and his left knee struck an upright rail support."

She told him what she had done and asked what she should look for. She concluded with yes, she was looking forward to Saturday, too.

Turning to Joseph, she asked for the latest on the weather and street conditions. He answered. "Sleet throughout the city. Do not drive if you do not have to. Sandspreaders will work throughout the evening. Temperature will be thirty-two degrees around nine o'clock in the morning. Schools delayed two hours."

"The medical report," she said, "we've done the right procedures. Continue the compresses for an hour. On and off every twenty minutes. Try to stay awake for several hours. If pain becomes very intense, we can call back. Oh, I should keep you warm." She looked down, then back to him. "How is the temperature?"

"I'd be more comfortable with my jacket off."

She jumped up. "It's time to take off the compresses. First, let me help you out of the jacket. Sorry I didn't think of it." Together, they eased it off. "How about the tie? I wouldn't want to save you only to have you choke in your sleep."

He grinned and grimaced as he sat forward again. "You do have a sense of humor."

"And you, counselor, recognize humor." She took the tie and folded it over the jacket, then unpinned the towel. "I'll hang these up and crack more ice."

She left him to remove the knee pack. In a few minutes she returned to get it and stick it back in the freezer. This time she came back with a bottle of ginger ale and two glasses. "Some liquid is all right." She filled both glasses and handed him one.

It had been many months since she had performed similar services for a man in the house. They still came naturally to her. Her arrangement had never been to wait on him or he on her, but the small courtesies that made everyday living congenial, being innate in both their natures, had been practiced. Nevertheless, she had spent many evenings alone there, as she was doing here. Recently, she felt her relationship with Joseph was friendlier, like tonight, because he had a girlfriend and she had several escorts. But she did not have a relationship such as she believed Joseph and Breear had, although theirs might be in abeyance now. For Joseph and her, it was more like a team-working relationship except on a few minor viewpoints and the issue of divorce. He repeatedly thrust an impenetrable shield between them whenever she mentioned her divorce or separation cases. A little tunnel in her brain was kept open, on chance that a remark by him or someone else could provide a clue as to his defensiveness. His vigilance against intrusion was puzzling. He was so adjusted in other aspects of his professional life.

She lifted her glass and discovered it was empty and realized she was staring at the fire. Reaching for the bottle, she glanced at Joseph. He was scrutinizing her. Again, she blushed and silently prayed he was not a mind reader, as she had been focusing on what were surely secrets of his life.

"Some more?" she asked, holding the bottle up. She knew her voice was deeper with a need to swallow, and her expression seeking the answer to more than one question. *You can't read my thoughts, can you?*

He pointed toward his glass on the table. "Please?" He continued to access her as she refilled his glass then stood up to hand it to him. He focused on her face as he took it; his hand on the stem partly covered hers. The glass was cool, her hand warm. Surprised at the contact, she took a quick breath with parted lips and eased her hand away.

His eyes widened. "Thanks. Are the twenty minutes up?" He sipped the drink.

"They are." She retrieved the gel pack and the iced plastic bag. "How about standing. Test the knee. Jarvis recommended flexing it, walking about every hour."

"All night?"

"We'll see. Come on."

Gently, he raised his knees, winced briefly, slowly inched forward in the deep chair to swivel his legs over the ottoman. When his feet hit the floor, he grasped the chair arm and hoisted himself to a standing position.

Clarissa stood nearby ready to assist. "Will the leg take weight?"

He took a step, favoring the left leg. "Not with ease. Ow."

Quickly, she supported his left arm and led him around the room. As they circled back to the chair, she let go and shifted the ottoman so that he could sit less awkwardly.

"Okay?" When he said yes, she asked if he would be more comfortable without his shoes.

He propped his right foot on the ottoman and untied the lace and removed the shoe, dropping it beside the chair. When he attempted the left, he groaned. Clarissa was ready with assistance. She placed the shoe beside the other one, walked over to the couch for an afghan, which she brought to the ottoman.

"I'm going to slide this back against the chair." He lifted his legs an inch or two up and brought them back down when it was in place. She unfolded the afghan and covered his feet. "When you get the gel pack back on, you can pull the afghan over your leg. Remember, stay warm." After those procedures were finished, she replaced the ice over his forehead.

"The mouse bump on your forehead should be hardly noticeable tomorrow."

"I remember that from the knocks I had as a kid."

That was the second reference he had made to his past. She waited for details, but none were forthcoming.

"I won't go to sleep, but I'll close my eyes a few minutes."

"You will tell me if the pain bothers you?" "Yes." "And I'll ask you a question now and then to be sure you're awake and coherent." "Thank you."

He squirmed around in the chair and settled into a comfortable position, then closed his eyes. She reached behind her for the novel and her reading glasses. She pulled her legs up under her and opened the book. Twenty minutes later, she inserted a bookmark and removed her glasses.

"Joseph, it's time to take the ice off." She stretched and went over to his chair. "Speak to me," she said, removing the towel from his forehead and inspecting it.

He cocked one eye. "Are you feeding the mouse?"

"The opposite. Decreasing its fluid. Are you feeling silly?"

"Is that a negative sign? That color is very pretty on you. Your skin has a lovely blush color."

"Rest your eyes again if you wish." She returned the packs for another cooling. From a chest in the living room she pulled out a lap quilt and threw it across her knees after she sat down again. She resumed reading. Joseph dozed.

Twenty minutes later she went back to the kitchen. Stepping to the door of the deck she flipped the outside lights on and saw sleet falling more sparsely. In the wooden planter, the wax myrtle branches and the slender leaves were sheathed in ice. The nursery had staked and tied the trunk and pruned the branches to minimize weight on the young tree, thus she trusted it would not split.

"Last cold applications," she announced.

Joseph opened his eyes. "And the dreams were so warm and pleasant."

She wrapped the towel and pinned it. "The mouse is shrinking. How's the leg?"

He lowered the afghan and they both inspected. "May I check

it?" she asked.

"A nurse's prerogative."

She knelt beside the ottoman. She blew on her hands and rubbed them briskly together before touching his kneecap. It was warm but not hot. She pressed and it felt swollen. "Does it hurt?"

"Not much."

"Tomorrow you could probably take aspirin. That helps with inflammation." She sat back on her heels. "I know you're uncomfortable. I don't have any male pajamas to offer, but you could remove your belt." He didn't reply while he unbuckled the belt and pulled it through the loops and dropped it by the shoes. She applied the gel pack, overlapping the Velcro strips and covered his legs again.

Looking directly at his eyes, she said, "It's about eleven. Would you like to see the news." Pausing, she added, "Breear is on this segment."

He picked up the remote and clicked power. "She was scheduled for tonight."

"Please, feel free to call her." She got up and moved the phone handset beside him in the chair. "I have a quick letter to write. You can bring me up to date about the weather."

Upstairs, she sat at her desk and rapidly wrote to Opal. She updated her on Windermere happenings and included what was taking place tonight. She ended I may not tell Mom. She would worry, not wanting me to repeat the Lester scenario. She would love for me to meet someone like Glen and have an All-American marriage. You Smiths have set the standard for the family. Oh, Joseph is not the marrying kind. And he's downstairs now watching his girlfriend on the nightly news.

She tucked the folded sheet into an envelope and went back downstairs. He was still watching television. The news was in its final minutes with a review of local weather. The sleet was very light. The major streets had been sanded as well as the thruways and other highways. Streamers crossed the bottom of the picture. Most were about schools, which held scant interest for either of them.

She gave him an opening for comment. "Anything I need to

know? Or of interest."

"No. You heard the weather. Breear had a report on an accident on one of the bridges. The station's vehicle was in the background. So she had a driver."

His mood was glum.

She walked into the kitchen and set about making coffee. She searched the cupboard for a snack, but found nothing as appealing as the cookies. By the time the coffee finished dripping, she had half-and-half in a pitcher, a bowl of sugar, two heated mugs, spoons and cookies on a tray.

"Clear the ottoman," she directed as she entered the room. He moved his legs over, dragging the afghan. She set it down. "Now, let's remove the packs for the night."

She took the one from his head and inspected. "Looking smaller. How about the knee?"

He handed her the pack. "Not much smaller, but cold as . . ."

She went to the kitchen and dropped the bag in the sink and the gel pack in the freezer. Picking up the coffeepot, she returned to the living room. "If we have to stay awake a few hours, hot coffee will help me. How about you? It's strong." She poured into one mug, paused.

"If you're offering, it must be on the doc's list." She poured another mug full and handed it to him.

She replaced the pot on the heating element and came back to her chair. "A cookie can be nibbled at. No choking that way."

Seated, she added sugar and cream, stirred the coffee, drank a few swallows then tilted her head back savoring the warmth, the flavor, breathing in the aroma. "Nothing like those first sips of freshly perked coffee."

"Nothing except one who feels the same way enjoying it with you." He saluted her with his raised mug. "To the best prescription I've ever tasted."

They drank in silence, each thinking their own thoughts.

He broke the quietness. Staring at his empty cup, he spoke in a low voice. "Breear drinks coffee when the mood strikes her. A stimulant. Not to savor."

Clarissa had no comment about that. After a minute, she asked, "Will she be able to drive home tonight?"

"She said a fellow from the station would follow her home." He was quiet for a while before speaking again. When he did, it was a chiding of himself. "She's out in this mess," he waved his free hand toward the window, "and I'm lying here enjoying more luxuries than in the past... years."

"Don't flog yourself, Seth. It happens to us all." She said this with understanding and compassion.

"I've hurt myself so many times, Clarissa, and just gone right on. Playing ball, running, working – and I've just gone right on. Here, I am laid up with a bump and a bang."

"Your limitation and your confinement, if you want to whip yourself, is the ice not your desire to go dashing off." With a little more force, she went on. "And you don't have a brave enough driver to follow you to wherever you were going!"

Startled, he jerked his head up.

In a huff, she strode across the room and came back with the coffeepot. "Do you want a refill?"

"Not on my head. In my cup, yes." He feigned fright, then eased into a smile.

"Well, put your mug up. The ceramic one!" Before she could pour, she began to chuckle and had to set the pot on the hearth. She started laughing. Laughing so heartily she dropped onto the chair, almost missing the seat and laughed exuberantly. He watched her in amazement. When she regained control of herself, she leaned back in the chair and wiped her hands across her eyes. She reached for the quilt and wiped her tear-streaked face and her hands.

"Sorry."

Joseph said, "No problem. But I need to move. Let me pour the coffee." Slowly, he eased into an upright stance close to the hearth. He found bending for the pot uncomfortable, so he sat on the ottoman and picked it up and filled the mugs and set it back down again.

He picked up his mug. "Seth. You called me Seth."

"It fits. It's from Joseph. Do you mind?"

"And I may call you Sassa?"

She thought about it. "Mine is only a family name." He didn't answer. She was reluctant to enter into personal conversation tonight, but she had an impulse to tell him about her name for him. "I thought of you as Seth the first time we met. At the interview. Joseph is a name to be proud of and it suits you, also. But somewhere I intuited another dimension in you, one inside the absolutely composed, confident, gifted and respected lawyer."

"Inside. Not besides." He coddled the words. Viewing her in a new perspective, he mused. "This has been an interesting and enlightening conversation. Seth. I like the way you say it. How about it in private? And you think about Sassa. Maybe you could agree to that in private. And forgive me if I intrude on your personal life but did your friend call you Sassa?" Immediately, he regretted the question. He saw the hurt in her eyes coupled with a shock that he might know. He called on his sharpest presentation skills to repair the damage. "You are too fine and lovely not to have had a special friend. And I would not presume to say many friends." It was the best he could do.

She refused to be humiliated and faced him without flinching as she regained the poise to answer. "It's only been family. Our staffs in Washington and Virginia were too large to have names not familiar to us all. In my family, Sassa is said with a loving spirit. Even by my brothers-in-law."

"It is a lovely name. I understand. Maybe someday. Now after hot chocolate and coffee, if you could tell me where the bathroom is."

She jumped up. "So sorry I forgot. Give me your arm. It's down the hall from the entry."

He allowed her to escort him to the entry, and then he made his way by himself.

Two hours later when he showed no alarming signs, she offered him the couch to stretch out. He refused, saying he was comfortable in the chair. She switched off all the lights except one in the hall. With that one and the glow from the gas logs, she could see him distinctly enough so that, if he awoke, getting to him would be no problem.

He fell asleep quickly. For half an hour she sat in the chair opposite, then quietly tiptoed to the couch and pulled the quilt about her. It was too short to cover her, so she went upstairs, pulled on a white robe, rolled up a comforter and went back downstairs.

The quilt she placed over Joseph's feet. His face was relaxed, peaceful, and quite handsome when he wasn't trying to focus on a problem or to ward off a personal encounter. His skin was smooth, tight and always closely shaved so there was no hint of the color of facial hair. His eyelashes were a mix of blonde and light brown like his eyebrows. There was only a slight swelling on the forehead.

Assured, he was in no danger, she lay on the couch to rest, fully intending to stay awake. About four o'clock, she was awakened, assumed the clock striking was the cause. She listened. There were sounds of someone talking or mumbling. She sat up and peered toward Joseph's chair. She could see he was tossing his head side to side.

She eased off the couch and walked toward him. Remembering from some source that a sleeping person shouldn't be wakened too quickly, she stood beside the chair and observed his actions.

His head continued to go left and right, then his shoulders drew up and his head tilted back. His upper body tensed. Slowly, she sat on the edge of the chair, leaned sideways and placed a hand gently on the left side of his face. His movements slowed. She slipped her other hand on the back of his neck and rubbed slowly.

He mumbled as if hurt or in pain. "Breear. Breear. No. No. Wait."

Clarissa felt his face. It was slightly feverish. She lowered the afghan and unloosened the second button of his shirt. He wasn't sweating. She continued to rub his neck and massage his shoulder. His expression changed from hurt to intense longing. Suddenly, he reached his arms around Clarissa and pulled her close, her hair against his face. She resisted the first instinct to forcefully back away, to push herself free. His breath was warm against her ear.

Through her knit top and heavy robe she felt his heart beat strongly. Continuing to rub, her hand inched up the back of his head very slowly.

This nursing process was out of her experience. Think. What to do? She sensed her own tension and rigidity. Relax. Maybe he will. Relax. She took deep breaths and counted slowly. In a few minutes his grasp lessened, his neck lost its tightness; his head ceased swiveling side to side. His breathing returned to a regular rhythm.

Cautiously, she withdrew her hand from his head and lowered her arm to her side. With the other hand she reached up and touched his face: It was cooler. She pressed both hands against the chair and began to back away. He pulled her closer and pressed his lips against her ear. His murmur sounded like *thank you*. Then his arms relaxed and she backed free and off the chair.

She smoothed her robe and went around the ottoman to lower the gas flames.

After getting a drink of water from the kitchen, she perched on the chair opposite Joseph to watch him, making certain he had not taken a turn toward fever and incoherence. Her analysis: He had dreamed about Breear. Perhaps he had been in the heat of passion and she had not. Or there had been an argument. Maybe she was out with someone else. Or he may have been concerned about her driving home on the icy streets. Surely, he wasn't dreaming the guy following her had come in for the night. Try as she would to disregard his grasp of her, it persisted at the back of her mind. The only way to eliminate it or put it into a perspective she could label and properly file away was to examine the situation and deal with the physical feeling of his arms around her.

First, he was dreaming. She firmly understood that if a pillow had been available, that he would have enfolded it. Second, she had tried to act like a nurse, a professional that was interested only in not awakening a patient in deep REM sleep. Third, the embrace was so sudden, so strong that she automatically tensed before pushing herself away. Fourth, that action wasn't in keeping with the second. Fifth, was there a fifth? Yes, she recognized she had to consider her feelings. After surprise, what? The power she felt in his arms. The strength of his heartbeat. The pleasant warmth of face, skin, his body even through his and her clothing. Even after the accident and during sleep, the movements were not awkward.

It was true, as she had imagined: He was having an intimate relationship with Breear. She viewed the relationship as a dichotomy. It has brought a relaxed, more open aspect to Joseph at the office and, she deduced, with his friends. But she was concerned that Breear's dearest dreams were, not of Joseph but, of becoming a top reporter or anchor in a major city. She wished Joseph well however the affair proceeded. And hoped he would not have to bear the disappointment–shoot, don't mince words, Miss Attorney, say them one more time – the grief, the agony, the pity.

At the moment, she wasn't far from feeling pity for herself. She had, as the locals were saying, many squires, each one distinguished, talented, financially well off, personable, and eligible. Although the pursuits were enjoyable, none had produced the spark that leads to an exclusive relationship.

The sky was gray in the morning and they both slept beyond their customary rising time. Clarissa woke first. After stretching on the sofa, she threw the comforter aside and tiptoed to Joseph, who was still sleeping, sprawled in the large chair. She took the comforter back upstairs where she quickly showered and dressed in slacks and a pullover sweater and flat shoes. She dabbed on a minimum of makeup, combed her hair and returned to the kitchen and put on a fresh pot of coffee. She laid a tray of cereal, fruit, milk and bowls and silverware with two large white napkins. Then she returned to check on Joseph.

He was awake and sitting up with his feet on the floor. "Hello," he said.

"How are you feeling?" she asked.

"A bit fuzzy-headed. A cup of coffee should clear that. I'll try out the knee," he said and started pushing himself up.

"Let me help." She hurried over and offered an arm. He put a hand out and supported himself with her assistance.

She walked backward and he slowly followed, favoring the injured leg. "Much better."

The phone rang and she backed to the desk and the phone. He walked with her and upon reaching the desk released her arm and rested a hand on the desktop. She picked up the phone handset.

"Hello. Yes, Jarvis. We are up and are just before having breakfast. No, he had no weakness. Any nausea during the night? Headache?" Clarissa looked to Joseph. He shook his head. "No, he's indicating with a head shake. Why don't you talk with him? He's standing next to me." Clarissa handed the receiver over.

He took it. "This is Joseph."

"I hear you stayed with my girl last night," Jarvis said.

"Your girl? You mean my attorney?" Joseph looked at Clarissa as if to assess any response she would make.

She lowered her eyes.

"I had good nursing care. We owe you a debt of gratitude for your input. And your quick return call. I trust we didn't interrupt you. Good. When will I be leaving? When do you consider it's safe for me to drive?"

"When the streets are passable."

"Yes, I'll wait until the street looks clear. This is a steep hillside. The ice should melt quickly with salt on it. If the temperature doesn't drop, it should be no problem tonight."

"It's good to hear you sound so cheerful. If the knee doesn't swell anymore or give you pain, you'll probably be back to running in a few days. But, Joseph, keep an eye on that big knot on your head. Hear?"

"I hear." He handed the phone back to Clarissa.

When she hung up, she asked if he were ready for breakfast.

"I am. And I'll be out of your way as soon as possible. Thank you for your hospitality. Will we be breakfasting by the fire?"

"Yes," she answered and went to the kitchen for the tray, as he assured her he could make it unassisted across the room

CHAPTER 22

Joseph McBaden had never sat through such a long church service in his life or heard so little of it. Beside him sat Breear Callum, the city's most attractive television personality. Today she appeared like a modern damsel whom young knights would always want to rescue. Yet it was a remnant from fantasy that such females who masked vibrancy, intelligence and career goals needed the charger or the sword.

The young man seated on the other side of her resembled the white knight of Arthur's time. He was handsome with a nicely shaped head and face, skin that appeared to be tanned naturally from the sun and bright blue eyes that were alert, kindly looking. Everything about him indicated a person who was open to life, and he was experiencing whatever came down the pike as opportunity for learning. He was wearing a seasonally appropriate, beige, lightweight wool suit and a white shirt.

When Breear called Joseph a few minutes before he was to pick her up, she dashed his hopes for a few private hours today. "Joseph, a friend of mine has just come in from South Carolina. I've asked him to come to church with us. That's okay?"

Driving over, McBaden had subdued his chagrin, but he wasn't prepared for the shock that awaited him when she opened her door and introduced Sutton Barnwell. He deliberately dropped his keys and used the time retrieving them to force a normal expression.

Breear watched the two men shake hands, looked back and forth at them, then asked. "Well, Sutton, what do you think?"

Sutton replied in a relaxed, warm voice, albeit respectful in tone. "Mr. McBaden, Breear just paid me a compliment. She told me that you reminded her of me, and that she was bold and spoke to you first."

Breear declared to Sutton, "Well, you are taller and somewhat leaner." Facing Joseph, she added, "But now that I see you together, Sutton's hair is much lighter and his skin, darker. You don't talk the same."

Sutton laughed good-naturedly. "No. But I've been out in the sun a lot and I may be permanently tanned on the skin and bleached on the head. And I've not endured the daily grind of the work world yet."

"And there are other differences. You're so casual and Joseph is . . . such a good representation of what's ramrod straight in the legal system."

McBaden seethed with the comparison. He was grateful that she didn't say and so much older, but he knew instantly she thought it. He sensed that boyish-looking reputation he had been accorded for a dozen years had just vanished from his face. He tensed to keep it from sliding downward. She had renewed his youthful ardor, and he would fight to keep it.

When the service was over, he told them he had a matter to discuss with the minister and he'd see them outside. They left by the front door and he stopped at the altar where Mitchell Rockland was greeting people. He asked to speak to him a few minutes and would wait upstairs. The minister recognized this unusual request and tried not to draw out the long-winded members' conversations.

While McBaden waited in Rockland's office, he let memories surface that he had squelched for years. When he and Frances had been in his youth group. When he and Frances had sought his help and been denied. The times neither Rockland nor he had been there for her. How could they have been! She hadn't told them what was going on. He could justify their absence. He could. Why did she make her decision by herself?

He heard the door open, Mitchell coming in and closing the door. McBaden turned and faced him.

"Take a look out the window, please," Joseph said. Then he turned away while Mitchell walked toward the window. When Mitchell didn't speak, Joseph asked, "Well?"

"What do you want me to see? There're only two people. Breear and a young man."

"Is he facing you?"

"No. Wait. He is now."

After seconds of silence, Joseph pled. "Does he look familiar?"

"I haven't seen him before." Quickly, Mitchell glanced at Joseph, who remained facing an interior wall, then walked closer to the window. After peering at the young man, Mitchell drew a deep breath.

Joseph heard and swiveled. "You recognize him!"

Mitchell's face was pale, his expression puzzled. "Joseph..."

"You see a resemblance!"

"It's like seeing you. As I last saw you. When? After high school graduation?"

Joseph shakily sat down in the nearest chair. "I know, I know." He dropped his head in his hands; his elbows propped on his knees. "I don't know. I don't know what to think."

Quietly, Mitchell walked around his desk and sat in a chair angled toward Joseph. Each man was collecting his thoughts, searching for correlation.

Joseph lifted his head slightly. "It was a shock. Have you ever thought someone suddenly hung a mirror in front of you?"

"What do you know about the fellow?"

"He's a friend of Breear's."

"You never saw a picture of him?"

"Never. The first time I met her, she started speaking to me as if she knew me. She decided she didn't. The second or third time, she... er, asked if I remembered her. I never saw her before she came to Windermere. She's not a girl you'd forget."

"How did he get here?"

"He chased some leads and located her."

"Oh."

"They met a year or two ago."

"The resemblance is very striking. How old is he?"

"Her age. Twenty-three or four."

"And you've surely kept your youthful looks, and not gained many extra pounds. Good living, Joseph. Not the daily family worries." Mitchell spoke lightly, trying to lift his friend's mood.

Joseph darted a questioning look. "Not since the accident. You think I've been free of family?"

"I was out of line. Sorry."

"Every severance has been a mutual choice. With Dad, Mom, Sis, me. Even Frances." They were silent. Joseph was delving; Mitchell, waiting. Joseph said, "Some nights those faces haunt me. Characters on TV resemble one or more of them, or they come in dreams. I get up. Get something to eat. Walk around the house. If that doesn't shake the gloom, I jot notes about a current case. I make myself visualize those people who need my help, my expertise. And work on solutions."

Mitchell surmised, "Now, you're working on this fellow's resemblance to you?"

Joseph nodded. "The age nags me. Me, Frances, the time. Her transferring. Her trip west. God! The trip west!"

"Joseph, hold on here. That's a big leap."

With a stricken look, Joseph made a fist. "There's a clutching hand deep inside, Mitch. I can't stand up," he moaned and bent over.

Mitchell grasped Joseph's shoulder. He stood. "Come on. Give it a try." He slid his hand down on Joseph's arm and pulled upward. "Try." He tugged again.

Joseph straightened his back and lifted his head. He struggled to his feet. Once up, Joseph mumbled, "Thanks." Then he cautiously made his way to the window. He placed both hands on the windowsill.

Breear and Sutton were in high spirits, laughing, and perched on the retaining wall. Her lovely legs crossed, her short skirt showing several inches of thigh. Her suit more feminine and flattering than those she wore on workdays. The pair personified the health, energy, and enthusiasm of youth. The two appeared oblivious to the rest of the world.

Joseph's face crumbled at the sight.

Breear threw her head back, welcoming the sunshine to kiss her face, mouth opened. He ached, knowing that pose so well. She tossed her head; her hair fell across her eyes. Reaching up to shove it back, she tilted her face toward the church. She spotted Joseph at the window, waved and motioned him to come down.

Joseph returned the wave and forced his facial muscles into a smile. He composed himself, then turned and spoke. "Mitch, I have to go."

Mitchell took a step toward him. "Joseph, don't let your suspicions run away with you. Think all this through before you draw any rash conclusions. Or speak impromptu."

"I've grown past that."

Mitchell put his hand out, placed it on the Joseph's arm. "If you want to talk, I'm here. Call me anytime. At home. I'm here for you."

Joseph cocked his head, stared at Mitchell's hand on his arm and searched for words. "Like twenty years ago?"

A visible hurt crossed Mitch's face. "I've matured, too."

Joseph looked intently at Mitch's eyes. "This has been a journey back in time, a rewind and a fast forward to the present. Now the reel is blank with the camcorder on. We're writing the script. All of us. God help us to get it right this time."

Mitch clasped both his hands around Joseph's, pressed them firmly and said, "Amen. May I walk down with you? Meet the young man? Sutton, you said?"

Joseph nodded assent. "He's only here for the day." The movement loosened Joseph's tight muscles, the walking allowed time for him to resume his public image—composed, steady, reliable, trustworthy, all the while alert. Mitch's casual chatter prepared him for conversation to come.

After greeting Breear and Sutton and introducing Sutton to Mitch, Joseph was quiet and listened. Breear leaned toward him. In an unusually beguiling manner, she said, "I asked Sutton to join us for lunch. I told him we were going to check out a new restaurant. That's okay, isn't it?"

"Certainly," he answered in the most sincere tone he could

muster.

Mitch took his leave, saying his wife was expecting him soon for dinner.

Sutton declared he would follow Breear and Joseph in his car and not lose them. Breear opened her mouth as if to offer to ride with him. The flash of annoyance on Joseph's face persuaded her to say, "Fine."

When they arrived at the restaurant, people were standing outside. McBaden excused himself and went inside to check on waiting time. The owner was reading the seating chart with a hostess at the pulpit-like registration stand.

"Looks like a full house, Will," McBaden commented.

Will looked up. "Hi! A good crowd."

"Church is out. How long a wait for a table for three?"

Will scanned the chart. "Your timing is right. A table for three should be cleared in about five or ten minutes."

"Three's the lucky number today. Thanks." McBaden said correctly, clamping his jaws.

By the time he returned to Breear and Sutton, he forced his host smile. "It'll just be a few minutes."

Breear noted the crowd had not moved. "Well, three must be the magic number today." She smiled at McBaden and Sutton.

Joseph did not smile, but tried to appear pleasant.

"That was a lucky call to your alma mater," Sutton grinned at Breear.

Breear clarified for McBaden. "Did I tell you that Sutton finally remembered my saying where I went to college? He called the alum house."

"They give out addresses?" he asked.

"Journalism school has taught him how to ask questions to get answers." She turned to Sutton, "Maybe you can give me some tips."

Sutton said, "Hey, Mr. McBaden is your man for that. Attorneys are tops in a language dual."

McBaden suggested they go inside. A waiter opened the door and called out, "McBaden party!"

"Here," McBaden answered.

When they were seated and had ordered, McBaden asked Sutton where he was from. When he answered California, McBaden asked, "How did you get to South Carolina?"

"I thought it was time I broadened my basis of reference. All my education had been there. All close to home. But a lot of stuff goes on here along the East Coast. And the university has one of the best journalism schools. Southern writing is well known all over the country. And I wanted to experience the culture firsthand."

"Is this a college break?" Joseph asked and sipped his coffee.

"Well, it is, but I don't get much of it. I have a part-time job with the local newspaper. I managed a few days off."

Breear forced a grimace. "And we only get this one day."

"I'm on my way north. Washington. I want to scout out some possibilities for after school. A friend has offered a room for a couple of days."

"Summer intern or do you finish this spring?" McBaden inquired.

"Graduate. So I'm looking around."

"He'll have a master's. Isn't that super!" Breear said.

While they were eating, McBaden watched Sutton closely. His gestures were unfamiliar; his laugh, unrecognizable. But the shape of his head, the backward growth of his hair, his high shoulders, the length of his arms and long fingers—he'd seen them all in old photographs. Where were they now? Damn, he hadn't kept any.

"This food is superb. Real whipped potatoes. The seafood is great on the East Coast. Has more flavor that what we get back home." Sutton gave a sweeping look around the room. "A nice place."

Breear enthused, "It is. Joseph, I think, it'll do well here. The chicken is excellent. How's your beef?"

"Very good. Is your family in journalism, Sutton?" McBaden knew he sounded like an inquisitor, but something inside urged him on.

He smiled broadly. "No, sir. Dad is in insurance, a great salesperson. Mom is his secretary."

"Have they come east since you've been here?"

"No, sir. They're not big on traveling. They go to some conventions connected with work. Dad says his forefathers moved west until they found paradise and put down roots. And he sees no reason to leave it."

Joseph tried not to utter the next question but heard it being spoken. "You were born there then?"

Sutton shook his head. "I don't know where I was born. I was adopted when I was six weeks old." He saw Breear's sad, almost pitying expression. "They're the best parents anybody could ever want. There are just the three of us. We have a good family life."

McBaden again couldn't squelch his question. "But you were drawn to the east?"

Sutton stared at McBaden's eyes. He thought a few minutes then spoke as if he had a revelation. "I was. It's been easy to adjust." He continued scrutinizing McBaden.

And McBaden had one of his rare yieldings and dropped his eyes first. He silently warned himself: "Be careful here! Wait until you have more evidence."

Breear folded her napkin. "Joseph, Sutton wants to see the studio, the station. I thought this afternoon would be a good time to show him around. Would you like to come?"

"Thank you, but I'll pass. I have some work to do at the office."

"Tell me the restaurant owner's name again. I'll jot it in my notebook," she said, withdrawing it from her handbag.

"The ever-ready reporter," he said to both of them. "Will Hamilton."

Sutton jested, "It's an extension of the journalist's hand. I'll wager that little book has everybody's name of any importance she's met since she came to town." He reached over and touched the book. McBaden noticed his fingertips resting on hers and his gaze lingering on her face. He turned to McBaden. "She said she met you her first day in the courthouse. You're probably at the head of the list."

"And you are to be one of the country's leading journalists, in print, someday. I'll make a note that this is your first trip to Windermere," Breear teased and scribbled a few lines.

McBaden lifted his hand and the waiter walked over with the bill.

Sutton offered to pay, but McBaden refused. He summoned all his self-control to keep a pleased-to-have-had-you-join-us face. God, he couldn't wait to get out. He'd never relaxed his guard in a public place. He knew so many of the people in the dining room. The owner was a client. The girl that he longed to hold had sat here and been caressed by this young . . . young . . . student. He walked quickly across the room and started to yank the door open. *Cool it, man.* He pulled the handle slowly and stepped aside for Breear, then Sutton to exit before him. Damn, if he would relinquish the heavy door to the young fellow.

Ahead of him, he could see Sutton speaking. The voice was too low to be audible.

Breear turned. She gave him a dazzling smile. "Joseph, since you have work waiting at the office, Sutton can drive us to the station."

He heard a question in that. She was learning how to phrase her decisions. "If you don't mind," he spoke to Sutton. "I'll see you later," he said to Breear.

She forecast, "It'll be early lights out for me tonight. I expect a full day tomorrow since we're short staffed. Maybe we'll cross paths in the courthouse."

As they walked away, he heard Breear elaborate, "I won't know my assignment until . . ."

"Well, that was a sweet kiss-off," McBaden fumed, as he jerked his car door open. He drove away without looking back. His mood was red. No way he could work now. A long run or swim. He opted for the run. He didn't want to be walled in. He needed to release internal heat, extinguish the burning sensation. And without any witnesses. Always without any witnesses.

Clarissa had gone to Virginia to help her mother sort through some boxes in the attic. Louise Bentley wanted to tackle the clearing-out in order to have room for more items not currently in use. Being a teacher of many years, she knew that spring was not a time to undertake such a project for there would be class field trips, projects, picnics and standardized testing at school. Also, the attic was unbearably hot in spring and summer. Thus, she announced her intentions and warned that any of the clan who wished to claim his childhood mementos to join the "attic attack" this weekend.

Opal came with Ellie and Ben, while Liza and Ralph begged off because of prior commitments.

Mid-Saturday afternoon Louise had boxed the few items she labeled to save and stacked the boxes neatly under a corner eave. Doug came up and surveyed the area. He pronounced the job well done. After he had his last armload of boxes for the trash barrel, he offered to take everyone out for dinner. The women and children accepted quickly.

Ellie and Ben were inspecting some boxes of the games that their mother and aunts had played years ago. They were eager to try their skills with them, so Louise took the two back downstairs.

Clarissa and Opal remained with the last box of discarded items to go through. Opal opened it and pulled out a stuffed bear.

She held it up. "Was this Liza's? Bears will always be a favorite, won't they?"

"Liza loved that bear dearly," Clarissa said, reaching over for it. "It's so bald," she said as she stroked the soft brown fabric. "From all that cuddling and loving, there's barely any fur left. Pardon the pun."

"What a way to go though." Opal pulled out a baby doll. "This was yours, wasn't it?" Clarissa nodded. Opal held the doll on her lap with one hand under its head. "She's about the same size Ellie was those early weeks. I miss holding a baby. Clarissa, have you ever sensed pleasure in holding something in the palm of your hand?"

Clarissa put the bear down and clasped her hands together on her knees. "An apple and an orange."

"Something live? Try putting your hands on your knees. Right. Now cup your fingers down and rub your knees. Do your palms feel sensitive? Cross your arms at your waist and tuck your thumbs underneath and your fingers over the top. Reassuring."

"My goodness, Opal! Whatever made you think of this?"

Opal's face brightened with a knowing smile. "Holding this doll. I remember how babies' heads felt in my palm. Such a perfect fit. I could raise my arm and bring the precious baby up, the fingers bracing the fuzzy little crown."

"Strange," reasoned Clarissa, "I thought the fingertips were the most sensitive to touch." She began to rub her palms together then made a fist and slid the knuckles across the hollow of the opposing palm and up the fingers. As she stroked a thumb crosswise on the opposite palm, she looked at Opal. "I remember how your babies would grab my thumb or finger when I put my hand out to them."

Opal shook her head. "It's such a typical remark. 'Look, how strong he's holding on.'"

Clarissa asked, "Do you think they found pleasure in holding on?"

"Then I thought it was a reflex. Now, I'm leaning toward the pleasure and interconnection with another person. Like flesh to my flesh."

"Your philosophical maturity surpasses mine." Clarissa watched her hands move; she brought the fingertips together until they pressed under the center of her chin. "I've seen Joseph do this when he's studying something or assessing someone."

"Assessing?" Clarissa didn't answer. Opal asked, "Does he have someone special in his life? The girl on TV you wrote about during the sleet?"

"I can't say. Let me put that another way. I don't know for sure. He has something that is bothering him. Mitch thinks that, too. He wants me to help Joseph, but I can only wait until he cracks the door and asks. He is very guarded most of the time. Meanwhile, I do what I can in the office. He's shared more about his cases lately, and I follow up leads, do research."

Opal had paid attention to her sister's answers. She reached over and took Clarissa's hand. "I know you closed the door solidly behind Lester, and I admire you for your strength and good sense. Soon though, I hope some Windermere fellow will be holding this hand. To me, handholding is a hallmark of courtship. It's so affirming, supportive, and pleasurable."

Clarissa squeezed Opal's hand. "Thank you. I shall meditate on your positive adjectives. You and Mom are so much alike. Your hands are always busy helping someone or creating something useful and beautiful. And yes, to your unasked question: I do miss having someone nearby. He may be just around the corner, and when the time is right, and we meet, just hope we are headed in the same direction."

Opal returned the squeeze, dropped Clarissa's hand and placed her own on Clarissa's brown hair. "You are the brains of the clan, my dear. You help others, too, only in a different way. I've always relied on you for factual and legal information. Mostly, I appreciate your rock-solid support in my many causes."

Standing up, Opal stretched her hands toward the box. "My, we'll be late for our dinner out at this rate. I see nothing here of Ralph's. What about you take what you want and I'll do likewise. The rest we'll mail to Liza."

"Agreed!" seconded Clarissa.

CHAPTER 23

As year-end bank and brokerage statements were received, people sat down at their desks to review their financial position. The time was appropriate for deciding whether to continue the course they were on, or to make adjustments. Many of Joseph's clients recognized that their situations had changed. Some had growing children and needed to plan for their education. Others wanted some assistance with overall estate planning. A few had complicated taxes to deal with.

Joseph had handled taxes for some clients while he was with Hadley Morgan, so he felt competent to advise most of them, even to filling out forms. The cases that he considered a financial planner's expertise would be a better choice, he told his clients. Deadlines being a couple of months away, he wasn't as pushed as he would be later; however, being consulted this early in the year, he was able to pencil in his calendar a block of days to work on the forms.

Across the hall, Clarissa was involved with new domestic cases as well as keeping in touch with Susan Phillips.

Susan had dropped by the office one afternoon to give Clarissa copies of her withholding tax forms from her employer and financial statements. She wasn't expecting any further information that would affect her tax situation, she stated tensely.

"Thank you for bringing these by Susan. Do you plan to file taxes yourself?"

"I do. I've filled them out before and they are still so simple, I'll do them this year. Has there been progress with Garvey's attorney?" Her tone was anxious.

Clarissa answered. "Yes. He has an appointment with Garvey tomorrow. The papers are ready for him to sign."

"That would be a relief," she spoke as if tired. "Will you let me know when he has signed?" Susan suddenly urged.

"I shall." Clarissa looked at Susan. "Are you getting along all right?"

She shrugged her shoulders. "Okay. It's just a strain. You know living back home with Mom. Dear as she is being about separation, and she's so supportive, it's not the same as having your own place. I don't see why Garvey wouldn't sign. When I read the papers last week, everything in them was exactly what we, you and I, had talked about. And you said his lawyer had been over all the issues with him."

Clarissa stood up, saying, "We'll think positive." Susan thanked her, gave a weak smile and left somewhat dejected.

Clarissa gathered Susan's tax information and glanced over it before inserting it in a folder from her desk. She stood with a concerned expression on her face as she tapped the folder against a palm.

Joseph knocked on the door. "Do you have a minute?"

"Yes." She answered but appeared preoccupied.

As he entered the room, he inquired. "A problem?"

"Several." She held the folder slightly forward. "Susan Phillips. She's not taking this as well as she did when she first came to us." She pointed the folder toward her desk. "Each of those clients – all women – are also having a difficult time."

He responded tersely. "Are they all in the same category? Domestic?"

"Yes. Separating. It's such a cold time of year. Indoors months and they need all their network around for support." She looked up with sympathy. "Christmas was very difficult for each of them."

"Well, that's over! Why do women make such a fuss over the holidays?"

Switching into an assertive manner, she replied. "Just because you don't like celebrations . . ."

"Whoa!" he flung up his hands. "You chose to handle these cases. And you knew the conditions."

She frowned at him. For several moments, they were locked in a tight-faced exchange.

"Why did you go into law?" Clarissa challenged. He glared at her. She continued. "Don't you know the profession deals with people?"

"With their legal matters," he shot back in his lowest tones, determined not to top her questions vocally.

"And aren't those matters personal to every client?"

"Personal, but not emotional," he kept his tone even. "Contracts, patents, copyrights deal mostly with the head. That's why they are called intellectual . . ."

"Honestly, Joseph, have you no deeper responses? No feelings?" Her exasperation bordered on anger.

"What a question! You're full of probing ones." He took a few steps and stood directly in front of her. "Yes, I have feelings, but I've learned to keep them in check. I think before I speak, before I respond." He tapped his head above his right ear. "I listen. I think. I stay focused on the issues." And his voice did rise.

"I do those things, too. But the clients' feelings are important. You have to listen to them with something besides your head to fully understand their words."

"In your specialties of divorce and buying homes maybe so."

"Somewhere there were passions that drove your inventors, writers, creative thinkers."

"Their final forms of expression are what we deal with. All those passions you speak of have been tied up neatly, sensibly, and handed to us in black and white. We help the creators, now our clients, to protect their rights. That's all. Isn't that what they ask of us?"

"Yes." She searched his eyes for any openness. "Don't you have any empathy or sympathy with personal problems? If you'd been married or gone through the agony of decision about a divorce, then feelings might be as obvious to you as facts."

He stared at her with hardness and anger. Before he could speak, she took his right hand and placed it on her heart. He jerked his head backward.

She registered surprise, but having taken action, she added,

"It beats, constantly. And warm blood pumps all over the body." She lifted her left hand, then dropped it to her side. "It helps to feed the brain."

Tensions she had expressed verbally now transferred to her body. Her eyes asked for understanding. She saw his anger submerged by the widening pupils in his renewed assessment of her. A man's hand had not been close to her breasts in a long time. How could she have forgotten the feelings its pressure brought? How could she have been so thoughtless as to place her boss and co-worker's hand upon her, and in the office? To have put them in position of compromise had anyone walked down the hall? Did she stop to think before yielding to an overwhelming desire to have him recognize there were issues that began in the heart, with feelings?

She stepped back and removed his hand. "Forgive me. I didn't intend to use such a personal gesture to illustrate my point."

He held his place. "Forgiven. I have feelings. I have a memory. The wretched situations we get ourselves in are of our own making. We try to get out of them by our reasoning, not as some people do by sudden or violent means." He looked hard at her. "What you don't know about me and my past, leave be. I've dealt with it. I've chosen my way. You've done the same, haven't you? Long-term relationships are difficult to forget?"

She responded with a glimmer of understanding. "They are. As you say, we can deal with them."

He gave her a long look and started to turn, hesitated, then narrowed his eyes once more. "You did tell me that *you* had not been married or divorced, didn't you?"

The air was still and tense with her silence. He spun around and walked out.

Late that afternoon he returned to his house, still smiting from his clash with Clarissa. He stripped his suit, shirt, and socks and pulled on his running clothes. As he laced his running shoes, the memory came to him at age eighteen of tying a pair of Nikes he had coveted for a year. They had been purchased with a gift of money for his graduation. He had felt good when he stamped about his room in them, flexing the instep, and then while stretching his leg muscles as he leaned against an oak tree trunk, the soles proved firm.

He had gone on a run by himself just as he was doing now. And he released the reins on that season in his past. He ran fast while names and faces and streets and ball games tumbled one after another like a traveling companion at his side. He ran until his breath became labored and his chest felt as if it would explode. He raced on, knowing that this would pass; he negotiated a turn and retraced his steps.

Tired and sweaty, Joseph sank on the top step to his front door. He wiped his forehead with an arm and flung the droplets outward. His lips were dry and tasted salty when he licked them. Salty lips. He ran his tongue over them again, shut his eyes, felt a cramp in his abdomen. Slowly, he stood up, took a single key from his pants pocket and unlocked the door.

Closing it, he leaned back against the wood, steadying himself. He needed the bracing to let what had escaped from his memory on the run be reckoned with. Names and places were not alone; there were associations. And after twenty years he should be reasonable enough to give them a moment of escape. To review them like postcards in an album. No more.

He untied his shoes, shuffled them off, and dropped his damp clothing on the bathroom floor. Reaching for the shower handles, a sudden impulse caused him to withdraw his hand. Don't shower. He licked his lips again and the salt taste reminded him of a scene and sensation still in the fuzzy area of his brain. Filling a cup with water from the lavatory, he peered at the mirror. "It's okay now. It's all in the past. Take a look at yourself. Older but not greatly changed in appearance. But wiser. In control. Stay in control and you can face anything," he'd been saying that for years. To be sure, it was a dominant trait now. That was almost as strong as being inbred.

He switched off the bathroom light, made his way in the darkness to his bed, and lay across it. The room was cool and the air felt pleasant against his skin. He stretched slowly several times and breathed deeply. His thoughts stood on hold while his body gave into the movements, the smoothness of the bedspread, the fresh smell of the room for a window had been left cracked open, and the quietness.

What is it that was like an evening long ago, he wondered? The stretching? The coolness. Realizing the room was becoming chilly and so was he, his hand sought the bottom edge of the spread. While pulling it over him, his memory triggered sharp as a gunshot.

The beach. Lying on a blanket in the sand. I had on a bathing suit. The air was chilly and we both tugged at the ends to wrap the blanket around us. Laughing. Why were we laughing? We were high-spirited. We were always that, but this evening was different. Yes. It was the first night we had drunk beer and far too many. We found it hilarious that the ends didn't quite cover us. As we faced each other, the ends scarcely reached down our sides. We tried rolling over and that didn't help. We stood up and wrapped the blanket around us with the long edges right side of me and wobbled back down.

The soft sand where we snuggled until our bodies made cozy indentations, the romantic three-quarter moon and the nearby fire we had built an hour or so ago still burned low with the ebbing tide and beach music on the portable radio – contributed to heighten our sensual mood. We began our usual kissing and petting. I remember she said I tasted like salt and I said she felt sandy. She kissed my hands and teasingly announced she was glad they weren't sandy.

She rested her head on my chest. For a few minutes she seemed as if she might be napping. I raised my head and saw none of our friends who had been strolling on the beach. We were alone. I tightened my arms around her. She tilted her head backward and opened her eyes.

"Don't you wish we could be like this always? I love you so, Joseph. I love the feel of you. I love you to feel me. Is that what I mean? Am I talking fuzzy? I'm feeling fuzzy. I want to love you some more." And she opened her mouth.

Joseph touched her chin and brought his open mouth down to hers. She shifted and brought an arm across his and up around his neck. Only her two-piece swimsuit and his bathing shorts were between them. Again, she moved and wriggled free the other arm that was under her. Her hand flipped forward and rested against his suit. She had never touched him there. They had confessed love to each other for over a year, kissed often and heavily, but never explored where they had been told would be places of no return.

As if predestined – they both vowed this later – at the instant her hand touched him, his hand slid under her suit. His motions became potent, fostering desires for a deeper connection. With the fullness of virility, he rolled over top of her, her back now on the sand. And that ended the virgin lovemaking.

They slept awhile, wrapped in each other's arms. When they awoke, the fire was out; they were cold.

"Frances, we'll get married when we get back home."

"Are you sure you want to, Joseph?"

"Are you crazy? We've always talked about it."

"Later. After college. You know our folks will never agree."

"That won't matter. This night wasn't planned, but it happened."

"Oh, Joseph. I'm so sorry. I started it, didn't I?" she sobbed softly.

"It was mutual," he said and kissed her eyelids. He waited until she opened them again. "It was better than I had imagined."

"For me too." She giggled. Softly, she said, "We never talked about it, but we both had it on our minds."

"It won't go away now, will it? The longing?"

"Not for me." She turned fully toward him. She shivered.

He squeezed her against him. "We should go in. You're cold."

"I have a cover-up somewhere over there near the fire."

"There's no fire. I'll go look for it."

The blanket fell away from him. She gazed at his form in the moonlight—his strong shoulders and chest, narrow waist and hips, and muscles that testified to his years of basketball and other sports. "I love your body."

She sat up and adjusted her suit. When he returned, he had his sport shirt on. He kneeled to put her cover-up around her shoulders. She said over her shoulder as she slid her arms into the sleeves and reached back around and encircled him. "The fire isn't out, not in me. If you still want to get married, I do, too."

After another long embrace, Joseph picked up the blanket, shook it and she helped fold it. Walking back to the cottage, arm in arm, he asked if she were all right.

"A bit different, but happy. Joseph, we never talked about it, but I don't take the birth control pill. And I haven't kept track of the days in the month. I wish I had. Will you forgive me?"

"Always. That settles it. We marry as soon as possible. We'll talk to Mitch tomorrow night after church. Doesn't it take only a few days to get a license?"

"You've very gallant, my handsome prince." She stopped and kissed him. As they resumed walking, she said, "But I know it's because you love me."

"I do. We'll work it all out. Telling our families. Going on to college. All of it." Joseph spoke with assurance.

CHAPTER 24

One evening in late February, Joseph was watching a basketball game on television when the phone rang. The score was tied so Joseph let the answering machine record the call. He leaned over and turned the volume up a notch.

"Joseph, I apologize for calling you so late and at home. But a matter has just surfaced that requires prompt attention. I'll give you my home phone number. I'd appreciate your calling me tonight anytime you get in. This is Marvin Hertford. The number is . . ."

Joseph hastily scribbled the number on a pad beside the phone then picked up the receiver before Hertford hung up. "Good evening, Mr. Hertford, this is Joseph McBaden."

"I'm glad I caught you at home. Would it be convenient for me to come by tonight and talk with you?"

Surprise showed on Joseph's face and he turned his mouth away from the receiver to clear his voice. "Why yes, it will be. Or if you prefer I can meet you or come to your house."

"Your place may be best. I'm bringing one of my sons with me. We should be there in about ten minutes. And thank you, Joseph."

Joseph replaced the receiver and sank back against his chair thinking what can this be about. Why me? Hertford will have all the big guns of Hadley Morgan standing ready to fight a cause for him. I never handled a case of his while I was there except as one of a team once in an intellectual property matter for his firm. Does he remember me? Why at home and not the office? It really must be an important matter. It doesn't sound as if he wants me to do some political volunteering like Monahan. And he's bringing his son so it isn't likely to be something about Hemley's Textiles where Marvin is treasurer.

Glancing around his study, he saw it needed some straightening before they arrived. First, he flipped on the outside lights then quickly stacked the newspaper sections and tossed them in the basket under a table. The files, having been pulled earlier from his briefcase, were shoved back inside. His glass and snack bowl were returned to the kitchen and put into the dishwasher. Next, he went to his bathroom and splashed cool water on his face and combed his hair. Debating whether to put his tie on or leave it off, he decided not wearing one was proper given the hour of the night.

Suddenly, he remembered he had promised Breear to pick her up at the station after the evening news. He slapped his forehead. Checking his watch, he concluded that would be an hour from now. Quickly, he decided not to be limited with the Hertfords.

Back in the study he pressed the television station news number. "Breear, please," he said when a man answered. She was on the line in a few seconds. "Breear Callum."

"I can't make it tonight. Can you get a ride from the station?"

"Is something wrong?"

He replied, "No. I have to see someone."

"A new interest?" she sounded a mixture of a tease and admonishment.

"Not a female."

"I'm curious."

"They'll be here in a few minutes. It's business. I'm really sorry to cancel."

"*They* must be very important."

Joseph, with impatience, said, "They could be, but I must hang up. The doorbell is ringing. Goodbye." He hung up without waiting to hear her say goodbye.

The doorbell rang again and he swiftly went to answer.

He opened the front door. "Good evening. Come in."

As father and son entered the foyer, Joseph shook hands with each and assessed first Marvin, who was fifty years old, the same height as Joseph, but fifteen to twenty pounds heavier. He was of a light complexion, with intelligent, gray eyes and thinning brown hair. He was wearing a sport shirt and a heavy sweater, no tie. The matter that brought him out was significantly urgent that he had taken no time for coat or gloves. Normally erect and unruffled by circumstances, Marvin appeared with a disturbed countenance and a tension in his body. His hand was warm despite the below-thirty-two degrees outside.

"This is my oldest son, Sidney. Sidney, this is Joseph McBaden."

"I'm glad to meet you, Sidney." Joseph extended his hand.

Sidney wore jeans, crew neck navy sweatshirt topped with a tan, all-weather, three-quarter length coat. The teenager had a firm handshake though his hand was much slimmer than his father's. Overall, Sidney appeared a younger, leaner version of his father. The variations were light blue eyes, more hair, and a couple of extra inches in height. Sidney looked straight at Joseph's eyes; his face was tense, his body poised in readiness for something. Joseph had no inkling what, but surmised the urgency had to do with this son.

"Come in." He pointed toward the open door of the study. Once in there, he indicated two chairs opposite his desk. He pulled up a side chair and they turned theirs toward him.

Marvin commented. "A nice study you have here. Very comfortable looking."

"Thank you. Sometimes it's good to bring your work home. A little change of view."

"I understand. It can give a different perspective to a problem, or a case for you." Marvin offered.

"And no interruptions from a cleaning crew," Joseph added.

"Well, I'm glad you were here tonight. Thank you for seeing us so quickly." Marvin turned to look at his son, then back to Joseph. "As we proceed here, you'll understand why I didn't call Hadley Morgan. This has to do with Sidney. It is a school matter, high school where he's a senior, but it has a bearing on college next year. He has been accepted at the university here. Acceptance still carries with it those limiting words – contingent on grades the final semester."

At this point Sidney sat back in his chair and lowered his head slightly.

"He's still making good grades. His mother and I are very proud of him. Sidney is one of three top finalists for the university's most prestigious scholarship. It is quite an honor to say you had this scholarship."

Joseph spoke, giving Marvin a chance to choose his words before continuing. "I have heard of this. Congratulations, Sidney, for being in the running. That in itself is an accomplishment."

"We agree, that is his mother and I as well as his teachers and guidance counselors. It's his staying eligible that concerns us enough to come to you now. After dinner tonight Sidney brought to me a publication with a poem in it. The poem is credited to a Zack Eaton. That is the name of one of Sidney's classmates. He is also in the same English section. Sidney, show Mr. McBaden the magazine."

Sidney pulled a rolled-up batch of papers from his coat pocket and handed it over. "The poem is on page twelve." While Joseph looked at the cover, then flipped to the dog-eared page, Sidney rested his elbows on the arms of his chair.

Marvin watched Joseph closely. When Joseph finished, he looked first to Sidney, next to Marvin.

"That's Sidney's poem." Marvin spoke firmly.

Joseph acknowledged Marvin's comment with a slight nod before looking at Sidney. "You wrote this poem?"

"I did." Sidney stated unequivocally.

"Tell me about the poem. When you wrote it, why, how many copies you made," inquired Joseph.

"In English class," the teenager began, "we have to do a senior project and turn it in a week before first semester exams. It counts for a third of our grade. I did one of versification, explaining a number of different verse forms, including when they were first used and, if known, who created the form. And I wrote poems to illustrate the forms I discussed."

"You are a poet?" asked Joseph with interest.

"It's a hobby."

"Are you going to major in English?"

Sidney grinned. "Lord, no. Excuse me, Dad. I've written poetry for several years. It's something I do when I can't sleep at night."

"Is this hobby well known to your classmates or your friends?"

"No. I never even talked about it until this year. Our teacher, Miss Ankers, has stressed poetry in class. We've had to scan a lot, do rhyme schemes, search for metaphors, irony – all that involved imagery. She's made it a challenge. Anyway, I began to think of doing this for my project back in late October and talked to her about it. At night I tried some of the new forms."

"Did Miss Ankers read all of the poems you wrote for the project?" Joseph asked, focusing on Sidney as he answered. The teen returned the attorney's direct look. "No."

"Did she read the one that is in the magazine?" Joseph continued.

"No."

"Did you show it to her?"

"No."

"Did you show any of the ones included in your final project to her before you turned the work in?"

"Yes. I remember three that I did. She made no suggestions for one, but she asked questions about two of them: She did not pencil in any corrections or mark through any words."

"What did she do? How did she make suggestions?" Joseph continued, aware that Marvin was listening closely to the conversation.

"In conference, she asked questions. I explained what I meant. She wanted to know whether I intended to make the metaphor overall or just in one instance. With the other, she called my attention to a switch in rhyme scheme and wondered if I wanted stanza three to vary from the pattern; and, if so, why and how it added strength, or was it weakened by the change. These were technical questions."

Joseph asked, "Did you make changes in those particular poems?"

Sidney answered promptly. "I did. I considered them appro-

priate. I used my own words."
"Did she see these reworked poems?" Sidney nodded. "She didn't ask to read all the poems before you turned the project in?"
"No, sir. There really isn't time for her to go over every student's work thoroughly. The conference is more or less to check that we have started early enough to do a creditable job."
Marvin leaned forward. "Joseph spent many hours on this project. He earned an A+ on it."
"Has Miss Ankers seen the magazine?" Joseph looked at Marvin then Sidney.
Sidney answered. "I don't know. She hasn't said so to me if she has."
"How did you come by this issue?"
"I was in the public library, the main branch. I had finished a report for history so I checked the magazines; there is a wider selection especially in poetry there than in smaller branches or our high school library. I thumbed through the latest issues of the journals. As I was leaving the magazine shelves, I spotted a stack of publications on the reference desk. I flipped through those until I saw a literary journal from another county – the one you have there. I was curious what they were writing." He said with some derision, "I nearly collapsed over the desk when I read this. You know how when you see something and you can't believe what you're seeing, you have to reread and still want to say out loud, 'No way, this is for real.' That's what I did. The librarian glared at me and shook her head."
"Sidney, was anybody with you when you discovered the poem?"
"Not right there. I went with a friend, but he was finishing an assignment on another floor. I copied the magazine at the library, in case I couldn't find another one."
"Did you tell your friend about the poem? Or did you show it to him?"
"No, sir. I wanted to, but something bugged me, told me not to say anything then." He glanced at his father. "When my friend dropped me at the house, I got into the Jeep and drove to our

branch library, but they didn't have a copy. Back home I read the poem in there," Sidney pointed at the pages Joseph held, "several times. I pulled up my poem on the computer. They are the same, word by word, line by line. I puzzled over how this could happen." Sidney threw up his hands. "I couldn't figure it out, so I went downstairs to talk it over with Dad."

Marvin interjected. "I'm glad he did. I asked him many of the questions you've just posed. I believe my boy, Joseph. I couldn't see any advantage in our delaying putting the matter before a legal mind."

"And Hadley Morgan . . . ?"

"Hadley Morgan does a lot of legal work for the university. They have many graduates of the law school in their firm. If I remember correctly, at least three of them have held that scholarship. You probably know many connections between the firm and law school. One is on the Board of Trustees. I didn't want to place them in a position of divided loyalties."

Joseph asked Sidney. "You said you weren't planning an English major. Are you considering pre-law?"

"I am thinking of pre-med, sir. I would like to be a doctor and will probably have a science major."

"Yet you write poetry? That's interesting."

"Poetry has structure and it's more involved than most people think it is. It's also a solitary pursuit. Everyday I'm with groups of people during school and after. For me poetry is a change, and as I said a challenge. You understand, don't you, Dad?" Sidney turned and looked earnestly at his father.

With sincerity came the reply. "I do. I read poetry myself at times, if I can't sleep." A silent rapport connected the two.

Joseph was inwardly touched and wished such an exchange could have been in his personal history.

He asked, "Sidney, did you know about the poetry contest in this magazine?"

"No, sir."

"When did you write the poem that's in this issue? The one signed Zack Eaton?" Joseph asked.

"Let's see. Last spring as best I remember, I started it."

"Was it freehand, typed?"

"I started it freehand then later entered it on the computer. Why?" asked Sidney.

"Well, it should be on your hard drive and should be dated," answered Joseph.

Sidney looked hopeful. "Great. I never check dates of documents. I'll find out how to do that."

Marvin appeared a bit relieved himself for the first time since entering the house. However, his face screwed again. "Joseph, I want this matter to be handled as privately as possible." He stopped and stared at Joseph, who nodded assent. "It's not something we'd want to take to court. You plan how you want to go about it. Call me anytime. If there's a point that needs clarifying and can be done without specific names being mentioned, you can reach me at the office. For more direct issues, call me at home. If I'm not there, leave your name and I'll return the call. Is there anything you want to ask either of us now?"

"Yes. Sidney, how do you think Zack got hold of your poem?"

Sidney threw up his hands. "I have no idea. I worked on the project seriously during Christmas break. All my poems are in a file on the computer and I kind of knew which ones I would use."

"Did you have any hard copies?" Joseph asked.

Sidney scrunched his face, looking much like his father. "Yes, I printed one of each after proofing and correcting, and after the line placement suited me. They are all in a folder with my original notes for the paper I turned in. I didn't write on paper everything that I turned in. I composed much of it on the computer."

"Do you have a copy of that?"

"No, sir." He shrugged. "It's on the computer if I need it." He brightened. "But I have the project back with Miss Ankers' comments."

Joseph commented. "That's good. Keep it in a safe place. So you never took a copy of the poem earlier to school, and Zack was never at your house?"

"No to both questions, sir."

Marvin stood and Joseph and Sidney did likewise. Marvin said, "We'll give all this some thought. If anything comes to us that is relevant, one of us will call you. Again, thanks for letting us come tonight."

After handshaking all around, Joseph said at the doorway, "I'll be in touch."

He opened the door and while holding it for the others to exit, he looked toward the road. The streetlight showed a dark sport vehicle parked at the edge of the driveway. White lettering read "CHANNEL 6 NEWS covers the Piedmont for you." Joseph's first instinct was to clinch his teeth and swear. Quickly, he imagined a cool scene, inhaled deeply, and forced a calm expression; otherwise, he knew from experience that he could be livid in color. He had presence of mind to shiver a moment, thankful for the cold.

Marvin had descended the few steps to the driveway when the sport vehicle moved forward slowly, then quickly increased speed and rounded a corner beyond sight. Jerking his head around, Marvin's face registered astonishment.

Before a question was put forth, Joseph said maybe someone was looking for an address.

"At this time of night? What would the station want to cover out here in a residential area?" He turned and looked around. "There's not a sign of commotion in the neighborhood."

"Marvin, I don't know, but I will find out. If it turns out to be suspicious, I'll let you know."

"I would like a call about whatever you learn," he stated.

Joseph nodded and the Hertfords climbed into the Jeep, Sidney in the driver's seat.

Back inside the warm house, Joseph still rubbed his upper arms as if he were thoroughly chilled. He went to the kitchen and drained the last coffee from the pot into a mug and reheated it in the microwave. He dropped sugar and creamer into the hot brew and stirred it vigorously with a spoon.

His initial pleasure at having Marvin Hertford for a client was overshadowed for the moment by seeing the vehicle in front of his house. He had no doubt that it was driven by Breear. Hadn't *he* suggested she drive herself home in a station vehicle? Why did she come here? Was she checking out his visitor? Didn't she trust him that it wasn't another girl? As much as he was smitten, even dazzled, by her, they had no holds on each other. She had dinner with other men. What did she say? She needed contacts and she couldn't be labeled as going steady with anyone right now. And she liked to add, you know how we feel about each other, it's not like that with anybody else.

He drained the coffee mug then went to his room and grabbed a sweater. The action helped switch his train of thought. "Think man, don't feel. Why was she here? She was snooping. Why? She's a smart cookie. Did she suspect that only an important matter would have someone come to the house at this hour? Not just an important matter– maybe an important person. Did she write down his license plate number? If so, it will probably be easy for her to check with her station connection. If she thought I'd seen her, she could get someone else to run the number by DMV. She had to know I saw her. What if she recognized Marvin Hertford? He had been one of the men I named for her in a restaurant.

Damn! That black notebook. She wrote everything I told her in that book. What did I say about him? Joseph wished it were daylight or not so biting cold that he could go for a run. He needed to move while he tried to sort out this situation. Really, both situations: Sidney and his project with the theft of his poem, and Breear spying on his house. She'd never been here. He speculated she had checked on his home address soon after their second meeting. It would be like her to satisfy her curiosity. Sure, it would! She had been bold enough to test her memory by kissing him that night. And for the moment, his body flushed, recalling her response to his kissing her immediately afterwards and all the other nights when they parted. He enjoyed the sensations before he resumed pacing about the lower floor of his house.

Enough! Think what she will do with the information. First, there's not much for her to go on if she ascertains the visitor was Marvin and a teenager. Second, what can she assume? *A*, that is his son. *B*, the son has a problem. The dad wouldn't bring a son along if the problem were his own. Okay, so what was his answer to her? That was simple, attorney-client privilege. What would he report to Marvin about the vehicle in front of his house? Don't get ahead of yourself. Talk with Breear first.

He checked his watch and decided to give her another five minutes to get home before calling. He continued to pace. Passing his fireplace, he wished he had a log fire burning. He climbed the steps to the second floor. There was nothing for him to see. The rooms were empty. He had never put any furniture in them. The maid service dusted the floors, the baseboards and windowsills and flushed the commodes every two weeks. His footfalls registered hollow and the unheated rooms were so downright cold, that he traipsed back to the study.

There he picked up the phone and pressed Breear's home number. After four rings the answering machine picked up. When the message ended and the buzzer was silent, he said evenly but with strength, "Breear, you've had time to get there. Please, pick up, otherwise I will call until I talk with you. I need to know you returned safely after my plans were changed."

"Hello," Breear's voice came on. "I'm just coming in."

"You commandeered one of the station's vehicles?"

"Yes. It's late. May I talk with you tomorrow?" There were sounds of a yawn.

Joseph thought that if either of them genuinely yawned, it should be he; after all, she was using an old excuse. "Why were you out front a short while ago? Please, don't say you weren't. The lettering was so bright and readable."

There was a silence, then a sigh. "A sudden impulse. That's all."

"Did you think I'd lied to you?"

"It's not like you to cancel the last minute. All right, the last hour. When I saw the men come out, I knew you had had an unexpected late appointment. You were so abrupt on the phone." Her last sentence was a scold.

"I had some tidying to do before they walked in. That's all."

"Joseph, that was Marvin Hertford, wasn't it?" Her voice inquired softly.

"Is that who you thought you saw?"

"Yes. Was it?" When he did not answer immediately, she continued. "That was probably the younger person's Jeep. Hey! Was that his son? Was he caught for a traffic violation? No! Wait. For that offense, Mr. Hertford would have gone to the police station to bail him out. It must be something more serious."

As her excitement and her interest mounted, Joseph broke in. "Breear, I can't talk about clients."

"Ah, Joseph," she caressed the name. "You can trust me."

"My trusting you has nothing to do with this. You know about attorney-client confidentiality."

"Well, I'll just keep my ear to the ground. I'll let you know any rumors I hear."

He couldn't decipher whether she was teasing or promising to pass along information to him. "Breear, what you saw tonight, please, keep to yourself. Don't shake any bushes trying to learn more. It is strictly a private matter. I want you to honor this request."

"I'll do my best. You have your job and I have mine. I will promise to tell you if there's a conflict. Okay?"

What choice do I have at the moment? he thought. "Thank you. What about tomorrow night? Dinner?"

"Sounds fine. Can we make it at seven? I need to be back at the station early."

"Right. I'll make reservations. And I'll pick you up."

"Lovely. I'm going to sign off. I'm ready for bed. Goodnight."

"Goodnight." He hung up wondering if she ever dreamed of him. He'd like to be there, lying beside her, watching as she slept. Was she a calm sleeper or did she toss and turn, trash about, talk in her sleep? What did she wear in bed?

He jumped up and rubbed his head between his fists. Get her out of your mind for a while. You won't be sleeping next to her until she gets good and ready. How long has it been since that first kiss? God, that was back in September. Try your only cure: Tackle a tough case, this Hertford matter. I can make notes while the conversation is fresh. Yeah, that's my solution for bad dreams and long-ago memories. Breear isn't a bad dream; she's a reality. I don't know whether I'm restless from desire for her or from anger that she came here and spied on me and whoever else was here.

Opening his briefcase and pulling out a new legal pad, he realized his confusion. He wasn't focused on the real problem. It was that she had compromised Hertford's trust in him. What was he going to say to the man tomorrow? Hertford had in no uncertain tones stated he wanted to know about the vehicle. Joseph considered making up a story but discarded that idea immediately. This was a fine, respected man. He was sharp and he could do his own checking. The honor he has paid me by the consultation doesn't deserve any falsity. This could be a very important case for me, not in terms of publicity, especially if he wants no trial, but the contact and the trust he has bestowed will be known. That's just the way life goes.

Joseph understood that Marvin didn't just draw his name from the Yellow Pages. Whatever respect Joseph had earned, he would keep only if the respect and trust continued. Damn, the spying episode. He'd have to be honest with Marvin. Call him and say he had to cancel an arrangement he had made to pick someone up at the station due to a late meeting. She had driven by to make sure he didn't have a woman friend over. She was satisfied when she saw two men come out and only one car in the drive.

Better to be embarrassed by a jealous girlfriend than the possibility of a news story.

CHAPTER 25

The next morning Joseph McBaden eyed the gold letters on his outer door and a feeling of pride joined his already-pleased countenance. Gretchen observed his entrance from her desk.

"It's a good morning, isn't it, Mr. McBaden?" She was placing supplies for the day on her desktop.

"It is. Any messages for me?"

"I'll have the faxes checked in a few minutes. I'll bring yours to your office. Would you like a cup of coffee, too?"

"Thank you. Yes, I'd like the faxes and the coffee." He swung his briefcase jauntily at his side. He gave a glance towards Clarissa's office. The door was closed so he knocked. There was no answer; thus, he moved on to his office, leaving the door open. He removed his topcoat and gloves and placed them on the tree. As usual, he emptied his briefcase and shoved it to a front edge of his desk.

He studied his notes remembered from the Hertfords' conversation last night on the legal pad. They made sense. He sat back in his swivel chair, steepled his hands and brought the ends of his fingers to the bottom of his lips. There were some unanswered questions. First, how did Zack get the poem? When did he get it? If he knew it was an original by Sidney, why did he enter it in the contest? When he knew he had won the honor of acceptance, why did he let it go to press, knowing the publication would be out months before graduation? Did he hope to gain some "honor" for himself? Or did he want to cause trouble for Sidney? If the latter were true, why did he want to do that? Was there bad feeling between them? Had Sidney won an honor previously that Zack had coveted or thought should go to him?

What kind of student was Zack? Who are his parents, what do

they do, where do they live? These were questions he needed answered. Now his job was how to collect all this without drawing suspicion. He might need some help. There were always private investigators. Was there another choice? Who could he work with whom he could completely trust? Breear would leap at the chance, but she would be too obvious asking questions. People would think it was for television news. Marvin would not like that.

This is a problem Samuel would be a good listener for. He could relate having teens himself. He could bring some experience and reasoning to the issue and people involved. But I can't put him in that spot. Or any of the other attorneys we know. Hadley Morgan is so big and every attorney will have at least one friend or acquaintance among the staff. Any reference made concerning my connection with the Hertfords will cause ears to perk, eyes to search more meaning and perhaps mouths to pose questions.

As he was thinking, he heard Clarissa coming down the hall and opening her door. He waited a few minutes for her to settle in for the day, and then he walked into her office.

"Gotta minute?" He looked at her. She was smartly dressed, ready for any business matter that surfaced. Her hair looked different, he wondered what she had done to it.

"Yes."

"Could you come to my office?"

"Yes." Before he turned away, she looked at his face quickly. It was not readable. There was a pull around the corners of his mouth in what she considered a controlled pleasure, but his eyes were narrowed and ironically with a slight glitter. Curious, she followed him.

Another surprise! He waited for her to enter his office then he closed the door. While she seated herself in the chair opposite his, he rounded the desk and sat down.

He leaned forward, looked at her, glanced down at his hands and finally leaned back in his chair, placing his hands on the arms, his fingers cupping the rounded ends. "I had a visitor last night. In fact two visitors. They came to talk with me at home. They have an urgent matter; one they want to keep private. It will not be easy to do."

He paused and looked directly into her eyes. She focused on his. He continued. "It is Marvin Hertford, treasurer of Hemley Textiles, and his son Sidney, a high school senior. Intellectual work gets pirated early."

The phone light blinked. Joseph pressed the intercom button, "Yes, Gretchen." He listened a moment then glanced toward Clarissa and said quietly, "Marvin Hertford."

Immediately she rose and indicated she would leave the room. He nodded. As she closed the door behind her, he told Gretchen to put the call through.

"Hello, Marvin."

"Joseph, again thank you for seeing Sidney and me last evening. I'm on the cell phone. There are some concerns about this literary work of Sidney's that I want you to be aware of. First, is Sidney's honor. His integrity is at stake. If this is not put right, there will be a stigma that will be felt by his brothers and sister. They are younger and will follow him in the same schools."

"I understand."

"Sidney is not dependent on the scholarship to go to college. However, at this point he is a strong contender; and, if he gets it, and this news is brought to the attention of the committee or the university – well, the scholarship will be withdrawn. Plagiarism at any level is unacceptable."

"I will do what I can to ferret the how and when starting today. Could you obtain schedules of Sidney's classes and Zack's? Would Sidney know Zack's grades in classes first semester? Oh, and what Zack's senior project was? I may need to talk with Sidney again."

"I'll get back with the schedules and grades. Let me know when you want to see Sidney. And I'll stay in touch. I'm at my destination now." Marvin hung up.

Joseph made some notes on his legal pad then spoke to Clarissa on the intercom. She came in immediately, this time with a legal pad, and sat down.

"You heard, that was from Marvin Hertford. He wanted to state his reasons for finding out how another student got hold of his son's poem. I admire his respecting his son by not pointing out in his presence last night that if his honor is discredited, then his siblings will feel the disgrace." He lifted the legal pad and brought the flipped pages forward. "Let me tell you from the beginning."

She listened and made notations on her pad. When he finished, she added a few more notes.

"Interesting?" he asked, stretching his arms and hands upward.

"Yes. Let's hope this can be resolved before the scholarship announcement. Did he say whether it would be by a letter or a phone call? If it's a call, then he, Sidney, would feel he had to inform the committee about the problem then."

Joseph made a note. "Good point." He put the pen down and with arms resting on either side of the pad, he said, "I need someone as a sounding board on this. Someone I can trust to keep the matter private. Possibly, to help gather data without causing suspicion. Information about the boys' classes, grades, what students think of them, is there a known hostility. Zack's family's financial situation."

"Private detectives?"

"Preferably not, but yes if necessary."

"Did the Hertfords bring you a copy of the literary magazine?"

"No."

"I'll search around at lunch. Can Sidney run a copy of the poem from his computer?" She asked.

Joseph wrote another question mark under his previous one. He didn't complete a beginning smile, but he did have a pleased expression when he looked over at her. "That's the kind of feedback I'm looking for. Pose a question and a pursuit for the answer. Keep thinking about this puzzle. The pieces are bits of information, the five *W*s, we need to complete the picture.

Who? Sidney or Zack?

What? Wrote the poem?

Where? On computer? Typewriter? By hand?

When? Was it first written? Received by the magazine?

Why? Did one of them steal it from the other? Or could there be a third person who sent it to the magazine? Simple newspaper style. State it all in first paragraph." Clarissa commented. "Right, as soon as we have the data." She paused a moment to review her notes. "Did Mr. Hertford agree to your talking with the teacher, Miss Ankers?"

"We didn't get into that, but she will have to be consulted. Marvin may have a preference where. If I accompany him, she may want an attorney."

"Does the school system have one?"

"Yes, but in this case with two students and conflicting stories and the clout heavy on one side, she may decide on her own attorney. And Marvin doesn't have in mind waiting around for a lot of bureaucracy."

"I'll get back to some paperwork if that covers what we know at this point. And, thanks for drawing me into this. It may be about high school students, but the consequences could be far-reaching for the school and the particular scholarship, as well as the families involved, especially the Hertfords." She was at the door when she turned and looked back at Joseph. "Could we get a photo of the boys involved?"

"I can ask. Why?"

"It would be helpful to identify them. Who knows, one of us might go to a basketball game and pick up some information?" She smiled.

His face, at first puzzled, broke into a grin. "I'll be damned. You have a conniving streak. I'll avoid that approach. Let's both go. The Littlegates have been after me to come to one of Sam's games. He mostly sits on the bench this year. This might be one way to question without sounding official. Pray these fellows play ball, or are in the band."

"Or fans cheering their team on. Ruth might have some slants. Didn't Mitch's son make the team?" She stood with her hand still on the doorknob.

"He did. Ginny will be there, and Mitch if he can possibly make it. I'll call him and find out when the next game will be." He picked up the phone.

She smiled at him and left the room with the door slightly ajar as he usually kept it.

Saturday morning Clarissa took a break from tasks and sat down to rest her body and let her mind wander. The cases before them at the office had been demanding, and she had been working off some pent-up energy.

Outside her study window, the sunshine was bright, the breeze gentle and intermittent. Staring, her mind free of thought, shadows of willow oak branches against the neighbors' east wall caught her attention. The movement was graceful and she watched the shadows changing shape.

After a while, she was unaware of time; the shapes began to take a pattern. As they moved back and forward, she yielded her imagination to the picture. The wall had become like a puppet stage, the shadows of two full-leafed branches the puppets. The left shape took the profile form of a female with shoulder length hair and a flared skirt, while the right shape became more masculine with a pronounced nose and chin. Neither shape had legs. The two faced each other with sunshine blazoned on the wall between them. The wind ruffled the trees and the figures moved toward each other. Briefly. A shift occurred. The right leaned backward, the left moved forward. The profiles touched briefly, before breezes blew them apart. The shadow puppets repositioned, as if anticipating another forward pull. The sequence of contact and disengagement continued, and she began to see herself as the female and Jarvis as the male behaving so similar to their partings. The space below the chin was always there.

A third image crept onto the wall far right. It was somewhat distorted and more active than the other two. It contorted and stretched into a semblance of a human form. What appeared to be a narrow leg, thrust toward the back of the male puppet, and projected a foot that continued growing. Its movement was unsuccessful as it awkwardly reached for the male shape. The pattern of the first two puppets continued: Breezes blowing them together. Face to face, lips to lips.

Clarissa focused on the third figure that had no distinguishing features, yet she intuited it was a man, and attempted to identify him. She interpreted his actions to be interfering with the male, perhaps to trip him. The trunk of the body was large or may have appeared so with possibly a cloaked arm extended. She mused whether or not that was a purposeful disguise or her lack of identification.

He would not be someone she had known before, she reasoned, for he was in the scene here in Windermere. Could it represent a man she had met here or was it a mystery person yet to be on stage?

The phone rang and she chatted for a quarter of an hour. When she returned, the wall was bright and blank – only sunshine bathed its surface.

Ah! So much for weighting shadows with dramatic riddles.

After lunch she took a long walk and stopped a few times to chat with neighbors. She sat for a while on a bench in the park and noticed that azaleas were heavily budded. Many early bulbs had finished blossoming, leaving only their green foliage spearing the clumps along the paths; whereas, in other beds short stems bore still tightly sheathed buds waiting for longer sunny days to show their petals in glorious color. The scene held promise of growth and beauty for the later spring. Even the air added a touch of a pleasant scent of pine. The new growth must surely be emitting oxygen to the air, she acknowledged and took a deep breath.

Refreshed, she briskly walked back to half-house and resumed her chores. She had the evening to look forward to and the company of Jarvis at dinner.

During the evening after an especially delicious meal, Clarissa and Jarvis lingered at the table savoring coffee and exchanging pleasantries. When the waiter approached and asked if they wanted coffee refills, he held his hand up.

"No, thank you."

Clarissa shook her head. The waiter placed the ticket on the table and departed.

"A fourth cup could keep us both awake." Jarvis's eyes twinkled.

Jarvis drove them to Hillside Street. The night was unseasonably warm. Neither was in a hurry and sauntered up the front steps and across the porch to Clarissa's entrance to her half-house. He opened and held the storm door while she moved forward to unlock the inside door. She had just inserted the key when his beeper sounded. Backing against the door, he withdrew his cell phone and punched in some numbers.

Clarissa unlocked the door, pocketed the key, and turned to lean on the door. Jarvis, listening to the caller, took a step toward her, with his back still supporting the storm door. Unexpectedly, the tension of the door moved him forward, smack against her, as close as they'd ever been.

He became slightly unbalanced. She gulped, recovered and reached over to steady him. Then she laughed and turned her head aside. He struggled not to do likewise and succeeded.

Saying into the phone, "I'll be there in a few minutes," he pressed power-off and replaced the phone in his pocket. As he looked at her, there was no sign of his usual light humor; instead, there was a hint of exasperation. Within seconds though, his expression switched into one of decisiveness.

"You're too luscious to leave, my dear. Not what I had hoped to do so early. A rain check goes with this short inspection," he promised and lifted her chin.

The kiss was firm, warm and moist. Caught between two doors at their backs, the contact was close, pressing, and difficult to back away from.

"Sorry about this early departure. Shall we call it an electronic interference?" he asked and walked away.

Savoring her lips, she stated too softly to be heard. "Or a providential pause."

She closed and locked the door. For a brief time, she glowed as a woman who had been enthusiastically kissed, been short-changed, then frowned as one who recalled a dream or image debating whether she had a clue as to a mysterious third shadow. Could it be an unknown person covertly lurking with a beeper?

CHAPTER 26

The rush of the morning was beginning to make itself known to Clarissa Bentley. A throbbing in her temples was a forewarning of a headache. As the elevator doors opened on the first floor in the courthouse, she exited and turned left toward the coffee service area. She dispensed a cup of strong coffee and took it to a rear table in the snack section. Not wanting to call attention to herself or to show any signs of a physical problem, she opened her legal pad and stared at the data recently noted.

Her mind was pulling up information that Joseph had shared with her of the Hertfords' first visit, what the guidance counselor and teachers had given with much reservation, and how some of Sidney and Zack's classmates had viewed the two boys. Her eyes didn't hold the notes in focus, so Clarissa was more in tune with remembering words she had heard than deciphering her written configurations.

Her name was spoken several times before she was aware someone was standing nearby. A level, sideways glance revealed a large brown, leather shoulder bag with cursive *BC* in bold, brass letters. It was slung over a stylish tan all-weather coat. Inwardly, Clarissa groaned. She knew to whom those hallmarks belonged. Before looking up, she cautioned her spirit and tongue to be pleasant, for the coffee had not had time to ease her pain.

"Miss Bentley, uh, Clarissa?" Breear spoke. "Do you have a minute?"

"Hello, Breear. Yes. Will you sit down?" Clarissa answered politely.

"Thank you. I hope I'm not interrupting you," Breear said, settling her bag then herself on the seat opposite Clarissa.

Closing the folder, she said no then waited for Breear to continue.

"I'm keeping an eye out for my cameraman," she said and glanced around the area. "This is exciting work, being an attorney."

"And often routine. Are you covering a particular case today?"

"We were scheduled to, but it has been postponed until tomorrow. Someone is ill." Breear paused, looking directly at Clarissa. "Could I ask you about Washington?"

"Yes. I'm not sure how I can help you. I came here from Virginia."

Nervously rushing her words, Breear said, "But you have worked there and have been associated with a major law firm."

"I started with the firm in Washington and later was assigned to another of its offices."

"Did you go into Washington for dinners, cultural events or shopping?" Breear spoke as if she were ad-libbing.

"Yes. Exactly what do you want to know?" Clarissa said curtly, her headache besting her usual code of courtesy.

Breear withdrew her notebook from her bag and leaned forward. "Do you like the city? Is it a fun place to live? Meeting people, is that easy?"

Clarissa leaned back. "Washington is an exciting city. It's one of the hubs of the world. There are fun things to do there, yes. If you have a demanding job and you're just learning to master it, time is short for after-hours events. Later, one gets to know the scene and chooses whatever appeals."

"Is living there expensive?"

"Most people say it is. Do you mind if I ask you a question?"

"No. Please do."

"Are you planning a trip up there or a move?"

Breear flushed and looked away as if searching for someone. Turning to face Clarissa, she answered. "Maybe go there to look around. Who knows when the media bosses will shuffle the personnel? Can you tell me a good hotel somewhere central? Not too pricey, but not a one star either." She opened her notebook ready to write.

"If you're driving, check the motor clubs. They can plan your route and help you with accommodations near your Washington destinations. Or you can buy guide books at most bookstores for the city you're interested in." Clarissa watched as Breear jotted a few lines in her notebook. Knowing she had said nothing unusual, she was curious if Breear had really asked what she sat down to learn.

"And what is the law firm you worked with?" Breear kept her eyes on the notebook and her pen poised above it. As Clarissa said the name twice, Breear wrote then asked who was her boss there and how did she get her job? She continued to write the short answers. Next, she posed, "Do you expect to be returning to Washington or Virginia?"

Clarissa studied the younger girl, wondering if the last question, or rather its answer, was her primary quest. "At this moment, I have no plans to leave Windermere."

"Do you go back to visit the city? Do you have any relatives there?" Breear stabbed somewhat as afterthoughts.

"Sometimes, I visit. My brother lives there." Not knowing why, Clarissa added that he manages a department store in Washington.

"Oh!" she looked up. "That's a well-known shopping Mecca. What's his name?"

"Ralph." She watched Breear write that down.

A young man walked hurriedly toward the booth. He stopped beside Breear. "Here you are. I got your message. We've got another assignment." He lowered his voice and leaned over the table. "A fire on the south side."

Breear closed her notebook and shoved it and the pen back into the bag and stood. Energy and enthusiasm surged as she thanked Clarissa for the tips. "See you around." Walking close beside the cameraman, Breear asked him for the details keeping her voice low. The word "fire" could cause instant panic if overheard.

Clarissa decided to take a couple of aspirin with her last swallow of coffee. She was still curious as to why Breear had sought her out or sat with her. With her head aching, she dropped the muddle and picked up her file.

Footsteps approached the table and suddenly stopped. A familiar voice spoke her name. This time she saw Samuel Littlegate looming tall beside her and just behind him stood Mitch Rockford, also a tall guy.

"Were you just being interviewed for the evening news?" He indicated down the hall where Breear and the cameraman had headed.

"Hello. Being quizzed perhaps, but not interviewed. Good morning, Mitch." She looked at both men.

Samuel humorously said, "You don't even suspect our good preacher is in trouble, do you?" Samuel's smile remained while his tone became more objective. "Mitch is here to support a youth."

Mitch stepped closer to the table. Clarissa said, "That's good of you. The family will appreciate your doing so. Are you having coffee?" She looked at both of them.

"Down here?" Samuel's jolliness returned. "Doesn't the lawyers' snack room have better coffee and more comfortable seats?"

"Samuel!" Harry Wooten, walking from the elevators called out. "Could I speak with you a minute?" He waved to Clarissa and Mitch.

Samuel met Harry mid-hall and Mitch eased into the seat across from Clarissa. He commented. "So Breear joined you for coffee."

"It was convenient for her to sit here while waiting for the cameraman. I don't know what she really wanted."

"Asked a lot of questions?" Mitch looked closely at Clarissa, who was tenser than he had seen her.

"Yes. In fact, she asked me if I had plans to leave Windermere." Her tone was close to hard.

"Oh? Is that a possibility?" His forehead wrinkled.

Clarissa moved her file folder about. "No. I think not."

"Have you talked with Joseph? Oh, not about leaving. Just talked with him?"

Now, she furrowed her brow. "I talk with him daily. Are you

thinking of some particular topic?"

"Well, other than office matters."

Carefully, she said, "Not any that I can think of. Mitch, does he appear anxious about something to you? Or depressed? Maybe, 'not settled' is a better term."

"He has a number of things on his mind. I thought he might have talked with you."

"Does one of them concern Breear?" She asked directly.

Mitch shifted on the hard bench and put his elbows on the table. "I really wasn't thinking of her. Why?"

"Mitch, you're his friend. You've seen them together." He stared at her. "Is something going wrong between them? If so, he wouldn't likely tell me." She rubbed her temples.

Mitch expressed compassion. "You must have a headache. Sorry if I added to it. Don't worry about their relationship." He reached a hand across the table but didn't touch her. "Trust me, Clarissa. Breear has been good for Joseph. I've known him a long time so I can say that. She's helped him get in touch with his emotions again. I never had a finer youth to work with. He was involved in so many activities, high-spirited, loyal, a good guy and a hard worker."

Instantly she quipped. "I know the latter."

Samuel rejoined them. "Well, Mitch are you ready to ride up and seek our man?"

Mitch rose and said, "I am." He turned and softly spoke to Clarissa. "Hang in there. He needs our support. And did I say, you are good for him, too?"

As the two men boarded the elevator, she tossed her empty cup in the trash container then scurried from the courthouse. Surprisingly, her headache was abating and it was time to return to the office.

At Price Tower Joseph got off the elevator on the sixth floor. Immediately, he recognized the short, squared figure standing in front of the first office in the left corridor: It was Pug Avery, who was holding his head very still and his left hand cupped beneath his right hand that was painstakingly brushing a letter on the door. Joseph stopped a few feet away.

"Eh, would that be you Joseph McBaden? I'll be finished gilding the name with another stroke or two." Pug said quietly out of one side of his mouth.

Joseph mused that painters may not stand very close to their work or breathe heavily to prevent excessive moisture on the work surface. "Are you psychic?, Mr. Avery."

"Not a smidgen. You are a soft-walking man. And this is your floor." He answered then stood back and scrutinized the lettering. "Finished," he announced with surety, wiped his brush and turned toward Joseph. "How're you liking your office?"

"Fine. And your work is going right along," Joseph nodded toward the door. "This is the last one on the hall, I believe."

"Are you about ready for me to add some names to your suite?" The sign painter continued to put away his supplies.

"Not yet."

"What about that fine-looking lassie who works with you? The talk is she's smart. Left a topnotch firm to come down here," he noted while closing his case.

"No partnership is in the works. How is the sign traffic downtown?"

"You mean Hadley Morgan and their slew of lawyers? You know they have changes on a pretty regular basis. Men in, men out. Course now, all of them don't get their names on doors, but if one leaves and his name *was* on a door, then that has to come off. Sometimes, it messes up the whole shebang and that means a heap of gold names to remove and reorder."

"Well, I'm glad to know you are staying busy," Joseph said and started to walk on.

"That new fellow who has some of your old clients doesn't seem too happy over there. Maybe you'll be looking for a new hand soon. He might be a good one." Pug scratched the bald area of his head then swooped his hand over the halo-like fringe of red hair.

"You hear a lot of news through those office doors," said Joseph.

"Yeap. Especially when they are ajar. Even standing in line for the elevators. Yeap, Grant Addison has the work piled up; and sitting right on top of it, he hears how quick that other fellow – that being yourself, Mr. McBaden – worked through the pile."

Pug walked with Joseph to his office and faced it saying, "That name appears mighty handsome up there. Reckon it needs another name or two. You know, Bentley is from the British Isles, well to be more exact, it's from Old English. Means 'from the moor.' And Breear, with one *e*, is French and translates to 'heather.'"

"I didn't know your specialty was the origin of names." Joseph opened his door.

"Just curious. I painted so many that I took to looking them up. Do you know what Joseph stands for?"

"It's from the Bible," Joseph said in a worn tone and stepped inside the office.

"He shall add." Pug nodded with a twinkle in his eye, turned and retraced his steps toward the elevators.

Joseph closed the door. "Gretchen, is Miss Bentley back?"

"Yes, sir. A few minutes ago."

He stopped at Clarissa's door, which was open, and knocked. She was unpacking her briefcase and looked up.

"Did you find any mention of the boys in the records?" he asked.

"Nothing on either boy. No traffic citations. No misdemeanors."

"That's good news. Will you type that up and we'll put it in the file."

"Yes. Do you have a few minutes for me to go over something with you?"

"Come in whenever you're ready," he said and walked to his own office.

When Clarissa entered Joseph's office, she had a file folder. Sitting in the chair opposite his, she opened the folder.

"This matter is really routine. The client could easily take care of this herself, but she called and asked if I could do it for her. It's an intellectual property filing."

He leaned forward and stared at her. "So?"

"This being your concentration, you may want to handle it." She leveled her gaze with his.

"Tell me about it."

"She is Reba Logan, a professor at a college here. During the past few years she formatted a set of lesson plans that she thinks could be textbook material. Perhaps a small volume by itself. She thinks registering the copyright would be the first step."

He sighed. "Before the Hertford case I would say tell her to get a manual from a library, and her college probably has one, and save a few bucks by filling out a form herself. But now, well, maybe she's right."

"Do you want to take it, or should I?"

Joseph thought a minute, swiveled his chair then faced her again. "You can handle it."

Clarissa sensed his struggle with this minor matter. Kindly, she said, "She has had a number of students in her class and there are many, who probably still have her notes. Some of her students have become teachers. It is a possibility one of them could write a book someday, refer to his or her notes and forget the material was presented and organized by Miss Logan."

"And she'll need the copyright if she has to prove infringement down the road. Timing is important, isn't it?" His question had a far-away sound as if he were considering more than this matter in front of them.

Clarissa pushed her chair backward and began to rise when Joseph spoke again, still in somewhat distant tones. "This is the season for student cases. Oddly enough, I had a grad student approach me yesterday as I left the law library." He looked across at Clarissa and she sat down again.

"He caught me at the door and asked if he may walk and confer. This is his story. This week he was tutoring an underclassman who was reading from a new textbook in psychology. One of the authors of the text is the student's teacher. This young grad fellow had the same professor. As they were reviewing a chapter, the grad found it was very familiar. He could almost quote the material without reading.

"The tutee, quizzically, glanced sideways at him. He joked the moment off saying 'Oh, you'll be able to recite lots of this later.' Well, as soon as the grad returned to his apartment, he rummaged among his old psyche notes and papers and found his final paper. It was the same as part of the chapter he had read in the textbook.

"Thinking back over that course, which was in his second semester as a sophomore, he recalled that some students had been asked to sign a statement that their material could be used in a textbook later. Grad student had not attended that final lecture. Said he had to finish work on another project. And he was never asked to sign anything."

Joseph paused and Clarissa asked, "Did he check the textbook against his paper?"

"He did. In the bookstore. The next day, he asked the tutee if he could borrow the textbook and copy a few pages. With an okay he did that. Copied the chapter that included his own material, the title page, publication information, and table of contents page with this professor's name, and finally the bio sketch of the professor. He was at the university the year grad was a sophomore."

"Does the grad student consider that it was an oversight?"

"Oversight?"

Clarissa restated the question. "The prof thought he had asked all the students for permission to include or refer to any work that had been handed in. Or could he have had an assistant who was responsible for checking permission signatures against papers?"

Joseph stretched his arms high overhead, brought them down and clasped the edges of his swivel chair. He leaned back then answered. "He doesn't know. Whatever the reason grad wanted to talk to us first."

"Meaning before he confronted the prof?"

"Right. Things have changed since my day. If we had a puzzle, we went to the professor and asked straight out. Perhaps we thought the man controlled his own class and course. Today, students may be more aware of the vulnerability of teachers and the teachers' anxiety for keeping their positions."

"The grad hadn't registered his paper?"

"No. It's not a step they usually have a need for. The registering process does take some time and students are often in short supply of that," Joseph noted.

"So he doesn't have prima facie evidence. And to be considered an infringement of the work and to get statutory damages, grad student would have had to register the work within three months of publication. The textbook was probably printed before that time." Clarissa surmised.

"From the grad's comments it sounds as if what was used of his work had been used verbatim. And that would have been easier to prove. This late, he has only the possibility of being awarded actual damages and profits. And the judge sets statutory damages."

Clarissa watched the furrows of his brow deepen and his eyes peering beyond anything in the office. Concern showed in his face and manner.

"Will you help him?" She asked quietly.

"We will. It may be this is where we can come in, the student years, and help sort out some problems. Can we find some non-violent, non-destructive paths that will speak to other students today and those who will follow? Show legal and acceptable routes without having to go to court? Or without costing so much that neither students nor parents can afford an education? And be fair to all parties." Joseph gazed directly at her.

"Did you expect anything like the three cases we have before us now, when you decided to delve into intellectual property law?"

He tilted his head back and laughed. "No, Miss Bentley. I worked in a sophisticated environment and with the most sophisticated men; thus, I never thought that we'd be asked to hobnob with clients who were in the throes of knowledge gathering, let alone, some not even in the salaried market."

She joined his lighter approach to the matters at hand. "It doesn't increase the credit side of your ledger, does it?"

"No." He shook his head and smiled. "But you know what, I feel needed at a critical time for these young folks."

"And fortunately, one of the youths has a parent with means

to see his case through."

"And you, how do you feel about aiding the teacher?" He quizzed.

"As you, I feel I can help someone. Perhaps it will only be to give her comfort-support. A protection before she needs it. Now, I should go and tackle some of these pathways you spoke of."

After she left, Joseph stared at the empty doorway, wondering how much that long-term relationship cost her – or how much she profited. Whatever, he was relieved that she did not appear in financial difficulties.

CHAPTER 27

The office was unusually quiet for late afternoon. Joseph was working his way through a stack of mail and faxes, jotting notes on a legal pad, concentrating as best he could. In her office, Clarissa was reviewing a defendant's first set of interrogatories and her client's replies and handwritten listing of property and financial assets and indebtedness.

Gretchen was engrossed with typing a number of cover letters to be mailed with packets that day. At 4:30 P.M., Gretchen answered the phone then buzzed Joseph that Marvin Hertford was on the line. He picked up the receiver. "Hello."

"Joseph, my wife and I are going to dinner tonight at the Plaza at seven o'clock. You mentioned that you dine there occasionally. Do you recommend it?"

"Yes. The menu is varied and every selection I've tried has been quite good."

"Fine. Perhaps you'll be there tonight, and your Miss Bentley? I hear she is a very capable addition to your staff."

Joseph thought quickly. "Yes, I had thought of going there. I have just asked Clarissa, that's Miss Bentley, to join me. Could you hold a moment? She went back to her office to check her calendar."

"I'll hold."

Joseph tapped Clarissa's extension on the intercom. She picked up. "Marvin Hertford is on the other line. He wants us to have dinner tonight at seven at the Plaza. Can you make it?"

"I can."

"Thanks," he said, clicked off and picked up again on the other line. "Marvin, we'll be there."

"I have a table for two, but we shall look forward to seeing you."

Joseph walked over to Clarissa's room. She looked up from the papers on the desk. "Come in." She waited for him to explain the call.

"An unusual conversation. He is a guarded man even on his cell phone. He and Mrs. Hertford will eat at seven at a table for two and looks forward to seeing us there. I trust this late arrangement didn't interfere with other plans?"

"It's okay. Should we assume he has something timely to share with us?"

"That's my take on it."

"He wouldn't be objecting to my helping you, or anyone assisting you?"

"Not likely. This is a matter with a deadline. And the quicker it can be resolved, the fewer people will know about it." He was reflective. "He spoke of the capable Miss Bentley. Could he object to someone with that qualification?"

She laughed. "Then I must commit to memory the facts and the personalities." She waved her hand over the papers on the desktop. "No matter how insignificant a notation may appear at first reading, it could well be the very one he will bring into the conversation."

"Well, I shall leave you to your review."

Clarissa's expression slid into a question. "Should I change before dinner?" She surveyed her blouse and skirt.

"Miss Bentley, you always look classy, like your namesake." Joseph nodded and left.

Sitting back in her chair, it struck her it was the first compliment he had given her since she walked into his office. Silently, she offered a thank you, kind sir, even if you did compare me to a car.

When she finished reviewing her notes, she clipped them together and inserted them in a folder, which she filed in her cabinet. She made a quick decision to join the five o'clock exodus from the offices and change clothes at half-house. Poking her head in McBaden's doorway, she told him she'd be back around six thirty and suggested he consider making a reservation.

He fretted but she had already exited and didn't see. After locating the number of the restaurant, he pushed buttons and reserved a table for two. He continued to work another hour before washing his face and shaving his light beard. From a drawer below the lavatory, he withdrew a fresh white shirt. After putting it on and tying his tie, he combed his hair. He folded the worn shirt and put it in his briefcase. He poured a glass of water and stood beside his office window.

The evening was dark. The cars below looked like models and their headlights like silent megaphones – translucent projections of light. Going home time. And to what were all these travelers returning? Warm hearths, fires in the fireplace, odors of supper cooking, the sounds of laughter, a dog barking? Or would many be like him if he were going directly home tonight? A cold house, darkness, no sounds, no aromas, and a lot of emptiness. But did any of this matter to him? He shook his head. He ate out most evenings, the house could be warmed in winter, or cooled in summer with a touch of the thermostat; and it would be bright and light instantly with a flip of a switch. What was there to question? There was a briefcase full of work for company any evening.

He finishing drinking the water and took his glass to the coffee area. He checked that the coffee machine was switched off and all was in order.

The outer door opened and Clarissa entered. Joseph noticed that she was dressed differently. She wore a matching outfit he had not seen before. It was a long jacket-type coat over a longer one-piece dress, which was just knee-length. The deep green color was attractive, being both restful and refreshing. She had combed her hair behind her ears and put on emerald earrings and pinned a modern broach on the jacket. She carried a small handbag. The effect was stunning, yet appropriate for dinner out.

McBaden breathed deeply; glad he had changed shirts.

They walked hurriedly across the street to the restaurant for the stiff breeze was cold, blowing off a front from Canada. Stepping into the warm and crowded reception area, they were doubly pleased they had a table waiting.

As they were placing their order, McBaden spotted the Hertfords being shown a table in an adjacent area. He gave no sign of recognition. In a few minutes, he said quietly to Clarissa, "The Hertfords have been seated. Upper level to your left. We'll let him make any overture."

She followed McBaden's lead. After all, it was a business arrangement, this dinner for two in a charming and comfortable establishment that offered a varied menu of well-cooked, attractively served dishes in an attentive manner. Any people watchers among the diners would notice the poised lady, stylishly dressed and perfectly groomed, was politely focusing her attention on her dinner companion and consuming the beverages and foods before her with gracious manners. And the companion was doing likewise. Their conversation was quiet and intermittent.

While the waiter was clearing their table, Breear was following a hostess and two other women through the room. Breear stopped. "Why hello, Joseph and Clarissa."

She leaned back as the waiter hoisted the dish-loaded tray and made his way toward the kitchen. "Clarissa, what's a good restaurant near the Washington Times office? For a friend going up." She fished her notebook from the front of the shoulder bag then placed it and a pen on the table in front of Clarissa.

Clarissa reached into her own handbag and withdrew a small notepad and pen and wrote a name. She heard Breear asking Joseph about his day tomorrow and an appointment. Breear watched Clarissa slide the paper on top of the notebook. She picked up the items and tucked them inside the bag.

"Thank you," Breear said brightly. "Well, I don't want to keep you. And my friends may wonder where I stopped. It's a birthday celebration for our programmer who keeps us on schedule." She spotted the waiter returning with two cups of coffee. She looked toward Joseph. "It is a good night for hot coffee, especially if you have lots of work to finish." She smiled and walked toward the table where her friends were seated.

Joseph saw her take her notebook from her bag and pause to jot a few lines.

Clarissa listened to Breear's parting words and noticed the absence of a touching gesture on Joseph. Without staring, she watched his eyes, which followed Breear then quickly dropped toward the tablecloth; he straightened it and the coffee spoon. When the coffee was set upon the smoothed fabric, he thanked the waiter without looking directly at him. She poured cream into her cup and held it forward with the handle toward him. Joseph took the pitcher, still holding his spoon tightly. His mouth tensed. Putting the pitcher aside, his eyes darted right where the Hertfords had been seated. They were not in sight.

As Clarissa and Joseph were drinking after-dinner coffee in silence, the Hertfords approached the table.

Marvin, walking behind his wife, stopped. "Dear!" She paused and turned around. "I want you to meet a friend of mine. Joseph McBaden, this is my wife Tricia."

Joseph stood and shook hands with Marvin. "I'm pleased to meet you Mrs. Hertford. Clarissa Bentley, this is Tricia and Marvin Hertford. Clarissa is my associate."

"Was that the Channel Six reporter?" Marvin asked first looking at Clarissa, next at Joseph with a more worried expression.

Clarissa picked up on the concern. "Yes. Breear Callum. She's not on a story tonight."

Marvin turned to her. "Oh?"

With a smile, Clarissa said, "She wanted the name of a restaurant I had recommended in Washington"

"Is she moving up there?" Marvin followed up.

Clarissa added. "Channel Six is owned by a media conglomerate that has stations in many states along the East Coast and has interests in D.C."

"She is an attractive young lady," Tricia noted. "Very articulate and energetic."

Joseph commented. "She covered some trials when she first came. We met in the courthouse. Just then she stopped by the table to chat with Clarissa, but she also was checking that I would have time for a friend of hers. A journalist on *his* way to Washington. He will be in town briefly tomorrow."

With a trace of concern in his voice, Marvin asked, "TV journalist?"

"I understand," said Joseph, "that he's a print journalist and a reporter with a Columbia, South Carolina, paper while he's getting his master's."

Marvin appeared relieved. "Well, he's tapping some good sources here."

"His parents are in California and keep primarily to West Coast and their state news. Being east, his interests have been whetted for a broader view. He's eager to learn more about government, federal as well as California and South Carolina," Joseph offered.

Marvin replied. "It's good he has someone he can talk his interests with. Maybe give him a recommendation."

"I don't know him well enough for the latter."

"I appreciate a successful attorney taking time with young men other than being involved with their misdemeanors, such as traffic violations." Marvin concluded.

Tricia had been looking at Clarissa as if she recognized her. "Have we met somewhere recently? At some function perhaps?"

Clarissa gazed more intently. "I think perhaps we were introduced at one of the medical functions. Or at another one with Jarvis Randolph."

"That's right. He's a good-looking man. I hear he's a fine doctor. Ruth Littlegate was there. She told me of your good taste in decorating the Price Tower offices and your house in the Historic District."

"Well, thank you."

"She liked your design for the downstairs draperies. Would it be an imposition if I asked you to come take a look at my dining room? The windows are a puzzle."

"Not at all. I'd be delighted to. Let me know when would be

convenient for you."

"How about tomorrow afternoon?"

Clarissa gave a cursory glance at Joseph before answering. "Tomorrow will be fine. Would four o'clock be suitable?"

"Perfect, my dear. I look forward to seeing you. We're on Timberland Drive, number 270."

The Hertfords departed.

Joseph said, "Thanks for the rescue. Marvin was fishing about Breear."

"You cinched it with the bit about the male journalist." Clarissa said and noticed Joseph's frustration.

Mid-morning the following day, the office was fairly quiet. Gretchen handled the phone calls, mail and package deliveries, and a minimum of foot-traffic business without having to interrupt Joseph or Clarissa. At ten thirty, Clarissa put on her coat and popped across the hall. "Joseph, I'm running over to an electronic store in the shopping center." She turned around as she heard the outer office door open. A young man entered. "This may be your journalist. He's not someone I recognize."

"Thank you," he said somewhat strained. Clarissa scanned him quickly, surprised at his manner. Even when he was busy or pushed for time on a legal matter or gathering data for a conference, Joseph rarely showed signs of tension that bordered on personal involvement.

As she slowly walked down the hallway, she wondered if this conference was problematic because of Breear's friendship with the young man or the matter that the journalist brought himself. In pulling on her gloves, he almost passed her before she realized he was approaching. She caught only a glimpse of him and tried to recall who he resembled. As he entered Joseph's office, she turned slightly to see the two shake hands like old friends who were comfortable with each other. She continued on her way, comparing this picture with the image of Joseph's anxiety a minute ago.

Closing the door, Joseph asked Sutton to have a seat and took his usual place behind the desk. "Breear tells me you're on your way to Washington."

"I am. There are a couple of positions open up there. The department head was aware of both of them, and I checked the school's placement office for details. They look like good possibilities." Sutton sat back easily into the straight chair.

"Do you have interviews lined up?"

"I do. One tomorrow morning and one early afternoon." Slightly shaking his head while grinning, he said, "No need to say I'm excited and apprehensive."

Sutton talked on about his professors and their advice and of what the two jobs involved. The more he revealed about his ambitions, the closer he leaned toward the desk with his elbows on the chair arms and his hands clasped, fingers overlapping. Joseph closely watched Sutton, assessing him personally and all he was saying. The revelations of his dreams, the correlation of his upbringing, his talents, his achievements and disappointments to date drew Joseph into camaraderie equal to any he'd ever experienced.

When he finished, Sutton's expression was one of amazement. He tossed his hands up, sat back and relaxed. "I can't believe I just said all that. Man, I feel better."

"Good. Now go into those interviews knowing what *you* want. But keep in focus what they ask for. Somewhere in between the wants and needs, you'll reach an accord."

"I can't thank you enough for letting me impose on your time. This is just great. Talking with someone who is successful, who knows what I'm talking about and who also knows what's going on beyond where he is. Dad is great, too; but, as I told you before, he's narrowly focused. He's happy and for him that's okay." He stood up in his slow, easy manner. "Well, I must be on my way if I'm to make Washington before the worst of the traffic."

"I wish you well tomorrow." Joseph said as they walked to the door. "Let me know how the interviews go."

"Thank you, sir. I will."

Clarissa was exiting the elevator as Sutton was boarding another. In the office, she paused at Joseph's door. "Hello. How did your conference go?"

"Fine," he answered, scarcely glancing at her.

"Sutton resembles someone I know," she knitted her brows as if trying to bring up a name. "It will come to me," she said.

Joseph kept his head down and attention on his papers. She pulled off her gloves and moved on.

At noon Joseph met Mitchell at Maple Street Café. The small restaurant was busy. They were shown to a booth near the back. The clientele included people working or shopping in the small business area and some nearby residents. Joseph spotted no attorneys.

After dispensing with pleasantries, Joseph inquired about resources for information of high school students. Specifically, he wanted to know any students who had their fingers on the pulse of who might be in trouble, or who had feuds brewing. He assured Mitch that he expected no divulgence of information learned in his ministerial capacity, and that two particular students he was interested in were not in his congregation.

"There are two senior guys involved in a matter that I'm looking into. This is being handled as quietly as possible. No one is thinking lawsuit, just trying to get to the truth so that reputations are not blighted."

"What are the interests of the two students? Are they active in sports or clubs? If we can narrow the focus, know where to start, getting some leads will be quicker."

"Time is important here. Something occurred at the end of the first semester and it needs to be dealt with as soon as possible. Your help will be appreciated."

"I've noticed the seniors are restless and unsettled until they hear from college admissions offices." Mitch drank his coffee and looked at Joseph.

Joseph nodded. "Dead right."

After lunch Joseph checked public records for Zack Eaton's parents, then drove by Mr. Eaton's business and the family's residence. The business was in a rented building, neat and well maintained on the exterior in an older section of town. The home was on a side street in a middle-class neighborhood on the edge of the school district that kids from upscale families attended. Joseph drove to the end of the block, made a U turn, and viewed the yard for signs of the occupants' interests. The only one was a basketball goal at the end of the driveway. No cars parked outside. While the property and house passed general inspection, Joseph noted that the shrubbery was overgrown, hiding the front and side windows, and that the house could use a coat of paint. That appeared the general condition of the residences in this block.

Returning to the office, he buzzed Clarissa and asked if she could come in for a brief conference about the Hertfords. Before she entered, he jotted notes about his impressions of the Eatons and entered the time on his calendar.

"I noticed a basketball goal outside the Eatons' house. I'll ask Mitch to check if his boys know Zack. Also, could you check the local sports microfiche or computer files, whichever are available at the library, for any mention of Zack? Thanks. How was your trip to the Hertfords?" He leaned forward with a fresh page of his legal pad topmost and a pen in hand.

"Bottom line. It's no more secure than anyone's house with children in and out. There's a full-time maid so it wouldn't be easy for a stranger to walk in and have a run of the place. But it is possible to enter and search a targeted room if you really want to. If a person is not a frequent visitor to the house and asked to come in for whatever reason, his appearance would be reported to the Hertfords. If a group of Sidney's friends were in the house socializing, it's possible one could leave the group and wander upstairs and rifle his desk, run a computer program or copy a disc, granted he knew the equipment and what he was looking for."

"Or would recognize some data that could be useful to him." Joseph added.

"Sidney came home while I was there, and I asked him to tell me dates when Zack may have been in the house with him. I asked him specifically whether or not Zack had been interested in his computer or his room in general; that's where the computer is."

"Did he remember Zack's being there?"

"Once. A group had come back to his house after a late-afternoon meeting at school. He thought that Zack had been one of the guys interested in seeing his new computer. But Sidney left the room for some reason he doesn't remember. He does feel certain he returned to shut down the computer and saw nothing unusual before the group left the house. Some were going for pizza and one or two others had jobs to go to. Zack was one of the latter.

"Mrs. Hertford showed me the last two high school yearbooks. She had already inserted bookmarks where Zack was featured. He appears to be in many of the same activities as Sidney. Mrs. Hertford says she knows who he is because she has attended activities Sidney has been involved in throughout his schooling."

"Did she say," Joseph asked, "that Zack had ever come to the house by himself?"

"I asked her, but she said no. In fact, he has only been there twice that she knew of."

"Um." Joseph mused.

"Sidney showed me and his mother the computer. He brought up the poem and printed a copy for me. I asked if he had saved it on a floppy also. He said no. Therefore, if Zack did locate the poem, run a copy, but didn't save it, there'd be no record of it. No timed recording on his hard drive."

"Did you check his computer for a time entry?"

"We did. It recorded the date as September 28 last year. And Sidney keeps a box of new floppy disks beside the monitor. One more point of interest is that Sidney and his brother each have their own password, so it could be a challenge for someone who wanted to snoop."

"Well, that date is good; maybe not strong evidence but it's a start."

"I learned something very interesting at the electronic shop." She told him what the manager, a skilled technician, had explained to her. "We'll have to investigate the matter a bit more."

Joseph nodded and rapidly took notes. Finished, he smiled grimly. "You might be on to something. Did this technician appear to be someone who could be called as an expert witness?" She nodded affirmative. He continued, "We need to check out Sidney's computer further. Thanks."

The light blinked on the phone. Joseph picked up. "Yes. Can you hold a minute while I get the folder?"

Clarissa signed that she understood it was a call for him to handle. She left the room, gathered her belongings from the office and headed toward her happy half-house.

CHAPTER 28

The plane rolled slowly along the runway before revving into its final stages for takeoff. Joseph McBaden felt that all the earth's forces were holding back the plane and his westward mission. The scene outside his window moved from the turtle pace to a hare-like hop, suddenly the landscape sloped and eagle wings took over. The plane was airborne. After baring sharply right like a boomerang, the plane climbed then followed a more linear course. The "it's safe to unbuckle your seat belt" light glowed. The mood lightened inside the cabin.

Joseph had splurged for a first-class ticket. He was apprehensive about the trip, more to the point about what he might discover at his destination. He gave his beverage preference to the inquiring stewardess and scarcely remembered drinking it. The empty cup was stashed in the holder by his seat.

He put his head against the seat back and closed his eyes. The memory of his conversations with Mitch during which he had told some of the details of his last high school weeks and of his college days was not totally clear. However, he knew there were some meaningful times he did not share, probably wouldn't, with anyone.

One memory he wished was clearer, just as he wished that particular evening in early December of his senior year, he had not been so weary. The events leading up to it started after study time the night before when he met some of his friends at The Campus Pub and had consumed more alcohol than usual. The next morning outside his classroom door he waited for the girl who was typing his final paper. She came dashing up a few minutes before class started, saying she had run out of ribbon on the typewriter and didn't have a spare last night. It was too late to buy another and no one on the hall had an extra. She had two classes that morning and could not type until afternoon.

He had been near apoplexy, he recalled. Waiting for the professor, he knew he would be ill-received stopping the punctilious man before class. There was no option. As expected, the prof was agitated. He tersely replied he would accept the paper brought to him in person before five o'clock that day in his office.

It was 4:30 P.M. when the typist paper-clipped the original pages together then stapled a copy. Joseph had proofed them as she unfurled them from the typewriter. Fishing the typing fee from his pocket and laying it on her desk with one hand, he opened a file folder, inserted the pages. His daily running served him well that afternoon as he raced across campus and handed his paper over before the deadline. He thanked the professor and apologized for the paper not being ready at class time.

Being stressed and sleep deprived, he made his way to the pub again. He ordered a hamburger, fries and beer. Some friends hailed him and asked if he turned his paper in on time. With minutes to spare, he replied more glibly than he felt. He sank down onto a chair at their table. The foursome one after the other toasted their luck, their joy, their good fortune and their benefits from handing in the last major paper for the semester. Next, they groaned about exams and toasted again.

Finally, Joseph was overcome by a desire to sleep. After bidding his friends goodnight, he picked up the file folder and stumbled to his apartment. The evening was cold and the sweat his body had generated from the overly warm pub was beginning to chill him beneath his jeans and the shirt under his bulky sweater.

He fumbled for his key, dropped the file folder, and swore as he picked it up. Unlocking the door to a dark room, he vaguely remembered his apartment mate had gone home after classes. He didn't switch on the light – all he wanted was to fall into his bed. Opening his bedroom door, he went first to his desk and laid the folder down. He located his chair, sat on some clothes and shoved them backward, and untied his shoes, jerked off those along with socks. His jeans, shirt and sweater he doffed and dropped.

Feeling his way along the edge of the bed, he lifted the covers and slid between the sheets. He turned over and felt a body. Slowly, his hand moved up the shape.

"Joseph, your hand is so cold." Frances declared. She took his hand between hers and rubbed it. "Let me warm them."

"Frances? Are you here?"

"Of course, I'm here. Can't you hear me?" She leaned over, whispered in his ear and kissed it. "Can't you feel me?" And she placed his warmed hand on her waist, then drew his other hand in hers while she moved closer.

"Did I know you were coming?" He asked, somewhat dazed.

"No. I finished my work early and wanted to surprise you. There was no one here. I haven't had much sleep lately. The nap was divine," she purred. "My side of the bed is all warm now. I'll share it with you. I've never known you so chilly, my love."

She scooted a few inches over, released his hand, and pulled him closer.

"God, you feel so real. So warm."

She laughed lightly and hugged him. "I am real and warm."

He murmured, "I haven't showered . . . brushed my teeth."

She sniffed his neck. "I've smelled you in the summer time. Nothing about you turns me off." She kissed his mouth.

There was something in his foggy brain that he wanted to ask Frances, but he couldn't put the words together. She was being so aggressive, more like their first days in this bed, not as she had been the past many months. Frances in this mood was irresistible. He welcomed her as the pursuer because he was so weary and not at his physical peak. Something about the pill he wanted to ask her. Still taking it? They hadn't been in bed like this for . . . how long? Their four years of secrecy were almost over. Are you ready for chances? A distant voice strained a warning. The questions never left him, for ardor overcame words. At the height of their lovemaking, a physical memory probed him, and he began to withdraw; she wouldn't let him and pulled him against her.

Settling on their sides and facing each other, she stretched her arms over her head and curved outward, her legs bent at the knee and feet backward. She returned to a forward crescent, her arms around his head. "Remember, the first evening on the beach? I loved you then, I love you now."

"Honey, you'll be cold. The thermostat is set low."

"Let's pull the covers up to our necks," she murmured softly.

"Pajamas? We're steamed up."

"Stay awhile in our own warmth. After a little snooze, we'll see."

Joseph couldn't truthfully say this account was verbatim. The night had been a highlight of their times together, and he regretted often that he wasn't more than fifty percent alert. He didn't see her again alone until after Christmas. Only a few times after that did they have physical intimacy. As he told Mitch, the final semester for them was pressured, harried and spent apart.

Frances and he did discuss announcing their marriage or perhaps going through another ceremony. They tossed around dates: soon after graduation or next fall before both entered separate schools. And they debated where to set up an apartment. Not reaching any accord at that time seemed okay with both of them. It was years later that he puzzled over why they left those decisions unsettled. He never had another girl and, as far as he knew, she remained loyal to their union.

The one contributor that he could eliminate regarding his fuzziness and lessened physicality was alcohol.

A second similar incident regarding a class was two weeks later.

In contract-law class, Joseph had been called on twice to answer the very exacting professor's question regarding a case the class was discussing. Dr. Hubler was predictable: He never called on the same student more often than twice in a row. He was tough, but he was democratic, giving each a chance to be heard.

So Joseph felt confident he had filled his quota for having a finger pointed at him for "his opinion." He had joined his friends at the pub and stayed late. The next morning, he slept later than usual and had to rush to get to the contract class on time. He raked his hands through his hair, smoothing it down after a windy run across campus. Composing himself while still relaxing more than usual in the hard, wooden seat, he brought up the narrow desk shelf, tilted the top, let it catch securely, and then placed his right arm on it. The professor entered from a door at the front of the room. Joseph reached in his backpack for his book and notes. He was fumbling for the pages concerning the next case, when he heard a deep voice penetrate the air.

"Mr. McBaden, what is your opinion on the contract between . . ."

Surely, he hadn't heard correctly. His still slumbering mind was playing tricks. Joseph looked around to see who was going to answer.

"Again, Mr. McBaden, have you an opinion to share with us? We are waiting."

Following the words was a deadly calm much dreaded in that class. If a student failed to answer a question the second time it was asked, the class could expect iciness so pervasive it burned the atmosphere.

To preserve his self-respect and a learning climate for the class, Joseph spoke the only words that came to him. "Dr. Hubler, I prepared the assignment but did not review my notes last night. May I defer to another student who is better prepared?"

"You may. Mr. Jones, are you prepared?"

After this failure to respond properly in class, he intensified preparing assignments for the remaining week of Professor Hubler's class. In fact, for all his classes and exams. No way could he afford to blow the scholarship at this late date. He'd have to drop out of school. He told Frances about the dilemma of keeping his nose in the books or losing the money for the spring semester. She understood and refrained from making demands of him. He didn't tell his friends, but he didn't hang out with them at the pub anymore.

It was a cold turkey giving up but worth the ordeal and resulting effects, no fuzzy brain and no excuses for being unprepared. He aced Dr. Hubler's class and earned across the second semester courses straight As.

In March, Frances and he were in a pizza parlor near her college dorm. When they ordered, she asked for ginger ale. She told him she too had given up drinking. He recalled jokingly, saying, "Ah! You don't want a fuzzy brain either." She smiled. "No, I don't." And he further remembered how glowing her face was and thought the wholesomeness agreed with her.

The next recollections weren't important to the narrative and remained private. "I reached across the table and squeezed her hand. 'This is a night we should be at my place. There's nowhere here . . .' 'No. In two weeks I'll be over.' She pressed my hand tenderly."

His stay at his western destination was short. Everything about the landscape and weather reflected the information he had received. The first was a view of jagged snow-covered mountains in the distance from both the flat area of the airfield and the center of the city. In full daylight the peaks were sharp spires evincing sunlight vividly against blue gray sky, and in twilight they were overcast by a haze almost ghostly. Second, the weather could not have been colder to Joseph. Personnel in the airport forecast more snow on the way. The secretary and the director of the school where Frances had been decades ago repeated the prediction.

When he asked to talk to someone who could help with information about Frances Smith, he was introduced to the director. She informed him that she could not reveal any part of the record. He had anticipated this answer and had rehearsed his reasons and brought his senior year high school annual, photographs of Frances by herself and of the two of them, their marriage license and her letters written to him from the school. Lightening the discourse, he told how he and Frances had laughed at the misspelling of their names and confusing the sexes in recording Francis on the male line. The director grinned. He explained the reasons for keeping the marriage a secret until they started first semester of graduate school. They had enrolled as single people and planned to locate an apartment soon afterwards. Also, he was planning to ask his dad for tuition money.

Their respective parents learned of the marriage soon after her death. Everyone was in agreement that a public announcement would be no benefit at that time.

The director listened and when Joseph was finished, she sat back, thinking and silent. Finally, she said that his seeking information about his wife all these years later was unusual. She admitted to having been a young teacher when Frances was there, and they became as close friends as possible, given their roles. After all, she recognized Frances as a certified teacher and not much younger than herself.

The director leaned toward Joseph, her hands clasped together on the desk. Keenly observing him, she asked, "Why do you think she came to our facility so far from her home?"

As if lighting struck him, he knew his answer. God couldn't have touched him and made it any clearer. "She was pregnant and she wanted a place, a safe, good place, to have the baby." For a minute he stared directly at the kind woman opposite him. What he saw in her eyes was his answer. He closed his eyes and dropped his head in his hands, his fingers clasped over his forehead. His breaths were deep, his shoulders heaved, his eyes moistened.

"She would have been such a good mother."

"Did you know before she came?"

"No. I wouldn't have let her. We would have told the whole world as soon as we knew."

"Why do you think she didn't tell you?"

"For all the reasons I've already said. She had to have thought of me first. My finishing school, getting the degree, being out from under my father's thumb. Oh, I wish I had known." He bent his head again then continued. "I'm responsible for her death. If she'd stayed east, she wouldn't have been on the road. She wouldn't have died in that accident."

She walked around her desk and sat beside him. "We don't know that an accident might not have occurred at that time somewhere else."

"But she did die all in the context of that situation. What can you tell me about the birth, the baby?" He turned and looked at her over his shoulder.

"For a first birth, it was not long and she did not suffer. She asked for an anesthesia to put her to sleep. She didn't want to be conscious until the birthing was over, and the baby had been taken to a secluded nursery."

"She never saw it? Did she know whether it was a boy or a girl? Was it okay? No problems?" He swiveled toward her.

"She asked not to see it or to know the sex. The baby was fine. Healthy as we see them and absolutely beautiful."

"Was he blond, blue eyed and fair skinned like Frances?"

She hesitated. "Why did you say *he*?"

Without any masking of his depth of anguish, he uttered. "I've seen him. He has come into my life – a few months ago. It's like looking into a mirror."

"What does he tell you of his family?"

"That he was adopted when he was six weeks old by a couple in California. He lived with them until he came east to college. He has had a good life."

"Do you want to claim him now? As a son?"

"I've thought of the possible relationship since I first met him. But it was too unlikely, too uncanny that if it were so, that the two of us would ever meet. All the way on the flight out, I've gone over every possibility. I know physically that it could have happened. I've counted the months backward. It was possible. I wanted to ask Frances if she was still on the pill, but I didn't until too late. And, she was incredibly beautiful the last months I saw her. I wish she'd told me."

"You said you thought about the possibility of a young man being your son. What decision would you make if you gained information reinforcing your suspicions?" She sat back, giving him space and time to answer.

"He loves his parents deeply. He says he has enjoyed a good life. He came east for a broader view of people and the world. He wants to know more about political forces and thinks about going to Washington, as he says, the hub of what's happening here and worldwide. He likes a girl I know back where I live. He's a journalist and she's in broadcasting and interested in the political scene as he is." He paused.

She prompted. "So?"

"There's nothing to be gained for him or me or anyone he's connected with if I lay claim as his natural father. I will not destroy his happiness or shake his foundations."

"That's quite admirable. Frances is apt to be smiling down on you this moment."

Joseph couldn't staunch the tears that flowed. He pulled a handkerchief from his pocket and held it against his eyes. When they had washed his face and cleansed his soul, he blew his nose. The salty taste was cathartic, purifying and healing.

She broke her rules and leaned over and touched his hand. "I have the top authority here to handle any inquiries about births and adoptions. The school has a written policy not to open sealed files. The rules have changed drastically in the past few years. Children are often favored if they seek information about their natural parents. Records are typically incomplete. Mothers often don't name a father. I was not in a position to know what finally was placed in Frances's file. What I know personally is as a confidant at an important time in her life. She was one of the bravest, finest women I've ever met. She talked about her husband to me, of how she truly loved him. Everything you have said today coincides with what I heard from her. There is something I thought of in retrospect when I heard she had died and, again, when I heard from you. She was happy in the present, but she didn't talk much of the future, certainly not the distant future. Doing what she had to do today was preeminent."

Joseph McBaden, tired and emotionally drained, stepped down from the Piedmont Airport shuttle bus and walked toward his car.

When he pulled into his driveway, he saw a dark and lonely house. He unlocked the front door and flipped the overhead entry light switch. He detected a faint odor of furniture polish and spotted mail stacked on the table, indications that the maid service had been in recently.

Picking up a memo, he read: Mr. McBaden, the furnace filters need changing. Too much dust. Maid Service.

Not only was it cleanup time in his life, but also in his house; ah well, he thought and put the memo down. He trudged to his bedroom and tossed his luggage onto the dresser, then walked into the study and pressed the play button on the answering machine. Dropping down on the sofa, he listened to the string of calls. When he heard Mitch's voice, he sat up and punched repeat.

"Hi, Joseph, it's Mitch. I don't know your return schedule. Just wanted to let you know I'm here when you want to talk. Clarissa phoned. She's concerned about you. Didn't ask questions, so no information was forthgoing."

Wearily, Joseph hit memory plus a number. Mitch picked up after the second ring. Joseph said, "You must have been right at the phone."

"I am. It's good to hear you. The flight back was on time?"

"It was." Joseph knew he must have checked incoming schedules. "I got your message. There's not much to talk about."

"You learned what you needed to know?" Mitch spoke without being invasive.

"Yes." Joseph hesitated. He knew what he had to say and he decided to be cryptic. "Suspicions confirmed. That's all."

"The story stops?"

"That's the wisest course for everyone."

There was a silence. Mitch broke it. "I understand, but I *suggest* if you feel inclined to share it with one person, Clarissa would be a good listener."

"Clarissa?"

"If you bottle up everything you've learned, will you be any freer of the past? Her not being a part of that could be helpful. She wouldn't be emotionally involved. I believe she cares for you."

"I'll sleep on it."

"I'm honored to call you my friend. You've always done justly. Sleep in peace."

Joseph replaced the receiver. With palms on the desk, arms ridged for support, he swallowed tears, sniffled back the overflow and bent his head. The echoes of *honored and justly* swam in his head.

CHAPTER 29

The following morning Joseph woke up early and couldn't get back to sleep. Groggily, he staggered to the kitchen and plugged in and switched on a pot of coffee.

Something about the last dream before awakening disturbed him. What he could recall had nothing of his old dreams of scenes of years ago. These images were of current people, but not a replay of some incident. The situation seemed futuristic and featured a beautiful blonde grinning and signing autographs. He saw himself standing at the edge of a crowd; she was in the center. A hazy figure handed her a paper to autograph. While the paper was being passed, everything shifted to slow motion and the paper took the shape of a dark notebook. Slowly, the blonde wrote in it then tucked the notebook into a large shoulder bag.

"Damn!" Joseph uttered and slammed his hand on the kitchen counter. "That's Breear! She's written a book. And used that damned notebook. Blast it all!"

He glanced at the clock on the microwave. Six thirty. He stamped down the hall then ripped off his pajamas, pulled on his running clothes and shoes and jammed a single house key into the pants pocket. The coffee was perking, the sun was rising, and he was hastening his preliminary stretching.

Up the driveway, down the asphalt street, cross empty intersections, and along sidewalks, lights were popping on in a few houses. In two living rooms he could see the blue squares of televisions already on, and from some sidewalks the morning newspaper had been retrieved. Other newspapers were rolled inside plastic sleeves waiting to tell the readers what was happening here, there, and everywhere. News. NEWS – information gathered from North, East, West and South. That took in everywhere on the globe. And who decided what was to be related or rather revealed to the public? He didn't have the answer. Maybe it was the city editor for this metro area. What was his yardstick? His criteria? Did his mood of the day affect what went in? Did someone upstairs dictate certain issues that were okay and others that were taboo?

Previously, Joseph hadn't given much thought to what went in and what didn't. There were some happenings he was aware of that could have been news for any of the local media but never were printed or broadcast.

How did Breear separate what she passed along to her supervisor from what she jotted down for future reference? What measures did she take to keep her notebook secure at the station? He had seen how quickly she stashed it in her handbag both on assignments and while dining. In her apartment she left it in her bag, which she deposited in her bedroom – a forbidden territory.

As he envisioned her living room, the desk with its bookends supporting a series of black binders caught his eye. What would be recorded on those pages? Would anyone be likely to place financial information in the most public place in her home? If she valued those notes she was always taking with intensity, would she leave them accessible?

He liked neither what he was thinking nor the nudges from his conscience to abandon the opposing thoughts. A mental dilemma but the desire to satisfy his curiosity was strong.

Now he contemplated two strong pursuits to be outlined this day. One was to form a strategy in the Hertford matter; the other, make a date with Breear.

He handled the latter first by calling her and invited her to dinner, making it clear he would pick her up at her apartment at seven o'clock this evening. The Hertford issue he would plot at his desk in the office.

After he had his ducks in a row, he called Clarissa into his office. Because she had been to the Hertford home and had a reasonable excuse to return, he asked her to search for some information, preferably with Sidney there. Joseph said he would phone

Marvin Hertford to notify him about what they were looking for and why. He intended asking for the search tomorrow afternoon or early evening. That would allow time for rehearsing any questions to be asked. Also, he had another agenda for himself tonight.

The remainder of the morning, Joseph stayed at his desk adding relevant data to some documents for Gretchen to type and briefly reviewing files for some afternoon appointments. He reached Marvin Hertford around eleven thirty. Marvin stated he had commitments for the next afternoon but could see him at 5:30 P.M. today at his home. Joseph agreed to be there, saying Clarissa could go at four thirty. Marvin said he would contact both Tricia and Sidney to be at home then.

Joseph hung up and pondered his time with Breear. There was only an hour and a half to consult with the Hertfords and drive to her apartment. Was that enough time? Well, it would have to be. The Hertfords had just reasons for settling this matter quickly; and he well justified attempting to reason with Breear. He could call her saying he'd be late if necessary.

Joseph intended to talk them through the data on Sidney's computer, then to back it up with figures on a legal pad if necessary. Clarissa would go over most of it with Sidney and Tricia prior to his arrival. He buzzed Clarissa and she came across the hall.

Before she could sit, he rushed into explanations of what had to be done. Her face showed surprise at his quickness of manner, the tension of his shoulders, and the seriousness of his facial expression as he leaned over the desk. A plethora of closed file folders and opened legal pads with pages curled back and tucked underneath were stacked in front of him. He held his pencil tightly over the topmost yellow pad like a wasp ready to attack.

His vigor caught her attention, penetrated her shield, and immediately drew from her a surge of energy and openness. She concurred with his plans and spoke excitedly about polishing her questions and presenting the findings.

Returning to her office, she closed the door and stood in front of her desk once more feeling the claustrophobia of the windowless room. She faced the door half-sitting back against her desk, her legs crossed and her arms folded at the waist. She deliberated over Joseph's demeanor. Why was he so uptight? The case, she recognized, was important for him. Positive results for Marvin Hertford could be a major benefit to his practice, potentially bringing in clients who were able to pay the fees needed to keep the doors open.

But something had nibbled at her usual legal cast of mind while in his office. Was her intuition interfering with her concentration or was it alerting her there's something else on Joseph's mind? Could it be personal? If so, she need probe no further until he was ready to talk about it; otherwise, aimless imagination and faulty cognition would cloud her mind, which required focus, sharpness and retention for the pressing legal issue she had been assigned.

At four o'clock she arrived at the Hertford home. Tricia Hertford answered the doorbell, greeting Clarissa warmly, and led her into the living room.

"Would you like a cup of tea? The kettle is hot for I find a cup restoring about this time of the afternoon."

"Thank you, I would," answered Clarissa.

Tricia returned with a silver tea tray laden with an elegant floral design on a white teapot and matching creamer, sugar bowl, cups and saucers. A maid followed her with a small dish of sliced lemon and a plate of cookies.

"Thank you Agnes," Tricia said then poured tea. "Please, add whatever you prefer." She sat down while Clarissa selected a lemon slice and dropped two scant spoonfuls of sugar into her tea.

After a few minutes of general topics, Clarissa asked about Sidney.

"He's keeping himself busy, but I can sense moments of tension in him," Tricia replied and sipped her tea. "He should be here very soon."

"This is an unsettled time for students. The last of the sports for their high school years and trying to keep up enthusiasm and finishing the offices they've held. They are quite ready to turn the leadership over to the juniors. As soon as they have acceptances from their college applications, they do relax quite a bit."

"You are quite knowledgeable about young people," Tricia said complimentarily, but with a slight lift of her eyebrows, denoting curiosity.

Clarissa smiled. "I have a sister who teaches elementary students while her husband teaches in high school. And I hear friends talk about the seniors."

The front door opened and footsteps were heard in the entry hall then coming toward the living room. Sidney called out. "Hi Mom, Miss Bentley. I'm not late, am I?"

"You're right on time. Would you like some tea or something else to drink," his mother asked.

"No, thanks. I grabbed a soda before leaving school." He looked at them as if asking if he should sit down or to get a clue what was next.

"Well, shall we go to Sidney's computer?" said Tricia standing.

Sidney started up the steps immediately ahead of them, saying, "I tried to straighten up a bit before I left for school."

"Don't worry about it. This was Agnes' day to tackle your room. She had strict instructions to leave the computer desk as it was. Truly," Tricia included both Sidney and Clarissa in her statement, "I think she is very concerned about this mystery of the poem. The possibility of someone entering the house and stealing something is very hard for her to accept. She is so careful not to let strangers in."

Clarissa said, "I can believe she is. One point I wanted to ask you both about is how many times Zack was here. Sidney said once and in my notes I have, Mrs. Hertford, that you said twice."

"I remember he was here once in early summer and later when there was a group of guys here," she replied.

As Sidney entered his room, he flipped on an overhead light, walked to the desk and switched on the computer. He turned and faced Clarissa.

"I think Mom is right. Zack asked to borrow a book I had. I

had already read it for our summer reading program. He was going away to visit relatives and hadn't been able to locate a copy."

Tricia smiled and her expression showed relief upon hearing the clarification.

"Sidney," Clarissa directed, "think back to that time Zack was here. Was he ever in the room alone? Maybe thumbing through the book while you left?"

Sidney clinched his teeth and drew his bottom lip up. He scratched his head, then his eyes opened wide. "Hey! I think he was. Let me picture that day. I handed him the book and he did open it. Checked the number of pages and scanned a few paragraphs, probably estimating the time it would take to read it. Then, someone called me. Mom, that may have been you."

"Yes, I have been trying to remember as you spoke. Agnes wasn't here that day, and the recycle bins needed to be placed at the curb. I asked you take it out." Again, she smiled with satisfaction.

"That's it. So Zack was in here. No more than ten minutes."

"Would you say that was long enough for him to search around your desk or get into the computer?" Clarissa probed.

"Sure. If you know what you want, it's easy. Only he wouldn't know my password," Sidney frowned.

"That's reasonable. What if you had your poem on the desk? Handwritten? Typed?"

"I had started it with a pencil, but had finished it on the computer. He had the whole poem in the magazine."

Clarissa continued. "Would you have run off a copy of the poem?"

"Hey!" Sidney enthused, "I had run off a copy to put in the poetry file." He turned and placed his hand on the desk. "The night before, I had printed several poems and placed them in a file folder, right here. I wasn't expecting anyone to be in the room, so I hadn't put it in the drawer."

"Would he have had time to hand copy it while you were out?"

"I don't know. That poem was on top for it was the last one printed."

"Well, could he have typed it on the computer quickly and saved it on a floppy disk?" Clarissa walked to the desk. "Do you keep new disks handy?"

Sidney reached to the rear of the desk and held up a box. "Always."

"Is Zack computer literate?"

"He is. And he's quick. We took computer together."

"Was the computer on?"

"I'm not sure. Unless I'm working on it, the monitor is off."

When the doorbell rang, Tricia excused herself and moved into the upstairs hall. She saw both her husband and Joseph enter. Agnes spoke to them and they looked up. Tricia waved and waited until they reached the upper hallway.

"Hello, Marvin. Joseph, thank you so much for coming. Sidney and Clarissa are making some interesting deductions." She led the way into Sidney's room.

"Dad, Mr. McBaden," Sidney spoke up, "we've remembered that Zack was in here alone one afternoon. Mom had called me downstairs to take the recycle bins to the street. My poem file folder was on the desk. And the poem in the magazine was the last one I had put inside the folder."

"That gives him the opportunity. Have you figured how he could have taken it from here?" Marvin queried.

Sidney looked at Clarissa. She nodded her head. "He couldn't get into my work on the computer because he wouldn't know my password. And it would have been a push for him to hand copy it. Zack is swift on the computer. There's always a box of new floppies on the desk here," he pointed to a box. "He could have typed the poem on the computer and saved it to a floppy in lots less time than he could have hand written it."

Joseph thought a moment, then spoke. "Sidney, could you go through what Zack would have had to do and let us time this?"

"Yes, sir," Sidney answered with enthusiasm and confidence.

"Clarissa, would you keep time for us?" Joseph looked around for a clock.

Tricia interjected. "I have a clock with a large face and a second hand. I will be the timer if Clarissa would prefer to concentrate on what is being demonstrated."

She left the room and was back quickly with a clock, pencil and paper.

While Sidney reenacted Zack's possible movements, Tricia recorded the time. When Sidney was finished, Joseph asked him to go through taking out the bins. Sidney commented that he remembered taking out at least two bins, as well as gathering newspapers from the den and another room. When he returned to the bedroom, Tricia noted the time.

"Well, timekeeper," Marvin spoke kindly to Tricia, "was there time for the poem to have been typed, copied and printed?"

"With a few seconds to spare. To fold and pocket the paper! Maybe a disk? A printer is noisy." She announced definitively and passed the notations to Marvin.

"You're right that printers can be heard," Clarissa said. "The poem typed directly to the floppy disk drive would be quicker and quiet. It could be saved with an unusual document name."

Joseph proposed, "Zack could have printed the poem later on any printer that was set to read the software."

Sidney's expression was one of relief; his father's of reassurance; his mother's of pride; his attorneys' of pleasure and anticipation.

Joseph, checking the clock, knew he had to move forward. "Sidney, can you bring up and print out for me the time you entered the poem in question? Also, the data about the systems on this particular computer, including any backups available?"

"Yes, sir," he responded eagerly, pulled up a chair and began pressing keys.

Marvin drew Joseph aside. "Sidney may not know that this computer has another back up. Most PC's don't have this feature. We use it in the office. I had it added to this one for the boys' use. Too often programs crash at very crucial moments."

"Thank you for that information. I think it will prove to be very valuable."

"I consider we have sufficient information to present to the principal. I'd like to take this matter to him tomorrow." He stared at Joseph.

"That would be the quickest approach."

"I'll call him tonight. I'll be in touch with you as soon as we set a time. I do have to be somewhere else soon. Thank you for being here." He looked over to Clarissa and thanked her, too.

Marvin left the room. Tricia offered to look on her calendar for the date Zack was there and Agnes was away. She wrote the date and time on a slip of paper and handed it to Joseph. After Sidney printed the information requested, he passed it over. He and his mother walked Joseph and Clarissa to the door.

Outside, Joseph handed a slip of paper to Clarissa. "Will you get back with the computer technician, ask him if the time of the first poem entry can be located there?" He pointed to a word. "And, if by intention or chance, it could be altered?"

"I'll stop by the shop on my way home."

"Also, ask him if he would be available to be an expert witness for us in this matter."

"I will." She watched him nod his head and go toward his car, observing even with the favorable findings here, that he appeared to revert into his earlier tension.

Breear opened the door soon after Joseph rang the bell. She smiled, saying, "I'll grab my bag and jacket and be right with you." She left the door ajar and headed toward her bedroom.

He walked in and closed the door quietly. His priority was to get her notes about him for personal reasons. And he wanted his comments about business and professional men because they may be misinterpreted later. He didn't want anyone harmed by his indiscretions. He had learned a lesson the hard way.

He had taken a few steps into the room when she returned, noticed the closed door, and frowned slightly at him.

"You're looking perky and stylish as always."

She replied, "Thank you. You did say dinner at seven?" She

eyed her watch.

"Correct. But I want to talk to you a few minutes. Okay?" He took a step forward.

"About what? Can't we talk at dinner?" She didn't step backward, but her body language leaned in retreat.

Joseph advanced, all the while assessing her anew. She became wary and shifted her weight slightly from one foot to another as if unsure what to do.

He said, "It needs to be private," and moved closer.

She shrugged and turned to the desk, where she laid her bag. Her jacket she placed over the chair. Putting a hand to her head, she shook her hair. "A minute." Then she looked at him pleadingly and femininely. "I really am hungry. It's been a busy day. And I have looked forward to a pleasant meal."

He closed the gap between them. He could see the black binders, standing center back of the desk. He directed his stare straight at her eyes.

"What do you have in those black binders?"

She blinked, swiveled her head toward the desk. An expression first of fear, next of shock that melded into one of defiance.

"What concern is that of yours?"

"Is that where you file choice pages from your notebook?" His voice had an edge.

"Those books could contain anything. Recipes, instructions, clippings . . ."

"Shall we see?" he challenged as he put his hand out.

She grabbed his wrist. Angrily, she shot back. "No! You have no right to come in here and look through my possessions. You may be the attorney, but I haven't signed any powers over to you."

He met her blazoned look and for a few seconds entertained diverse thoughts. He'd never seen her in this mood, and his muscles tensed as he felt the heat of her anger, the strength of her protection of her property, the defiant fight in her. Her face glowed with intense emotion. If only he didn't come for one primary purpose, he'd like to seize her and kiss her until she surrendered.

Forcing his mission uppermost in his consciousness, he declared. "You're up on your rights. So I'm going to ask you. Are you going to tear up your Windermere notes and journal pages?'

"Why?"

Joseph squared his shoulders. "When you leave here, they will no longer be relevant."

She said with strength and self-control. "Please, step back. Over by the sofa. Thank you." When he complied, she lifted the binders and placed them in the deep drawer of the desk, locked it and held the key in her hand.

"The people, the problems and issues remain germane to the local scene," he said.

"Oh, well. I may browse through them again. As a reminder of our meeting and dinners," she switched on a sly, sideways glance toward Joseph.

Not ready to be fooled, he asked, "Any other reason?"

"What reason?" She returned the question for him to defend.

"Information concerning a number of people, men of rank, perhaps."

"Joseph, writers keep notes, journals they're called."

"Would you give me the pages about me? And the men I commented on in the restaurants?"

"It's getting late and I have lots to do after dinner. Shall we go?" She walked toward the door. He briskly rounded the sofa and blocked her path.

"Will you?" he demanded.

Breear drew in her breath and leaned backward, head up without moving her feet. "No. The journals are my work!"

"But . . ."

Breear held his stare. "I wrote the words. The observations are mine. My intellectual property!"

"I see." He returned her triumphant expression with one of exasperation. "You learn well." Reassessing her, his face shifted to a decisive look. "The notes may be yours. You may shape them into an apprentice's manual or as the first chapter in your journalism expertise. For whichever form you consider for publishing them, here is a word of caution. Guard them and all future notes. We never know how anyone will use or interpret our words or observations. Journalists are steady targets for libel suits." His eyes shuttered any subsequent meanings.

He walked to the door before turning toward her. "Excuse my ungentlemanly behavior. I will still escort you to dinner, although I'll understand if you choose to eat alone."

"I'm too exhausted to go now. By the way, I had a message from Sutton on the answering machine tonight. He'll be in about noon tomorrow." With a sigh, she added, "Will you be in the office if he wants to touch base with you? He's quite excited by his tone."

"I'll be in. I know you're hungry. What about my stopping for pizza and have them bring you one and a salad, and whatever you want to drink?"

"Thanks. A Pepsi, please. And Joseph, you've been good to me. Sorry we have to stand on opposite sides of . . ." she flung up her hands.

He finished the sentence. "The notebook." He walked out and closed the door. Moving toward his car, he felt drained. Tasks remained for him. First was preparing for the conference with the school principal and others tomorrow morning. He had no doubt that Marvin would be granted his request. Now there was a visit from Sutton to anticipate.

He couldn't recall an angry scene like the one he had just had with Breear, except maybe the ones with his father. He recognized he had forced all the episodes, even a few with Clarissa. Yet, Clarissa in her armor had never been so defiant or flinty. His personal life was stilted with secrets, confrontations, and career demands.

CHAPTER 30

The telephone rang just as Joseph was snapping his briefcase. He had expected an early call at home and was prepared to leave for the office or elsewhere.

"Joseph, Marvin Hertford. I talked with Paul Monroe last night about a meeting today. He phoned a few minutes ago that the guidance counselor and Della Anders, the boys' English teacher, and Zack Eaton's father – all agreed. The school system's attorney may also be there. Everyone involved will be in Monroe's office at ten o'clock. Does that still fit in with your time frame? Good. Do you have any points we need to cover beyond what we talked about yesterday?"

"The computer's extra feature is in our favor. We have a computer consultant who is willing to be an expert witness for our side. If anything else surfaces, I'll be in touch. Thank you for calling," Joseph said then hung up.

Although he felt confident with his computer findings, he could never be certain that the opposition did not have some other fact that was unbeknownst to him or his client.

Arriving at Price Tower, he pulled eagerly on the handle of the heavy, brass-framed glass front door. There was no revolving door entry. He felt good during the elevator ride to the sixth floor. As he moved down the carpeted hall, he admonished himself not to feel so important about the height of his office. There were taller buildings in Windermere and other cities. Approaching his own doorway, he eyed the gold letters and paused.

He felt a sense of self-respect, akin to pride, for what he had accomplished, and he did not consider it was a sin. Constantly, his guard was up not to be arrogant or proud.

What was it Pug Avery pointed out to him? Your name looks

lonely. Was he lonely? He didn't know. He hadn't taken the time to think about it.

He opened the door then closed it behind him, believing that would shut out the words "looks lonely." But the room was dim. Gretchen hadn't arrived to put the offices into working mode. After he switched on the overhead lights, he walked down the hall, glancing briefly at Clarissa's closed door, and went into his own office.

He dropped his briefcase on the desk then hung up his jacket. The briefcase was of fine leather; the jacket bore a well-known label; the furniture in his office was constructed to last for years. All of these material objects were purchased not only because he admired them, but also for what they represented to him and to anyone who came into the suite of rooms: They bespoke success.

Yet one desk stood alone in this office and the other across the hall. A single name was gold-lettered on the entry door.

Who was he trying to impress? The people of Windermere? Or was he trying for reassurance that he had made a name for himself. In spite of the hardships he had had in getting his degree? The sacrifices he had made in those early days? The denial of being a husband and a . . . ? He couldn't say the word that had been emblazoned in his head as deeply as that little school and infirmary were nestled in the bottom of the bowl surrounded by tall, jagged mountains.

Why can't I say it? Why can't I? Is this the legacy of my family? Was my role model so hard, so strict, and so authoritative I can't bear to continue it? Am I cursed? Am I responsible for the abrupt ending of a life I held so dear and loved so intently . . . all the while denying her a title she was so fit to bear? Have I chloroformed sections of my memory in order to achieve accolades of "well done!" and demand a handsome sum? If I had been more sensitive, more aware or alert to another person's needs, could I have changed any lives? To the past ones, I am denied an answer. To the present, there are choices to be made. God, help me to choose right this time.

He sat still, eyes closed a few minutes. Suddenly, a noise startled him. He visually surveyed the room, cocked his head. Nothing.

No sound. He shook his head, poked his forefinger in an ear, but there was only silence. With his arms he pushed himself out of the chair and went to splash cold water on his face.

Revived, he kept on track until it was time to leave for his ten-o'clock meeting. He added the note Clarissa had left him after her talk with the computer consultant.

The meeting progressed as evenly as anyone could expect with two young people claiming authorship of the same poem. The father of each boy supported his own son. The school personnel attempted to remain neutral although Miss Anders, who was familiar with Sidney's work, appeared to favor his claim. There was talk of bringing in the journalism teacher from the other school who was advisor for the literary magazine, but the conflict was solved without that being necessary.

The Hertfords were appreciative of Joseph's thorough work and grateful to be able to put the episode behind them. Sidney and Zack went to their class, as did Miss Anders. Mr. Eaton apologized to Marvin and Sidney for his son's action and for the inconvenience they had been caused. He stated that he would see that Zack wrote the retraction that evening and would post it by certified and registered mail to the school principal and the magazine advisor. And, he added, one to Sidney. Paul Monroe told them the plagiarism would be presented to the Faculty Committee on Honors and Conduct though the action occurred at another school.

Joseph was pleased with the outcome of the meeting and the settling of the matter in the short time and in a manner that Marvin had wanted. However, his enthusiasm and energy began to wane by the time he was back in his office.

After he removed his coat and loosened his tie, he sank in his desk chair and slumped into a lethargic posture.

"Are you all right?" A voice came from the doorway.

"I don't know." Joseph answered in a distant tone, unaware he was speaking aloud.

A soft rap of knuckles on the door was followed by a quiet

tread into his office. "Joseph?" the voice asked in low tones of concern.

"Yes?" He turned his chair and saw Clarissa at the other side of his desk. "Pardon me. What did you say?"

Scrutinizing him, she repeated the question. "Are you okay?"

"Yes." This time the inflection was level and louder.

"Gretchen has fresh coffee ready. Would you like a cup?"

"Thank you." He stood.

"I'm going for one myself. May I bring you a cup and you can update me on the Hertford case?" She waited. He replied, "Thank you." As she left, he unsnapped his briefcase and pulled out the notes about the meeting at the high school.

When Clarissa returned, she reached across the desk and handed him a mug.

He stared at it and asked, "What was it you said, being thankful for coffee on our table in the morning?" He lifted the cup and took a deep drink.

"Coffee, yes." She added, "And the other simple things."

"Amen." He took another swallow then set the mug aside and gathered his notes from the morning's meeting into his hands.

Clarissa held her warm mug and concentrated on his face, ready for his words.

He related in clear tones the chronology of the meeting. Monroe stated the situation succinctly, for to his knowledge details were somewhat scant and secondhand. The magazine was presented then Sidney's paper. Next, Zack was asked to explain the poem's inclusion in the magazine from another county.

Zack told them that he had needed a class that he couldn't schedule at his regular school due to a conflict with another he wanted to take. Thus he had stayed with relatives in another county last summer and enrolled in the class in a high school that offered it for summer term. He had cleared it with the guidance counselor and the grade had been transferred to the school office. He was reading the poem to some of the members of the summer session when the journalism teacher came in and heard it. She asked if he wrote it and he had answered "yes" thinking it a joke – just a boast. Well, he was surprised when the end of term came and she stopped him in the hall one day and asked if she could submit it to the student staff of the literary magazine. He said "sure," thinking it probably wouldn't be chosen. He went to the typing room, typed a copy, and left it with the school secretary to place in the teacher's mailbox. That was the last he heard about it until he was sent a copy of the magazine a few days ago.

When Monroe asked Zack if he wrote the poem, Zack said "yes," then Marvin and Sidney sat up straighter and taller. Sidney had a scowl on his face. Monroe asked Sidney if he had something to say. And, of course, Sidney claimed he wrote the poem. He gave the date he started it on paper and the date he completed it on the computer.

Then Zack challenged him how he could prove that date. Sidney told him he could open the list of documents, move the cursor over and entry dates were displayed. Zack smugly countered that dates could be changed similar to the way time can be changed or set, when computers are plugged in.

His father almost smirked with his son's apparent superior knowledge of the computer.

And to make the story shorter, and that is really in the spirit this whole gathering was intended to be from Marvin's prospective, apparently, the fewer harsh words that were exchanged, the easier the boys could sit in class together the remainder of the year. I asked to make a comment and the discussion yielded to me. Your notes from the consultant were really the clinchers. When I informed them that Sidney's personal computer had a back-up tape that automatically backed up whatever was entered, the Eatons started to protest. I talked a bit louder, and, when I mentioned our "computer consultant," they stopped to listen. The computer consultant, I continued, stated it would be almost impossible to change that date later. Then when Zack resumed his objections, I countered with the news that the consultant had a computer compatible with Sidney's and could locate the original entry date on the tape. And, furthermore, he would appear as an expert witness in the matter. The computer consultant is not and has never been employed by Mr. Hertford and would be a neutral witness. Also, I pointed out that Zack went to Sidney's house in the summer to borrow a book. He was alone for ten to fifteen minutes in the room with Sidney's computer.

So Zack had no other avenue open and hung his head. His father appeared shocked and asked him if he wrote the poem. Zack shook his head. When his father asked him how he obtained the poem, Zack looked at Mr. Eaton and said that he opened a file folder, read the poem, then turned on the computer and typed a copy of it and saved it on a disk. He had no idea what he would do with it. Nobody at school knew Sidney wrote poetry. Zack felt he had made a real discovery. Copying it was an impulse, the same as reading it to the students last summer and saying okay when the teacher asked him to let her submit it to the magazine staff. His ending comment was not received too favorably. "Gosh, it's a small, county high school compared with ours. How could I ever expect there would be an issue in our main library! What are the chances a thing like this could happen?"

Monroe asked Sidney and Marvin if they had any recommendations for handling the matter. Marvin stated he wanted Zack to notify the county school principal and magazine advisor of the real author of the poem and to retract his claim to having composed the poem. He also wanted letters of apology to both Sidney and himself and to Monroe and Miss Anders. And if ever a question came from any college or scholarship committee now or anytime in the future, a letter concerning this incident would be on file in the school administrative office to be sent immediately to any such inquirer. Furthermore, he wanted no reference to this incident to be in Sidney's file either for the current year or in his permanent file.

The requests were noted and Monroe would be in contact with Sidney and Zack and their parents later.

"So, thank you for your astuteness to suggest consulting an expert in the first place and for your follow-through," Joseph said to Clarissa.

"I have no doubt that the Hertfords and everybody else in that room thanked you," she promptly touted.

He shook his head and breathed a sigh of relief. She stood up and thanked him for letting her join him in handling the matter. Sensing his energy was ebbing at the moment, she took the mugs and left the room.

She had hoped he would have a short respite before his next appointment. But that was not to be the case.

Leaving his office, she looked down the hall as Joseph's next client entered the reception room. The outer door had scarcely closed before it was reopened by Sutton, who walked a few steps toward Gretchen's desk and waited for the man ahead of him to gain her attention. She was taking notes while engaged in a phone conversation. Clarissa pivoted back into Joseph's office.

"Joseph, your next client is here. So is Sutton."

Before he could answer, the light blinked on his desk phone. He tapped the intercom and the message was audible on the base speaker. "Mr. McBaden, your next appointment is here."

"Thank you, Gretchen. Tell him I'll be with him soon. Ask him to have a seat and offer him coffee." Joseph turned to Clarissa. "Do something for me, please. Go out and talk with Sutton and find out how much time he has."

She nodded, left the office and returned quickly.

"Well?" asked Joseph as he drew a folder from the file cabinet.

"Not long. He has to be back in Columbia for his job in about six hours and it's a five-hour drive."

He nodded toward her and picked up the phone. She left the office, leaving the door open. "Gretchen, send Sutton Barnwell in." He adjusted his collar and tie.

Joseph walked to the other side of the desk. Sutton strode in, beaming and handsome, his clothes rumpled from travel, and extended his hand.

"Thank you so much for seeing me again on such short notice."

"It's good to see you. Have a seat. How did the interviews go?"

"Great. Better than I could have imagined." Sutton sat on the edge of the chair.

"That's good news." Joseph returned to his chair, put his arms atop the desk and gave Sutton his full attention.

"Yes, it is. I know your schedule has to be full, so let me give you the bottom line first. Both firms talked positive offers." Sutton spoke exuberantly and focused on Joseph's face.

"You can't beat that, can you? Two interviews, two offers. Do you like the terms?" Joseph asked and leaned further forward.

"I do."

"You didn't make a verbal commitment to either one?"

"No." Sutton frowned slightly and fidgeted with his arms on the chair. "I told both of the personnel officers that I would think about their offer and asked if I could let them know after I receive a mailing with details about employment with the companies." He angled his hands outwards. "I also asked the deadline for answering. It's a week."

"Well, that sounds generous from what I'm hearing companies are requiring nowadays. It appears recent graduates are shopping around and revealing how much someone else is offering."

Sutton laughed. "Yes, sir. I guess we are doing that. After all, if it works, we might as well keep trying. But really, sir, I'm pleased with both offers." He paused and rubbed his hands together, showing signs of travel weariness.

"How about some coffee?" Joseph offered.

"That would be great. I'll be hitting the road as soon as I leave here. Just black, thanks."

Joseph buzzed Gretchen and asked for two coffees, black. "So what's the difference in the offers?"

"It boils down to the job descriptions. One will be for a small publishing firm that is devoted to travel magazines and brochures. Writers and or photographers gather facts and send photos of interesting places. The firm has writers who find an unusual, different slant and work up an article. The carrot is that after a while I may have the opportunity to go to the locations myself. Work up some of my own features. The editor liked that I am familiar with both the West Coast and the Eastern Shore.

"The other will be with a large newspaper. I may have mentioned that. The paper takes several new people each summer, as well as interns, and the competition will be keen both for news assignments and for staying on as reporters."

The door opened and Clarissa entered with two coffee mugs. As she handed them out, Sutton stood and Joseph introduced him to her. He added, "Clarissa worked in Washington several years before she transferred to an office of the law firm in Virginia."

"Hey, that sounds interesting. Maybe the next time I'm here, we can talk," Sutton said.

"I look forward to seeing you again," she said and left the room.

Although the exchange was brief, Joseph noted the admiration on Sutton's face and the enthusiasm in his voice as he spoke to Clarissa. "What type of writing do you want to do, eventually?"

"Political reporting."

"Which of the two positions will more likely lead to that?"

"Well, the travel sounds like I can learn about many places, and politics starts on the local level?"

"Is there a possibility of landing a political assignment with the newspaper?"

"Yes. The personnel officer said there would be a vacancy on that beat when a reporter retires next month. Someone already on the staff will fill his position. What the new hire will get will be down the line, as I understood," Sutton clarified.

"Well, you have some aspects to consider before giving an answer to the firms." Joseph asked, "Will there be a minimum trial time to find out if you and the company are well suited; or will you both be free to break the contract under conditions agreed to, at anytime? Is it an open-ended contract, or is it to be renewable yearly?"

"Gosh, I'm not certain about that." Sutton looked perplexed. "Sir, it's not really a contract at this entry level. It's what I would call a verbal agreement."

"Did you talk work hours and salary?"

"Yes."

"So you will be agreeing to those verbal terms?"

"That's the way we left it. When I get whatever they mail,

could I fax a copy to you? Would you look it over? This would be hard to explain to Dad." Sutton looked seriously at Joseph. "I know he will take care of the fees," he added quickly.

"Don't worry about that. Yes, I'll be glad to look at whatever you send. Add any comments if there's a statement that you're not sure about, or something you may want to look into changing or negotiating."

"Thanks, Mr. McBaden. I really appreciate your doing all this. Even though we've known each other a short time, I feel comfortable with your advising me about these offers. I look toward the day somebody will look at me and say, 'Sure, you can write my story, report my piece cause you are so confident, so trustworthy.'"

Almost simultaneously, both men arose. Joseph came around the desk, saying, "I'm glad to be of help. I'll be looking for the fax. Gretchen will give you our phone and fax numbers. Leave with her your address and a phone number where you can be reached, and a fax number."

Sutton extended his hand. "I will. Oh, I chatted briefly with Breear this morning. She said to tell you hello. You may know that she's an energetic person and prone to push herself too hard. I'm glad she knows someone like you to take an interest in her while she's here." He grinned.

"She has her sights on D.C. herself, doesn't she? Maybe she'll be up there . . ."

"She does. And she may be before long. There are openings in TV, and she has professional experience now. She'll be wanting more than the basic entry level."

"Sounds promising," Joseph offered. "Keep in touch."

Sutton displayed his youthful bright smile that bespoke of affability, self-confidence and an eagerness to be engaged in life. He lifted his hand in a jaunty, will-do salute and left the room. Joseph approached the open door, grasped the brass knob and very slowly and quietly swung it toward the frame. He stood with the door slightly open until he sensed the outer door being opened and closed. Then he homed his own office door into the frame and listened for the lever to click into the faceplate.

"I have closed something. I have blocked a relationship." His eyes scanned the top of the solid wood door, right to left, then created a zigzag pattern down its width to the floor. His hand was hot against the round metal knob. He stared at his fist that clutched the means to open and close the barrier between him and another human form. He questioned was the knob hot or his hand? That was not the dilemma: It was had he shut the door against Sutton, permitting him to leave in ignorance, or closed the door to help assure his own continued self-esteem and sense of whom others judged him to be?

Furthermore, Joseph agonized whether he had denied himself a chance for a flesh and blood kinship, or did he continue the secretive pattern that had become second nature to him. If the latter were true, how could he continue to be effective in a profession that upheld legitimacy? Upheld the truth and sought right action? Sought justice! And who was to say either had been reached? Or the final one, justice, administered? And who was the ultimate judge about human conditions and human actions? Was it someone seated in the government court?

Joseph pressed his forehead against the door. The wood was warm against his skin. Its surface smooth, but hard, rigid, unrelenting. Nothing gave to his pressure.

Through his shoes, his feet felt vibrations against the carpeted flooring approach, then halt on the other side of the sturdy door. He remained tense, immobile, his heart beating strongly, his breath bated. After a few seconds, the footsteps resumed, quiet, faint, inaudible. Joseph knew something on the other side had empathized with his loss.

The remainder of the afternoon dragged on for the three of them. The atmosphere was tenuous. Clarissa and Gretchen walked quietly and spoke a minimum of words and those very low-keyed. Joseph kept to his office with the door closed. Gretchen was grateful that there were few incoming phone calls and those she could answer competently. At five o'clock, she left quickly as possible, telling only Clarissa goodbye.

During the next half-hour, Clarissa experienced a bout of tiredness and brewed a cup of tea. She felt relief physically for a few minutes then became anxious about Joseph. It was atypical of him to stay so long closed in his office. She cleared away the tea things, listened in the hallway, and returned to her desk; but she couldn't buckle down to any work. She felt they should be celebrating the outcome of the Hertford situation.

Walking again to the hall, she listened and heard no sounds. Deciding to take a last look out the windows, she went into the conference room. The springtime scene was fresh and somehow quieting. She couldn't feel the soft breeze or hear the gentle brushing of leaves against each other. Nor could she smell the fragrant fruit blossoms. But the images wrought their magic; and she relaxed, emptied her mind of legal matters and personal problems and acquiesced to her imagination.

She stood a foot from the window looking out. Twilight was creeping across the landscape. Her countenance was transformed.

Joseph walked past the open door, noticed her, and moved on. He turned, retraced his steps, and paused at the doorway. She was silently staring at the view. Quietly, he entered the room, stopping beside the conference table. Was she all right? He wanted to ask, but restrained speaking in case it was a very private moment for her.

He adjusted his gaze as the twilight deepened and sought her expression in the tinted window. It was a different Clarissa face that he saw. He opened his eyes widely to fathom the image, but he did not know this face. It was as if she had left this room and journeyed to some inner space. He could read neither where that was nor what she was thinking.

Not knowing what to do or say, he simply yielded to instinct that echoed from some memory of years long ago. He did not count the minutes that he stood still watching her reflection; time was unimportant. Perhaps she might need someone or something, and he was the only person there. With his own problems so weighty he didn't know if he could take on any more, but he felt he should stay.

The sun was steadily dropping, and the sky was increasingly

being flooded with awe-inspiring flames of orange that spread over the horizon and merged as immense clouds of gold and amber. He had never noticed them.

Had he missed other beauties, other offerings right in front of him? He asked himself.

She spoke softly. He strained to hear.

"The trees are lovely. Graceful. The flowering fruit trees just across the road are at their most beguiling season. The growth is still in the springtime stage, fully leafed, but not the immature green. Their color is truer to the species. Is this what the Garden of Eden was like?"

A rhetorical question, he knew it to be.

"If that were an apple tree, it would soon be forming the fruit that Eve would know." She blinked her eyes and reentered the room. She did not meet his eyes in the window. She slowly rotated toward him. No lights were on in the room, but he could discern her features.

Directly, she returned his gaze. "The apples were there. Why apples?"

"Temptation? Testing?" he answered.

"Apples for their redness? Their thirst-quenching juice? Their roundness to fill the palms of her hands? Their freshness?"

"Their being forbidden?"

"Apples still hang on trees."

"Are we talking about apples?"

"The thoughts just came to me," she confessed.

Joseph fully lifted his eyelids and focused on her face to read all she was saying. Thus Clarissa had abandoned her trance-like state. Whereas her eyes had shielded a private world, they now as fully revealed a soul exposed. He waited for revelations.

"Do you think Adam himself was ever tempted by the apples?"

"Are you asking if men are tempted?"

"Are they?"

"By some things."

"Even forbidden things?"

Joseph prolonged his wide-eyed search of her face. Does she know the turmoil I've been in? How could she?

"Is it probable that apples are a symbol of all that man should not know? For knowing about many things means to have bitten into, fully savored the flesh and juice of the fruit. To have been temporarily nourished. Not fulfilled. There are many apples on a tree. Might each represent some bit of this world it is best to avoid? Each one, tasted, holds knowledge. Could each one hold different bits of God's vast inventory?"

Joseph stood spellbound by her utterances, as if he were witnessing a birthing. She continued, staring soulfully at him without demanding any answers. "Is knowledge forbidden? Does it fall into one category or another, good or evil? Should we stop trying to learn?" She paused. "Is there a choice now? Once Eve ate ... Isn't there a thirst in one *to know*, to discover for oneself knowledge?" Her eyes were pleading a response.

"And for man because he ate, too? Yes, man wants to know. And to know more as he matures and can absorb more." Joseph said.

She smiled just slightly and her voice tone changed. "Do we know the sex of the serpent? What would be your first reply? Was it a male or female?"

"What questions you are asking, Clarissa!"

"First guess, please."

"A male. God only knows why I chose that!" He moved for the first time, stepping over to her side of the table. "Will you answer the same question?"

"It's only fair. I agree with you, counselor."

"Well, that's unity for the legal team. However, I've not thought about it long enough to swear by."

"Isn't it likely the first response is the truth?"

"Come now. We both *know* – oh, that word, forgive me, do – that would call for exploring." He half-laughed as he stood two steps away. His eyes, however, were fully assessing this new presentation of Clarissa. Here was a deeper insightful person with an exploring theological dimension and a magnetic aura that he had not previously countenanced. God, what challenging conversations we might indulge in! Thank you.

They remained looking at each other. He narrowed his focus;

she resumed her noncommittal demeanor. Both stepped back a pace. She said, "There's a phone message in your tray." She turned and went out of the room.

Left alone, he thought to take one more glance at the springtime scene. To see a fresh, renewing site, to add another point for his choice of office space. But he had waited too late. The sun had almost set. Someday, he promised himself a longer surveillance.

CHAPTER 31

The afternoon had stretched at a snail's pace for Joseph. He had reviewed some cases, telephoned clients for information, and afterwards filled a legal sheet with astute points in intelligible legalese. Drawing on his years of habit, the familiarity with the subjects discussed and applicable laws, he pulled off his role without a single perplexed expression during the conversations.

However, following the last notation on the yellow pad, he shoved it wearily onto the stack on his desk. He sat back in his swivel chair like an ancient scribe who might have just completed a handwritten translation of an Old Testament book. His hands were cramped, but they were not numb with cold or stiffened with clutching an instrument that had to be repeatedly dipped into an inkwell. Alas, he didn't have to go to evening chapel service and sit in an unheated room. His concentration was waning; his movements, sluggish, giving the appearance depicted of monks of old.

"Thank God, I don't have any dinners or business meetings tonight." He muttered then stretched. He swiveled his chair and slowly stood up. He jammed a few folders into his briefcase. He spotted his coffee cup on the desk, sighed and forced himself to return it to the service area. The hall and reception rooms were quiet. He briefly listened prior to looking at Gretchen's desk. It was tidy, ready for tomorrow with no Gretchen in sight. He ambled back to Clarissa's office where the door was shut. He knocked but there was no response.

Joseph cogitated as he rinsed the coffee cup. "Have they ever left without checking with me first?" Surprisingly, answering the question was a strain, so he let the matter be unexplored. He did notice that the coffeepot had been cleaned and the unit turned off.

Back in his office, he fumbled with putting on his jacket. His trod down the hall toward the outer office door as one who had been overstrained by the complexities of the day. Flipping the light switch off and vaguely experiencing the grayness of the evening, he shivered almost imperceptibly as a mode of emptiness pervaded the usual atmosphere of friendliness and helpfulness. He turned, opened, exited, and closed the heavy wooden door. He twisted the brass knob, making certain it was locked. His gaze was caught by the gold lettering on the door. His name, Joseph McBaden. Now it spoke to him. One name. One man. A lone legal light in the growing world from whom needy people came seeking help and answers and favorable judgments. Each client had to justify to him–the attorney–that there were sufficient claims or grounds to proceed with the issue brought for consideration.

This evening Joseph paced his steps down the corridor, as a teacher of ancient days may have done, strolling and lecturing along the colonnades, only Joseph played the roles of teacher and pupil.

Ah, what a wearisome day he had experienced. Starting with Hertford and his scheduled request before office hours, briefing Clarissa, an appointment and Sutton arriving simultaneously, and the meeting with Sutton which demanded the ultimate restraint, the interview concluding not with closure of relationship but with establishing and maintaining an ongoing connection. Then the phone conversations he had with clients who beheld their problems as worthy of immediate attention, and rightfully so. And the last exchange with Clarissa about apples and serpents climaxed the day.

The elevator doors opened. He entered wearily. The doors closed and Joseph, with his heavy burdens, descended.

Night was approaching as he pulled his car into the stream of traffic. Joggers ran in place on the sidewalks at intersections as they waited for a break in the passing parade of vehicles. Joseph empathized with the men in shorts and running shoes, but he squelched his inclination to stop and allow them to cross the street. Did he have the right to delay drivers steering their course behind him? Maybe some of them, maybe he himself, might be headed home to change and hit the runners' paths?

Where am I headed? Since he couldn't answer, he drove up some familiar streets and down some others, aimlessly eating away the miles. He braked the car at an intersection for a family of four, two of whom were small children, to cross the street. To his right he saw First United Methodist Church. He lifted his elbows and placed them on the steering wheel. Staring at the façade and at the stone pillars that bore the church name in bold capital letters.

"Well, Mitch, what advice do you have for me tonight?" Joseph cocked his head as if listening for a voice. There was only silence. The family had moved out of sight. No other cars were coming. As the Baptists might wonder: "Has the Rapture come and left me behind?" Joseph shook his head, turned left and steered the car in the opposite direction from the church.

The street lamps began to glow block by block; the traffic was intermittent; the yards and porches were vacated. Not knowing where to direct his car, Joseph made his way to his house. Lugging his briefcase, he unlocked the door and walked to the study. He dropped the case, pulled off his jacket and went into the kitchen. Opening the refrigerator door, he gazed at the lighted interior. Nothing called out "eat me." He pulled the milk carton forward and poured himself a glass.

He walked into the dining room and stared out the picture window. The lawn was green and closely cut. Neat and tidy were words he customarily liked to say about the yard; however, tonight the words sounded hollow and without personality. He grunted a laugh, followed by a question, "Is that like me?"

His answer was a question also. "Do I mow low any signs of growth trying to maintain a pattern of conformity?"

Brushing a hand across his lips and wiping any milk moustache, again he laughed derisively. "And the cows didn't even get the clippings!"

In the kitchen, he rinsed the glass and put it in the dishwasher. Glancing out the window above the sink, his eye was drawn to the swooping of birds down to the short grass. He watched as they hopped about and thrust beaks to the ground and up again with backward tilted heads. Some broke rank and darted hither and thither. "What are you looking for?" he asked through the window. Unheeding his question, the birds continued searching with heads cocked for a closer view.

Joseph unlocked the outside door unable to recall when he had last exited this way. The wooden platform he stood on was not big enough to be called a deck. It was a narrow landing with steps to the concrete walkway where trash containers stood at the end of the driveway to the side of the house.

Even in his tiredness and state of questioning every thought and scene that crossed his mind or eye, he recognized that the lawn had a pleasing lay with its contours along the boundaries and a gentle slope away from the house. The green of the grass and the few clusters of shrubbery, as well as the spring's bursting tree crowns, were calming to his sight. After a few deep breaths he appreciated the freshness of the scents.

Quietly, he watched the birds persistently pecking amid the blades of grass. Were they looking for something not yet found? Another type of grass seed or juicier worms or water? He had no seed or worms to offer, but he could provide a bowl of water. He returned to the kitchen and found a bowl, which he took outside and filled from a faucet. Placing it on the grass, he stepped back and watched the birds hop forth to investigate. After a few drinks, the first sippers flew up to low tree branches and other birds winged their way to the bowl.

Deep inside there was a stirring sensation that he had done a selfless kind act. He experienced a slight relief of his low mood. Yet that was not sufficient to raise his spirits. Climbing up the steps and reaching the landing, he turned for another look and was rewarded, through a gap in the trees, the last glow on the horizon. A few stars blinked, teasing lights against the creeping night.

Those faint, faraway suns flashed one after another until Joseph sensed they were sending him an encoded message. A broader, deeper undertaking was necessary. He wanted to talk about what had been unspoken for twenty years. He needed to release the pent-up emotions. He longed to share what had made him who he had become. Then he knew there was someone who would listen with an open mind and, perhaps, an understanding heart.

He reentered the kitchen and locked the door. At the sink he splashed cold water on his face, rinsed his hands, and dried off. Without switching on any lamps, he went out the front door and got back into his car. The evening was dark except for the street lamps. Through the windshield with its upper inches tinted against the brilliance of sun upon its rising and setting, the stars were not visible to him; still he had faith they shone whether or not he was observing them.

He drove at a slow, steady speed with the extent of concentration he could summon on deeply inhaling and exhaling and clearing his mind. Neither rehearsed speeches nor explosive confessions would serve the purpose. No rhetoric would be needed.

He parked the car with the wheels cut toward the curb to prevent a swerve down the street in case the brakes did not hold. He got out and locked the door.

Lights from the Hughes' glass front door and windows cast yellowish rectangles upon the gray porch flooring. Around the side at Clarissa's entrance shined similar patterns. The doorbell pushed, he stepped back. Soon the sound of heels clicking on the hardwood, interior floors beat upon his attentive ears. The exterior overhead light came on. Seconds later, the key clicked in the doorplate. The door opened slowly.

Clarissa stood on the other side of the storm door; she was still dressed in the blouse and suit skirt she had worn that day to the office. She pushed the storm door out. "Hello," she said with surprise.

"Are you getting ready to leave?" he remarked.

"No. Will you come in?"

"Thank you," he said and pulled the storm door fully open and she stepped back. He closed it. "The door?" he nodded to the inner one.

"You may leave it open. It's such a lovely night." She commented as she turned to the living room.

"It is. Would you like to walk?"

"Yes. Let me change shoes."

"Sure." As she rummaged in the front closet, he stood looking about her comfortable living room, remembering that he had spent a night here in what seemed a long while past.

Sitting on a bench, she discarded her heels and donned walking shoes and socks; then standing, she pulled her sweater around her shoulders.

"Sometimes it's cool in early evening," she explained and walked toward the door. "Ready?"

He nodded and opened the door. "The key?"

She held up a ring of keys then pushed them into her skirt pocket.

They walked in silence for three blocks. She stole a few glances sideways at him. Sensing he had some need, she waited for him to start a conversation.

"You're not too chilly, are you?" he asked, stopping at a corner.

"I'm fine." She replied and surveyed him long enough to see he had not changed clothes, which were now somewhat rumpled.

His mood was as atypical as his appearance. In his quietness and slow-paced gait she detected an effort at self-control coupled with a need to communicate. As they crossed the street, she matched his pace and continued to wait for him to speak.

He coughed, cleared his throat and spoke. "I want to talk with you. Do you feel up to hearing a life story?" He kept his eyes focused ahead.

"Yes," she answered, "Joseph," she added low and softly.

"It will be quite a lengthy tale. I have no preconceived idea how this will come out. I shall try to unfold the essential facts in chronological order. If they get convoluted or sound disjointed and make no sense, just tug my sleeve and I'll back up, clarify or whatever. Okay?"

"I'm listening," she said simply with openness.

They strolled down the sidewalks hardly aware of others walking leisurely in the neighborhood. Occasionally, Clarissa nodded to passersby and Joseph halted his story. Once he reached for her elbow as they were crowded toward the curb, but released it when the sidewalk no longer had to be shared.

He had begun his talk with a few details of his growing up in Eastern Carolina and his family without glossing over his hard treatment from his dad, his love of his mother and his admiration of his sister. He told of fun in high school, his switching to the Methodist Church for its kinder and more appreciative manifestation of a loving spirit, and his dating Frances.

Pausing to clear his throat again, he resumed stating only that after a weekend at the beach, he and Frances decided to get married the following Monday. He turned toward her as he said that they asked Mitch to marry them but he wouldn't without their parents' consent. Thus they drove to South Carolina and were married by a justice of the peace and a marriage license was signed with a mixup in their names. "People sometimes joke about my dotting every *i* and crossing every *t*. Now, someone knows why." He again looked at her.

She nodded.

"We never told anyone. At least I didn't. Mitch told me recently that Frances had called him while we were in college and wanted to talk to him, but they never got a chance." At this point, he swallowed and told her about the violent scene with his father in the presence of his mother and sister and of his never having spoken with his father since that day. And about Frances's fatal accident.

His face was grim. Clarissa reached over and touched his sleeve, squeezed his arm then slid her arm around his. They walked on, only now she was guiding him down the street that curved beside a park. At the entrance she pulled slightly on his arm and they took the meandering path until they came to a bench backed up with azaleas.

"Joseph, let's sit here." She directed courteously. Still with her arm looped about his, she began to sit and he offered no resistance.

He brought his hands up and lowered his head. "I told her parents and my mother after the funeral. All of us agreed to let her remain as she had been buried – Frances Smith. Except for Mitch, no one else knows. I never thought it would help to talk about the marriage or the wreck. I never thought the secret heavy until now."

When he lifted his head, she slid her hand up and touched his palm, which was moist. "I'm so sorry, so sorry."

He clenched his fingers over hers. "Thank you for listening. But that's not the end. I want to tell you the rest," he implored.

"Go on, when you're ready." She pulled the sweater more tightly around her shoulders.

"You're cold," he said and helped arrange the sweater. "Shall we walk back?"

"No. I'm okay." She sat still.

"Since then my whole life has been devoted to law. To finishing school, passing the bar, learning from the best in the profession and now striking out on my own. Everything seemed in place. There was nothing to go wrong. Until . . . until . . ." he wavered.

She slipped her hand from beneath his fingers and placed her arm around his shoulders. Her other hand she laid on his arm. Though her hands were calm, a noticeable tension was evident in the upright position of her head, her lifted shoulders, and her tightened abdominal muscles. Her breath was slow and shallow.

"Yes," was all she said.

"Until Sutton came to Windermere. Clarissa, it was like looking into a mirror when I saw him. Mitch said Sutton looked just like me at that age. I had to deal with the possibilities. His age matched up with the time Frances went west for the summer. He told me he was adopted when he was six weeks old."

Then Joseph recounted his search for the school where she had gone to work, his visit there and his talk with the director who had been a friend to Frances. Now he had no doubt about Sutton's real parentage.

"Can anyone imagine such a chance encounter for two people from the farthermost points in our country or on this continent? If I have acted remote, withdrawn or even unapproachable the past few weeks, this explains *why*. There is no precedent for me to follow."

"No, there probably isn't. Joseph, the dilemma is yours. I know you will make the right and just choice."

With unshielded soul, his eyes met hers. "You're a good person. That man you left relinquished a treasure."

The street lamp shined on her face and highlighted the tears on her lashes.

"It won't be fair to rob his father of the relationship he has with Sutton. It could do nothing favorable for Sutton to disturb his whole life as he is ready to face a career full of optimism and purpose." He stopped, thought then continued. "And what can putting my findings to him do for me? Make an honest man of myself two dozen years late!"

"Have you been dishonest?"

"If not that outright, then let's at least admit I've lived a lie."

"To whom have you lied? Not to me. Not to anyone I've spoken with. Not to your parents or hers. There was concurrence all around you said." She took a breath as one on dangerous, invasive ground. "Has Mitch chastised you?"

"Not once. He is saddened by his part, of his being young and inexperienced in handling such a situation."

"And you've forgiven him?"

Considering before answering, he admitted, "Yes. Yes. I know it now, but without your question, I may not have addressed it directly." He reached up and back and squeezed her hand. "Thank you."

"Will the secret be hard for you to live with?"

He shifted his weight and hunched then relaxed his shoulders. She dropped her arm and pulled it between them, laying both her hands in her lap. He said, "I'll be okay. You've let me share the others with you and I don't expect to have a problem with them now. Verbalizing and putting them in a timeline was invaluable. And I'm making the decision that knowing facts is not always necessary." He scrutinized her face this time as if seeking some particular response.

She permitted the scrutiny and responded. "Later, if there's a need for him to know, you'll discern that and have a chance to talk."

He rejoined: "There are written laws . . ."

She finished: " . . . that can be amended."

He stated. "And verbal agreements that . . ."
She completed: " . . . are not binding."
He proposed: "And physical laws of attractions . . ."
She lamented: " . . . that become antipathetic."
"I've hurt you again. Can you forgive me for the times that I've done that?"

Closing her eyes and bending her head, she barely nodded. Both were quiet with their own pondering. Without lifting her head, she asked, "And Breear?"

"She's a good match for Sutton. They are both ambitious, aspire to similar careers and talented, educated young people prepared to move where the action is and jobs to be had."

Those were comments the Joseph she interviewed with would have made, but with the compassion and clear-sightedness of an emotionalized Joseph.

"I don't have to ask if you're all right about the life you left. Everyday I see your confidence and composure. And the response from everyone who meets you is positive. Only a centered person could extrude your qualities." He appeared to fold after those statements.

Quickly, she stood. "Well, it's time to walk back or else I will have to go fetch the car and come for you." She extended a hand, which he reached for and raised himself. "I'll wager you haven't eaten since lunch, and that you may have skipped with those doubled-up appointments."

He attempted a laugh, but was too spent to make more than a mild squawk. With effort they climbed back up the sloped streets; and upon reaching his car, he bid her goodnight, refusing her offer to fix him a snack.

He drove directly to his house and parked the car near the front door. He entered and once more found his way through the house with only a minimum of light shining through windows. In his bedroom he took off his shoes and socks, discarded his suit, shirt and tie, then walked into the bathroom where a small nightlight was always plugged in and turned on the tap. After a quick tooth brushing, he filled a glass with water. The birds are right to seek water; he mused and drained his glass.

Immediately, he turned down the covers and slid into bed, barely aware of the pleasure of clean, fresh linens smooth against his skin while he pulled the top sheet and lightweight blanket over him. He drifted easily into the deepest sleep he had known in years, dreamless throughout the night.

CHAPTER 32

The following morning Clarissa was sitting at her breakfast table enjoying the fragrance and flavor of freshly perked coffee. The robins were returning in flocks from their winter havens and were intermingling with the chickadees and juncos that she expected would soon be on the wing to other regions. Now all were in search of nourishment to break the night's fast. The ever-faithful cardinals and blue jays were much in evident in their year-round domain, flashing their bright red and brilliant blue feathers in the air, on the tree limbs, and on the green lawn.

She watched as a tiny chickadee couple took turns taking food to a nest tucked under an eave above the deck. Spring mating had been productive for them, she believed. Her pleasure in the schemes of nature turned melancholy. Not for me and not for Joseph, she regretted the outcome of their love relationships. She pulled the freshest layer of memory forward and heard his voice revealing long-kept secrets and was as deeply affected as she had been last evening. What ways to help him, she could not answer yet. The news was too recent for her. In spite of the sorrow for him, warmth had nestled in her center, perhaps her heart, for his choosing to unburden himself to her. That had been no impulse, no "caught in a situation of speaking before thinking," no panic because there was no one else to talk with. He could have turned to Mitch, who would have been there in an instant; even his sister or Breear, certainly Samuel Littlegate would have been a listener.

The telephone rang, and she went over to the wall phone almost relieved to have her contemplation interrupted.

"Good morning!" The sonorous voice of Jarvis Randolph said.

"The same to you," she forced a cheerful tone.

"Hey, I like that friendly sound. I'm in the car and have just picked up a gourmet breakfast for two. One has your beautiful name on it."

"You're a dear. I have a fresh pot of coffee, but nothing else to the ready."

"As long as you're ready for the food . . . and me, I'm almost there, my dear Clarissa." He pushed *end* and hung up the car phone.

She quickly applied a little lotion and lipstick, smiling as she did the latter and wondered if this new color would pass inspection. It was a pale pink; an appropriate selection for early morning especially as it matched the pants and pullover she was wearing. She combed her hair that had grown long enough to fluff and frame her face.

Ring. Ring. Ring. Joseph groggily turned to his side and listened to the noise. Was that the alarm clock? No. The sound was too far away. What time it was, he had no idea. The answering machine should pick up, his brain told itself then drifted into a half-sleep, a fourth groggy and a fourth struggling to open his eyes.

Some time later, he was reawakened with a bell ringing. Not the phone. The doorbell. After repeated rings, there was a loud knock on the front door.

Joseph with tremendous effort raised himself to one elbow, shook his head, which felt two sizes larger, before trying to kick off the sheets. Somehow his feet were entangled in the bedcovers, and he had to upright his body in order to separate the layers and yank them off one by one. He threw his legs over the side of the bed and got up. He pulled his robe from a hook inside his closet door, put it on and tied the sash as he reached the front door.

Mail lay scattered on the floor beneath the slot in the door. He leaned over and bunched it in his hands. He needed both hands to unlock the door; thus, he placed the mail on the hall table. Opening the door, he looked out but no one was there. He peered up the driveway and toward the street where there was no sign of life. Only a couple of birds were signaling to their flock. He went back inside.

He raked his hands through his tussled hair, squeezed his eyelids tightly a few times and yawned. Opening his eyes and viewing the mirror, he immediately realized he needed a shower not only to bring him fully awake but also to restore some decent image.

After showering a long time, he shaved and put his robe back on then made a pot of coffee. Strong. Going again into the bedroom, he saw the unmade bed, walked around it and spread the covers neatly. Not until he was looking into his closet did he think about the time. Angling backward, he peered at the clock on the bedside table. It was ten thirty.

He declared, "No way! I slept the hands around the clock! First time such a stretch in bed. That's why I was so out of it when those bells were going off."

He wasn't sure what he would be doing today. Nothing had been scheduled, so he decided to wear khakis and a blue shirt that would have him presentable for most any event that he could anticipate. Last he shoved his feet into socks and loafers. The aroma of coffee drifted into the room and he made straight for the kitchen.

After filling a mug, he opened the back door and walked out onto the landing. He leaned his arms across the railing holding the steaming mug until the coffee cooled enough to drink. Looking down, he saw a covey of bobwhites bobbing their small heads; and, leaning over, he could see that the water bowl was dry. Placing the mug on the railing, he sauntered down the steps, refilled the bowl from the faucet, and bounded back up to the landing. He picked up the mug and drank deeply. The coffee had cooled more than he liked, so he returned to the kitchen and added more from the pot.

In the study he noticed the light blinking on the answering machine and pushed play. "You have three new messages."

The first one came on, from Breear, telling him that a courier was bringing him a package on Saturday morning. He walked back to the hall table picked up the mail and returned to the study and sat on the couch. At the bottom of the stack was a brown envelope almost too large for the slot and that most likely provoked the courier into the last knocking. It must not have required a signature, Joseph decided.

He ripped the flap open, tilted the envelope, and the contents spilled out. A packet of white sheets was tied together with a green ribbon, which he untied. The top sheet was blank white stationery with an embossed CB centered near the top. The next sheet had been torn smoothly along perforations. It was dated last fall; and, as he read the first entry, he knew it was the initial encounter she had with him in the hall of the courthouse. She had written exactly what had happened and what he recalled she had asked. *Have we met before?* Another page recorded their first evening in her apartment when she kissed him and asked, *do you remember this?* And his negative reply and his kissing her and her answer. He flipped through several other pages reading more closely the names and comments she had made regarding the men Joseph had identified for her when they were dining out. He didn't want to read them all. Now, he had to trust her that she would not withhold any notes. Later, he would read them in entirety. A name on one of the final pages caught his eye. *Sutton.* The comments that followed were personal and the words touched him at many levels. One was the manner he felt about holding her, knowing the feel of her under his hands with the duality of her longing and resisting. Another was his position and knowledge that could help her in her job, with his willing to be used and to give; for hadn't she chosen him when there had been so many others who would have eagerly done the same. In spite of her occasional coyness, hadn't she basically been honest with him? And most importantly hadn't she been the link with a part of himself he may never have known. *Sutton.*

As he was inserting the retied sheath of papers, he glanced into the envelope and noticed a four-by-six white card. He let that fall out before enclosing the papers. The card was embossed like the stationery. In Breear's handwriting was a question: "In return for these requested notes, may I ask that the temper of our times together remain just for us to know?"

After reading the card a second time, he dropped it into the envelope that he placed into a small safe behind one of the doors in the wall cabinet.

Refilling his coffee mug and munching a day-old bagel, he returned to the telephone and punched in the speed dial to connect her apartment line. When her answering message ended, he said, "Thank you. In answer to your question 'yes' the times will be as you request." As an afterthought he added, "Best wishes for the future." He hung up.

The answering machine light continued to blink. He tapped the button once more. "Joseph, I called your office first in case you were in this Saturday morning. I left a message on your machine to call me at home when you had time. I'm leaving the same message at your home. Marvin Hertford."

Joseph pressed Marvin's home phone number. After four rings a teenager answered the phone. "Hello."

"Is this Sidney?"

"Yes, sir."

"This is Joseph McBaden. I'm returning your father's call."

"Right. I'll get him."

Shortly, Marvin picked up. "Good of you to call back so quickly, Joseph."

"Good morning, sir."

"I have another matter I would like your help with. It also concerns intellectual property. The client would be a nephew of mine. He's a designer and there is a possible copyright infraction involved. Are you interested in talking with him?"

"I am indeed and I thank you for thinking of me."

"If you have a few minutes now, I could tell you the basics of what he told me last night."

"I do," Joseph answered pulling a legal pad and pencil from his desk drawer and sat down.

Marvin began. "A year or so ago my nephew who is a freelance designer did some designs for a major furniture company. He had a contract with the company to be paid royalties on his designs. During that time he designed full suites for living room, dining area and bedroom. He presented the company with concept renderings, and the company head took the drawings. Later, the head returned them to my nephew stating that they were not a good fit for the company. During the time of the contract, no action was taken on the designs and he's never heard that there was a change of plans. There has been no request for a full set of designs. No news has filtered down to him of similar designs being manufactured."

Marvin paused. Joseph was making notes and flipping yellow sheets backward as fast as he could. "Is your nephew still under contract with this furniture company?"

"No. There was a parting of ways. No drastic disputes, nothing unusual."

"Okay. I'm with you."

After clearing his throat, Marvin continued. "Recently, he has seen brochures for a hotel showing a suite that is furnished with pieces that are almost identical to his renderings. He's interested in pursuing the matter quietly, gathering data and such before confronting the former employers. How does this matter sound to you?" Marvin asked.

Joseph added to his notes rapidly and paused a minute before replying. "Excuse me for not answering immediately. I was scanning what I had written. Now, I want to turn the question back to you. How does it sound? As if he has reason to investigate?"

"Right."

"Do furniture manufacturers still place their name somewhere on the finished pieces? Say with a stamp or a label? I have seen them in drawers and cabinets and on bottoms of chairs."

"They may do that."

"If the hotel has a facility nearby, has he been in to look at the furniture?"

"Not yet. He has considered that, but decided the first course of action was to get some legal advice. And there's not a hotel of that chain in our section of the state."

"By all means, the matter should be looked into. I'll be glad to talk with him. I'm assuming he has a copy of the renderings and of his contract with the company. If he keeps royalty rights for his lifetime, that should have a bearing on his claim. Does he live here? When can he come by?"

"He lives in Eastford. He can arrange to come most anytime. I appreciate your being willing to see him. As you know, Eastford's major industry is furniture, and my nephew could have difficulty getting a top firm or attorney to take him on. I expect he'll be in touch with you Monday." He ended with giving Joseph the name and phone numbers of his nephew.

Joseph replaced the receiver. "Well, this is a momentous day." He scanned the clock, which had both hands on the twelve. "The bewitching setting for midnight, but a golden opportunity time at noon," Joseph declared and threw his head back and grinned.

He jumped up and padded about the house, thinking all the while that this well might be the big case he had hoped would come along. The small guy up against the big firm with a legitimate claim for recognition and reimbursement. And a super-nice man who was showing his appreciation had contacted him. Joseph. "How much better can the day get?"

He wanted to tell somebody – to tell someone who would be happy for him, who would care about what it could mean to the practice; to tell someone he cared about, someone who cared about him. Suddenly, he stopped mid-room. He turned fully around taking in his study; stopped again and gazed out the window and into the treetops, lush and lovely. He knew whom he would call, and he knew what he would do and what he would say. His hand reached for the phone.

The bell rang twice before Clarissa could answer. Hurrying, she opened the door to a smiling Jarvis Randolph with a napkin-covered basket in one hand and a dozen pink roses wrapped in green florist paper in the other.

"Good morning," he said cheerfully with a gleam in his eye.

"The same to you, flower and breakfast bearer," she responded, opening the storm door.

As he entered, he turned to face her and kissed her soundly on the lips. "I'm starting with inspector duties first." He held the roses close to her face. "Um? Did someone alert you to the color I was bringing? It matches the roses exactly. For my intuition, I merit another sample, I'd say." Impulsively, he leaned toward her, looked first into her eyes and then brushed her lips softly with his. "Um. More tasty than the breakfast promises."

She took the roses and said, "I'll help you. Now, head for the kitchen, sir."

They took the meal out to the deck on a tray. Clarissa placed the roses in a graceful china pitcher and he carried the coffeepot and two mugs. They chatted and savored the food, listened to the birds and admired the springtime greenery of the trees and gardens.

The sun warmed them, and their talk was easy and comfortable. Finally, Jarvis stood. "This has been delightful, but there are errands I must run. I'll take the tray back in. Then I have something to ask you."

She held the door for him. As he passed her, he bent his head slightly, then drew back. "No. I'll wait till we get all of this out of the way." He went inside and she followed with a few items. They were setting the things on the kitchen table when the phone rang.

Clarissa crossed to the wall phone. "Hello." She listened. "Yes." "I think so." "Yes. Half an hour will be fine. Goodbye."

Jarvis looked at her intently. She blushed.

"That was Joseph, wasn't it?"

"How did you know?"

"On Saturday. He's coming over?"

"You said you had to run errands."

"Correct. So you think you'll stay on with him, pardon, his firm?"

"Yes. Why? Have I indicated otherwise?"

"You still consider him a good attorney?"

"Oh, I do. More so than when we first met, talked. I mean . . . he and I interviewed . . . oh, no, I mean when you first asked me. I've seen him being very kind and very professional to young people, young men."

"I see."

"Did I signal somehow I was leaving and without telling you first?" she queried.

"No."

Somewhat vexed, she said, "Jarvis, does it bother you that I admire the legal skills of someone I work with? Surely, there are nurses and other women around the hospital who admire you equally so." She stared at him. "You have no reason to be jealous."

He walked and stood in front of her. "You think not?" He put his arms out and drew her against him. He kissed her fervently and long, then easily and softly before leaning back and looking into her face. "I've wanted to do that for months. From our first meeting I felt there was a chance for us to be a long-term couple. Our backgrounds are similar, we understand each other; and, I believe that we respect one another. Clarissa, you're all a man could want for a lifetime companion. And, as a bonus, you're beautiful and intelligent, and people love you."

Clarissa brought her hand to her face. He moved back.

She exclaimed, "Jarvis, you never said anything about your feelings. All you told me or asked me was about the pace. It's been fun and romantic and . . ." She stopped.

"I didn't make a wise choice in giving you time, did I? That's rhetorical, my dear. Somehow rushing you didn't seem appropriate. And, Clarissa, I had already planned to kiss you as I did, before the telephone call."

She looked at the wall phone and blushed again.

"A half-hour you said. It's time for me to leave." He took a step toward the door, spun around and said. "If I ever find the woman who talks about me in the voice you do about Joseph, I will marry her."

She was aghast and didn't follow him to the door. She heard it close firmly. Dashing to clear up the kitchen and running upstairs to change clothes and wash her face, she stumbled on her discarded shoes and nearly burned her hands with the too-hot tap water. The doorbell was ringing before she finished pulling a green sweater over her head. Quickly, she ran a comb through her hair, scolding her tousled appearance.

Running down the stairs and jerking the front door open, she was breathless as she faced Joseph.

His face showed surprise. "Am I too early, or have I interrupted something?"

She shook her head and began to push the storm door outward. With her free hand she indicated for him to enter. He finished pulling the door open and followed her inside.

"Are you sure you're not busy?" He asked again. The flush on her face, the carefree hairstyle, and the bright green sweater enhanced her appearance in an attractive, casual manner. There was an expectant aura about her that was unusual and excited him, yet aroused his curiosity.

"No. Yes. Oh, I mean I'm not busy." She appeared flustered then regained composure. "You said on the phone you wanted me to see something."

Narrowing his eyes in an interested manner, he replied, "I did. May I have a drink of water first." He turned and walked toward the kitchen.

"Of course. I can get it for you," she called, but he was ahead of her. The first object she spotted was the tall vase of pink roses on the table. She glanced at him and he nodded.

"Beautiful flowers. Not from the garden, are they?" He said as he drew a glass of water.

"No."

He turned and looked at her. "They are quite suitable for you. Though not as rosy as your blush this morning."

Her head straightened, her color heightened, her eyes returned his gaze. But her voice was mellow when she commented. "He's a friend, Joseph. A good friend. That's all." She swallowed and waited. Inwardly, she had no certainty why she had labeled her relationship with Jarvis so unequivocally.

Joseph placed the empty glass on the counter and strode to face her. "Good. It's good to have friends. May we go now?"

"Yes." She turned and they left the house and he drove them in his car.

As she had done the evening before, she waited for him to

reveal whatever was on his mind. She showed no discomfit today upon staring at him. Although he appeared relaxed and tidier in his fresh clothing, much of his confident air had returned. An apparent difference was that this new confidence was more approachable, not ridged and holding people at bay – or at least not her. Amazed, she almost verbalized *attractive*.

"Thank you for listening to me last night," he began, turning briefly to her. "I've made a decision about Sutton. I won't tell him anything I have learned. I can't see it could benefit him in any way now. He needs all his wits for beginning the high-powered world he plans to enter. And he's asked for my help professionally. That's the best role I can serve now."

"It's an admirable role," Clarissa said.

"In these circumstances, we have a good rapport." He was quiet. Then he said evenly, "He and Breear knew each other first. I only reminded her of him. He considers me a friend of Breear's. One who has kindly helped her the first months in Windermere."

She reached over and touched his arm. "You have been kind to both of them. If circumstances change in his family, with his parents, you can consider your options again. Just as you have left the door open for your mother and sister. Perhaps your family will be closer to you now." She moved her hand before he could reach across and touch it.

He turned the steering wheel and drove into the driveway at his house. Stopping and switching off the motor, he pivoted in his seat.

"I had an unexpected telephone call this morning from Marvin Hertford. He's offering me a chance at a big case." She drew a breath, but before she could let it out or exclaim, he rushed on. "Now, it's only at the discovery stage. It may involve a copyright violation; we'll have to have a few more facts to be certain. But Hertford is no fool and wouldn't ask if I were interested unless there is a reasonable indication of wrongdoing."

"Joseph, I'm so pleased for you!"

"For us. For the firm. Knowing me as you do now, are you planning to stay? In Windermere? With the firm?"

"Do you want me to?" Her brows knitted, emphasizing the question.

"Yes." This time he reached out and she met his hand halfway, and he quickly squeezed and released it.

He got out of the car, came around, and opened the door for her. As she stood facing the house, he said, "This is my house. This is what I wanted you to see."

She took a long look at the façade then slowly turned full circle and inspected the grounds. She nodded. He walked with her up the steps, unlocked the door, and they went inside.

After he had led her through the upstairs rooms and those downstairs and stepped out onto the landing for a surveillance of the backyard, they continued their silent walk back inside. She retraced a path to the dining room. He stopped.

Clarissa walked to the window that overlooked the backyard. "It's lovely."

"Not much has been done to it."

"The lay of land is nice."

Joseph crossed over. He opened the window. Although he stepped behind her, he extended his arm and placed his hand on the window frame. The fresh air blew in.

She said, "The house has your traits. Sturdy, reliable, shows planning, comfortable."

"Do you think you could . . . ?" he began.

She interrupted. "Have you ever had . . . Did she ever come here?"

"No. I've not brought any other . . ."

She shook her head slightly. "That's all I wanted to know. Yes, I could."

Joseph drew a deep breath and slowly exhaled. "Did I ask you to marry me?"

Clarissa turned her head and he peered over her shoulder. With an affirming tone and warm expression, she answered. "I believe you did."

"And to live here?"

She faced the window again. "The lawn has lots of possibilities. Dad could design a lovely rose garden."

"He's welcome."

"I'll always be close to my family. We love to see each other. Not just at holidays, but anytime we can. Will you be comfortable with that?"

His hand tightened on the window frame. "I accept the ties. And I want to know your family, as family."

She leaned her head over and pressed against his arm. He brought his hand around and touched her shoulder. She lifted her head and turned in the embrace. With eyes filled with tears, she spoke. "Did I say the house also has your trait of being very attractive?"

"Both of us appreciate your praise and acceptance. The long wait for a mistress is now validated. May our pleasures be mutual."

"There's so much to talk about. The practice. Will it stay the same? The announcement, when and how? A wedding! Moving?"

He backed a step away, keeping his hands on her upper arms. "Stop a minute. We'll cover all that. Right now, let's tend to a fundamental. Seal this engagement."

He pulled her to him and kissed her. When he loosened his grasp, she looked at him, batted her eyelids until she regained her breath. "It's a good tactic to wait until your proposal to do that. You are one persuasive guy."

She lifted her arms around his neck. "Please, resume."

He did as ordered, being that to do so was desirable. And the absence of resistance stamped the action *justifiable*.

ACKNOWLEDGMENTS

I thank friends with a variety of experiences for reading the manuscript and making suggestions. Your time and comments were appreciated: Andrea Decker, Libby Freedman, Alice Noble, Jean Poston, Sarah Rhodes, and Jane Taylor.

Stephen McGee continues to explain the complex world of word processing and the computer.

Sarah Reynolds Dixon sketched the landscape and skyline of Windermere, N.C., a fictional city.

Thank you, Jean Beam, for being a faithful supporter and right-hand assistant with various tasks.

For four special attorneys who answered my questions about legal matters, and those whom I saw in court trials, I choose old-fashioned, honorable words to describe them: fine, good men.

BVG

Made in the USA
Monee, IL
19 April 2022